"**This literary work is fiction, but the facts are real, and shape a world I have not experienced in other WWII accounts**. The author uses the direct first person to connect readers with Ingrid, a heroine whose complexities and courage are enhanced by the secret fears she shares with you. This book stays in the forefront of your imagination every second you are away from it. Taking care of mundane chores, loving your children, and putting away groceries become privileges. You bless everyone in your family with gratitude while you reflect on the horrible quandary Ingrid faces, as did those who lived through the Holocaust and French Occupation. Ingrid becomes a friend and role model. Sometimes you want to shake her and other times you want to defend her, but you always admire her fortitude. *The Résistance Between Us* is an excellent example of how literary fiction at its best reveals a higher truth."

**Elizabeth Hurd, Special Correspondent, *The Daily Oklahoman,*
www.okartsceneandhurd.com**

"**Ingrid's thrilling story is a scary ride, expressed sharply as she maneuvers herself and her life forward creatively**, using her education and high-born class. Sensing her destiny she hides much muscle behind her mirror."

Karen Krause, artist, photographer, NYC

"**In *The Résistance Between Us*, the reader is immediately drawn into the scene and mindset of its main character, Ingrid Fellner**. The textures, smells, and nuances of her surroundings are palpable. One becomes caught up with this woman and what she faces moment by moment as her journey unfolds. Like a canvas where each brushstroke has its place for the painting to succeed, each word, phrase, and chapter of this historical novel is carefully placed and layered to create a truly beautiful literary work of art."

Corinne Didisheim, artist, www.cdidisheim.com MO

"It was a great read. It has been a long time since I enjoyed a book this much. I did not want to put it down. Historical fiction is something I always love. The characters came alive in my mind. I was right there with Ingrid during WWII. The depth was real and passionate. The twists and turns of the plot kept me guessing and hoping things would turn out well for Ingrid and her daughter. Like so many women she gave completely of herself out of pure love . . . a courageous woman in a horrific time in our history."

Shelby McGuire, Myrtle Beach, SC

"An exciting journey of personal growth and sacrifice as well as a raw look into the French Résistance. This read prompted memories of my dad's stories of his military experience—captured in France and sent to a German POW camp with Russian soldiers in WWII."

Michael Mooney, Pinckney, MI

"*The Résistance Between Us* resonates with our desire to be part of something greater than ourselves. Ingrid's saga was deeply introspective for me . . . a much-needed eye opener about WWII and its stark reality for my parents' generation."

Nancy Mooney, Pinckney, MI

"A gripping story of a French World War II heroine who hid Jews in her basement who were en route to safety. The story unfolds in such vivid detail that the reader can almost see and feel the action firsthand, and the characters come alive on each page. The dialogue is filled with historically accurate facts and covers the gamut of human emotion and experience. I couldn't put this book down! It is historical fiction at its best, and so brilliantly written."

Grace Schuler, Personnel Consultant and Entrepreneur, Philadelphia, PA

The Résistance Between Us

Ingrid's Wars: Book One

Phyllis Kimmel Libby

Mary Ellen Cooper, Mistral Editions
Permissions, Rights, Sales
711 East Mansur Avenue
Guthrie, OK 73044
merctoo@aol.com

Publisher's Note: This is a work of fiction. Names, characters, places, and incidents are a product of the author's imagination. Locales and public names are sometimes used for atmospheric purposes. Any resemblance to actual people, living or dead, or to businesses, companies, events, institutions, or locales is completely coincidental.

Cover Design, Phyllis Kimmel Libby

Book Layout ©2017 TheBookmakers.com

Ordering Information:
Quantity sales. Special discounts are available on quantity purchases by corporations, associations, and others. For details, contact the "Special Sales Department" at the address above.

The Résistance Between Us/ Phyllis Kimmel Libby. -- 1st ed.
ISBN 978-0-9987441-0-0

Dedication

"I can't burden you. It's too dangerous. Anyone who does this has to be strong and self-contained. You act from unconditional love—or anger must propel you. Either way it's a commitment from the heart. You reap gratification in the precise measure you live the terror. You can't have one without the other. If you think twice about it, you're not cut out for it."

Dieter, 7 November 1941
The Résistance Between Us, Book One: Ingrid's Wars

In memory of Reginald Backus Libby
Corporal, USS Marine Corps
Semper Fidelis

Contents

Foreword

There are times in life when you have to break all the rules. You don't want to. It would be easier to do nothing, but you can't live with your conscience because what's wrong is too wrong. It doesn't matter that you're not safe—or that it's a huge risk.

Suddenly the world has become too ugly. Organized hatred and xenophobia have quietly woven their evil agendas into your physical, emotional, and moral landscape.

When do you speak up about it, and what can you do to stop it?

Phyllis Kimmel Libby

Acknowledgments

I am indebted to my Ukrainian Jewish, Czech Catholic, and Hungarian Lutheran family and the Yiddish, High and Low German dialects spoken across their cultures, religions and politics at our dinner table. Courage and love guided each struggle in the journey that brought them to America.

I thank my corps of readers: Eva and Dr. Giancarlo Salmoiraghi, Dr. Laura B. Ousley, Corinne and Ariane Didisheim, Dagmar and Francis Lai, Antoinette West, Nancy and Mike Mooney, Mary Lou Gwozdek, Lillian Stinnett, Mickey and Beverly Kalman, Carla Fellers, Grace Schuler, Judy Katz, Angeline Leiker, Dr. Catherine Rött, Elizabeth Skala, Janet Caputo, Kay Gately, Elizabeth Hurd, Karen Krause, Karen Kimmel, and Shelby McGuire. Their support prodded me to write the second and third books that continue the heroine's dynamic journey.

I am especially indebted to my friends of Swiss background, Corinne and Ariane Didisheim; and German and French background, Dagmar and Francis Lai; for their help with historical accuracy and the foreign languages in the novel.

For Antoinette West, the manuscript evoked tragic memories when, as a seven-year old, she traveled to Oradour-Sur-Glane with her grandparents a few hours after the Nazis massacred and burned the entire town, and before the world knew what had happened there. I'm grateful for her candor and courage as she shared her past.

I was humbled to meet the late Elisabeth Sevier, one of the youngest women in the French Résistance to be decorated by de Gaulle. She inspired me to search the heart of my heroine, who, like Elisabeth, sought peace and reconciliation after her honorable service.

This novel germinated for decades after a brief visit with Dutch Auschwitz survivor, Anna Sara Fels-Kupferschmidt in Amsterdam in 1968. Anna taught me how the pain of profound loss marks us, and we persevere with love despite it.

I thank my Polish colleague, Bozena Bejnar Slawow, for introducing me to Poland, and making it possible to put my feet into the Black Sea, in the Ukraine of my Jewish grandparents. I have been blessed to teach and coach Swiss, Italian, French, German, Austrian, Polish, Ukrainian, Latvian, and Russian families in addition to my Nicaraguan and Honduran families with brain-injured children. I thank each of them for their dedication, trust and hard work. Their values play a significant role in my heroine's journey.

Learning Cranial Sacral therapy with the Upledger Institute inspired my writing, as did Carol Bowman (Author, *Children's Past Lives* and *Return from Heaven*), whose Past Life Therapy Course helped me deepen my characters' relationships.

I am grateful to Chuck Schrunk at MacMan in Moore, Oklahoma, and Carol Barber, for their never-ending patience that helped me so much with software. I thank Amy and Sarah Hurley, whose help over the last fifteen years, behind the scenes, freed me to focus on writing. They made foreign travel achievable without drama. And, speaking of drama, I thank my classroom of live drama and extraordinary excellence for twenty-three years—the Pollard Theatre of Guthrie, Oklahoma.

I am indebted to Michael B. Neff, founder of Algonkian Writers' Conferences and author of *All the Dark We Will Not See* for his incisive critiques and support during rewrites (after I thought the story was complete). He showed me answers that were already in the text, but had escaped my awareness. A tough job, almost always thankless—but I thank you many times over, Mr. Neff.

I also thank Adam Davies, editor and author of *The Frog King*, who listened to my last read-aloud and final edits. Thank you, Adam, for your insight and energy. As a playwright, Adam understands the immediacy of Ingrid's voice. I needed that confirmation when I read his upcoming play, *The Bathrobe Club*. His characters, bigger than life, unfold their universal message, at once grand and intensely private. Adam's play taught this writer it's okay to grab the truth in life and make it into art.

My third and most patient professional ally is Mary Ellen Cooper, who, in cooperation with Random House, Doubleday, Simon and Schuster and *Encyclopaedia Britannica*, published bestseller *How to Teach Your Baby to Read* and following titles in 18 different languages. She was the founding editor and sometime author of *Rug Hooking Magazine*, an international magazine also available in Canada, Great Britain, Australia, and Japan, and editor/publisher of the award-winning book, *A Passion for the Creative Life, Textiles to Lift the Spirit* by Mary Sheppard Burton. She edited *The Résistance Between Us* with thorough, gentle guidance—listening to the story, and working with me for fifteen years to manifest it on paper. She inspired me to paint with a medium of words when my history was brush and pigment. She respected the story's voice: that of an aristocratic woman born in 1900, well educated, but alas, a rich, naïve trophy wife whose haughty exterior hides a fierce, loving heart. Without Mary Ellen to guide me, this story would not have reached the world.

I thank Joel Friedlander, Tracy Atkins, Abigail Dunard, and Joel's devoted team at The Book Makers for their high standards, craftsmanship and consummate skill that saw this book through its completion to market.

P. Kimmel Libby

1941

Chapter One

The Universe Casts the Bait

4 November 1941, Tuesday

This is my time to honor unwanted guests, and pray for the day I can make them go home. Pardon my scorn, but these guests are the enemy. Not the Germans I grew up with, nor the man I married and lost. This enemy is a rigid, twisted, oddly obedient criminal lot everyone fears. We French were asleep when the lethal infection next door grew overnight into a Teutonic Juggernaut. I slept too, preferring my ignorance. Now I grovel in servitude like everyone else.

People whisper about a local Résistance, but no one is sure who's in it. We talk among ourselves when our overseers are out of earshot. Our liberty, equality and fraternity are lost.

My widow's soul is frightened. The mother in me knows my daughter's life is not safe, even here at the foot of the Jura Mountains.

This morning I'm on the shore of the Doubs to check my boat's mooring. Our river crested in a storm last night, and dumped all manner of trash on my banks. I stand here in its eerie mist with my boots sloshing in the shallows. Nothing appears amiss on this bloated artery . . . except a stench of rot that smacks my nostrils.

South of us, the storm's upstream current must have pulled an animal under and it landed here. I pursue the foulness, and tread carefully around tree limbs, fishing line, and torn river grass.

My nose leads me to large mounds that protrude from the mud. I break off a sturdy branch to move the rubbish aside. Pulling at a piece of bark causes it to peel away from a tree stump like old skin. The ripping sound alerts my senses. With sickening urgency my hands scrape the muck aside. Then, poking around, I feel something soft and familiar.

What *is* this? What's underneath these mounds? I dig madly at the mud before I numb, anticipating. . . . No, this can't be happening. Oh *Mon Dieu*! There is one, no, there are two yellow stars, two people. A Jewish couple has washed up on my shore! Conservative black clothes cover their blistered skin. They're still—like the inanimate trash around them. My heart constricts. *Aye*, I touched them with my bare hands, and twitch with revulsion. Nausea rises up in me. I can't stop staring at their soulless bodies. Their indignity is so alive.

The warm vibration of my flesh wants to defend me against these two dead people, but my mind is cold and my heart is in shock. I panic, turn away, fall to my knees and retch.

When I look at my visitors again, sadness carves hollows inside my chest. My whole world convulses. Sobbing, I grieve for their lost lives.

Were they the phantoms that called me from sleep last night? Their groans left me floating in a menacing darkness in this *cauchemar*, this nightmare that is here, this evil omen at my feet. Cold terror creeps up my spine. The finality of decay that replaces their youthful dreams—will it worm its way into my life?

This war has come too close.

I get up slowly and look back at the stands of trees on the riverbank. A few moments ago, I was rooted in this noble nature. Its energy filled my cheeks and stood me upright like the saplings around me. Now the water's gentle waves lap a dark refrain on my clotted shore:

Your freedom is just an illusion.
Death has visited you again. You have read a bitter future in its debris.
You have been chosen.

Chosen? Why? For what?

Fright pounds in my ears. I back away and take flight. My stately home thrusts above me from the sheer lime hill. My feet squish in my boots as they grab its mushy slope. A dark foreboding colors the uneven breaths heaving from my chest. I shudder. I'm unsteady. The gruesome fingers of death reach up to pull me backward toward the river.

I cry and curse this degrading Occupation and my pristine refuge that has betrayed my trust. My feet slide on wet pine needles littering the steep private path. I run past weeping willows and stands of young pines. My legs slow at the last thirty meters to the top of the ridge. I pause, gasp in disgust, and scrape my heels against the sharp edging stones along the public walkway.

The inert intruders are mere specks on the shoreline from this height. What shall I do? What if my daughter asks Guy to walk with her down there?

Moving forward, I shove open the heavy blue gate to my high-walled yard. A bitter gust of wind scurries me past barren fruit trees and vegetable-laden cold frames. The rusty hinges on the château's basement door groan as they welcome me into its warm corridor. I look around uneasily, and pray aloud,

"Please God, let me feel safe in here." But the familiar fragrance of drying lavender can't erase the mildew of death that comes in on my coat.

I look down at my muddy hands and feel odd, distant and afraid. I catch sight of myself in the large cracked mirror in the corner. *Mon Dieu*, my coat is covered with mud. I've been upset and hadn't noticed. I rinse my hands in the stone basin and remove my coat, socks, boots, and skirt. I wrap myself in a large towel and tiptoe upstairs.

Still estranged from my surroundings, I stop on the steps, realizing the dead are not just victims but also uninvited guests. I have removed their mud, but not their message. Their presence has also stolen the peacefulness of my château and the beauty of my forest.

Before today I felt protected here. My thoughts flowed freely within these walls and outside over those steep lime hills to garner nature's forgiveness toward me—her stubborn seedling that grew among the rocks. Now, it's as if I'm exposed, my heart is found wanting and I must prove myself.

I am like my dubious river Doubs. This river is filled with doubt about who *she* is. Less than half her distance is navigable. Three times she deceives us with changes in the direction of her flow—with her twists, turns, and doubled waterways.

I had hoped the Nazi takeover would be temporary, and end in a quick, winterkill freeze.

Now I fear we are in for a long and terrible siege.

I'm still shivering a few minutes later in the receiving salon as I stare into the glowing fireplace, my mind in a trance. My social and financial advantages have insulated me from this war. I have not had to confront change or take responsibility for anyone beyond my family. Yet my life of wealth and privilege is useless to prevent tragic deaths. I cringe, and a new darkness creeps toward me with a poignant message I cannot interpret. It is *my* turn now, but for what?

My eyes fix on the photograph of my late husband Emil on my writing desk. The Jews on the riverbank remind me of him, dead, crumpled in the snow almost two years ago.

I couldn't save him. I couldn't save them. Is there anyone I could save?

I came upon today's carnage alone, in isolation, but will now, no doubt, be publicly exposed. I wring my freezing hands anticipating the provincial commentary this tragedy will unleash between the visiting Visigoth and our native Gaul. I can't ignore this. I must do what's right.

I dispatch my butler, Guy, to alert the authorities while I sit here, waiting, in shock.

I feel the carnage on my shore infuse its details into my sitting room. The soft feminine shades of garnet-green upholstery meld into dark mire. The soft, white wallpaper turns grey. From now on the dead will permeate every aspect of my life. They foretell a bittersweet future that begins with male voices riding the wind when I open the rear balcony doors.

"Madame Fellner, down here, if you please."

"Coming."

I give my lips a quick once-over in the powder room mirror. My cheeks are rosy, clean and tight from the cold wet day and a good wash downstairs. Long brows are knit in a sentimental frown. Dark, grief-triggered circles below and around my green eyes confirm my lack of sleep. I tame my mess of wavy auburn tresses from the damp, and whisper to my reflection,

"Dear Emil, the beauty in this mirror atrophies for want of your love. . . ."

The riverbank mocks my trivial preoccupation with feminine middle age, and a wave of guilt sweeps over me for being intensely alive against that couple's solemn warning. My eyes scan the leafless trees above the young pines. A crowd forms on the shore. My hands shake, tightening the belt on my black mourning coat, as I descend the spiral balcony stairs for the second time today.

The Jewish corpses hover in front of me as I recall a casual conversation at the bank a week ago. I shared my frustrations with the loan officer. He agreed we French have to wait it out. I decided to take Marta to visit her Grandmaman's idyllic farm. But there, instead of peacefulness, doom haunted my haughty but vulnerable heart. Our family interlude was not safe.

There is no way to escape the shame of Nazi bondage.

And now my forty-one-year-old widow's world wobbles like a child's top near the end of its spin.

Dieter Van der Kreuzier, a music colleague, meets me at the gate. He takes my hand as we descend the pier path and sidestep puddles to the few solid areas at the river's edge. Dieter towers over me as he takes giant strides.

What is he doing here and why is he moving quickly? I can barely keep pace as we pass a crowd of onlookers. I nod to local farmers, fishermen, the Agricultural Prefect and a few neighbors drawn to the somber scene. Their murmurings rise in little grey clouds like a cold morning air of wasted breath.

"Dieter, thank you for your kindness to escort me."

His chivalry goes beyond the divisive boundaries of French caste still held dear in this provincial backwater. Yet he barely acknowledges me, distracted today. The rest of these men smirk at their town's widowed aristocrat. They stand in a colorless clutch and wait for me, their land-owning empress, to falter at the sight of our first Vichy-authorized deaths. Annoyed, I swallow thickly against the rotting odor and tuck my black-and-white silk scarf into my coat.

Within a few meters of the two bodies our Duchamps' Police Prefect, an avowed anti-Semite, commiserates facetiously, leering as he pulls on his wiry mustache.

"The river has played a ghastly trick, Madame Fellner. Sorry it's upon your doorstep."

How pompous he is. Why am I bothered with such Vichy vermin?

"Really, Monsieur, Le Préfet? The river did it? Indeed. Let me see."

I watch the swollen current in the distance as it carries debris north, and ask myself, if the Doubs carried these bodies to me despite the flow of the storm's current—where did these two come from, if not up north? It's strange. They journeyed so close to the Swiss border, yet did not cross to freedom.

I bend low for a closer inspection next to Jacques Devoir, the coroner, who turns over the bodies to expose their backs. Seeing them a second time is less shocking but no less gruesome, except, wait,

"*Mon Dieu*, bullet holes! They were murdered, yes?"

Devoir nods sadly and looks up at Alain Duvette, the town's senior doctor, a shy, edgy man. Duvette glances at Dieter and chews his lip as he flicks cigarette ash to the mud. The three men are silent, but I'm furious.

"Sshh! Madame, we don't want the whole town to know now, do we?"

Small wonder that the Gestapo officer is pleased and his French marionette is *nerveuse*. That chameleon of a mayor has the gall to scold me. The little toady wants me to shut up so he can stay on good terms with the Huns. He's so ordinary; he uses his authority to cover a spineless mentality. A far cry from the days when men like my Emil ran Duchamps. This town had class then as it did when Dieter was mayor before him. What has made us complacent?

"And why not, sir?" My raised voice grabs the rabble's attention. I will use my thespian charisma on my neighbors, the only audience I'm ever likely to entertain.

"Two young people are lying here, murdered, on my property, if you please."

"They were *Jews*, Frau Fellner," the Gestapo agent finally presses his authority, after quietly observing his prey.

"Really! And that makes their murders acceptable? Well, who are you?"

Upset at his violation of my pristine landscape, I give this Teuton an aristocratic tone before catching Dieter's glance. Kreuzier's delft blue eyes bore holes in my skull. Much taller, he stands behind the Nazi, and frowns, then shakes his head imperceptibly in a "no" that tells me it's best to change my attitude.

But speaking out was worth it. The German becomes more pliable.

"Allow me to introduce myself, Madame Fellner. Erich Heisler, head of Gestapo in this region. A pleasure to meet you."

A pleasure indeed—a trifle astonished by my candor would be more accurate. His mouth twists into the shy smile of a handsome blonde Aryan. How sad, when good looks are wasted on a specimen of the Super race. He performs a robotic military salute and clicks his German heels. I wince at his mistake. He digs his boots deeper into our muddy French terrain . . . and splashes the hem of my dress.

The French bystanders snicker.

Heisler's men about-face and take aim at the crowd!

The townspeople gasp and step back. The SS leader is flustered at this ridiculous piece of hyperbole and orders his men "at ease," excusing himself for soiling my dress. He blushes as I wipe away a bit of the stain.

This is my first encounter with an overseer of our French defeat. How can anyone seriously sport that adolescent Totenkopf, the skull and cross bones insignia on his hat and the three pips with lightning stripes on his collar? And I have to appease this Allemande harlequin when everything in me resists. *Quelle théâtre!*

Annoyed, I answer in flawless German. He's surprised and appears delighted with my distinctive Bavarian accent. The French authorities and my neighbors can't follow our conversation. He becomes relaxed as I hiss in his language . . . perhaps too relaxed. I feel his eyes rove my slim waist and shapely calves above my rain galoshes. He undresses me with his eyes while these two innocents at our feet plead their cause in decomposition.

I kneel down to touch the woman's cold grey hand. I shed a silent tear for her, when suddenly, as though she were still alive, I feel called upon to defend her and snarl an unexpected revelation to the Swastika, Heisler,

"You killed three people, Obersturmführer. She was *enceinte!*"

Immediately, the coroner kneels down to inspect. He hadn't noticed she was with child but will confirm it later. It takes a woman to sense new life—even when it's dead.

Jacques helps me stand. I scowl at Heisler and announce to the crowd,

"She never had a chance to fulfill her love with their child," then turn to the SS and town bureaucrats to finish with, "Damn this war and everyone in it!"

I have risen too quickly. The hot roll of stomach acid teases my throat. The tiny unborn corpse and this Nazi fool's bristling Aryan supremacy make my head reel and eyes roll up. My body sways toward fainting. Dieter and Jacques rush forward to steady me.

I revive to the undercurrent of murmured support from the crowd as Dr. Duvette passes lavender scent under my nostrils. I have a vague idea that a beautiful female has insulted her new German master and garnered enough public support, this time, to get away with it.

Then Marta's call wafts over us from the small second story balcony like an eerie angelus, "Maman. Maman. What is it? Who's there? May I see?"

We look up from the bodies. My eight-year-old never misses a chance to satisfy her curiosity. My eyes open wide as the Nazi spies on her through a miniature telescope. His voyeurism elicits my protective lioness. A deep, contracting pain radiates from my groin into my chest. Enough tragedy, I can't breathe.

"Excuse me, gentlemen, my child must not see this carnage." I give the predatory Kraut a cursory glare and casually wave my hand to dismiss him. His face is impassive with boredom for his Franche-Comté territory, but his eyes burn to conquer.

Provoked, I bark with authority like a general to a lowly foot soldier,

"Whatever legalities are necessary, Obersturmführer Heisler, you may see me later."

I call to my pigtailed gamine with overplayed maternal sweetness, "I'm coming, Marta. Stay there, *mon ange.*"

Cold and perspiring, my nerves shudder me back to family concerns. She must not climb down that narrow outdoor staircase on her rigid, jerky left leg.

"Begging your pardons, Messieurs. . . ."

I hold my head erect with Gallic pride as Dieter offers his arm to escort me to higher ground. The fickle gawkers part to give their new 'Marianne' a path.

"Are you all right, Ingrid?" he asks quietly when we're a short distance from the crowd . . . as if he knows my conscience is fast losing an argument with my heart.

"I'm bilious and angry but I'll survive," I whisper, and mix an ironic laugh with a sour cough, "And you, Dieter?"

I search his handsome face. Dieter manages a sweet smile but his eyes show worry. He appears distant, as though his mind sees his body swathed and his eyes blinded in some future occurrence, perhaps even more ominous. When I shake his hand, my "Thank you for your help—and regards to your Amélie," fall on deaf ears.

Until today, mourning for Emil shielded me from the death of France.

Now, I feel raw inside. My riverbank has abandoned me, and murdered Jews diffuse their sorrow upon my peaceful domain. Their ghostly presence initiates my heart into the nail-biting consciousness of wartime Europe.

What shall I say to my daughter?

Once inside I run past her into the powder room and deliver up the rest of my breakfast. She follows, tugs at my arm and chirps like a hungry baby bird with a nest full of questions.

"Maman, why are you sick? What happened out back? Why all the people? I'm scared, Maman. Why were the police here and Gestapo and Monsieur Dieter? Will the Nazis take us away?"

"No, Marta. We're safe," I cough out answers between dry heaves, "How do you know enough to think that way, *chou*?" Pursing her lips she raises her eyebrows but says nothing.

"Are you listening to the French war broadcasts over the BBC? Answer me, *ma fille*."

"Oui, Maman, just as you do. With a water glass against the closet wall in my bedroom when you think I'm asleep. Don't be angry with Grandmaman. She showed me how."

"What a clever little princess," I rinse my mouth, dry my face, and smile into her question-mark eyes. No one controls my mother's enthusiasm for her granddaughter.

"All right, angel, let's talk. No, wait. First get Marie up here with a cup of peppermint tea for me, and a buttered tartine for you with hot cocoa."

"Ah oui, Maman, I'll tell her. She just came home."

I watch Marta teeter toward the street floor kitchen. Her left foot turns in more today. She touches the furniture and walls for balance.

Cocoa is a rare, hoarded treat under rationing. It keeps her at bay when I need to think. I am at the end of a huge tin I purchased last year before the war.

I sit listening to my heart race and knees knock from the casual evil of the Gestapo and the town's sniveling bureaucrats. The couple lay still, her dead baby rotting inside her, its tiny soul gone elsewhere. Why did those poor wretches choose me, and this place?

My sprite interrupts my reflections. A stern-faced Marie walks behind her; she's worried I'll dismiss my princess when her questions can't be answered. Then it will be Marie's turn.

"Maman, tell me now; here's our tray."

"Yes, in a moment, Marta." Still freezing I stand to stoke the embers in the hearth.

"Uh, well, some people were injured on the riverbank. I went down to confer with the police." No use lying completely, she's too smart for that.

"Why didn't they bring an ambulance if they were hurt, Maman?" She deduces the truth too quickly, "Maybe they were *dead*, Maman?"

"I don't know, Marta. It's over. Get your schoolwork and we'll correct your test."

Marie raises an eyebrow as she leads Marta out to get her materials. It's harder and harder to fool my little stick of a girl these days—to protect her innocent spirit and rigid flesh.

It would be easier for us to live with her Grandmaman. I tried to be comfortable in the mountain countryside, but I need my independence here even when the loneliness is unbearable.

If I had the courage to help people like that young couple, except for my widowhood and this war, I'd have everything I ever wanted. What have I done with my life? Given away money. So what? It costs nothing to be a philanthropist. I hide my light under a bushel basket while my daughter watches me like a hawk. Before this incident on the riverbank I was content to shake my head at the war from a distance. Now that cauchemar shames me, and that young family's death will become my recurring nightmare.

꒰ꩌ꒱

An hour later, the nightmare continues. The two young Jews lie draped on gurneys inside the rear autopsy room of the morgue. Jacques and Dieter sit with me in the public salon. We three are hushed like its sparse funeral décor, thinking on these first tragic deaths in our area, wedged on my shore.

The coroner, a Freemason, is fourteen years Dieter's junior. He has great respect for Kreuzier's skill to mediate the conflicting politics of rural Duchamps. He wields his influence on behalf of farmers and local mercantile families years after he was their mayor. The region's powerful families oppose him, and support the fascist puppet, Pierre Laval. The same high caste families who have tried to coerce me to join in their collaboration.

The Nazis behind ultra-conservative Laval washed out our free-thinking societies. Rumor says the fledgling Underground here is a mix of Masons, Socialists, Communists, Protestants and Catholics. They are bound by love for Free France, respect for the dignity of human life, but most especially by their unfulfilled revenge left over from the last war.

Dieter's shrewd insight appears to level the wake of everyone's political churning now that our neutral Swiss neighbors can no longer wade legally across the Doubs' border. We lost our Swiss labor that helped produce our *Comté fromage*, our largest and oldest medieval agricultural cooperative. Today the elderly and youth make our cheese for the Wehrmacht.

I came here to the morgue to deal with death certificates and bureaucratic Vichy papers, but the bodies and their implications for my future distress me. Helplessness chafes my integrity. I voice my disgust,

"How can we be expected to live like this?"

Jacques looks up at me warily, and Dieter appears curious.

"What do you mean, Ingrid?" Kreuzier asks, as if fishing for something.

"If I do nothing, gentlemen, I'm a collaborator who agrees to the annihilation of Jews. It's inhuman, dishonorable. My family businesses, my personal rights . . . damn Laval and Pétain! They do Hitler's bidding and reduce us to slavery. Where do I sign?" I growl at the papers.

"Here, Ingrid, I checked these lines." Jacques points and I press an angry scrawl. Then I excuse myself to use the toilette. Upon my return, outside their door, I overhear my name in their conversation. Jacques paces, anxious to confirm the woman's condition, and says,

"Strange how secluded we are here while the north is pillaged viciously, Dieter. How do you think those bodies got down here from up there?" Hearing no response from his comrade, Jacques says in a louder voice, "You're too quiet, Kreuzier. Planning something, aren't you? No, don't tell me. It's the Fellner widow."

Dieter sounds surprised, as though Jacques knows he guards a secret and has figured out what it is. Dieter doesn't want to answer and says clumsily, "Yes, well, no, ah, not really."

"*Mon Oeil*! My eye! You can't fool me. You're thinking of pulling her into the group, aren't you?" Jacques interjects. I suppose he's certain his friend suffers a serious lapse in judgment to even consider involving me. "Why should Ingrid help us? Her father came from fence-sitting aristocracy. She's too comfortable. She only mixes with you because of your common interest in music."

"Come on, Jacques, her Emil was my closest friend. I knew him long before he followed me as mayor of this town."

Ooh la la . . . he's defensive; I'm amazed. I will wait until they finish before reentering the room.

"I'll be a few minutes, Dieter. Have a stronger drink if you like. Look, don't take that pretty widow too seriously. One needs cunning to deal with the damned Doryphores."

Jacques presses his concern that his friend is smitten—with me? Really?

"Be careful, Dieter. She's wealthy, and powerful, but innocent. And she has a partially paralyzed daughter to care for. If she didn't volunteer last year when everyone else did, why would she do so now?"

"I guess you're right, Jacques. But I keep wondering, could she fit in?"

Chapter Two

Dieter's Proposal

6 November 1941, Thursday

Thursday the sky is dark, rainy and forbidding, like Tuesday was on the riverfront. The octet finishes rehearsing the Christmas concert. Dieter puts his violin into its case while I sort sheet music. Everyone else has left. The ancient church is empty.

"Ingrid, may I speak with you a moment?"

"*Oui, bien sûr.* Certainly. What is it?"

"Sit down, Ingrid. It's very important." His serious tone intrigues me. I've tried not to think about what I overheard at the morgue—but have naturally thought of nothing else.

"Ingrid, I want to propose a way for you to help the Jews. Are you interested?"

"Ah oui, of course, but, are you talking about the Underground?"

"I can't answer directly, you understand."

"All right. I see. Look, you may be wasting your time. I'm a spoiled rich woman, good only at playing the role of a dutiful wife. And since I lost that job I'm only a dutiful mother. What? Do I shock you, Dieter?"

His nostrils quiver at my self-deprecating tone. He winces as if my ambivalence and self-pity have ambushed him. I confirm it with a hint of sarcasm,

"Well, Monsieur Van der Kreuzier, I was just an ornament on Emil's arm. Even if you didn't see it then, it's better you know it now."

He thought he knew me, but had yet to see my underlying anger and self-indulgence. Does he wonder how he will break through my wall of pride?

He seems unable to believe a capable woman could be hard on herself. He must know we *femmes* swallow our opinions like good little passive French breeders.

"Ingrid, you were upset the other day on the riverbank and. . . ."

"What do you need, Dieter? Money? Certainly, I can give the Résistance money. Just tell me how much."

I try not to hear him. He hasn't divulged any details of his mission and already I am upset. I think I want what he's selling but unrelenting panic answers for me. Horrible, how I want to do it with money, not with heart. I hate my queasy solar plexus. I have to do whatever he asks of me.

"Sorry, I barely give you a chance to speak and interrupt to avoid what you're asking of me."

"No, ah, I, I'm sorry Ingrid, please, excuse me."

Is he angry because I have read his thoughts, or because Jacques Devoir's judgment was correct? He stands to leave. I'm sure my attitude thoroughly frustrates him, but my fear crests in waves and fights my desire to do something bold and useful. I berate myself whispering under my breath,

"You fool. You're impossible!"

"What did you say?" he asks, bewildered by my unexpected performance.

"I can't let you leave here thinking ill of me. Forgive me; please don't go, Dieter."

"Yes, well, I'm sorry Ingrid. I must not burden you. It's too dangerous. Anyone who does this has to be strong and self-contained. Either you act from unconditional love or anger must propel you. It's a commitment from the heart either way. You reap gratification in the precise measure you live the terror. You can't have one without the other. If you think twice about it you're not cut out for it. Sorry to have bothered you."

He's made a terrible mistake and wants to leave before revealing things that are supposed to remain secret. He looks embarrassed and disappointed. As he picks up his violin case I grab his arm and look directly into his eyes. My cheeks flush. I surprise us both,

"Please, Dieter, let's start over. You've known me for years. I'm ashamed and afraid but I want to help. I've had nightmares for two days. I can't get those young Jews out of my mind. I waste half my life in mindless luxury while death was their only dignity. They had nothing but faded clothes on their backs and yellow stars over their hearts. They died for what? For following the wrong religion or being too industrious for their neighbors? Are we no further than the Dark Ages? It's obscene. Teach me what to do, Dieter!"

I wait anxiously, search his face and think all the right things but can't say them. His eyes bore into my shallow soul with awful silence, evaluating the risk.

"Please, Dieter, I can't live without a purpose beyond Marta. I've read about the Eastern massacres in the Underground tracts. Something is pulling me to do this."

"All right, Ingrid, calm down. I take a chance telling you." He has never seen me this emotional.

"You can trust me to be silent."

"Really?"

"Yes. I've been alone a long time. The friends I trusted are married to pro-Nazi financiers. A few even bought Jewish businesses up north. All Vichy, I can barely eat at their *soirées*. Their conversations are full of excuses and self-serving attitudes. The real traitors use their French wines, grains, cheese and truffles to protect their Nazi interests. My Emil, a German-born, would have been furious. I shouldn't judge, but. . . ." I shrug my shoulders.

"Yes, all right. I'm glad you're ready to come down to earth, but to follow your heart means you will shatter connections with your social rank. Yet you will still dine at their tables. You will have to pass the woman you think you are and not resist the woman you will become."

"I understand."

"*Vraiment?* Really? Can you deny yourself for someone else?"

I pull back. He is so brutal. I respond sneering,

"Well, I, I've done it my whole adult life. I'm a woman after all. Buried myself, and my dreams of a musical career in Paris for the sake of my family, as expected. But it kills me, Dieter. I want to help. I'm ready to try."

"Can you put your life ahead of Marta's to save a stranger?" He stares through me not yet convinced.

Now I pause, "I'd die if I put her in danger, but what good am I if she sees me act like a loveless coward? That's worse. I can't leave her with that legacy. Teach me what to do."

"Ingrid, this war isn't like the last one. You won't know who to trust or who will denounce you. This game is a civilian war with a brutal enemy. We have to teach ourselves, and it will be worse when Hitler gets fed up with Vichy and takes over all of France."

"You think that will happen?"

"It's only a matter of time. We hope he makes the same mistake Napoleon did in Russia. The few of us awake must stay ahead of the Krauts."

"Keep them ignorant? I saw that on the riverbank. They're strangers here. Your biggest problem would be the locals who abet them like that Fritzie Police Prefect, right?"

"You learn quickly, Ingrid."

"Yes, well, I can see one has to be alert at all times." I hope he's relieved a little bravery surfaces as I calm down. "What must I do to help?"

"Entertain their high command, Heisler and his cohorts. Have dinners, liquor, music, and female companions. Invite them when we need you to and let them escort you to parties and public ceremonies. The picture for a Nazi sympathizer is not pretty. You'll be hated until the war's over, but while you distract the Doryphores—Jews and political refugees will cross here safely."

"You mean very close contact. Fool them into thinking I'm on their side."

"Precisely."

"I don't know. It's not a matter of ethics. I agree wholeheartedly with the cause, but—am I strong enough to handle that evil?"

"I think you are but if you're afraid to do what your heart tells you. . . ." He looks me square in the eye again.

"No, you're right. I mustn't be afraid."

I couldn't collapse on him midstream.

"I take a terrible risk finding out what you're made of, Ingrid. Innocent lives will depend on you. Please don't think anyone will hold you in less esteem if you refuse. This work isn't for everyone. Remember, once you're in, you can't get out."

His proposal is no mere conversation with a vanity mirror at midnight. I will have to act on the spur of the moment. I take a deep breath to reassure my nerves as he continues,

"Ingrid, the Gestapo is stuck here. The Résistance is their enemy and as long as we're hidden, they can't touch us. They don't speak French very well and fewer of us speak a decent German. You're multilingual with high social and financial connections. That's important for the Underground. None of us have your resources. We funnel refugees east and south to Swiss and Italian borders. The only reason this part of France matters is Besançon's railway. The Maquis are the real SS quarry. They sabotage Boches' rail tracks, engines, and munitions sites. The Gestapo has enough problems fighting Maquisards. When we entertain Nazis they want to relax, they're not interested in hunting Jews. Berlin hasn't sent us hardened butchers like a few hundred kilometers north, at least not yet."

"Yes, Dieter, I understand."

"Do you?"

"Well, ah, what are the consequences if I am denounced?"

He studies my face. I try to picture this role but can't foresee the danger of cavorting with an unpredictable enemy that disrespects our civilian life. Does he believe I think my wealth will insulate me from the ugly machinations of war? How long could the Occupation last? Now that he has made the offer, perhaps he wonders if it's a mistake?

"Harboring enemies of the Reich is treasonous, Ingrid. The range of what an SS would do depends on your encounter face–to–face and how you handle your interrogation."

"Anything from a slap on the wrist to deportation to a foreign work camp. It depends on how I play it? From house arrest to death, right, Dieter?" I say the words with no idea, really, how my path could unfold and lead me to such a perilous end.

"Look, Ingrid, no one has been caught in our region. We are only of agricultural use to the Reich. The problems come to us from north and northeast where the SS leadership is harsh. There, sabotage and hiding refugees result in deadly reprisals. The Waffen SS conscript French Alsatians and order them to badger their own people."

"I see. May I tell my stepson, Stefan?"

"Absolutely not! No one's permitted to share what he does with anyone else unless it's set up that way from the beginning. Only Guy and Marie will help you."

"Why not Stefan? Being his *belle-mère*, step-mother, complicates our relationship."

Dieter clenches his jaw, not used to having his authority questioned.

"Your *beau-fils* is a young hothead. He has a keen mind but I can't trust his attitude. It's better if he hates you. Thinks you're a traitor. He's only trusted to, sorry, Ingrid, I can't say."

I feel sick withholding my position from my stepson, but Dieter's in charge. He watches me react. I hear myself turn the corner.

"All right, Dieter, I'll do it."

"Good. Wait until the Obersturmführer comes on Monday for written confirmation of the 'drownings.' Deal with him in your home first," he pauses, sizing up my courage.

"Then you'll tell me if you're ready to join the Underground."

Dieter leaves preoccupied; probably thinking I'm too complicated a woman for his mission. I wonder who else works with him? It's odd how I never thought about that before the Jewish couple showed up dead. No doubt Dieter compares my hesitancy to the silent dedication of others taking bigger risks than he asks of me. I'm sure he sees me as a typical upper-class woman of leisure. The Résistance will be an opportunity to waltz myself into a new romantic role. Does he imagine I'll seek adoration for pouring out my largesse?

I know Dieter well enough to predict his answers. He isn't telling me how to act. He is judging my discretion and honesty. This is about me, and my choices. I am on trial. If I do this, the person I am today will be dead and gone tomorrow. Is this what it means to be chosen? I can neither see what I have to surrender—nor the price I might have to pay.

Chapter Three

Encounter With Heisler

10 November 1941, Monday

Marta performs her therapy in my late husband's study on the first floor above street level. Here, for many months, my wounded princess has walked six meters back and forth a hundred times a day. Portable waist-high railings that crisscross the middle of the sunny, pale-blue room support her.

This space was cleared of furniture except for a honey-blonde art nouveau table and built-in shelves. Marta's old crutches (borrowed from the orphanage) lean on the table's gentle curvilinear woodwork. The shelves hold Emil's history and law texts, my philosophy, spiritual and religious texts, Maman's old horticultural encyclopedias, and Marta's Latin classics, Greek mythology, French, English, and German poetry and novels. The table and bookcases stand in stark contrast to her rough angular railings, oddly symbolic of our life together, pre- and post-1939.

Ammunition from a different war sits on a nearby tray: bottles of strong scents and flower essences, sponges for massage, bells, cymbals, whistles, a barrage of gear that lifted Marta from unconsciousness after the ski accident that injured her and killed her father.

Maman and I stimulated Marta's senses day after day in our desperate attempt to rebirth her from a skull fracture and blood clot. For hours we made loud noises, passed strong odors under her nose, rubbed her flesh pink, talked to her and played music. I even pressed her fingers into the keys of my Maman's antique portable harpsichord to play her favorite Bach melodies.

It took two months to do what the doctors said would never happen. We succeeded and for what? So she could be considered defective? She was injured, not born that way.

Recently, in town, a street urchin imitated Marta's jerky walk before slipping into an alley, laughing. I gripped her slightly rigid left hand to restrain her. The neighbors stared at her gimpy left foot. Marta glared back, defiant.

Hitler's obedient medics euthanize children like my Marta, and under Vichy's blind obedience her imperfections fill my heart with worry for her safety. Multiply that street urchin's taunting behavior many times over and what kind of a society will France have?

Aye, Mon Dieu, will we bury the heartless among the Aryans before they can be enlightened?

This morning I recite Victor Hugo's poetry as Marta orchestrates the muscles moving her left leg. I smile as she purses her rosebud lips and her dark blonde pigtails bob and arch from the sides of her head like parabolic antennas with red bows. She wears an oversized green woolen sweater drooping over her thighs. Her thin limbs are immersed in black woolen leggings that wrinkle down over tightly laced leather shoes. She is small-framed with long delicate fingers, the right hand strong and the left hand and leg still slightly weak.

Marta is the joy of my life—the only joy these days.

My childhood friend, Germaine, has joined us to cheer her efforts. Germaine is a difficult personality with a big heart who looks at life so directly few can stand her company. She tends to think only after opening her mouth, and quite often her foot is already in it. She is highly critical—but no more of others than herself.

I have grown used to her in our thirty-odd years together. Yet, if we had met yesterday I'd have to dismiss her personality as unsuitable for friendship—too brash and overbearing. I forgive her because she supports me through thick and thin. She enjoys watching Marta conquer her body, but too often is carried away with emotion. Germaine loves well from a distance. I don't take all her opinions to heart.

We sit in the sunny room sipping *tisane*, herbal tea. Marta walks and chatters, performing her best with our adoring attention. Germaine encourages,

"Good, Marta, lift that old leg. Easy now. I'm proud of you. Ingrid, promise me you'll get her away from here now that the war is spreading. Will you go to Mathilde's estate in the mountains?"

There's no point telling her I tried that option weeks ago. We weren't safer hidden away since the SS visits there, too.

She admonishes me sternly, not waiting for a reply, "You have to protect Marta from all this fascist rage, you know."

"I hadn't thought of it seriously, Germaine, until the backyard."

"Ay, Maman, will it happen again? Will more people die near us?" Marta asks, worried.

Sacrebleu, I wince. I should have known better than to mention the yard with my daughter present. How quickly she dives in after it. I want to keep her ears pure of that incident.

"Now Marta, you remember, we discussed all that," I shake my head.

"Well there, you see, my dear, certainly you can't have her witnessing any more unpleasantness like those drowned lovers. Damn butchers. Following those poor Jews into France, spreading their hatred and fear all over the continent. And those Anglo-Saxons at Mers-el-Kébir who sank our innocent French boys, ach! Dreadful! Lucky for you that Stefan has that inoperable hernia. At least you didn't lose him."

"Oui, I see your point. I'll certainly consider it, dear. I appreciate how much you care."

"Nonsense, Ingrid, it's the right thing to do, and above all, the safest. Let the men, the stupid fools who concoct these horrors, live with the consequences, I say."

I cringe at her chauvinism but understand its roots.

"Oh, the time, dear. I must be going."

Marta gives her a hug and kiss on her way out. I smile at how hard Germaine works to obscure her caring nature.

>ᴛᴛᴀ

Barely two minutes pass, and we're interrupted. Marie is deep in the basement; I answer the door. Germaine must be returning for something. But no, she's not. Instead, I come face to face with my future. How did Dieter know he would come to see me?

"Guten Tag, Madame, I'm SS-Obersturmführer Heisler. We met a few days ago."

Marie calls from the stairway to ask if everything is all right. Apprehension in my voice tells her no. If I accept the life Dieter offers, every time the doorbell rings it could spell disaster for us, and anyone we protect. I try not to think about it but my stomach gnaws on itself.

"Guten Tag. Bitte, come in, Obersturmführer."

As Heisler turns into the receiving salon, Marie's loving, questioning, bright-blue almond eyes give me an icy stare. Her thin lips harden into a sharp line and her forehead wrinkles like a mother fretting over an adolescent child.

But just as quickly Marie's face becomes emotionless and her movements practiced, as a housekeeper's anonymity requires. She's been with me through my marriage and Stefan's traumatic childhood, Marta's birth, Emil's death, and Marta's recovery. Worn like a second skin: stern and courageous. She's a spirit sent to protect me. We have few secrets from each other.

Marie's hard, fleshy hand grabs my shoulder as she whispers in a serious tone,

"Be prudent, Madame, please. I will bring tisane and check on you."

She turns abruptly and plunges her right hand into an apron pocket quietly fingering her rosary beads. Before I ask, she escorts Marta downstairs to the kitchen.

Marie knows my inexperience is the real danger in everyone's path.

I enter the front salon in work clothes; a woman in pants is socially unacceptable according to Vichy morality. On horseback or at home, provincial paternalistic decrees on appropriate fashion for this French *femme au foyer*, housewife, are not obeyed. Pants are easier when helping Marta bend her left knee during therapy.

Heisler stares, "Madame Fellner, sorry to bother you. I have documents about the incident on your property." He produces the papers: business-like about death.

Erich Heisler unnerves me. He is very smart in uniform with his sandy-colored hair, clear skin and blue eyes.

"Yes, of course. *Ja, natürlich.* Where do I sign?"

Hmm, he sounds official, but when I speak German, he relaxes. I watch every gesture and listen for a change of tone in his voice, an opening to take him off guard. He soft-peddles those outrageous murders. Why? Because the death of Jews doesn't matter, or he has to be nice to a simple French widow with a lot of money? Is he pursuing me? No, just too far from home. He enjoys his native language on a foreign woman's tongue. That's it. He loves the authority bestowed by the Nazi hierarchy, even if it is only a few kilometers of French territory to fuss over. He has to be lonely.

I sit at my writing desk, pen in hand, and feel his military guard drop as he leans over to point out where signatures are needed. Attracted by my skin and hair, men are all the same regardless of their national swagger. Heisler is wary of "frontier French," unsure if I am pro- or anti-Vichy, despite the name Fellner and my fluent German. I act the widow in mourning to befriend him platonically. What's next? Ah, yes, offer him schnapps, then sit and talk.

"Where do you live in Germany?" I ask, pouring his drink.

"My people come from a small town near the border with Luxembourg. My older brother married a French woman seven years ago. They live in Lyon. He runs her family's business in Germany."

Ah, oui. The first-born married money and this second fiddle has nothing.

"You're married, too?"

"No, Madame."

No, he's too poor to attract a rich woman, unlike his brother. Bashful, he enjoys my interest. He's in his late thirties. Maybe he loved once and was rejected? Had to be his limited financial position. Maybe his brother made it too easy, and gave him a small section of the wife's business to manage as a mere wage earner. He joined the Gestapo to find excitement, adventure, and power. Brainwashed, obedient without sentiment; he isn't a man of deep conviction, neither educated nor ambitious. I detect a hint of bitterness. His body went rigid at my question about marriage. He changes the subject.

"Your late husband, Emil, was known to me, Madame. My brother and I had dealings with him. Our family's retail business sold his wines in Germany."

"Is that so?" Emil's name from this German's lips pulls a raw nerve.

Marie knocks and brings in the herb tea. Her eyes sweep through the room and take us in like furniture to be polished in her daily routine. Marvelous, how disinterested she looks. Yet I tremble, slightly self-conscious in her presence. I note her fixed stare and arching eyebrow that tell me my thin blouse is too revealing and I made a mistake serving the SS alcohol too soon. Only then do I realize Heisler is thoroughly obsessed with me. I pull the cardigan over my bosom. He'll stare rudely if I don't keep him focused on our conversation.

"Um uh, yes, my late husband had German business dealings as did others in this area."

Next, Heisler cranks up Teutonic arrogance while Marie pours tea. I wonder if the reality of killing Jews sank in only after he was well installed in the SS.

"Yes, Madame, a pity that France couldn't see the Reich's point of view."

Oh no, it spills out—the Deutschland, Deutschland *über alles* propaganda. How self-righteous. Marie has heard enough and leaves the salon without catching my eye.

"Well, Obersturmführer, I take a dim view of politics. Each of us has to do what's right. I prefer to accept each person as they come. You know the Biblical scripture, 'Judge not lest ye be judged.'"

"A romantic, old-fashioned idea, Madame," he laughs confidently, "Maybe you can afford such dreams of a tolerant world, but for me it's not practical. I have to make harsh judgments every day."

He takes a sip and finishes his drink, still staring. And in this home, there are no photos of his Führer adorning my walls.

How am I to entertain this brute if we can't have a decent conversation? He knows nothing of life's refinements. I need a woman to service him and will have to let it happen here as Dieter says.

Oh good, he looks at his watch and announces he has to leave. I walk him to the door and reach out for an unnecessary casual handshake. He is gallant with a formal smile. Hesitantly, he raises my hand and bends low to kiss my fingertips. What a surprise!

"Until we meet again, Madame Fellner. *Auf Wiedersehen.*"

He's gone. Thank goodness. I rub his Nazi kiss off on my cardigan, and return to the front salon relieved he entered and exited without a "Heil Hitler." But my solar plexus wrenches painfully. I feel queasy, like a hunted animal that has run out of options for safe hiding.

Later I sit upstairs at the piano writing notes on Marta's sheet music— her next challenge to regain her precocious keyboard talent. My mind drifts back to Dieter's proposal and the uncertainty of living on the edge of my nerves. I don't realize I've already agreed to it. I've been too well behaved, and too generous, to a man who represents death.

My informal chat with the Nazi opened my door to his future visits. I haven't understood that the Third Reich is now in command of everyone's life in France. This isn't the same as identification cards and ration books. The reality hasn't sunk in despite two Jewish corpses on my riverbank. But now, since the moment Heisler rang the doorbell, a gnawing fear deep in my stomach never leaves me. No longer free to act, I can only think. And thinking is useless unless action follows.

I feel poorly equipped to carry out a deception of Herculean proportions and regret my political apathy during the years the Nazi Juggernaut gathered momentum. At least a few people are already engaged in the silent business of night crossings. Certainly, although I do not know this for sure, I must shop in their stores and depend on their services; families I've probably known all my life. Can I do what they're doing? Or, will I be a bystander and play it safe?

Inaction is tacit agreement with Hitler's tyranny. If I do nothing, when the *Boches* squeeze their Nazi trigger, my French hand, hidden under theirs, will squeeze it too.

My beloved husband would have resisted the enemy alongside his dearest friend, Dieter. That should be enough reason to act. I put down my pen. The notes become fuzzy as my eyes glaze over thinking of Emil.

What about Germaine's warning to keep my daughter safe?

I run these arguments over and over while practicing Marta's new piece. My fingers percuss my angst into the piano keys as my heart succumbs to Mozart's dark rolling arpeggios, anticipating the sad haunting melody in his first "Fantasia." The music's anticipation speaks the language of my nerves.

When I breathe deeply to suppress fatigue my mind goes blank: floating like a curtain of breeze-passive lace. Flesh disperses into space and the eye of God opens in a warning like a silver slit in the clouds. Trembling, I drop to my knees. My eyes search above the door, through a veil of tears, for great-grandfather's antique Alsatian pewter crucifix. I haven't prayed with such urgency since Emil lay dead and Marta lay near him bleeding and unconscious in the snow.

"Dear God, bless thy servant who desires to serve Thee upon her own cross. Today I believe beyond what I see. Help me tomorrow when my faith may not be strong, and I may spend hours, days, weeks . . . perhaps months . . . in pain and disbelief."

⤙⤚

I had very few close friends before this war. Only one, Agnes, defends my behavior with the Gestapo. The first rumor to destroy my reputation is based on Heisler's official visit to my home. Perhaps my former friends, who pant at the goose-stepping heels of Heisler and his Doryphore hier-archy, overheard my name in SS dinner conversation where the Nazis congregate . . . at the LaFrance Hotel. In that *haute cuisine* inn lately the favorite soupe du jour is petty *French nouveau-riche à la Vichy-soisse.*

Pro-Hun hypocrites live comfortably off German investments in munitions, precision manufacture, chemicals and French industries converted for the Reich. Agnes Balfour and her husband are different, originally from families of Swiss watch manufacturers across the border in La-Chaux-de-Fonds. I suspect the Balfours are converts from Jewish mercantile people who invested wisely generations ago to accrue sizeable wealth.

Agnes is sweet, a recent grandmother, a little round-shouldered, with curly greying hair and dimpled cheeks. We share philanthropic interests in the Duchamps' Home for Orphans and Sick Children. Her sister's French husband has had a nephew living there for decades.

Agnes, Germaine and a few others are several years my senior with time on their hands. I've strayed from their luncheons and dinner parties. Marta's condition and my widow's education in financial matters allow little leisure. They also provide legitimate excuses to avoid everyone.

Marie describes an incident in the *boulangerie/pâtisserie,* where brisk foot traffic and a deceptive yeasty aroma leaven the weight of gossip in its ration lines. Most loaves have ground oat or bean husk fillers that make the bread taste like the tasteless talk. How pure your dark wheat loaf is depends upon what political side you're on. It's worse in urban cities, even Paris, where sawdust is the usual filler.

Bells attached to the baker's narrow double-door entrance chime all morning to signal the long queue. Inside, Marie listens while she knits around the corner in a seating area reserved for the most scandalous chitchat—the kind that demands an ersatz coffee and serious *tête-à-tête.*

My "friends" position themselves at marble-topped tables and chairs with heart-shaped backrests along a pale-yellow wall near the sparse pastry display. The rising warmth from the basement ovens stokes their malicious hunger for details of my life. Wooden floorboards creak with dismay as bogus blather replaces the butter they once spread on their bread.

Jeanne, the baker's wife, is a shrewd, silent woman. Her husband Mirek sculpted figures and portraits out of bread dough every week and displayed his baked creations in the window. After *Kristallnacht* in 1938, he made Hitler's head with half a hardboiled egg in each eye, and a dark pumpernickel mustache glued on with egg white. His clientèle appreciated the Führer's yellow eyes. Marie told me Mirek stopped his artwork in 1940, fearful a protest would endanger Jewish "guests" hiding in his basement. No one questions Jeanne and Mirek's political affiliations. The best bakers in town are too valuable to lose.

Marie overhears Agnes having a chicory coffee with Germaine, who's being self-righteous as she discusses my life. Marie recounts their conversation word for word at my insistence.

"Their conversation began like this, Madame, 'So Agnes,' Germaine grilled her, asking, 'Do you know about that Nazi overseer's visit to Ingrid last week?'"

"And Agnes responded, 'Oui. Something to do with bureaucratic formalities related to that poor young couple on her riverbank.' Agnes is always dutiful, Madame, but she avoided looking at Germaine and opened her silver compact to redo her lipstick and adjust a stray lock of hair."

"Marie, none of these people, Germaine especially, can know why I'm building a rapport with Heisler. Dieter said the Underground plan has to unfold."

Marie nods in agreement. "Oui, Madame. Germaine's eyes narrowed and her penciled eyebrows arched. The way she applies her peach-colored pods of powder that dot her *foie gras* cheeks—they wrinkle with her testy grimaces every time she makes a nasty comment, like, 'Do you believe that?' Her suspicion is clear like the beauty mark stenciled on her upper lip."

"But Marie, what did Agnes say?"

"Agnes was adamant, Madame. She said, 'Certainly I believe Ingrid, Germaine. Why wouldn't I?'"

"Germaine was huffy, 'Because she's behaving like a tramp with the SS, dear.'"

Marie asks me to excuse her cattiness. "Madame, Agnes snapped back at her, indignantly, 'You're digging where you shouldn't, Germaine. Let poor Ingrid alone. That was a terrible nightmare for her. How can you be this cruel?'"

"Germaine accused Agnes of being blinded by her loyalty to you. She says you are weak and helpless, always a pushover with men. Even Monsieur Emil dominated you."

"Emil knew Heisler in peacetime, Marie."

"Oui, Madame, I remember, and Agnes reiterated that. But Germaine was rude when she said you had no morals, that you were falling for this SS and your actions were at best misguided and at worst, self-serving and outrageous."

"Ooh la la. That wasn't nice. How did Agnes respond, Marie?"

"She said the heart doesn't know political boundaries and it's your affair and no one else's. She said instead of judging you, Germaine should worry for your safety. But Germaine said she would never invite you to her home again. Agnes was quiet after that. I think she suspected Germaine was envious of you receiving a younger man's attentions. Madame DeVillement eats, drinks and smokes to excess. It has sucked her youth dry and stolen her figure. She resents your good looks. And I think they forget you're younger, Madame."

"Oui, Marie. My dear Germaine has drawn her petty social battle line against me. I'll survive her and the others, but she should never say 'never.' Her life may change as well."

"When Jeanne had your bread order ready, Madame, incensed as I was at Germaine's nastiness, I smiled benignly passing their table, and pretended I hadn't heard them. Agnes recognized me and said in a low voice, 'I hope she didn't overhear us.'"

"Germaine replied loudly, 'What if she did? She had better get used to it.'"

Meanwhile, our first Jewish escapees cross through my basement, staying two nights. I prefer to call them my Old Testaments. Lately, the word

"Juif" has taken on a fearful, negative connotation. I'm not proud of being too afraid to meet them. They know me by my *nom de guerre*, Madame Henri. I hear about them from Marie, who's disappointed I avoid them. The irony is they are German Jews. I speak their language, and could make them feel welcome, but am afraid to let their reality touch me. I give of my home, food, clothing, money and medicine, but will not meet them. Guy and Marie attend to their needs alone.

I didn't tell Marta they were in the house. She's not allowed to go down to the servants' kitchen on the floor below street level unless accompanied by an adult. Her poor balance and coordination since her accident forced me to install rough rugging for traction. It covers the front and back stairs from the street floor up to the first and second floors above the street, where she spends most of her days. Her paralysis makes it easier to keep the basement operation secret.

During these two days my mind never leaves my vestibule, and plays tricks that pluck at my nerves. I wait for Heisler to ring the doorbell and watch the Gestapo's evening curfew checks from the second story window. I worry, but in some ways it's amazing how easy it seems to hide people when no one suspects you work for the Résistance.

Yet, the fear drains me. If my guests are caught, I'll pay the price. While they are under my roof, the image of the murdered couple on my shore haunts me.

Then suddenly my lodgers are whisked away in the dead of night, across the Doubs or south to Italy—and I must find courage to face the *next* wave of refugees.

At first the three of us simply act on our orders, thankful for the freedom and anonymity to do so. As time goes on, I feel quite guilty. The equality we share in this effort to shield the Old Testaments is limited because I'm Guy and Marie's employer.

I can't let my house servants do all the unpleasant chores while they also serve me, and my daughter. Marie despises the Germans since the last War, and Guy says very little. They risk their lives daily. It's clear they are pleased to be involved in my mission.

However, the physical residue of refugee presence needs extra tending: laundry, dishes, and the rest. I take my turn, burying incriminating evidence, the refugee refuse.

I haven't secured a trustworthy plumber to install a new basement commode and repair the backyard privy. Chamber pots don't allow the waste and odor to be dispelled quickly in the basement, and we can't use the plumbing on the upper floors in case of a raid. The bath and toilette in the servant's quarters are right under the receiving salon. Their normal use by Marie and Guy raises doubt from Heisler, who's unaccustomed to sit amidst wealth with servants moving about.

My only choice is to fertilize my flower gardens all winter. Dealing with putrilage is as much help as I can give without actually meeting my lodgers face to face. Hopefully, astounding blooms this spring will mean my odious *arbeit* will have been worth the effort.

Later this week, Agnes stops by. Marie is delivering medications to other Résistance families for the pharmacist, Philippe. Guy calls me from the balcony. I leave my gardening buckets, climb the stairs and remove gloves, apron, and boots before I enter through the balcony doors. I give my hands a good wash, quick sniff and a slather of lavender oil.

"Bonjour, Agnes, good to see you, my dear."

I greet her with a kiss on each cheek, a bit disheveled in my stockinged feet. What I was just doing would be beyond her comprehension, but I love her for caring. "How are you? What's new?" I ask with genuine interest.

"Oh well, not much. But look at you," she surveys my disarray.

I give her a lame gardening excuse for this time of year, except luckily it's a warm day outside. She seems satisfied and runs through the usual rumors, then stops short.

"I, uh, I had a terrible experience with Germaine earlier this week, Ingrid."

I don't have time to listen to her drag it out in bits and pieces. Marta has a piano lesson; I have more manure to bury, and laundry to finish with Guy. I keep it light-hearted. "I know why you're here, Agnes. Marie overheard. Thank you for standing up for me. Germaine's jealous. Now, how are your boys?"

I divert the whole conversation and our visit is done in less than thirty minutes. With another kiss and a hug, she leaves feeling better.

It's all I can handle. I've examined my haughty attitude since joining the Underground. Although nervous for the risk, I'm more comfortable within myself, and less driven to be rigid or perfect. Bowing to others' opinions without mutual respect is easier when living my own truth, if only in secret. The way everyone's tongues wag in town my good name will soon be so slandered that even Agnes won't want to see me anymore.

If she only knew how exciting my new life is now! Hurled from the boredom of throwing backgammon dice in the LaFrance gaming room to the humbling thrill of burying human refuse in my yard.

It's much cleaner to bury *la merde* than to accommodate Gestapo officers. But where will my ignorance lead me?

Chapter Four

Exacting the Full Price

30 November 1941, Sunday

We play Russian roulette with the SS every time the front door opens. The pressure to act with a calm and casual air whenever Old Testaments are in the basement is almost too great a deception to pull off. Guy or Marie can cross the frontier between the basement and upstairs receiving salon to inform me of "forbidden guests" arriving. But I don't know what's happening in the rest of my home unless one of them alerts me.

Guy and Marie have learned to shield their emotions on the job, but I have not. To ingratiate myself convincingly to Heisler requires a focused performance. Slight disturbances make me apprehensive—when I hear Marta on the stairs or Marie knocks at the salon door. On stage at all times, it's even worse when I'm alone with the SS in the house.

We design an elaborate front door bell system to protect me from suspicious Gestapo and SS officers. Guy installs a second chime that hooks into the downstairs kitchen and the basement below it. He hides its buzzer in the embossed copper frame of a face mirror hanging in the front vestibule. Marie places a spray of lavender over it.

We push the secret button before opening the door when we see Boches through the narrow side windows. We alert everyone in the basement and kitchen before we usher the Doryphores in. And then, we fuss over them without the delay that arouses their knee-jerk instinct to raid for Jews. One buzz means one Nazi. Two buzzes mean two Nazis. Two short presses and a long one means refugees must hide in the cellar chambers immediately with no talking.

Bouquets of drying lavender and garlic bulbs hang near the basement windows of the outer rooms. There the refugees take their meals at a long table used to prepare food for canning, pickling, drying and smoking. Against the cellar walls we have locked floor-to-ceiling cabinets stocked with preserves, canned fruits, wine, vinegars, fermented vegetables, hand tools, smoked fish and meats, dried herbs, tinctures, and olive oil. The crosswise wall rotates on hidden rollers for easy, quiet opening. Up to twenty people hide behind it. This false facade and the buzzer fortification upstairs put me more at ease.

The Obersturmführer is well behaved during our initial encounters. I have no choice but to "invite" him when he asks to come. On some of those evenings a group of Old Testaments hide somewhere in town, often in my basement. Tonight Guy and Marie tend to our downstairs guests while upstairs Heisler enjoys a good dinner, cigarettes and liquor.

We listen to music. Sometimes I sing Schubert "Lieder" at the piano—alas, the only bit of aesthetic sensibility in the man. Otherwise I listen patiently as he tries to convert me to the Reich.

Dieter asked me if he wanted a prostitute. I casually suggest it to Heisler each time he comes but he isn't interested. I think he has someone in town, but I grow more skittish each time he comes for dinner. I tell Dieter I'm afraid he's pushing me to have sex, but deny the seriousness of the situation.

Heisler restrains himself as long as possible. Then finally one night, he grabs me for a kiss. As I resist it dawns on me that he thinks I'm a lonely young widow who desires him and that's why he is invited. How foolish not to perceive the situation from his point of view.

How did I make such a dreadful mistake? I should have been brusque and refused his visits occasionally—and had another woman here from the start. I was much too naïve, bound up in my noble mission to save Jews. I refused to see his deviousness. Now I have to pay the price for not living in the present moment. Ach, Ingrid, you fool.

There is something else odd about him. He knows more about me than what I have told him. There is no way to substantiate where he gets his information. Knowing someone else in Duchamps is behind him makes me more apprehensive. However, each time Dieter instructs me about crossings I also neglect to say someone feeds Heisler background about me.

On three different occasions Heisler shows his impatience to claim me as his spoil of war. I hesitate to tell Dieter. I think my dilemma is small compared to finding safe hiding places for Jews. But the daily worry is a pressure that chews my stomach and clouds my judgment. Stupidly, I let it slide.

To complicate matters Heisler is clumsy and insecure with women. Perhaps he believes I secretly hate him. Naturally, it never crosses his mind that if I do it's because I'm a captive female. All women are captives for this Hun. Nor does it matter if I dislike his politics. Heisler wields power as if he's entitled to the world. I cannot foresee how my ambivalence and fear will destroy my safety. Instead I worry that everyone else in the household is vulnerable.

I interject my painful widow's memories between us to fend off Heisler's advances. I avoid . . . and then tease him as the pressure to succumb increases. By the eighth visit he demands small sexual favors. He holds my hand. I have to accept an embrace. Finally I must accept a kiss. Each move is initiated with adolescent sincerity and inexperience.

It becomes harder to ignore the usury until one night he holds me in his arms, laughs and threatens to raid my home for Jews. My heart almost leaps out of my chest. My body tenses the moment he uses the word "raid."

I see how porous the wall is between what he knows about me and what I'm actually doing. I project instant aristocratic hauteur at his preposterous warning to convince him he has insulted me. How can I protect myself from a needy boy who craves power and lusts for attention behind his Teutonic obedience? I'm sliding into an inevitable abyss. I refuse to face it and deny where it could lead me.

I stop protesting to Dieter. He doesn't hear me. I try to handle everything alone; afraid to tell him I freeze at Heisler's touch, and that I slither from his arms to destroy his amorous moods. Again I mention a woman to Erich, but he's annoyed. It's too late in the game. I've done everything short of letting him satisfy his desire and still keep my distance.

My vacillation is ridiculous and adolescent. I avoid sex yet act like an alluring slut mystified by Aryan supremacy. Heisler doesn't believe an intelligent woman could be motivated to risk her life for Jews. He has to think I'm a wealthy pro-fascist type.

Yet there's always that hint of mistrust. He has a jealous nature and keeps tabs on me like a secretly obsessed predator. Is this an inherently controlling nature or a maniacal overlay of Nazi indoctrination? Or both? I think he dreams of marrying me when the war is over. Naturally he dreams Germany will win the war.

We never talk about anything important. Heisler's unwritten law is a woman can't hold up her end of an intelligent conversation. Like many women in rural households throughout France—my feelings never matter.

In a desperate move to avoid sex but maintain his visits, I teach him ballroom dancing. He needs to know how to dance if he expects to mingle with the Vichy set. It works until the night he succeeds in leading me around the room with a sense of rhythm. His hands begin to rove the contours of my torso. I manage to separate myself after the dance with a suggestion of liquor.

We finish our brandies. I sit forward to rise from the divan and walk him to the door to end the evening when he pushes me back down onto the seating. Immediately he presses himself over me and forces a hard kiss. I push him off me. I try to make my rebuff a casual but conclusive 'no.' He grabs me again and violently bites my breast through my clothes. I cry out defiantly and wriggle away from him. I can hardly catch my breath—afraid he'll be a beast.

"*Jamais comme ça!* Never like this, Herr Heisler!"

Humiliated, he narrows his eyes and dictates like an overseer to a social inferior,

"*Keine Weigerungen mehr!* No more refusals, Frau Ingrid! No more playing with me. You will have me! *Sie werden mich haben!*"

"*Nein! Ich werde nicht!* No! I won't! I will not accept such coarse behavior from you or any man, Obersturmführer. You will make love and not rape, Herr Erich."

"*Das hängt von Ihnen ab, meine Liebe!* That depends on you, my dear!"

His voice is rough with lust in both languages. I've never been so demeaned. It frightens me worse than his hands ripping away layers of my clothes and grabbing my soft, vulnerable flesh. I pray my passivity will mitigate any physical pain but my compliance excites him. Tears of lost pride pool in my ears, as my taut dry womb resists his thrust.

He consummates himself on my salon divan. The sex is clipped and mechanical. My skin ripples with revulsion until the shock of his orgasmic grunt encases me in ice. I can't look at him and send him away gruffly with no further submission to his SS authority. He doesn't care. He got what he wanted.

What else could I have done? Marie was upstairs with Marta, who was in bed with a cold. Guy was somewhere in town.

I can't report Heisler to the local Vichy authorities. They would spy on my home and threaten my secrets. If I don't accuse him, I'll be forced to entertain the brute like any local prostitute. If I do refuse him, I can't expect benign neglect from the Pétainist locals enamored of enemy investments. Heisler could implicate my mother and me in an extortion scheme—blackmail us—and force us to join the collaborationist *Parti Populaire Français*. We're the only non-fascist upper caste partners in our local Fromage Cooperative. No one wants to align with Vichy, but many good families with adolescent sons must capitulate or face financial ruin, and the possible loss of their home. I have no choice but to submit to Heisler to protect my political independence and my lodgers.

My body rides a new emotional seesaw of opposing personas. I'm uneasy, short-tempered and confused. There is only one sparing grace after Heisler's victory: I continue to avoid meeting the Old Testaments that come through my basement.

My innocence has made me reckless. Fresh resentment wells up inside me. How much more abuse will this game of survival exact? How much violence can one person bear with a peaceful heart committed to rescue a few people?

I'm desperate to wall off my new grief in a corner of my mind reserved for widowhood and feminine adversity. But this rape doesn't fit anywhere. Until Heisler, Emil was my only lover. Gentle, my husband knew how inexperienced I was. He taught me how to love him. It was part of our attraction. I was afraid to trust any other man. Now I retreat, hiding my loving heart behind a stiff, snobbish exterior.

The next morning, alone in my bedroom, I stare out the window at the apple orchard. Suddenly I hear the pop of gunfire and see a doe wildly crisscrossing the neighbor's field. I feel the deer's urgency and relief when she finds camouflage in my apple orchard, and escapes a second bullet that would have heralded her death.

Chapter Five

Exposed

8 December 1941, Monday

The Americans are in the war. London BBC radio reports the Japanese bombed Pearl Harbor in Hawaii. I hope *les Amis*, the Americans, will not delay helping us because of it. I fear a long siege if that great nation has to fight a war on two fronts.

For our small part, Guy and I reorganize the large backyard: a space about one hundred by eighty-five meters. We have to hide increased wear from the refugees, install more steppingstones and gravel walkways. Footprints are too obvious on the dirt paths.

We build up flowerbeds with brick walls to keep the soil in place when it rains, giving more room to bury waste. Bags of lime to degrade manure are hidden under the false bottoms of large attractive planters. We place them conveniently among the flowerbeds. Luckily, we have a few clear December days this year. Guy and I do the outdoor work ourselves.

I'm thankful for Guy's strength and mechanical skills. He is a paradox. Gentle and kind, he sometimes appears simple-minded although he's actually detached in service. His rough facial features are in direct contrast to his baby-fine grey hair. He is an attractive man despite cheeks marked by childhood smallpox.

Guy's discretion will ground me in the coming months when people reveal their weakness as though he's invisible. He sees human nature with uncanny accuracy yet rarely dislikes anyone. Guy carries a German Ausweis identity card. It permits him to be out after curfew to deliver medication for our apothecary, but he also uses it for the Résistance. He moves through the long nights, bending with the seasons, and never compromises his principles. His manly presence rests my mind from the constant worry of a raid.

I don't let myself believe Marta notices my agitation after Heisler's visits. She's a child and doesn't understand adult affairs. Well, that's my lie to avoid the topic and hide the abuse. Marie keeps us apart after my relations with Heisler, waiting for the cold compresses to shrink my swollen red eyelids back to normal.

For weeks I avoid telling my angel about the Old Testaments passing through our basement because entertaining the SS at the same time makes me self-conscious. I'm responsible for Marta's safety, yet she and everyone in the house are in greater danger if she doesn't know the truth. Eventually the reason for protecting our fortress becomes impossible to hide. I have to trust that my daughter's intelligence will allow her to analyze and act as quickly as an adult.

Her paralysis is my greatest concern. I nurse a morbid fear that her rigid left leg will bring terrible tragedy upon us, despite her physical progress. I question my objectivity—driven by the pressure of possible exposure and denouncement from my neighbors.

When I finally include Marta in our secret communication, her hearing proves to be sharper—and her vision much keener—than any adult. She is the only one who can hide on the small upstairs kitchen balcony obscured by ivy. There she peers through binoculars hidden in the vines with a good view of three-fourths of the yard. This balcony is accessible to outgoing refuse pipes from the tiny kitchen upstairs. The pipes reach down into the basement. This tiny kitchen also has a dumb waiter that moves from the serving kitchen on the street floor to the main kitchen below on the servants' floor. Marta creates a code on the sinks' pipes similar to the front doorbell system that alerts the basement. It's her idea and becomes her responsibility. I'm grateful for her ingenuity. She's found a way to alert the household without relying on her slow legs and poor balance on the stairs.

Without a profusion of fragrant flowers, crossings in the winter are harder to obscure. In spring and summer, rose arbors and espaliered cherry trees create a maze of shapes interspersed with walls of fragrant sweet pea, bean vines, delphinium, bergamot, and giant sunflowers. Spiked heads of digitalis stand tall, a riot of colorful bells cascading amidst fennel, borage, and hedges of lilac and evergreen. These make a search too confusing unless one is familiar with the yard's hidden spaces. A few pathways lead to the house. We plant new rows of large flowering shrubs for extra cover in winter.

For years we placed a board over the refuse hole in the old outhouse to store garden tools. Now the privy is back in service to relieve pressure on my home's ancient plumbing.

People who walk along the river path at night outside of my high walls are vulnerable to Gestapo curfew patrols. The SS searches for Jews who cross the river. We time the use of the outhouse for lodgers to be safe. The flower fragrances easily obscure refuse odor in spring, summer and autumn, but in winter it isn't that simple. Nevertheless, we do all we can to "beautify" the property.

And then one chilly moonlit night our efforts are put to the test. The river moves lazily. The willows hang low, their dense branches, although bare of leaves, conceal the shadows of a small rowboat cutting through the silken water. A gentle breeze softens the loud, rhythmic tinkles of water dripping from its oars in a countdown to an ominous curfew. Precisely timed, a Jewish family disembarks at my pier.

I peek out the balcony window as I lower the black bombing curtains.

Heisler will arrive shortly. Through the trees under the one light by the dock, I watch the oarsman unroll a mat of light burlap onto the short muddy path between the pier's dirt walkway and the steep climb to our back gate. The family walks on it quickly in silence. A minute passes and they ascend the hill. Guy unlocks the gate and ushers them in. The oarsman rolls up their footprints in the mat, turns off the light, and rows downstream. The whole operation takes less than two minutes. The ground appears untouched.

I was told the Stumachers are gifted German musicians with family awaiting them across the Swiss Border. The father, Nathan, is a well-known violinist of the disbanded Jewish Orchestra of Stuttgart. His wife Paulina plays piano. Their nine-year-old is a piano prodigy and the six-year-old plays flute.

The family made a harrowing run from their home in 1940. They hid in a farmer's silo rebuilt with a false floor suspended about halfway up. The Stumachers gave their life savings in exchange for their hosts' silence. They had to leave once the grain supply feeding them was diminished. Time was running short. Suspicious neighbors threatened their host family. They moved on, and will lodge with us for two nights.

Evening commences when Heisler arrives at 7:00 p.m. for his customary entertainment: dinner, cigarettes, liquor, music and sex. Downstairs Marie prepares a cold meal for the family, heats water, carries linens and trays of food to the area in front of the false wall and then readies the chamber pots. Guy serves us upstairs while Marta practices on an upright piano near her bedchamber—also upstairs and around the corner from the tiny kitchen.

I turn on my gramophone to cover any sound made in the backyard. This permits Guy to carry a railroad lantern outside without detection as he guides our refugees quickly along the garden path to the rear door.

By 8:00 p.m. Heisler is relaxed with brandy and distracted by foreplay. All proceeds smoothly except Marie calls through the door that she needs a word.

"What is it, Marie?" I whisper in the hall to handle this interruption quickly.

"The father has diarrhea. He wants to use the privy outside. What do we do? He's too embarrassed to use a chamber pot. His family will eat in the same area. He's ill. The odor will be bad. He can't use my toilet. It's right under this room. Heisler can't be suspicious."

"All right. Guy can take him to the outhouse but he has to stay there until the curfew check at 8:15 p.m. is over. Give him an extra sweater. Tell Guy to listen for the SS before he returns the poor man to the cellar. Go quickly, the check is in a few minutes."

But of course, being upstairs, I have no idea what will actually transpire. Music drowns out the noise outside and I always lock the door when Heisler wants sex. Tonight I'm very uncomfortable, but dare not show it or the Nazi will suspect a cover up. I shouldn't appear distracted but I do. Heisler has to think I want him even when he's only interested in his climax. That makes our usury contemptible and painful. I light a cigarette for him and button my blouse not a moment too soon.

The front door bell rings.

I don't hear Guy or Marie on the stairs. I excuse myself to answer. I'm worried. I need them. Through the narrow window I see another Nazi uniform. What's this? Quickly, I buzz to alert the basement, and open the door. My job is to acquiesce under all circumstances.

"*Gute Nacht, Offizier?*" A young SS stands there, awkwardly, an underling not an officer, but maybe if treated as one he'll leave promptly with his ego sufficiently inflated.

"Offizier, ah. . . ."

"Krieger, Madame," he replies, staring over my shoulder. Both the receiving salon and inner vestibule doors are ajar; he sees a sliver of light.

"What can I do to help you, Offizier Krieger?"

I'm increasingly paranoid. Why is this man nosing around if this isn't a raid? Then Heisler's voice calls from the front salon, annoyed, "Who's there and what's taking so long, Ingrid, my dear?"

At the sound of his superior's voice, the young Boche's eyes open wide.

"Forgive me, Madame, I don't wish to intrude upon your evening," he blushes, turns and walks briskly back to the street before I utter a word. I close the door and take a deep breath, return to Heisler and say nothing. He leaves a few minutes later.

⤙⤚

I think all is well until later that evening, after the Stumachers have retired to bed. I meet with Guy, Marie and Marta in the servants' kitchen to review what was an almost catastrophic exposure of our basement operation.

Guy is a bit shamefaced telling me his part in the story, "Madame, I was walking back to the basement when I tripped on a steppingstone that lifted up in our last rainstorm. My hand caught the metal watering can and I fell."

"You fell, Guy? Oh my God! Are you all right? Why didn't I hear it?"

"Because the gramophone was playing Heisler's favorite tune, Maman, that demonic '*Ride of the Valkyries*' by Wagner. All that Allemande horn bluster must have smoothed out the metallic clatter of Guy's fall. His brass lantern hit the metal watering can at just the right moment! Wunderbar, Maman! Wagner is on our side, *n'est-ce pas?*" Marta cackles, jubilant at the divinely inspired timing. I sit in disbelief at how protected we are.

"The flame in the lantern went out," Guy continues sheepishly, "and a Gestapo agent on the other side of the wall heard me, Madame, and banged on the gate."

"Right, Maman, and I was upstairs next to the kitchen, practicing. Just as I paused to turn the page of my sheet music, I heard Guy's fall outside and raced to my post on the balcony. I scanned the yard through my binoculars and followed the beam of a Daimon torch back to an SS! Oh, Maman, I was shocked to overhear Guy talking with a German officer. The back gate was open and our garden was exposed."

"What did you do, Marta?" (My legs start trembling beneath the table.)

"I galloped to the kitchen pipes under the sink and grabbed the wrench and tolled the alert. Marie, downstairs, heard my warning. Right, Marie?"

Marta puffs with pride over her fast action.

Marie smiles and concurs, "Oui, I heard Marta, and pushed the children and mother into the far recesses of the chamber. We grabbed pots, pans, and food to put in the rear. I closed the family behind the false wall, gave the room a quick sniff, and ran to the back door.

"I was worried for poor Herr Stumacher. He heard the crash. I was afraid he'd leave the privy. Later, when he returned to the basement he told us he had wanted to help Guy but was weak and couldn't get up from his crouched position. Poor man, helplessly lightheaded and chilled, he overheard Guy talking to a Nazi only thirty meters away! He was sure the SS would discover him. He broke into a sweat and nearly passed out.

"I opened the door from the basement and called sweetly to Guy. When he didn't respond I panicked. Either I could do nothing, or take some bold action to show we're innocent of hiding Jews. I couldn't let the Nazi enter the house."

"That's right, Marie, and meanwhile, Maman, I banged the pipes again to say the SS had no dog. When you heard that you decided to step outside, right, Marie?" My Marta is so proud of herself.

"Oui, Marta. I gathered my wits and walked down the path trying to be calm, and said, 'Good evening, Offizier. How can I help you?' He asked me who I was. I told him the housekeeper for Madame Ingrid Fellner and Guy was my husband and her butler. 'Is there a problem?' I asked.'"

Marta interrupts to play the part of the Nazi and takes over telling the tale. "Maman, this young SS announces, 'We have evidence of people on the river path this evening. See here, footprints.'"

"Then Maman, Marie says, 'Oh, Offizier, Madame Fellner had a load of stones delivered today. Look.'" I saw her point to the nearby wheelbarrow weighed down with stone, sinking into the soft soil, surrounded by footprints and heard her say, 'Perhaps that's what you saw, Offizier?'"

Marta interrupts herself to digress, "Hey, Maman, this permanent fixture wasn't convincing tonight. We need to do something else. Guy was at a loss for what to say next. The SS insisted on coming into the yard to look around. Your turn, Marie," Marta grins, "Listen to this, Maman! This part is incredible!"

"Yes, I challenged him, Madame, I said, 'Excuse me, but do you know where your superior is?' It was crazy, but I was desperate to keep the Nazi out of the basement. Guy stood behind him and shook his head at me in a 'no,' but I ignored him. My forwardness surprised the SS. But it worked."

"Oui, Maman, he asked, 'Madame, what does that have to do with this?'"

Then Marie says, "Well, SS-Obersturmführer Heisler has just eaten the dinner I cooked for him and Madame Fellner upstairs, there."

"Marie said it with such authority as she pointed to the balcony, Maman."

"I was exasperated at my wife's candor, Madame Ingrid. Zut! Because then my Marie asks the Nazi, 'Perhaps you'd like to see for yourself? You know, come in and report to your superior directly?'"

"Really, Madame, only a woman could get away with such nerve!"

"Oui, Maman, then the SS answers, 'Oh no, Madame, that's fine, I wouldn't wish to disturb him. Excuse me.'"

"I heard it all from the balcony, Maman. Marie did a great job. You should be on stage, Marie." Marta bubbles over, continuing, "And then Marie says, 'No problem. We are happy you do your job faithfully to keep us safe. Good evening, Offizier.'"

"You should have seen Marie curtsy and raise her eyebrows for Guy to edge the German out. Marie made him curious enough; he went around to the front door. It was brilliant, Maman!"

"Just how did you see Marie's features, young lady?" I ask amazed.

"With daddy's binoculars. Guy and Marie were standing under one of the bright new street lamps you had installed. It was easy. Oh Maman, Marie was very convincing. Guy led the SS out and bolted the heavy gate. I saw you, Guy, when you grabbed her hand and smiled at her in the moonlight. Then you two checked on Herr Stumacher."

"He was too weak to stand on his own, Madame, so we helped him into the basement. I knocked three times on the false front to alert Nathan's wife. She came running and cradled her husband's perspiring head in her arms. He almost fainted."

Marie continues, "His wife asked if we could help him with his ailment. She fears it will kill him and leave the family destitute before they cross into Switzerland. They're exhausted from pursuit and starvation. We gave him tea, lavender salts and heavy blankets."

After this dangerous exposure we decide on a spoken code. New lodgers with medical problems requiring immediate attention will be referred to as "leaks in the plumbing." Approaching Boches are to be known as "neighbors in need across the way." This is how we will protect ourselves in our civilian world of clandestine warfare.

Before taking a little hot chamomile we hold hands across the table and give thanks for our lodgers, our good luck this evening, and the innocence of young Nazis. Marta suggests we practice meowing like cats in case we knock over anything else in the yard at night. She volunteers to test her accuracy on the neighbor's cat. Her childish jest is a welcome relief.

It's past eleven but the evening isn't over. Marie talks to me after Marta goes to bed.

"Madame, the parents are weak and malnourished, their bodies are beginning to break down. We should keep them here for a week. Amélie can give them tonics and remedies to rebuild their strength. They face a long trek through Les Planchettes after crossing the Swiss border. Please let me help them."

"Oui, bien sûr, Marie, I'll ask Dieter to arrange for the next people to stay elsewhere until the Stumachers are ready to travel."

My voice is flat and dry with fatigue. Marie is relieved but her hands are fidgety.

"What is it, Marie? You're not satisfied?"

"Madame, please, can you come down and meet this family? I know they would be so. . . ."

"No, Marie, I'm still shaking from tonight's confusion. I ah, I'm barely able to handle deceiving Heisler and his cohorts."

"But Madame, it would mean a lot. We have a hard time communicating. For you it's easy. The Gestapo doesn't come in the mornings. Please give a few minutes to answer their questions? It would help us," she smiles sweetly, but her voice holds a hint of reproach.

"Marie, for you it's simple to see what I should do. I agree. I can handle Heisler alone, but if my fear affects what I'm juggling here I could make a mistake in his presence and say or do something to give us all away. Please understand. I'm not aloof and unloving, just terribly frightened."

I lower my head in shame for exposing my inner turmoil. Marie's eyes become red, filled with remorse, as she plunges her hand into her pocket, probably to clasp her rosary.

I think, dear woman, I numb myself every time Heisler demands relations. I must defend against wanting the warm loving arms of my husband to stay rooted in the present.

"You don't understand, Marie, this is more than enough sacrifice. Sorry to disappoint you. Please, don't ask again."

She touches my arm as I stand to leave, too drained to say good night, and suggests,

"Perhaps if I bring you a note written in German, do you think you could answer the family by writing back to them? I could be your courier, Madame."

Undone by my housekeeper's sincere devotion, I whisper, *"Oui, bien sûr. Bonne idée."*

<hr />

It's Thursday, December eleventh, and Dieter brings me instructions for new travelers when I haven't recovered from Monday evening's escapade with Offizier Krieger and the Stumachers. He seems less preoccupied than before when I tried to speak about the Obersturmführer. He sits on the end of the divan. A small reading lamp sheds a soft glow over the cobalt blue sweater that highlights his eyes. His cheeks are red from the damp cold night. He warms his hands with gifts for my supine service— hot English tea and whiskey. I sip a small glass of port and sit on the edge of the rocker.

I'm tired and uneasy. My emotions have been brewing since Heisler first touched me. In only a few short weeks, everyone in town is convinced I'm a Nazi sympathizer. Dieter's razor-sharp sensibility knows I want to unburden myself. I gather courage to tell him.

"Dieter, I can't go forward any more with the Résistance. I'm sorry. I have to back out."

"You can't do that, Ingrid. It's too late. There's no safe way for you to stop seeing Heisler. You would put yourself, the Jews and the whole operation at grave risk."

"Yes, I know and I'm very sorry but I can't fake the rest of this game. He's put pressure on me to . . . um."

"Go to bed with him?"

"Yes." My eyes open wide at how easily Dieter figures out my dilemma. "So?"

"*So?* It's *so* easy for you to agree that I must do it? How dare you treat me *so* lightly!"?

Anger rises like a fiery ball from my stomach. I want to blame Dieter. The far recesses of my conscience won't let me, but my mind takes over and for a few delicious seconds I surrender to childishness. His response, catching me by surprise, is harsh,

"Ingrid, nothing about this war is easy. I waited for you to say something. I could have gotten a woman to satisfy him. You never came forward. What do you want from me now?"

I stare at him, lashed to pain and frustration, stymied by images of rapes that occurred exactly where he sits on my divan.

"I had no idea you were hiding all this. How many times did you think I'd ask if you needed help?" His voice softens with pity as my face stiffens with anger.

"Hiding? Dieter, you knew this would happen. You watched me go through this hell for a month and did nothing before it came to this." He won't rescue me.

"Right," he groans, "This is the seed I've sown?"

Surely it is, I think. My regal arrogance is transfused with weeks of shame, all wasted, germinating in silence. I've saved my pain for tonight.

"Dieter, I'm not a man. I'm a woman. For mercy's sake, how could you throw me to this German dog like a piece of old meat?"

"But you didn't say anything, Ingrid."

His words hang between us like a death sentence. My disgust will explode in another second. He warned me; now he reaches to hold my hand. Will he condescend and say this isn't the end of the world?

"Ingrid, dear, can it be all that bad for you?"

"What? *Zut!*" Anger spews in a stinging slap across his face. He grabs my wrist.

"Don't touch me!" I pull away, insulted.

"What are you doing, woman?" Astonished, Dieter fingers his blood streaked cheek and glares at his spoiled, unrepentant acolyte, then laughs bitterly, "Did you mean to snag me with your diamond wedding band?"

He insinuates I'm throwing his friendship with my late husband at him when he and I shared a deep attraction despite our marriages to people we adored. I've never flirted with him since my widowhood. How loose does Dieter think I am—or does my SS debauchery fit his fantasy?

"I can't believe this is happening," I whisper, humiliated by his scornful laughter, "How dare you assume it should not be *so bad* for me? Yes, you asked about supplying a woman for Heisler, only once, early on—when I had no inkling of his intentions."

I was too flattered by them and regret my stupidity, but am too angry to be contrite.

He addresses me as if I'm a troublesome brat, "My dear girl, I'm sorry, but good men kill every day in these times."

"Oh, that means I should lie down for this bastard and sacrifice my feminine dignity on the altar of the French Résistance? Don't preach to me about honor. How could you be such a brute when I trusted you, Dieter?"

"Come on, Ingrid, men are trapped in a web that's not of their own making. I regret you've had to stoop so low to secure safe crossings for innocent victims. How I wish it weren't necessary."

"*Necessary?* It was a foregone conclusion this would happen?"

"No, I'm sincerely sorry this happened. Please, Ingrid, I thought you knew how bad this could get. You're part of it now, up to your beautiful neck. You're a soldier on the same battlefront as any of us. If you retreat, the SS will know you're in the Underground. They'll use you until you're totally degraded, or arrest you and then who knows what they'll do? You have the upper hand as long as you play along."

"Upper hand for being molested?"

"No, Ingrid, to pass Jews to safety under their noses." He rolls his eyes heavenward, "Forgive me, woman, I can't control what happens. Look past your pain at the real mission here."

"But Dieter, how could you let me live in a deluded, idealistic little world when you knew it would come to this?"

"Sorry to say this, Ingrid, but *your* reality and *your* feelings are *your* problem, not mine."

"How dare you behave like some low-life bar-room bully?"

By refusing to let me get away with self-pity, he avoids facing his underlying guilt. He grasps my shoulders and twirls me around to face him. Dieter runs his hands down my arms and envelops my tiny wrists, shaking them with emphasis as he insults me.

"Stop it, Ingrid! Don't hold me responsible for the ignorant romantic notions you concoct sitting alone in this château with Marta day after day!"

As he drops my hands at the end of his patience, I turn to stare at the fire.

"Damn it! What do I do with you now? You're such an innocent. I had no idea. You had to tell me, Ingrid. *Sacrebleu*, I have too much on my shoulders."

He sighs, frustrated, and touches me lightly on the arm—afraid I will hit him again. He whispers in my ear, sweetly contrite,

"Ingrid, I'm sorry. Please accept my apology. I can't lose your friendship."

"Get out!" I reply starkly, suddenly rigid to his touch, "I won't do this any longer. I won't be a *Feldmatratze* for the Third Reich!"

I face him, "Damn you, Van der Kreuzier. You just drank SS payment for my erogenous field mattress duty. You manipulated me into your confidence then left me to fend for myself. Me, be *your* friend? I can't risk it. Go home!"

He grabs my shoulders, unable to leave us like this. His eyes sear my tear-stained face, exasperated, "Not before I tell you how much trouble you are. I have to be your teacher, confessor, even a good propagandist all at once. You're so difficult. Like a frightened young fawn separated from its mother for the first time."

My word, he has had confidence in me. His voice has an almost obsessive need. I feel intoxicated as his hands radiate warmth in my arms and must suppress the nudge to surrender to him. He, too, distances himself and mutters, "How do I soften your stony heart?"

Our eyes are riveted to each other. We circle like gladiators in a mental arena. He can't let me bow out. It's too late. He appeals to my intelligence when my feminine neediness disarms him. He's defensive and reinforces the leitmotif of my existence with a blunt reminder,

"Listen carefully, Ingrid. Those dead Jews chose you and you can never forget it. You took the sword at that moment. You walked away from your comfortable, sheltered, aristocratic world to discover who you are. You're breaking with the past and it hurts."

My silence encourages him to dig deeper.

"You still see those dead Jewish newlyweds in your mind's eye every day, don't you?"

"Yes," I agree, never thinking he'd throw this at me. I deserve it. I'm behaving like a shrew.

"Well then, take responsibility for your decisions and your mistaken notions about the Gestapo. About *all men,* for that matter. Let those two dead people lead you forward. Ingrid, you're a mature woman, a daring human being despite your attempts to shield yourself from this war and your part in it. Don't be afraid to live from your heart and all will go well."

"How can you utter such romantic drivel? I don't believe you." I pull free of him, my jaw is firm and my eyes flash defiance, "How easily you sway me with your ideals. You aren't the one who has to spread your legs for Gestapo scum. This is military rape, Dieter. I have to live with myself. I retch when I think about what I'm doing and have yet to do until this war's over. And my daughter must never know. I'm dreadfully ashamed."

Rippling with anguish, I frown, expecting sympathy, but instead he drives me to the truth of my actions. "Right; admit you were blind from the start."

"Oh, now, that's a very male way to keep yourself clean, isn't it? Next you will insinuate that I was easily persuaded because I wanted sex and now deny it? I've been widowed for over eighteen months with never a glance at another man. Maybe you think this is how I'm coming back to life?"

"Well, Ingrid, if the shoe fits?" He's annoyed but falls into my trap. I have him cornered.

"I understand now. You need to justify yourself and dismiss me as a pathetic widow or a bad actress. You didn't consider my reaction to your scheme, or where it would lead us, and now you can't be bothered dealing with your mistake. You can't make me disappear. If you had known I'd be this prim and proper you never would have asked me to join your ranks."

Dieter's face flushes red. He presses his hands too deeply into my shoulders. I become rigid with fear before he drops them.

His tense voice whispers hoarsely, "You're right, Ingrid. Except now you could expose us: Guy, Marie, Marta, my wife, and people unknown to you in the Résistance whose stores you shop in."

His words flay my pride. He invited me in, but I have to get myself past this shame. He won't let me back out. He has pushed me as hard as he knows how. He will let me lick my wounds in private and hope I can restrain myself.

Still, he blurts out angrily, "What can I say, Ingrid? Naturally it's repulsive to have sex with the enemy—so stop acting like an outraged Virgin!"

"What?" My chin quivers but he subdues me with more.

"You mean to tell me you don't have enough self-control to act this part without letting it scar you? You were married joyfully to my best friend and are as strong as he was. You're still young, only forty-one and a beautiful woman. Who knows, Ingrid, maybe you'll marry happily again some day."

"I don't know, Dieter. I'm repulsed by this ugly affair."

"Ah, at last," he sighs, "the first bit of truth from your lips."

What makes him think I can master this? He feels badly, but if he lets me see it, he knows I'll keep pressing him to release me. He'll persuade me, no, he'll *shame* me into continuing. With his next argument Dieter builds upon my strength and not my insecurity.

"For God's sake, Ingrid, go down to your cellar and look at your Jewish escapees running like dogs. Then tell me your sacrifice isn't worth it. You're a woman of the world, a brilliant actress. You have the whole town fooled. The SS eats out of your hand."

"No, Dieter." Fuming, I put up my hands, palms outward, to stem the flow of his argument, "your praise isn't worth my sacrifice to Nazi lust on behalf of total strangers!"

"But Ingrid, you're the most vital link in our chain to save these people. No one else can do what you're doing. All of us, the boatmen, the walkers, the drivers, the forgers, the farmers, we're expendable. Someone else could do our job, but you're unique. Let the sex go. Get past it, Ingrid. War makes us do outrageous things, but one day it will be over and we'll go back to a normal life."

"Ach, Dieter, stop. I live a *double* life and you tell me one day I'll get over it? Just like a man. You know better than that. I'm scared to death on this stage. How do I keep sane with all this pressure?"

Then I laugh, and a strange ironic smile exposes my inner strength. But I don't realize it. I can't feel it, too numbed in my heart.

"I said it before, Ingrid. Remember how you felt when you uncovered the murdered Jewish couple. Your acquaintances still think they accidentally drowned. They rest easier believing that lie."

"But. . . ."

"But what? Can I help it if they washed up on your property? That you saw she was enceinte? Don't you wonder why this horror was brought to you and not to ah, Germaine deVillement, for instance? Let your outrage inspire you to be sly like a fox. Stalk the Krauts artfully, and they won't know what's happening."

He thinks I'm rational. He's almost right. I'm listening, but my fear is still palpable.

"*Ça suffit*, enough, Dieter. What happens in the end?" (I try to separate myself from my whoring persona in this pornographic sideshow.)

"Will you be there to redeem my reputation in front of my former friends, and Stefan? You've pimped me in front of my neighbors, Dieter. I've lost everyone, but Stefan's disgust is the worst. It cuts me like a knife. I want badly to tell him and dare not. Living with constant suspicion from everyone in this town wastes me away like a disease, Monsieur Van der Kreuzier."

"Sshh."

He puts his hand over my mouth and reaches over to turn off the light. We hear a sound outside on the pier. He gently pulls back the heavy drapes to see who is there. "It's only a dog. I thought it was Jews or Nazis. I've stayed too long. Amélie will worry."

"What does she think, Dieter? About my joining your ranks?"

His expression pulls inward. He hesitates. "She said you could be a lot of work. You're a sleeping lioness. Your contribution could change us all, her mostly. Don't ask why, I don't know. *Bonsoir, mon amie.*"

For a second, he can't help but follow the lamp's highlights over the firm contours of my figure. Blushing, he looks away then takes a step closer. I let him cup my face and kiss my forehead. He winces, afraid I'll hit him again and restart the battle. As bait for the Boches, I'm his prisoner too.

Finally, his voice is helpless with remorse, "Sorry, Ingrid, I have no easy answer for your tender soul. No one else sacrifices security and self-respect as you do."

Some ancient vulnerability deep within him provokes a Lancelot obligation to protect me as he did on the riverbank. It transforms his face and draws on his masculine nobility. His features become more defined and powerful. I'm uneasy, certain he hasn't felt a tug at his heart like this for years. Maybe Amélie doesn't need him this way anymore.

He whispers softly, "You have no choice but to continue the affair. Your secret is safe with me, but please, Ingrid, meet your lodgers. Talking with them will ease your sacrifice. I promise to listen to you rant and rave, but let's save these unfortunate wretches without detection. Betrayal is all around us." He hesitates, "Are we still friends, Ingrid?"

"I don't know, Dieter. Sorry to detain you. Go quickly. Curfew is in ten minutes."

I retreat to discourage him. He's disappointed when I'm cold, stern and sullen. We're no further along than when we began. I keep returning to my self-pity like a boomerang. How will he explain the cut on his cheek to his wife?

He says good night. I watch him disappear into the darkness from the rear salon window.

The wound on our friendship is raw—cut open by his demands *and* mine.

Perhaps he's listening, but he has no answers.

Chapter Six

Escaping Detection

12 December 1941, Friday

On a blustery afternoon a few days later, I go to the cemetery to be away from everyone. I can't keep up the pretense of sexual interest in Heisler. I need to free myself from the fear of meeting my Old Testaments. Dieter says I should balance my debauchery with their love and respect.

Why do I resist their gratitude? Because I am afraid if I love my lodgers they won't make it to freedom.

Perhaps if I can lay my condition of soul at the foot of my beloved's grave I might return home a new woman, having exorcised my anguish. Otherwise, with my secret operation endangered, my fear and bitterness could conquer me and my odious Nazi arbeit will have beaten me.

Outside the ruins of the medieval town wall, I see Dieter on his bicycle. I'm driving my late husband's Citroën, a commercial coal burner made before the war in 1938.

Dieter's tall figure pedals rhythmically toward me, close to the roadside. His violin and satchel of sheet music are strapped over the rear wheel in his special contraption to hold such paraphernalia. I would prefer to bike also, but I would not be safe: too highly visible and unprotected moving around Duchamps.

I make my way to the far entrance of the cemetery, remembering how often Dieter and my Emil rode their motorcycles together out here. What do I say now in anticipation of passing Dieter, after we argued bitterly because I threatened to quit the Résistance?

As he nears me, I think that either we must pass each other waving—or pause briefly to exchange pleasantries. But without warning, he stops dead in his tracks and brings his hand to his face. I stop and open my door.

"Dieter, are you all right?" He turns with his left eye closed, tearing badly. It's windy; huge gusts come down the mountain and push cold air into the valley along the Doubs.

"Ingrid, *bonjour*, I didn't recognize the car. I'll be fine if I can pull this plank out of my eye. The wind kicked up suddenly."

"Come inside. Let me see if I can get it." I park by the edge of the ditch but must keep the engine running. He leans his bike against the driver's side, walks back around to the passenger door and slides in.

"It's raw out there. Tell me, is this car yours, Ingrid?"

"No. Emil bought it new just before he died. Remember? Maman and I share it now. Let me see your eye, Dieter. I have some water here, and a first aid kit." I reach across him to retrieve it from the glove box. "Wait. Lean this way. Move nearer the window, toward the sunlight."

I kneel on the edge of the seat. My head faces the rear window as I stare into his large blue eyes. "Whatever's in there is quite small. Sit still now, please." My hand must be quick once I see it.

"There, I got it." I hold it in my palm.

He smiles and comments wryly, "Here is the little plank you had to pluck from my eye as payment for my harsh misjudgment. I couldn't remove it myself. Bless you, dear woman. Am I forgiven?"

I'm embarrassed. He's too charming. This time I can't refuse and grin, almost laughing, "You are forgiven, Monsieur."

Very quickly he takes advantage of lifting my spirits and grasps my hand, kisses it and murmurs with genuine gratitude, "Thank you, and please, Ingrid, continue to help us."

"Don't count on it. I had no choice to do what little I could, Dieter;" I remove my hand hastily.

"Then why didn't you introduce yourself to them?"

"What? Who? My lodgers? How do you know? Marie told you, didn't she?"

"No, Ingrid. The people who receive them after they leave your place told me. You're the only person who hasn't worked directly with the refugees. Why?"

He manipulates my feelings to interrogate me. I'm an easy mark; I'm compliant. The more I talk, the angrier I become, as he sits there casually staring at his eye in the rear-view mirror.

"Why does it matter as long as I keep the Gestapo satisfied? Look, stop this, will you? I drive here to visit Emil's grave for peace and quiet, in his car the Gestapo allows me to use as a reward for *ma service obligatoire.*"

Dieter stares at my clenched jaw when I speak of my *Feldmatratzendienst*—work as a German field mattress. "My obligatory service" is a lie, like Vichy's phony excuse will be to ship hundreds of thousands of French laborers to their deaths in Germany to appease Hitler.

"Leave me alone, Dieter." The irony is crushing, "All you good people wring your hands because I don't behave like everyone else, but *I'm* the one who entertains the enemy and lies down to be. . . ."

"Sshh."

His hand covers my mouth. I freeze. An official Mercedes approaches from behind, five hundred meters away, just clear of the old town wall. Dieter and I see it in the side mirror.

"That's not Heisler's sedan, is it, Dieter?"

"Yes, it is. Wait, they don't know this car, right?"

"Right. But if they stop, he'll become suspicious if he sees me with you. He's never seen me with another man. Heisler's jealous. I had to swear he's the only man I've known since Emil."

"Heisler may not come out of the car for a simple spot check of our papers if other officers are with him. We have a chance to escape detection. Let's be French and get busy."

"What do you mean? Shall I leave?"

"No, it's better to play to their prejudice, be seen as harmless lovers oblivious to them and the war. I'm sorry Ingrid. We have no choice. Let me handle things."

"Yes, but what are you going to do?"

In the rearview mirror, I see the Nazi vehicle slow to a stop. A driver, and a man I assume to be a French informer accompany Heisler. He's in the back seat. He must be reviewing paperwork. He waves a hand as if annoyed at the delay. We listen as the car doors open on the Mercedes. The two men get out. Before walking toward our car, they stop to talk for a moment. We hear their voices carried on the wind.

"Do you want us to investigate, Obersturmführer?"

"I don't recognize that car. The windows are fogged and the engine is running. Well, it's a *gazogène*. Someone's inside or maybe taking a piss. Do a routine check for papers. Be quick about it. I have an early dinner engagement."

We're prisoners now and can only hope we're doing the right thing, and that the Citroën engine doesn't stall out. We dare not lose our foggy windows.

"*I'm afraid. . . .*"

"Sshh. You will have to trust me, Ingrid, and forgive me all over again."

Without explanation he forces me down onto the seat. His hands pull on the top buttons of my heavy sweater coat and my blouse. The weight of his chest crushes me as his lips move against my bare collarbone. I squirm under his hands and mutter angrily into his ear,

"What the hell are you doing? You have to be kidding, Dieter. . . ."

He puts his hand over my mouth and whispers, "Ssshh. We have to look like lovers or they'll suspect us of having a rendezvous to exchange information! They know who I am. I won't hurt you, Ingrid. Please help me, don't fight me: moan, or do something—act like you're enjoying it."

I'm so upset that I shake until I hiccup suddenly and then laugh. Dieter finds my mouth and kisses me. I hiccup again in his ear. He grabs my buttocks, pulls my skirt back, and pushes my left leg toward the dashboard, and the right one to the ceiling, as the Gestapo agent and his French informer's footsteps come closer. Oh God, they must be staring into the car. The windows are very foggy. They can't see our features clearly, but they know in a flash what we're doing.

"Ooh, la la! Very nice legs, eh, Schuller?"

"*Was ist das? Och, sex speilen? Ja!*"

"Oh no, Schuller, take your hand off that door. Let's watch first. How often do you Germans get a front row seat to our French love-making, eh?"

Dieter begins to rock me as if we're coupling, hoping a simulated performance will embarrass the men into leaving us alone. Instead they are glued to the spot. There's no way they can tell Dieter's pants are not undone and my underwear is still on. He whispers into my ear, "Ingrid, moan and breathe deeply. They should have opened the door. Damn, they're waiting for a climax. *Fake one, woman.*"

I begin to moan and cry out as Dieter follows me with deep heaving breaths in my ear. We're still undisturbed. Maybe they will wait and get us when we stop? Oh no, I'd better not stop. I keep on going and pretend to climax several times in a row, with a little pause in between to hear if they're opening our car door. All the while Dieter moves me, my legs are straight up in the air and fatiguing. Then my right calf cramps and I scream in real pain, masking it with a vigorous rhythmic jerking to work out the cramp.

In the pause of my screams and grunts, we hear the Frenchman say to the German, "Très bien, Schuller. Vive l'amour, my boy! Those two have more important work than the war. Thank goodness someone does. Let's get back to Heisler. We don't need to share this with him."

We hear their car doors open and close. Their engine springs to life. We lie there catching our breath and wait until they pull away.

Dieter's head is on my chest; perspiration beads on his forehead despite the chill. An unfamiliar calm settles over us like two lovers who bask in a safe valley below the height of their union. At first I soak in the peacefulness. There is nothing else, no war, no Occupation, no concubinage, just Dieter and me. The feeling grips me completely. I cannot think.

Then I hiccup again, loudly. Reality hits and immediately I must suppress the luscious pleasure of his scent and the pressure of his torso bearing down on me. I hiccup again and we laugh together. God forgive me but I don't want to give up this moment.

I look at my footprints on the ceiling with a twinge of grateful giddiness and say sarcastically, "Why does it all boil down to sex, eh? My real job in this war is on my back, no?" and I hiccup again but this time I can't laugh.

Dieter raises himself up on his elbow and looks down into my face, smiles and nods his head, "You're great, you know? Formidable."

I blush and look away as he lifts himself off me. I pull my skirt down and sit up. He reaches around my shoulders and helps me with my sweater. I button my blouse and straighten my hair. He sits quietly and stares out the window while I adjust my stockings. I wish I could guess what he's thinking. I'm embarrassed like a schoolgirl.

"I'm done with my stockings, Dieter. You can turn around now." I try to block out the wonderful peace of being held in his arms. Afraid the longing for more shows on my face, I reluctantly pull myself back to widowhood.

"Come with me to the cemetery, please Dieter," I ask plaintively. His face looks serious. For the first time he has invaded the ironclad grip of my loneliness and can better understand how I feel.

Our performance saved us from a mindless invasion of our privacy. It could have led to a French detention camp. Instead, it frees me to rescue myself from the past. His sorrowful gaze fixes me to his eyes. He has unlocked my hidden chambers of widow's pain.

Slowly he reaches out his arms and I move into his embrace. He holds me tightly and kisses me passionately. I can barely breathe. His touch releases a contraction deep in my uterus. It winds upward through my solar plexus in a searing hot cramp, up my esophagus and out my larynx

in a terrible primordial groan. I cry out, pull his hair and dig my fingernails into his shoulders as sobs heave from my heart. A tumor of loss,
fear and loneliness for Emil empties its toxin.

If it upsets Dieter to see me out of control, from lighthearted laughter
to thrashing like a wild, dumb, wounded animal, he doesn't show it. He
supports me with loving detachment, calms me, and gently massages my
shoulders with tender reassurance.

⌒

I return home empty, woozy and nauseated, having shed an old skin—
my widowhood. At first my head pounds, unwilling to accept its new
freedom, until I eat voraciously and stop worrying about the doorbell
ringing for the next four hours.

This latest ruse with Dieter was too reckless.

We foiled the enemy again, but for how long? Had Heisler discovered
me with Dieter, we wouldn't have gotten away with admitting a casual
affair. Dieter said Heisler suspects him. I would be deported to a work
camp if seen as a spy. Marta would be taken from me. A double agent
pays with her life. I sigh a halting uneven breath.

Heisler passed us traveling out of Duchamps toward the next village.
That means peace and quiet for a day or two, long enough to ground
myself again. I'm grateful my Vichy persona is still safe. Assured of a
solo evening I retire early, relieved but uneasy.

I catch myself reliving the heightened sensation of Dieter's body
brushing against me. Friction from our layers of clothing increased my
desire, but the fear of SS detection smothered it. When Dieter lifted
himself off me, I realized my flesh had rejoiced with the scent of his
caresses, and I was fooled into thinking he loved me for a few stolen
moments. I resist tucking the excitement of our intimacy away . . . into
the back of my mind.

With Heisler I move like an automaton devoid of feeling anything
beyond abrasion. Our unions are staged acts of public théâtre. My SS
client is exceedingly repressed. He's oblivious to his damsel's feigned
delight for the pornography that passes between them.

Chapter Seven

The Concert

22 December 1941, Monday

O ver the next ten days I still cannot make up my mind about the
Résistance. I avoid Dieter outside of rehearsals and decline to see
Heisler twice for dinner. Citing illness worked once. The second time the
Nazi became annoyed and suspected I had another lover.

I'm quiet and reserved during the last few days of concert rehearsals
with Dieter, Amélie, and the other musicians. Neither of the Van der
Kreuziers touches on the issue of my work for the Résistance. Everyone
concentrates on the music.

When I think about what has happened in the weeks since I uncovered the dead Jewish couple on the riverbank, began servicing Heisler,
and backed out of the Underground after my argument with Dieter—
my mind returns again and again to that afternoon on the road to the
cemetery.

Dieter and I fooled the Nazis by pretending to make love. After our
passionate kiss he stowed his bike in the back seat and drove us in close
to Emil's grave. The engine had barely enough fuel to get us inside. I

watched him load the coal in the burner and gave him bottled water to wash his hands.

We walked the fifty meters to Emil's grave in silence, my hand on his strong violinist's biceps. Dieter's warm body sheltered me from the wind. He steadied me with his hands on my shoulders. The wind blew against his kiss, still moist on my lips. We stood before Emil's headstone lost in our memories. I was astonished. I felt nothing. The grave was cold and dead. I had no life to give it to keep the image of my late husband alive. I had let Emil go.

The Citroën was my car now. Back inside the car, I sat in the driver's seat waiting for the motor to build up enough pressure to get me back to town. I remember the distant look on Dieter's face as he got in beside me, his eyes appearing irrevocably tied to my heart. He said, sadly,

"I can't go into town with you, Ingrid. People must not see us together."

The Catholic Church's interior is stark this evening. Only a few potted plants and bouquets of fresh evergreens scent the air around the Crèche. The last eighteen months have found the citizens of Duchamps grateful they're not starving like towns up north in the path of Hitler's army. Nevertheless, with the strain of Occupation, this gathering will be quite sober.

We have dispensed with the traditional dinner afterward. Most people hoard their rationed food in root cellars. A few use it to feed Jewish families. There is no food for festivities. Many attendees leave their children at home instead of bringing them to this usually joyful occasion. No one feels especially safe or festive these days.

The singers and musicians ready themselves in the side chapel. Twenty in the choir of older men and women adjust their gowns and warm their voices.

Dieter and a young farmer from an outlying district stand in the narrow corridor near the sacristy door and talk in hushed tones. I'm returning from the toilette and overhear their conversation. I freeze at the words: "There's a rumor the Germans are preparing a raid as soon as this concert is over."

Who's the informer? I wonder. Oh scrub that thought, Ingrid. If you dwell on betrayal, paranoia will consume you. Just listen.

"Stefan has to move quickly tonight, Jean Claude. There's no way to know if the Boches will stay for the whole concert. We have to tell him in time."

"Sir, I thought we had a woman in town to entertain the Doryphores afterward. We need at least an hour more to cross everyone safely or it's too risky. Most of his passengers will be children and adults with babies. Stefan says the roads will be clear, but tomorrow evening the snow returns. The Swiss *passeurs* say no one will move for a week. He has to be on time to meet the smugglers at the border."

"Sorry, Jean Claude, we don't have that woman's help anymore. It's now or never. Send the other men inside. I'll give them the cue if all's well. Alert the few faithful farmers who help with babies. You'd better go. I have to get ready for the performance."

Dieter slides back into the dark narrow corridor a few meters behind me. I'm sure his eyes watch me swish gracefully through the door in my long black dress. His veiled conversation stings my memory with the argument we had about me backing out of the Underground. I can't acknowledge him and have no doubt he shakes his head in disgust for misjudging me, a mistake he rarely makes.

I take my position at the harpsichord and notice Jacques Devoir, the coroner, standing with the baritones as the choral master taps his baton. The coroner smiles a hello I return, recalling him at the Doubs shore and the morgue. He's a mysterious man with a good voice.

"Places everyone."

Dieter plays an "A" and the musicians tune, rehearsing for another minute.

This performance is a tradition in Duchamps, without a mass or a sermon. It alternates yearly between Catholic and Protestant churches. Tonight many in the audience of four hundred stand, in a church barely seating three hundred.

The Romanesque gargoyles, remnants from the original structure, look down menacingly from their thirteenth-century cornices. They spy on the company below, anticipating the anti-Christ.

One minute before the concert begins, the huge wooden doors swing open to admit a sudden blast of cold air. Gestapo officers enter with Vichy locals fawning at their heels. Heisler marches in the lead and unties the special ribbon that reserves the first pew for him and his henchmen. The subdued audience is visibly uncomfortable as the enemy sits down among them.

A colorless mole of a cleric, Fr. Beauverger, welcomes the Protestants and out-of-town visitors, our German conquerors. Predators sit amongst their prey, the local farming populace. Frenchmen swallow hard. A few narrow their gaze and frown at the obsequious cleric's remarks aimed directly at pleasing the Swastikas.

When Beauverger completes the Catholic salutations, the Protestant Minister gives his traditional ecumenical blessing and the concert begins.

Dieter plays violin, and Amélie, the flute. They sit in front of the octet. I'm in between them at the harpsichord. A French horn player, oboist, cellist, second violinist, and viola da gamba player surround us. The program begins with Bach and will remain almost all German composers for the evening. I extend my harpsichord solo by five minutes. Dieter stares. I return twice to embellish the main theme. Perhaps he thinks I forgot my part instead of intending to lengthen the program.

In the second choral selection the choirmaster decides to repeat the first verse of "Cantique de Noël" in his attempt to do the same. The choir's blend of rich harmony rises to fill the church's high ceiling, then drifts down to soothe the nervous Résistants in the audience.

Heisler is attentive for the first half hour. Toward intermission he glances at his watch every few minutes. At the break he catches me by surprise as I return from the side chapel.

"Good evening, Madame Fellner; how lovely to see you again." He's sly—on public display—and says nothing to unnerve me.

"Obersturmführer Heisler, so good of you to attend. I hope you like our mostly German program."

"*Ja, ist es gut.* I hope to see you soon. You look quite well tonight, Madame."

"Yes, thank you, I'm feeling healthier. Excuse me, we are about to begin the second half."

Dieter watches our interaction with interest. Strained, he's hopeful now that the SS will stay for the full concert. I return to the harpsichord. Dieter rises to play an "A" for us to tune but mistakenly plays a "G" first. A few people are unsettled and get up to leave abruptly, but to most the "G" is just an odd mistake. Heisler is oblivious to the error and settles down for a nap while the second half of the concert plays on.

Strong applause and shouts of "Encore!" awaken him at the end. He seems surprised to hear a round of enthusiastic appreciation from a provincial audience. Most everyone remains seated. The Résistants peppering the audience look at us musicians. Their expectancy suddenly electrifies the air as Heisler stands to leave. They want an encore. They *need* an encore. They know a terrible secret the rest of their neighbors sitting around them do not: tonight the SS has an appointment to catch Jewish children in their desperate race to freedom.

Dieter looks distracted. Amélie whispers for him to begin. The choral master turns around to look for direction. A few long seconds pass but no one moves to stop the Obersturmführer. Worried farmers are unsure whether to get up or sit still.

I can't stand the suspense. I see my *beau-fils*, Stefan, out in the cold, driving himself and his Jewish refugees into a Nazi trap.

In an instant something pushes me to behave in a most atypical manner. I stand up from my chair behind the harpsichord and open my arms in a grand sweeping gesture that causes my shawl's long tassels to wave. The motion catches Erich's eye as he turns to walk down the aisle and out into the night. With a smile I hiss at Dieter through clenched teeth,

"Quickly, play 'Silent Night.'"

"What?"

"You heard me, I'll sing to him in German. Damn it. Dieter, do as I say."

Amélie immediately picks up her violin from its case on the floor and plays the opening bars, before Dieter understands what I'm asking. I'm thankful for her intuition to tune her instrument at intermission when she had arranged to play only flute.

I step forward into the light of the candelabra in front of the musicians on the lower steps of the altar. Heisler watches as I allow the black shawl hiding my *décolletage* to slip slowly from my shoulders, revealing a deeply scalloped bodice with a hint of separation between my breasts. The old women in the front pews, rosaries in hand, sit back, raise their eyebrows and gasp. Their husbands lean forward to leer and snicker.

Church is not the place for base allurement, but I have no choice. We're desperate to keep Heisler in here as long as possible. Other faces are riveted to the back of Heisler's head. A general air of relief floats softly over the pews as the Nazi pauses and returns to his seat.

I gather my breath and begin *Stil-le Nacht, Hei-li-ge Nacht* in a deep contralto. My voice has the power to fill this huge space as never before. I struggle to remember the verses in German, Italian and English in addition to French: grateful my Papa's rigid ideas about education included Swiss boarding school in Basel.

The old carol works its spell. Heisler is glued to my chest. He sits forward as I take deep breaths to climb the soprano heights. My heaving bosom anesthetizes his addiction for Jewish blood for the moment, but I need to sing something else to hold his attention.

The Germans applaud loudly as I finish, the French only sporadically. A few old timers leave. Naturally, the old women and my envious friends like Germaine, who expected at least one French composition for their encore, exit pretending to be insulted when they will munch on this scandalous tidbit for weeks.

I've just reinforced their judgment. I'm a whore for Hitler.

As I make a deep curtsy, deliberately bending forward to show my cleavage again, I whisper to Amélie to play one of Schubert's "Lieder." She knows which ones I can do since we practice duets. We have no piano, so she opens on her violin and Dieter follows her lead. I sing Heisler's favorite songs, stretching them out for forty minutes until my voice begins to strain from the fear behind it. The concert ends an hour later than predicted.

As I take my final curtsy, everyone rises. Heisler marches toward me, bows, takes my hand and kisses my fingers. Darts of Occupied frustration are aimed at us. Yet, strangely, a few people smile and exit the church quickly, as if late for a pressing appointment.

The Van der Kreuziers come forward to thank the Obersturmführer for attending. Dieter listens as Heisler asks to escort me home. He knows what that means. I accept and give Erich an alluring look to root him to the spot until I return from the toilette.

Dieter corners me in the dimly lit hallway just behind the altar.

"How did you know to do this?" Apparently my performance was mesmerizing.

"You should be more careful where you have your conversations, Dieter," I reply stiffly, "I overheard you before the concert. Thank goodness your wife was here. Amélie knew what was needed. Thank her for me. I wouldn't have succeeded without her accompaniment."

"Does this mean you are with us again, Ingrid?"

"No, don't count on anything beyond this night, Dieter. I'm afraid for Stefan. I couldn't live with myself if he's the next sacrificial lamb to be butchered with innocent Jewish children, especially if he dies hating me without knowing the truth of my sacrifice."

I turn to leave and he grabs my hand. He feels me shake. I sound strong, but inside quake with fear, anticipating the rest of my evening.

"Thank you for your help on behalf of the Underground and the children you've saved tonight who'll never know you, Ingrid. I'm so grateful. I know what. . . ."

"*What* do you know?" I interrupt indignantly, on the verge of tears, "What the rest of my evening will be like now that I've surrendered myself like bait on *your* hook?"

As I speak, heat pulses behind my eyes and my cheeks flush. The sudden genuine release of Dieter's gratitude pierces my heart. He adds, head down, still holding my hand firmly,

"Please, forgive me, Ingrid. I didn't realize how this could hurt you."

"Don't beg, Dieter, it doesn't become you." I can hardly force myself to be rude in the face of his overwhelming charm and concern, but seeing myself flat on my back for the next hours makes it easier.

I pull my hand away roughly and turn quickly to avoid his face. He is so crushed with shame; I could break down and cry. His sadness follows me as I close the door and return to Heisler with a cardboard smile pasted on my lips.

The church is nearly empty, except for a few stragglers praying at devotional side altars. Erich is excited. We're alone in almost total darkness. He stands too close behind me. I feel his body aroused as he places the heavy, black velvet cape over my shoulders. He leans over and kisses my bare collarbone and nips my ear, as his left hand presses my abdomen. The gargoyle above us is asleep on the job. This demon behind me is much too eager to subdue his victim in her house of worship.

As we walk down the side aisle, a few old women praying their rosaries interrupt the singsong cadence of their "Hail Marys" to mutter vile, unchristian epithets at me.

The rustle of my long taffeta gown blasts the timeless, ethereal quiet and follows the click of Heisler's boots in the stilled, darkening church. With each step I'm swallowed up more deeply by the night, physically and spiritually.

⤙⤙⤙

Riding home in Heisler's black Mercedes, I feel proud that my Stefan and twenty-five Jews, mostly children, will be safe. But my flesh crawls with dread. Heisler wants sex. In the car Erich is excited that I will be under him, even if I'm limp and numb. I'm revolted, and will hardly pretend to be passionate. But he will have enough passion for an army and ravish me.

All through the night my mind will run amuck. Images and conversations with Emil, Dieter, and Erich will swim together. I won't sleep . . . fearful I'll say something to expose my clandestine operation.

Marie worries and keeps her distance. She hears his familiar footsteps in the room above her quarters. No one greets me. The house is dark.

I survive Heisler's pawing, but over the next weeks lose weight and seethe with anger. I still resist meeting my Old Testament lodgers in the basement. Now I'm afraid if I do, I'll shoot Heisler the next time he comes to my home. He insists on more time in the boudoir, and with many crossings over the winter, spring, and summer, I must accept.

I send word to Dieter I've resumed my *Feldmatratzendienst* status for our good cause. At Christmas I wallow in bitterness at Maman's home, but cannot tell her why. Back in Duchamps my eyes and ears are open, ready for more rounds of insults from my neighbors.

Since the concert, old women wag their spindly arthritic fingers in my face. They curse and spit at me in the street while old men pander vulgar propositions. I squirm whenever I pass Duchamps' elderly. I expect their behavior—a Christmas gift for my new life hidden from them in the Underground.

I guess which shopkeepers are Résistants. They're annoyed with me as with other pro-Vichy townspeople, not knowing I'm one of them. Only the baker, Jeanne, suspects, because Marie orders more bread than we can use. And the pharmacist, Philippe, sells Guy first aid medications Marta and I never need. The Résistance shopkeepers are part of Marie and Guy's circle. They have no idea of my role since everyone's sworn to secrecy. Of course, I pay the bills.

One day, I'm embarrassed in the *charcuterie*, the meat shop my family has frequented for decades. The owners have prepared their last delicious batch of *foie gras*, goose liver paté. It's being bought up quickly since there's so little as the war drags on. I'm next in line, in front of a large marble counter with an ancient, brass-knobbed cash register. Only a few salami and *jambon* slices sit in the glass case.

I can't accustom myself to the public scarcity of food. Before the war, the pale blue ceiling and white walls in this shop were festooned with imported Italian prosciutto hanging interspersed with fresh wreaths of white garlic heads. Displays were rich with the aroma of homemade products: fresh roasts, prepared croquettes, pork wursts and other spiced delicacies. Shelves held colorful tins of condiments, bins of horseradish, dried mushrooms and mustard seed. Aromatic herbs evoked memories of festive meals and incited a cook's imagination for new ones.

The German Wehrmacht intensifies the rape of our French agriculture and leaves us very little to buy, unless we shop *au noir*, at the black market.

"Bonjour, Madeleine," I greet the shopkeeper's granddaughter behind the counter while surveying her jambon and hesitate, "I ah, would like some *foie gras*. . . ."

A stout older woman I don't know steps in front of me and snarls snottily, "Well, I'm sure Madame Fellner can get her foie gras for a cheaper and more exciting price from the Boches, Madeleine. Why don't we let her do that? Agreed? You can't spend your Reichsmarks here, anyway, Madame Fellner. This is a French establishment."

Madeleine falters. This woman is a customer just as I am. In this small town, Madeleine knows everyone and is upset to have to serve her when she's so rude. The woman looks familiar but in Duchamps this is often the case. The three of us stand here suspended in social sourness when Germaine, who stopped communicating with me after the concert, walks to the counter from the rear of the store and glares at me. She overheard this woman's insulting remarks. I thought I'd have her support but instead she rubs salt into my wound.

"Oh, Ingrid dearest, how convenient that you have many sources for your satisfaction while the rest of us rely on ration cards."

I stand here silent, scandalized by their conspiratorial vulgarity, insinuating I'm a paid consort of the Reich. I suppose the Gestapo's regular gifts; chocolate, liquor, and coffee are payment, even when they eat most of it at my dinners. I am beyond resentment but pity poor Madeleine. I've known her since she was a babe in arms. These two delight in bullying an unsophisticated farm girl, knowing she's alone in the shop. If her mother were here, this wouldn't be happening.

Madeleine wraps the last bit of the delicacy and places it in front of me. Ignoring the other two, she challenges them to grab the package.

Germaine's friend plunks down her francs as I anticipated and nearly knocks me over taking my order in the process.

The two women purr contentedly and proudly hold my foie gras aloft as they walk out. Madeleine's face reddens with embarrassment as she places their money in the cash drawer.

"Excuse me, Madame Fellner. I'm very sorry. I didn't think she'd be that rude or I would have handed you the package."

"It's all right, Madeleine. You did the right thing."

"Oh, Madame, please, I've always admired you. Some of us know you can't say anything, but *mon grand-père*, ah, he ran out of the concert when Monsieur Dieter played a 'G' instead of an 'A.' You understand, oui?"

"Ah, did he? Bless you for telling me, Madeleine."

I purchase a few items and leave the store with my eyes brimming. I vow not to shop anymore until the war is over. I can't fight these people or risk making a scene. Let them slander me so I can protect my lodgers.

Their hypocrisy is infuriating. The Reich has drained our agriculture and manufacturing industries for the last nineteen months. The Jewish question doesn't bother most French, but growling stomachs awaken everyone's conscience. After today I send Marie in my place to face the gossipmongers.

I avoid the retail shops, but still have to go to the bank on a monthly basis. After today, however, I will no longer bring Marta with me. I think people will respect my daughter, and control their tongues in her presence. But I'm wrong today, as always. . . .

We enter the bank and go to the far side of its very elegant foyer. Built in grand Napoleonic style as a private home, it stands out against the town's quaint architecture as a monolith to the wealth and bombast of a bygone era. High ceilings with large windows and oriental carpets anchor pillars on either side of semi-enclosed areas. Tellers are on the left and personnel offices are on the right.

Marta sits patiently by a column and looks down the center aisle as I calculate my monthly withdrawals. I have to disguise increasing amounts spent on Old Testaments. As a French widow I am allowed a personal bank account, but my late husband made Stefan oversee my withdrawals against the family business profits. It's an increasing annoyance to be at the mercy of a stepson half my age. He must not become suspicious. Nothing will change as long as Vichy and the Church relegate French women to intellectual incompetence. If this war ever ends I hope for the right to vote and control my finances.

In the midst of adding expenses my attention is distracted momentarily by a dull thud. Édouard de Villement, the bank Vice President and chief loan officer, runs out of his suite with a client. Marta jumps up and grabs my arm excitedly.

"Maman, someone's sick. Go to them. You have the lavender salts. Go!"

I have no idea what she is talking about, but give up on the transaction and shove my papers back into my folder. She drags me away . . . digging into my purse for the salts. After seeing her father lying dead in the snow, my poor little dove becomes frantic at the least emergency.

As we get closer I am surprised to see Stefan kneeling over an old woman. She is wealthy, judging from the quality of her clothes and the diamond rings on her fingers. Her large-brimmed hat has fallen over her eyes and nose. The men appear uneasy with the idea of removing it—and the wreath of furry, stuffed minks with menacing little eyes that guard her shoulders. Stefan and Édouard gently jostle her to revive her but she is unresponsive, and needs more stimulation. The coward in me fights my desire to engage in simple social contact with Stefan and Édouard to help this poor soul sprawled out on the floor. I know I must act. My Résistance persona, however, is apprehensive.

"Oh, the poor dear. Here gentlemen, let me try this."

I remove Madame's hat and open her collar, pushing her little chimeras aside to pass the lavender under her nose. Oh my—I recognize her. The same woman who took my foie gras two weeks ago at the charcuterie! I would prefer to leave the smelling salts with Stefan or Édouard and depart immediately, if only for Marta's sake. Instead I steel myself for another onslaught of vitriol when she rouses. My collaborator persona ensnares me completely.

Édouard struggles to cradle her in his arms, but her large girth dwarfs his thin, delicate frame. He winces, trying to shift her weight off his weak leg. The leg makes his posture quite wooden. He behaves as if in pain.

Stefan kneels to help Édouard and raises her head higher so I can pass the lavender under her nose. His eyes pierce mine as I force a smile, our faces only centimeters apart.

I greet him . . . while keeping my eyes on her, "Bonjour, Stefan, good to see you. Sorry it's under these circumstances. I hope you've been well."

Too afraid to continue the conversation, I do not wait for his reply and ask Édouard,

"What happened?"

Édouard replies with a note of sadness in his voice, "She had bad news about her sons, lost them recently in an accident up north. I fear her heart's broken. She's one of our oldest clients. You know her daughter. She left Duchamps for Paris years ago. This is Madame Josephine La Farge. Her family owns vineyards in the Rhône."

Madame La Farge looks up at the three of us and sees me holding the salts under her nose. I do my best to smile and pray that Édouard will address her. He does.

"Madame La Farge, are you all right? Do you have any pain? Do you need a doctor?"

"No. I'm fine now, thank you, Monsieur Édouard."

"Oh, but you have to thank Madame Fellner here. She revived you with lavender salts."

Édouard looks pleased with himself for complimenting me. Stefan watches my every move. I wait for her to attack.

"You! You had the cure, did you, my dear? Trying to make up for your hidden life, eh Madame? Really, I don't care what you did. Get away from me." She sits up, steadies herself and reaches out to both men, who lift her to her feet.

I step back and push Marta behind me as though hiding my child will protect her ears. Édouard appears embarrassed by Madame La Farge's lack of gratitude for my simple act of kindness.

"Pardon me, I think you're mistaken. Madame Fellner is a highly regarded philanthropist like you. She donates a great deal of time and money to the orphanage."

"No, Monsieur. You didn't go to the Christmas concert this year, did you? Certainly not, or surely you would understand my disgust."

Madame rearranges her hat, scarf, gloves and minks. Édouard has no idea what she is talking about. Her insult passes unchallenged, since she's his client. He utters a lot of trite, subservient nonsense as he leads her to the door. Then he returns to Stefan and pulls a starched white handkerchief from his lapel pocket to wipe his forehead. He rubs his hands with it and presses it through his long, unmanly, fingers repetitively . . . as if he has just touched a deadly poison.

Édouard apologizes profusely for the old woman's unkind remarks. This surprises me since he knows his adoration incurs my revulsion.

Poor Marta's icy stare means she is angry—I haven't defended myself. She's too young to understand why adults mask their behavior when trapped and forced to accept lies for a good cause. She asks naïvely, in a rare defense of her mother, "Monsieur deVillement, that lady wasn't nice to Maman, and she only tried to help her. Why was she so ungrateful? And why did you apologize for her?"

"Hush! Marta. I'll explain to you later. Sorry, Édouard."

I blush, bid the men *au revoir* and clasp Marta's hand very firmly, digging my fingernails into her palm. As we head for the door I grit my teeth to hold back tears. Outside, she badgers me again as she pulls her hand free.

"You knew that lady, Maman, I could tell. Who is she?"

"Stop it child, I can't explain to you now." I push her brusquely into the waiting car.

Please, God, just shut her mouth for one moment. I need some peace and quiet. Guy drives on while Marta glowers from the back seat. I bite my lower lip and look out the window to avoid her eyes. It's hard work diverting my flood of wounded ego to a reservoir of silent service. I have to cut myself off from my daughter for a few minutes. I despise myself for lying to cover my Underground tracks. Wedging the Résistance between us is hurtful but I have to survive, too.

I cover my face, embarrassed in front of Guy. My jaw quivers and my tears flow over the levee of my mind. I pull out a handkerchief and fake a sneeze to blow my nose and wipe my eyes, still looking out the window. She pouts. I've spoiled her. She has no boundaries when she crashes into my world.

I'm weak in the early days of Feldmatratzen service. The framework of lies that supported my mental state as a young married woman crumbles against widowhood. I dwell in petulant rage. Marta's purity invites my anger. Dieter avoids me. Guilty about my despondency and resentment, he relays messages about refugees through others.

Eventually I grow a tougher, more honest skin but the first seconds of anyone's chastisement flay me anew. I resent this unspeakably inhuman *mauvais théâtre* that catapults me into adulthood at forty-one. I'm defensive like a child nursing her stance when she can't get her way. Indeed, I am a child very much like my daughter.

My double life gnaws at my appetite and sabotages my rest. After the bank scene it's even harder to sleep. In a nightmare that harasses me, I stand over Emil's twisted body at the scene of his accident in 1939, frightened by his broken legs that are torn at the knees. His neck and collarbones are broken but he doesn't bleed. He lies there limp in the snow with his beautiful muscular physique crumpled like a piece of paper.

As I gaze at Emil in the dream, images of the dead Jewish couple on my riverbank overlay Emil in a milky transparency. First they are faint and he's solid. Then Emil becomes transparent and the Jews are solid. Alternating from opacity to transparency, they chase me as I run, searching for a safe place to hide. I run and run until I trip over another body—my Marta. She's broken too, but warm, bleeding and unconscious. I want to be near her but am pulled away by the huge hands of a mysterious stranger.

Next I'm naked, with wrists and ankles bound to a wall in the morgue. My body is hanging over Emil who is stretched out on a gurney below me. A piece of my flesh flies off to cover his nakedness every time I look at him. I'm almost without flesh, yet still alive.

Marta appears again as a sleeping angel. Her eyes are closed, ears are blocked and her body floats through space encased in ice. Her embrace envelops me in frost but strangely she feels warm to my touch. My skin grows back when it comes in contact with her body.

It's raining blood. When we leave the morgue, deep red blood is everywhere. I can't avoid stepping in it. I carry Marta in my arms and run again. Something follows us, but I can't stop to look over my shoulder to see what it is. It gets closer and closer, breathing an evil smell of death. Startled, I hear Marta scream and awaken.

Marta is, in fact, actually screaming here in the house at 3:00 a.m.

I get up, still caught in this bizarre dream state and go to her room to help her rise to consciousness. As she convulses, I rub her feet, pull her big toes, gently cuff her face, pull on her hair and shout in her ears. She comes around in less than a minute, opens her eyes and reaches for me, crying, "Papa's dead, he's dead, he ran from me!"

She has wet herself and is drenched in sweat. I calm her, "That was a long time ago, mon ange, he's in heaven now." I wash her in the tub, and dress her in clean pajamas.

The entire time I'm locked inside the hideous image of running in the blood storm. We return to my bed. I cradle her in my arms under the comforter. Again bloody figures pursue me as I drift into a restless torpor. Each scene establishes a terrified, wounded man or woman fighting against violence and starvation. My heart sees a relationship between Emil and the Jewish phantoms. My mind accuses me of deserving this nightmare because of my sexual indiscretion with Dieter. I am not convinced this dream *is* a nightmare. Metaphorical yes, but by the next morning at breakfast I remember it as the "blood dream."

I guess its dark prophetic message will be revealed if I continue my clandestine mission.

1942

Chapter Eight

Dinner at Le Petit Chat

1 March 1942, Sunday

Maman and I are halfway through our main course in the rear of the Le Petit Chat dining room when Dieter and Amélie arrive and sit at the front. We had no idea they would be coming. And here I am, having disgraced myself at the Christmas concert when I seduced Heisler from the Church altar singing his favorite Schubert "Lieder" for an encore. Entertaining the Swastika is a saga: so is my vow to get out of the Underground, the trip to the cemetery, the concert, and now, meeting Dieter here. What will *this* encounter bring?

Dieter and Amélie look very much in love. She wears a beautiful dress. Her hair is braided around her ear on one side and a sprig of silk flowers cascade to her neck. A lovely violet wool shawl covers her shoulders. No one would guess such an earthy-looking woman would possess prophetic powers. She certainly has cast a long spell over Dieter. It's their thirty-third wedding anniversary. It's easy to see why he loves her. They're so opposite in temperament.

Maman notices me brooding and probably concludes, erroneously, that seeing a happy couple upsets me. I know she worries about my weight loss and thinks I'm sad to excess about losing Emil. As far as I know she has no idea about the SS. I haven't been able to tell her, yet I see her every week. I'm ashamed and afraid she'll disapprove. We finish our meal drinking real coffee in lieu of chicory, my contribution to Yves and Yvonne this evening—compliments of SS Heisler's payment for my services.

Dieter passes our table on his way to the kitchen. I hide my face but he recognizes Maman. "Madame de Vochard, so good to see you," he kisses her hand.

"Ah, oui, *mon fils*. How are you?" (Every grown man under seventy is "my son" to my eighty-four-year-old mother.) She recalls Dieter tuning our piano and harpsichord twenty-five years ago.

"And I see you're here with Ingrid. Madame Fellner, so nice to see you."

I'm forced to acknowledge him. Dieter kisses my hand very formally, but his eyes beg forgiveness all over again. He still carries shame for my disgrace when my ignorance tripped me into the role of victim for Nazi lust. How debonair of him when I blamed him unjustly.

Now all I want is my freedom from Dieter and this town.

"I hope you'll grace us with a visit soon, Ingrid."

"Yes, perhaps. Please give your Amélie my regards."

He hesitates and excuses himself, looking wounded by my curtness. I want to leave immediately but Maman insists on going into the kitchen with Dieter to say "au revoir" to Yves. I walk to the front of the dining room to say hello to Amélie, who sits alone.

She looks up and smiles, "Ingrid, so good to see you. There have been a few babies to birth and I haven't seen Marta at her piano lessons. How is your sweet little girl? I miss her charming nature. Is she walking better?"

Amélie is tender, a charitable woman. Her round eyes and delicate brows express what she says as much as her words. Still a natural beauty though approaching her fifties, her strong white teeth hold her youth when she smiles. She is easy to talk to.

"Oui, she makes great progress," I pause and add, "ah, you know, Amélie, I never thanked you for the encores that night at the Christmas concert. You were a great blessing."

"I knew what you were up to, my dear, all in the line of duty, n'est-ce pas? The price of learning self-reliance, eh?" She winks at me.

Her casual air about my affair with Heisler makes me think maybe I have been too prim and proper. She knew the Obersturmführer would take over the rest of my evening after that concert. I love Amélie's directness, her womanliness. One never feels any probing or animosity from her. She makes you the center of her conversation.

As we talk, my eye catches Maman, Yvonne, and Dieter together at the back table. All three smile in my direction. One of the diners (they all know each other in this crowd) pulls out a chair and helps petite Yvonne, the owner and cook, to stand on it. She announces,

"Mesdames and Messieurs! *Attention, s'il vous plaît!* Tonight we have two special guests, my benefactress, Madame Mathilde de Vochard and her daughter Ingrid Fellner. I know you want to join me in thanking them for their support of my petit bistro d'haute cuisine Française, food prepared with integrity and love for free France!"

At this, Maman and I are handed glasses of wine to join the toast.

I'm speechless as Dieter and Amélie lead the men and the women, including ma mère, in raising their glasses toward me and chant in unison, "Vive La France!"

At first I don't know why; but looking closely, I recognize a few of the male diners who ran out of the Christmas concert just after Dieter played a "G" for tuning before an "A." They grin with a knowing look, especially one very old gentleman, Madeleine's grandfather. I blush and smile demurely. Apparently they are the outlying farmers who are so grateful for my *collaboration horizontale*. Ironically, my downfall is their protection.

"A moment, you two love birds," Yves, husband and devoted dishwasher, enters and proposes a toast to the Van der Kreuziers on their wedding anniversary, declaring "Vive l'amour." He sits at the old upright piano and plays a few bars of "The Wedding March" by Mendelssohn after Dieter kisses his beaming Amélie and salutes the whole establish-ment, "Vive l'amour et Vive La France!" The diners raise their wine glasses to the toast.

Yves follows, breaking into a rousing introduction of our forbidden "Marseillaise." Trusted neighbors in this neighborhood in such a tiny "cheese pocket" town will not denounce us for singing our verboten national anthem. Maman and I stand behind Dieter and Amélie. We join in as Amélie reaches back and pulls us forward into the circle of dedicated Résistants, so focused on love and decency. Despite her wealth and aristocratic bearing, Maman is aligned with them and sings fearlessly, leaning on her cane. I turn away to dry my eyes.

Amélie cups my shoulder and whispers, "Ingrid, many here know the sacrifice you make for them and those they shield. They appreciate that you could have chosen to sit out this war and do nothing. This is a lonely journey, but they honored you just now. Come back to us, dearest. Make peace with Dieter. We love you so much."

"I'm embarrassed and confused, Amélie. I can barely look at you, yet I'm grateful for your attention. This moment is a treasure for a weary heart."

I hope my memory of this small community's love and respect endures for the duration of the war, but it's not enough to bolster me against the struggle to push away or ignore my shame. I give in to the urge to escape to the toilette at the back of the eatery.

Who is that strong part of me that mocks this purging epiphany even as I try to hide my shame in a public bathroom?

In self-deprecating *humour noir* I converse with my mirror image inside the tiny water closet. I splash water on my tear-stained face and wipe my trembling hands.

"Trust your actress self to be the Résistante, old girl. You can detach from worry over your brain-injured daughter, forced sex with the enemy, and this Vichy servitude, ah oui . . . even the rest of your nightmare life . . . and not lose who you are."

Dieter said I would have to pass the woman I thought I was and not resist the one I would become.

Then I hear the Kreuziers outside the door, "What's the matter, my sweet? Is your best student blaming you for her loss of honor with the Obersturmführer? *Pauvre chéri*."

"Stop teasing me, Amélie, I'm sick at heart over her attitude and how that SS abuses her. She helps us but takes her pain out on me. I've never made such a bad error in judgment. If we survive this war, Ingrid Fellner will never speak to me again."

"My love, I'm sorry, but you needn't worry. She'll be back sooner than you think."

"How do you know that? She refuses to see me. I send her orders through others."

"Oui, but tonight, Dieter, I planted a different idea in her head. You saw how she reacted to being honored. Just wait. She'll contact you this time. And don't think on her so much. Ingrid is groping for security and has yet to discover it's living in the moment with God."

"How can you read someone's heart like that, Amélie?"

"She's a woman, my dear, and frightened to be alone. You can't understand. Give her time and don't force her into some new role now. She'll resist your efforts and try your patience fighting against her desire to be submissive," Amélie laughs heartily, teasing, "I know you like your women meek and needy, Monsieur Van der Kreuzier, so don't give me cause to be a jealous wife. Ingrid is my friend, too."

Dieter embraces her passionately after that because the door to the bathroom leans against my grasp on its latch. I was about to push down to open it and now can't budge it.

"I'll show you how much I love you, woman. It's our night to celebrate. You needn't worry. Kiss me, Madame, before we go home."

Amélie moans softly as the entire length of the door moves against its hinges from the pressure of Dieter's body against hers. I hear the sound of her silky skirt moving side to side as she purrs something into his ear. Dieter lets go of her, and the door frees up with my hand still on the latch. Amélie giggles and whispers again in his ear.

My cheeks flush at the power of their intimacy. I am a voyeur of their marital bliss and must not torture myself with the memory of Dieter's embrace. Without warning the latch releases and my light clicks off. I'm in the dark with the door ajar, free to act on my own. I hear Amélie laugh, and see her throw her shawl over Dieter's head and slip out of his grasp, pushing him away before he can see where to find her.

When I think about it later, Amélie's comments to my face and behind my back were accurate, but had they come from Dieter's mouth I would have been angry and defensive. I conclude it's imperative not to be judgmental or self-indulgent. I can't live in the past with so much risk in the present, so I contact Dieter—agreeing to be amicable.

Small groups of Jews, especially children, have crossed through our countryside. Marie, Guy and I have continuous rounds of dinner guests: the predator upstairs and his prey in my basement—while the wagging tongues in town observe my every move.

No one else is holding me back now. The resistance I must overcome is my own.

Chapter Nine

Heisler to Mueller

22 July, Wednesday, to 22 December 1942, Tuesday

One late July afternoon Marie knocks lightly on the receiving salon door during Heisler's visit. I answer reluctantly. She peeks in timidly and realizes it's not a good time. I scan her face quickly and excuse myself, leaving the Obersturmführer alone.

Marie and I whisper in the darkened hallway.

"He's here, Madame."

"Who?"

"The jeweler we waited for. Shall I give him the brooch to remove the engraving?"

"Yes, please, but why bother me? We discussed this months ago."

"Guy thought perhaps there were other pieces? While this man is with us, we should take advantage of his skill. What do you think?"

"Ah oui, bonne ideé. Get the box in my bureau upstairs. Take the other two rings I never wear. They're moderately valuable but too gaudy. They'll fetch a fair amount of money. They're also inscribed with a family crest to look like the originals. The Underground can use the money since le Rafle in Paris. I must go or my guest will begin to nose around in there. Bring refreshments when you've given the pieces to the jeweler so I know everything's all right, yes?"

"Oui, Madame."

A few minutes later Marie enters with chicory coffee, biscuits and a knowing look. I am triumphant and another step closer to personal freedom. The pain of selling my jewelry is gone.

A week later Guy pawns my brooch and rings a few towns down the Doubs. The jeweler gives him a fair exchange and wonders where the *bijouterie* comes from. He's so impressed with the main piece he places it in the shop window as Guy leaves. Money is terribly inflated and limited to necessities. Only a few French and German officials can afford to buy luxury items. The rings sell quickly but the brooch sits in the window for four months attracting attention—but no buyers.

⤙⤚

Meanwhile, from August to November of 1942 the tide outside of Occupied France begins to turn against Hitler. The British and Americans pummel Rommel in North Africa as the Soviet Deputy Commander Zhukov encircles the Huns in Stalingrad. Like Napoleon, Hitler is fighting a war on two fronts. And like Napoleon, we hope he loses in both places.

Churchill tells us over the wireless on November 10th, "This is not the end. It is not even the beginning of the end. But it is, perhaps, the end of the beginning."

On November 11th French tempers are raised because Hitler breaks his 1940 Armistice with us. He lost El Alamein to the Brits and Amis and overnight his army occupies all of our beloved 'Marianne' in a vengeful squeeze—an Axis versus allied tit-for-tat. This change gives Huns like Erich Heisler more power, but makes him more vulnerable when Berlin reassigns his Gestapo underlings to the Wehrmacht. Occasionally I see him driving his Mercedes around Duchamps by himself.

On Tuesday the 8th of December, I travel with Guy to a neighboring town to deliver a large parcel of food to one of Maman's elderly friends and check how she fares for other necessities under rationing. Afterward, Guy goes into a shop while I sit in the sedan.

Then I spot him . . . Heisler. Oh no, he sees me and makes a beeline for me across the street. I look away but he will not allow me to ignore him. People stop and stare, raising their eyebrows. Their viperous tongues will chew on this encounter forever.

Heisler glares at me through the window. I refuse to roll it down so he opens my car door. His breath smells heavily of liquor as he leans over to offer me his gloved Nazi paw.

"Madame Fellner, so lovely to see you. Bitte, you will accompany me back to Duchamps this afternoon. I shall have schnapps at your home, of course, ja?"

Never does he ask permission. He owns me, the bastard, and gets away with it.

Our affair is a year old and this SS wants to cement his relationship avec moi. Guy says I've been a very good actress. It's sad that Erich believes lifeless usury can lead to anything serious. Maybe he thinks he can win over a French woman like his brother did? But how, when he's so rude? Underneath his Aryan arrogance Heisler must fear his easy life in France will end soon. His Führer is losing everywhere else.

I must get out of the car to go with my SS master. He takes my hand—which makes it look worse—and leads me to his Mercedes. He's oblivious but I can't close my ears to this town's embarrassing catcalls. The entire Doubs region knows my family.

I hear a snide commentary whispered in rural Patois French no Hun can follow, "Et voilà, Madame, the latest souvenir tied to your bedpost, n'est-ce pas?"

With no choice I ignore the old biddy but wince at her crudeness. She will gladly tell Guy where his mistress went and with whom. To avoid her anger-slit eyes and cursing jaw, I look up at the sky and down to the ground like a small child expecting a reprimand for my infraction of social conduct.

Once I'm in the rear passenger seat, Erich leers at me in his rearview mirror, then starts the Mercedes and lurches us toward Duchamps. His voice slurs from drink, "Ingrid, *meine Liebe*," making his usual demand sound casual, "I haven't seen you for days. I expected a dinner invitation."

I say nothing. As we drive deeper into the countryside, light beads of sweat dot his upper lip. I conclude he's anxious driving alone on this isolated French road. In the past he could afford alcoholic excess, but Guy told me yesterday Berlin transferred his driver to the front, without a replacement. Usually Heisler is the cat and we French are his mice, but today he's nervous and en garde. At least this way he isn't likely to pull over on the side of the road and force sex on me.

While that is a relief, large rain clouds have descended from the mountains over the entire region. I fear he will have an accident since visibility in the hills becomes poor, about ten to fifteen meters. Dense fog conceals sudden sharp curves on narrow, high mountain roads that catch locals by surprise. As we climb higher his car pitches us forward when he downshifts too quickly around twists and turns. As he descends toward the valley on the edge of the forest, he rubs his forehead; no doubt a headache is coming on from nerves, alcohol, and his lousy driving on this circuitous route.

Moisture-laden air blankets his car and the windshield fogs up with sleety rain when he starts moving through groves of dense dark evergreens.

Well, here I am, his prisoner in his car, looking forward to a night servicing his pleasure . . . even if right now I am safe. The worst part is my town believes I enjoy my concubinage, despite all I have done as their noble philanthropist, mayor's wife, professional musician, and keen businesswoman looking out for the interests of farmers and their herds in our Franche-Comté fromageries. I take a few deep breaths to reposition my rage for the next few hours.

The ruts in this road pull my attention to our descent into the older low-lying evergreen forest where the soil is slippery with decades of needles. The farmers deliberately leave the road surface degraded and unattended. Most ride bicycles or drive horse-drawn field wagons. Gazogène lorries are tough enough to get through mud and shallow streambeds. The farmers hope the Nazis' Mercedes and confiscated French and Vichy-ite vehicles have accidents. Small acts of revenge have to satisfy their servitude.

Heisler is sleepy. He drives too fast and overcorrects too severely on curves and potholes without . . . finally, oops, damn, he's lost control. Merde! We're airborne and . . . Sacrebleu! We hit a really large rut. The car has veered off into a ditch and now refuses to go forward. He tries several times to move out of it but his rear wheels only spin deeper into the mire.

He curses our French mud and gets out to survey the damage.

The forest is quiet; a few birds chirp. There are no sounds of human life. The wind begins to hum softly through the pines to lift the fog. He looks through the trees searching for a clearing or some sign of habitation. There's nothing. He lights a cigarette and waits a few minutes.

Opening the car door to get back inside, he hears the sound of a lorry in the distance. I remain silent, grateful he has ignored me. Anything I might say could backfire. As the vehicle approaches he takes out his Luger and stands in the middle of the road. He overplays his aggressive stance—but Heisler is alone on his watch.

I whip my head around quickly at the familiar sound and recognize Marcel Beauchamp's scruffy, grey-bearded head behind the wheel. He is only twenty meters away and slows the lorry very gently. The old WWI veteran must be driving a small band of Old Testaments hidden in the rear of his "convert" coal-gas truck.

He and his assistant must have a rendezvous near the Swiss border. The younger man is freckled and fair-skinned with red hair hidden under the slouch of a—oh no! Stefan, my stepson lifts his head and pulls back his brown béret. He hates me because he doesn't know I am a Résistante. For sure they have Jews in that truck. He sits forward in the front seat next to Marcel. I pull out my small cosmetic mirror and hold it up, pretending to fix stray tresses, but really trying to read Stefan's lips without turning my head. They stop. I see him mouth,

"Merde, gun the engine, Marcel."

What will they do now with this Kraut in a ditch? Slowly I roll down my window to hear what they say. Fortunately Heisler seems so nervous he has forgotten about me.

The two get out of the truck speaking in our old Jura dialect no Nazi can understand. Marcel has a shovel in hand. Heisler is confused. They're maybe fifteen meters from the SS.

"Sonny," the old veteran smiles at his acolyte, "let's be nice and help this gentleman get his vehicle back on the road. It looks like there's no one with him, except your belle-mère."

"You have to be out of your mind, Beauchamp."

"Sonny, if we had passed him he would have emptied that pistol into our tires. He would have identified us, and we would have been arrested. The whole operation in this valley depends on what we do in the next few minutes. So don't dare act surly toward this bastard. Be nice and friendly, you know, 'freundlich.' Isn't that how you say it? Remember to speak your best German. He knew your father, Emil." Marcel is increasingly upset with Stefan, who eyes me with disgust.

"Right, and he beds my stepmother too, the. . . ."

"Shut your mouth, Stefan. That's not important right now."

Old Marcel's hazel eyes glisten as they crinkle into crow's feet when he smiles cunningly. He squeezes a deep vertical wrinkle between his thick, wiry, arched eyebrows. As the two men near the enemy, he warns his Underground comrade,

"Stefan, we want this guy to relax and put his gun away. It should be easy unless he discovers our cargo and we have to kill him. We'll have no choice then. But he doesn't know that. We must make him think we're politically indifferent, just good Samaritans on the road."

Old Marcel pauses. With bitter nonchalance, he inhales deeply and scratches his broad belly where his itchy woolen sweater rubbed it against the steering wheel. Stefan breaks out in a cold sweat. The reality of this deception sinks into my neophyte stepson, who regards me with disdain. Nevertheless, old Marcel made sure I heard his message.

"Don't worry, sonny, just do what I tell you. I'll do the talking. Do you have your documents?"

"Oui, bien sûr." Stefan shuffles his feet in the mountain's late afternoon chill.

If there are Jews in the rear, they must be very tense. Their transport always tells them how long a drive will take, and if there will be any stops. Clearly this stop is unexpected. I can imagine them huddled inside a cramped, crate-like section piled high with baskets of root vegetables and potatoes to camouflage their secret space.

Switching into modern French, Marcel and Stefan stand a few meters in front of the Obersturmführer, when old Beauchamp offers,

"Guten Tag! Well, Obersturmführer, what's the matter?" waving his hands in a friendly gesture he smiles with congeniality that surprises Heisler. The Nazi is anxious and keeps his gun aimed, not trusting anyone who speaks a Patois he can't follow.

"Your papers first, Messieurs."

Marcel surrenders his documents to Heisler and Stefan follows. The SS glances at Stefan's photo and recognizes the last name. Thankfully he doesn't draw me into the situation.

"I seem to be stuck in this ditch. Can you help me?"

"Perhaps. Uh, can I have my papers back, please?" Beauchamp nods to Stefan who translates for him. The farmer hands Stefan the shovel and winks at him to be on his toes.

"You'll get them when you've completed your task for me and the Reich," the surly Hun replies with authority. Heisler is unsure whether the farmer is naïve or arrogant. He does a poor job concealing his insecurity at being outnumbered, even if he has the upper hand.

"All right, Obersturmführer, my assistant here can dig up rocks to put under your wheels for traction. Let's see how deeply you're in the mire."

Heisler barks an order before the old man bends down, "Just a second. First, you, young Fellner, throw that shovel over here and stand next to him while he peers under the vehicle." Heisler's impatient, and curious about Stefan. He checks Marcel's identification while the farmer looks under the car.

"Oh ah, Obersturmführer, I think you need to see the damage here before we do anything. Please look. Your car is leaking something."

"Nein. Das ist nicht recht!" Heisler's unnerved at the prospect of his vehicle being immovable.

Stefan translates for Marcel, "No, this is not right," and says to Heisler, "Sorry, sir, but this old farmer knows he is right. He knows engines. We only want to help you, sir."

Heisler grits his jaw. He'll be forced to travel with these two Frenchmen. He asks through clenched teeth, anticipating the temporary loss of his precious Mercedes,

"So, what do you recommend I do about it, old man?"

Erich won't risk looking under the car. The farmer pulls his head out from under the bumper, "As I said, let my assistant place rocks under here, but you've lost fluid, and, well, you may have problems steering, braking, shifting or the engine might. . . ."

"That's enough!" Heisler snaps, "All right, stand up old man and you," motioning toward Stefan, "take the shovel and dig."

As Heisler tucks their documents into his breast pocket one small folded paper flutters to the ground.

"Ah, *und was ist das?*" he picks up the note and reads it. Instantly he crushes it into a ball and his face darkens with anger, "So, you're Résistants and you have Yids in that truck. And she's one of you. That rich bitch!"

Stefan reaches for the shovel as Heisler turns toward me. I am so consumed with the violence shooting from his eyes that I pee my panties. He ignores the two men.

He has recognized Madame Henri's handwriting and is alarmed. Beauchamp is livid, realizing Stefan's sloppiness has exposed us. He and Stefan must know I'm as good as dead now. Stefan reacts swiftly. He raises the shovel and swings at the Kraut with great force. Stefan hits him with the shovel just as Heisler fires one shot. As he falls, his gun drops from his hand and the ominous paper hits the mud.

But the Doryphore rises, wobbles and scrambles for his weapon just as old Marcel kicks it away, leans over and grabs it. Stefan prepares a second blow to Heisler's head. The Kraut escapes the full force of his swing, but Stefan has grazed him.

"Enough!" Marcel hollers.

Dizzy from the impact, Heisler looks up to see Marcel aim his own gun at him.

"What the hell did he read just now?" Marcel seethes.

"I don't know. I didn't look at it. I received it from. . . ."

"Shut up, you fool, he isn't dead yet." Marcel's angered by the unnecessary complication.

Heisler laughs and sneers at the young man's incompetence. He's delighted to reveal the contents of the note.

"I'll tell you, old man. It's a list—a prescription for remedies for Mendel Levine, one of the Jews in your lorry. And guess who wrote it?" he nods toward the car without taking his eyes from the two men.

Just then a baby's cry comes from the farm truck and the German turns toward it.

"Perfect timing," Heisler smiles.

Marcel frowns, keeping the gun on the SS, he calls to Stefan through clenched teeth,

"Quiet that kid."

My beau-fils trembles, realizing the Nazi's death is at hand. The old farmer doesn't want to kill the German with Stefan watching. He waits to squeeze the trigger until my stepson is behind their vehicle.

"Damn it!" The gun misfires giving Heisler a chance to beat them both.

The German's rage powers his lunge toward Marcel and his punch sends the old farmer grunting and reeling backward onto the Mercedes' trunk. Marcel is no match for this professional killer. Stefan hears Marcel's groan and tackles Heisler from behind before he can grab the old veteran again.

Oh God, I can't watch this, but I can't look away either.

The two roll on the wet ground in a furious struggle. Marcel's jaw is jammed and his left cheek is red hot. He regains his breath and pulls out his own pistol. He can't get a clear shot at Heisler. Then, Stefan rises to his knees, clutching his own throat. It appears my beau-fils maneuvers himself to face the lorry, so Heisler's back is to Marcel and the Mercedes.

"Shoot, Marcel, please, shoot!" I scream. Heisler looks in my direction and sneers—then looks down at Stefan, "You're not her, but you'll do for now, you feckless French idiot."

The Nazi pulls the old scarf around Stefan's neck in a garroting grip so tight, the young redhead's hair and face are the same color. As seconds tick away Stefan's eyes bulge and the whites are blue. His face swells and drains of color as the death squeeze cuts off his airway. Tears spring from my eyes; my throat closes—but my body is frozen into the seat.

Heisler stares into my stepson's rigid eyes and concentrates all his strength on killing him. The SS sways Stefan's life-draining body from side to side like a rag doll. He has only a few seconds left. Heisler foams at the mouth and growls like a rabid dog.

Marcel can't miss this shot. He aims at the German's neck and squeezes the trigger. The forest resounds with the echo. Heisler's body lifts up reflexively from the force of the shot at close range. He sprawls forward across the muddy road with his arms out at his sides. Blood spurts from his neck and mouth. He hits the ground as a dead weight. Madame Henri's prescription lies under him in the French muck. His German blood blurs my message.

The old farmer sneers and spits with avenging finality.

"Now we've completed our task for you and your Reich, you Nazi prick. And you have our *Genickschuss* in your neck as our final payment, you bastard." He turns over Heisler's corpse to retrieve their documents.

Stefan lies nearby in a fetal position, gasping and spitting convulsively. Slowly he rises to his feet, reeling. His breathing is labored. He coughs up phlegm. He's numb and in shock from the attack and the murder.

I want to go to him but am afraid he'll revile me. I stay still in the Mercedes, wishing I were invisible.

"We have to get out of here now," Marcel declares, gently moving his sore jaw.

The two men breathe heavily as they gather their wits. Stefan stares at Beauchamp whose image as a gentle country farmer and mentor is erased from his memory forever.

Marcel senses it and laughs scornfully, "Ha ha. Still a virgin, eh, *mon camarade*? Start the stinker while we clean up here."

Marcel spits a clot of blood from his cheek at Heisler's corpse, "Now he'll pay his debt to France by donating to our Résistance!" He picks up the shovel and Stefan's scarf, watching his somber young novice load and start the truck's cooker. Then Stefan returns to search Heisler and removes a small parcel from his breast-coat pocket.

Beauchamp opens the glove compartment in the old Mercedes and pulls out a small high-powered German telescope and battery-operated torch.

"Hey, get the tubing and the containers. There's almost a full tank of petrol."

The two men quickly empty the tank into portable jugs. They leave Heisler on the ground, taking his boots, gloves and hat, anything not bloodied they can use for a disguise. Stefan stoops down to give the German one last look.

"Hurry, Stefan; we can't take him with us. We could be stopped again by another Kraut. Merde! I fear some poor innocent souls will pay for this. At least out of sight the Hun buys us time to alert other farmers before the Gestapo finds him."

The two men kneel over their enemy. Marcel gently closes Heisler's eyelids before concealing his body under thick low brush. Stefan covers the Boche slowly with a few shovelfuls of earth. Staring at Marcel he coughs out his first words,

"How could you do it?"

Marcel replies bitterly, gazing far off into the past.

"It's been twenty-six years since I killed a man. And then it was another Kraut. He finished off my twin brother next to me in a trench at Verdun. We were both wounded. I played dead, but Étienne spat at the German. I waited for the Kraut to turn and killed him with my pistol. We Frenchmen wore uniforms with pride in that war," his voice wavers as he makes the sign of the cross over Heisler and himself.

"Come on, mon fils, let's go." In a gruff but fatherly way Marcel puts his arm around Stefan. His face contorts like a man who forces nausea and blood from a fight, kill, and unresolved memory down his throat.

"How's your neck, young man?" Marcel asks gently, as they open the rear doors of the truck to assure the Jews they're safe.

Stefan, in a rueful moment admits, "I guess I deserved it, sir."

Marcel smiles. "All right, then you drive for a change. It's what you do best. We're late and it's hard to move quickly on this damned washboard they call a road. Take care of the passengers back here."

Marcel comes to me, everyone's pariah, and opens the Mercedes door. I know him from childhood and am so afraid of what he must think of me, of what everyone in this valley thinks, and keep my head down, ashamed.

"Madame Henri," Marcel whispers, tenderly, "I know who you are. But your boy here apparently doesn't. He was too nervous to put it together. Give me your hand. Let me help you up. This has to be so hard for you, my poor Bonne Jeanne."

His kindness is so stunning it lifts my spirit immediately, and I take a deep breath to force back tears, thanking him, "You are so sweet, Marcel, merci." Then I add, fighting my fear to restore myself with dark dry humor, "You know, my old friend, embarrassing as it is," pointing to my skirt soaked through, "if the only attack I ever make on the enemy in this war is to piss on the seat of his Mercedes, at least I've done that." Marcel chuckles, and then is serious when I add, "I thought Stefan was listening to Heisler accuse me of being a Résistante, but now I think he must have been so scared that what the SS said didn't sink in. Please don't reveal who I am. It's a miracle Heisler never read my code name aloud."

"Your secret is safe, Madame. What's between you and your beau-fils isn't my business."

He walks me slowly to the rear of the lorry. "Sorry you must hide back here, Madame, but we have to avoid any risk to your safety and our cover. If we're stopped again by Gestapo, your story is we found you stranded on the road, oui, ça suffit?"

"Oui, bien, but where? It has to be far from the abandoned Mercedes."

"How about along the edge of your Maman's property that borders on mine? I can say you were overseeing the fromagerie there and your car wouldn't start and you were walking the half-kilometer back to my place. We are only a short distance from there right now."

"That's perfect, Marcel."

"Bien sûr, Madame. When we arrive I will alert your fromagerie manager. He will cover for you without asking any questions. And if we need it, Guy can drive the car there."

Since Stefan is out of hearing and can't see us at the back of the lorry, I grab Marcel's hand and squeeze it, reach up and kiss his scruffy bearded cheeks. His warm fatherly smile cancels my tears when he replies,

"Ma chère femme, if I were twenty-five years younger you would no longer be a widow!"

I smile as he helps me into the rear of the lorry. He positions me up against the wall and shows me a tiny sliding wood panel about 8 by 6 centimeters he engineered that opens to the truck's cab to allow a driver or passenger to give directions to a third person in the rear. That person fills the cooker with wood or coal when the fuel runs low. Stopping the gazogène would waste too much valuable time. No one else knows about it, except Stefan. Marcel made the hole appear on the outside to be part of the cab's ventilation system, but it's to bring in clean air to the refugees inside their closed chamber next to me. At last I'm peaceful for a few minutes and pray for a safe journey the rest of the way.

Beauchamp climbs into the passenger seat and Stefan takes off without a word. We maneuver a few kilometers over the deeply rutted gravel lane. I feel groggy until I hear Marcel ask to see the parcel Stefan removed from Heisler. He hands it over. The old man opens it.

"Ooh la la! What a beautiful piece!" He holds up the jeweled pin for Stefan to see.

"Oh no, that's Ingrid's. That son of a bitch had it!" Instantly he's infuriated.

Marcel humiliates Stefan, twisting his voice into sarcasm, "Hey, sonny, relax. You don't know how he got it. At least it will fetch a good sum at the pawnbroker in town. Unless you want to give it back to her personally?"

A long silence follows. That guilty little boy in Stefan's heart at long last shames him to hold his tongue and keep his eyes riveted to the road. The two men drive the rest of the route without saying a word.

I think on these months servicing Erich Heisler and am relieved that he was his own worst enemy. He never did too well with our French mud, staining my dress with it in November of 1941 and ending face down in it in December of 1942.

Marcel stops at his farmhouse for me to clean up a little, and gives me a shot of whiskey. He has a phone call from another Résistant, Jean Claude de Voisin, just before we leave. Marcel lets me listen with him as de Voisin uses a code I do not understand.

"The tractor left a lot of debris on the circle that was identifiable from the brown clods where the grains were gathered."

Marcel later tells me the phrase means Jean Claude saw the mound covering the Nazi's body, surmised what happened and collected every scrap of Stefan's torn scarf left behind in the rush. He will report this to Dieter, but he recognized Marcel's tire tracks. Marcel will change the tires. He has spares in the barn. Nazi vengeance in outlying regions is always harsh. We must be prepared.

A small package arrives in early evening. I sit by the fireplace in my receiving salon to unwrap it. Shreds of Stefan's scarf surprise me. Dieter received these last bits of evidence and sends them with a brief message that Heisler is dead. I quickly deduce that Marcel hasn't told Dieter I was there at the scene. Stefan never reports to Dieter and is forbidden to tell anyone what he knows, since he's only a junior driver. That should protect my secret. Not that I really care what Dieter knows.

I'm thankful Stefan is safe. I gave him that scarf just before I married his father eighteen years ago. He loved it. He was a kind little boy then and felt safe with me. After I married Emil, his attitude changed overnight. I still do not know why.

I asked Emil many times what happened when his wife, Hélène, died in the boating accident. Emil never had an answer. Stefan was so young. Maybe something haunts him from that time? Emil didn't agree that Stefan's ambivalent behavior toward me was atypical. Stefan must have a terribly dark secret he's afraid to confide. He held so much tension in his young eyes in our early days.

Perhaps that fear holds him back from loving me? Now my *feldmatratzendienst* appears to have crystallized his anger from whatever that old wound is. Being a field mattress for the Reich appears to justify his stance against me. His mistrust fillets my heart worse than sex with the enemy.

I'm grateful he was saved from detection but worried that he left damning evidence behind. Everyone in town knew Stefan by this scarf. The last bits of it burn in my hearth along with Dieter's note when Marie enters and announces in a shaky voice,

"Madame, SS Heisler's replacement is here to see you."

I turn from momentary reflection on family matters and my blood runs cold, gazing up at the next brutal chapter of my life.

～

Franz Mueller is a beast in every way: portly, fat-cheeked with an Adolph mustache, a bloated boxy nose and small shifty eyes. He's an obese version of Reichsführer Himmler and definitely not Aryan. His large hands are hairy. He makes me nervous, knowing in due time I will discover his whole body is hairy. He bulges with a thick layer of pork fat on top of his powerful musculature. His teeth are bad and skin is greasy—altogether he's vulgar and repulsive.

The rumor about town is his kin work for saloonkeepers and butchers. He has a wife and four offspring in Germany. He trained under men who led the Eastern Einsatzgruppen massacres of Jews in 1940. His arrival coincides with Germany's takeover of France's "Free Zone." Whatever little freedom I cherished before will live only in my private thoughts now.

Mueller introduces himself and questions me about his predecessor's disappearance. I find him dull yet shrewd, and a hard-of-hearing mutterer.

His violent and vengeful nature terrifies me. A farmer who lives near the road where Heisler was found has already been tortured (he proudly announces)—and will be deported to a labor camp in Germany. Mueller could have had ten others shot in reprisal, but this farmer martyred himself by confessing to save his sons and neighbors.

Heisler is the first SS murdered in our region. Everyone has read of the recent Nazi reprisals in Lidice and Ležáky, Czechoslovakia. Two Czech Résistants assassinated Reinhard Heydrich, der Führer's head SS Reichsprotektor of Bohemia and Moravia who was his architect of the Final Solution. Both towns were burned to the ground. All the men were murdered. The women were separated from their children and both were sent to death camps. Family pets and farm animals were slaughtered.

Der Führer's revenge opens the door for Mueller to treat us French as personal playthings he can dispose of at whim. We've heard that he hasn't tasted our blood yet, and only has power as our overseer. It's the most prestigious position he's had thus far. Nevertheless I am nervous my neighbors will betray our local Résistance because they fear Fritzie vengeance will strike them dead here in Duchamps as well. The Germans were better behaved toward us earlier, when they were winning their battles. Now that all of France is under their thumb, we are treated much like other conquered nations.

As time goes on, I realize Mueller has wheedled the truth out of Heisler's cohorts. They must have described how Erich bedded me in intimate detail. Mueller is a sadist; he wonders if he should expose me—or gain intimacy. He calculates his torture on a psychological battlefield. He steps in, ostensibly, to see if I'm a spy.

By now I've cut myself off from feeling anything for anyone. Such defensiveness protects my flesh but dulls my ability to perceive the little ways an enemy reveals himself and his secret agenda.

SS Mueller immediately tries to lure me into sex but I decline. Next he softens me with candies and black market trinkets. He's eager yet unwilling to push me since I'm well worth sweetening for conquest.

Heisler at his worst was a worm going along for the ride while this SS is a low-life bully. I detest his blind love for der Führer.

One December afternoon, he arrives unexpectedly, finally satisfied I know nothing of Heisler's demise. He makes a great effort to be friendly because I'm concerned he saw Marta going out as he came in. I've tried to keep them apart. During our previous meeting we had an argument when he implied she was defective. He's jealous of my attention to her and of my past relationship with Heisler.

As an independent woman bred to the higher classes I'm not the type he goes to for sex. I'm afraid he will expect me to do things I will not consent to. He continues to soften me up as he pushes me into a corner.

"Mein *Schatz*, I've brought you a small token of my appreciation for your friendship, a Christmas trifle."

"That's not necessary, Obersturmführer."

"Oh, but it is, dear one."

He feels very uncomfortable in my presence. I have great difficulty concealing my contempt. Everything about him revolts me. I'm certain paid prostitutes have treated him the same way. I try to find something about him to like. I'm becoming hard and coarse in the process of defending my basement operation. I hope Mueller perceives none of this. He hands me a small parcel and like an eager puppy awaits his treat.

My fingers tremble as I fiddle with the box. I feign a cough—fearful I'm giving myself away.

"Och, mein Schatz, are you cold?" He moves closer and I move away coughing a little more to keep him at a distance.

"No, no, it's nothing, just a little chill from the rain last night. Our wood supply is low these days. The war takes it all."

I pause to see if the lie's convincing. He accepts it. Good. Now what the devil is in this damn little box?

"Oh, my goodness!" I gasp and gaze in disbelief not sure whether to laugh or cry. Mueller has brought back my brooch. I can only hope that he's unwittingly contributed to the Résistance with his purchase.

"Well, do you like it?"

"Oh, ah, yes, ah, what a beautiful brooch, Obersturmführer. You shouldn't have gone to so much expense."

I sit back and stare at it. Mueller leans over and takes it from my hands to pin on my dress. I relinquish it without a blink and travel back to the time Emil gave it to me. Then suddenly I snap to attention and take it from the Hun.

"Oh, no. Please, no. Not yet, Obersturmführer. Let me admire it first. Please, it's been many years since anyone has given me such a lovely gift. Excuse me, I'm overcome."

Mueller's happy I'm pleased but he wishes for a warmer show of gratitude. He wants me to consent to sex as his reward for this gift, today, now, here on this small divan. His intentions are so primitive. I can't bear the idea of him touching me, or the brooch, let alone pinning it to my dress, so I play the sweet passive female who cries softly,

"Forgive me, Obersturmführer, I'm sorry. These are tears of happiness."

A complete lie; they're tears of profound sorrow. I remember my departed husband on the sunny afternoon when he gave me this brooch. It was a family heirloom and not quite my taste. Emil apologized. It was all he could give me at the moment. He had just proposed marriage. I was euphoric and laughed. Immediately he pinned it to my dress. I recall the vivid image of our passionate embrace and the lovemaking that followed. I have grown to adore this antique. And now this brute will pollute my fondest memories with his Blitzkrieg for military rape. My stomach rides a wave of bitterness.

"I'm so long without love in my life, dear Obersturmführer, you'll forgive me for indulging my emotions at this moment, please." I wail and push myself to look him straight in the eye with a pathetic expression of female weakness that makes men squirm.

"Ja, mein Schatz. Take your time," Mueller replies uneasily and stands abruptly to pace the length of the room, unsure how to handle me or perhaps his erection. Serves him right for fooling around with a rich widow. I pretend to be sorrowful for my lost love and sprout a few tears after overhearing him mumble at my wedding photo over the writing desk,

"Should have taken her on that damn little sofa and been done with it. Ach. Now she's crying. I'll have to get it somewhere else."

He crosses the room to sit next to me. "There, there, don't weep, Schatz. I'm awed by your sensitivity. I'll do whatever you wish." He touches my hand. I give in reluctantly.

A second later I say abruptly, "Oh, look at the time. So sorry, Obersturmführer, forgive me. I've taken you from your work," sensing he has not subdued his sexual arousal.

He frowns, very frustrated, as I look toward the door. All this time spent on my feelings. Now he must leave and suppress his desire. He rises from the divan unaware I overhear him whisper again under his breath, "Will I ever get it in this slippery dish?"

"Did you say something, Obersturmführer?"

In an unusually compliant tone he recovers quickly and smiles, "No problem, my little Schatz, I shall see you tomorrow. We'll have more time to enjoy the afternoon."

He looks into my eyes, bends over, takes my hand and kisses it hastily in a pathetic attempt to be debonair. He must have learned that move from Heisler's gossips too. His reenactment of that first fateful flattery almost makes me choke. My innocence and vanity have cost me dearly. I cough a little from revulsion, but disguise it to reinforce the potential for illness coming on, while actually quite bilious from our encounter.

"Forgive me if I do not see you to the door, Obersturmführer."

"Yes, tomorrow for sure."

He marches out obsessed with the loss of his conquest. Marie must have noticed him rearranging his pants as he passed her in the hall. She enters warily, a right hand over her quickening heartbeat, and her face transparent with a mind full of ugly imagery. She finds me weeping and laughing in a crazed manner.

"Madame, are you all right? Did he hurt you?" She comes quickly to my side.

"Oh no, Marie, but the universe has paid me back. Look, Marie, *look!*"

I open my hand and hold out the brooch.

"Where did it come from? From him?" Then her face brightens and her eyes light up, "Oh Madame, it's a sign. A wonderful sign."

"What? How can you say that?" I'm angry and sit bolt upright, "It's horrible. To see it again when he's the person to return it. How can you say it's a good sign? I will be sick."

"No, no Madame. Step back for a minute from your pain, please, and listen. That brooch paid more than once for the Underground."

"How?"

"Well, Madame, I shouldn't say, but the brooch garnered a large sum already. Mueller giving it to you means it doesn't matter how it happened or was returned, only that it's here."

"No, Marie. It does matter. You didn't think Mueller would be the one to return it, did you? I see it in your eyes. Tell me who bought it before him. You know, I'm sure."

"Yes I do, Madame, but the less you know the better."

I say a few names and her eyes widen as I pause at Heisler's.

"So it was bought twice, paid twice, and both times the Fritzies donated to us?"

Marie smiles. "Oui, but it means more than that, Madame. It confirms that your work to help escapees is the right thing to do. The Underground got the money and the SS returned your jewel in the bargain. You should be happy."

I snap back from the past and hear her clearly for the first time. I'm still attached to the pain of forced intimacy with Heisler and my fear of sex with this SS brute. I remember Dieter's warning to pull myself together or the ugliness will cloud my judgment.

"So you're telling me the universe is on Dieter's side regardless of how I degrade myself for the cause? Well, if God can hide His Face from me I suppose I must appreciate this satire."

My voice trails off as I reconstruct the brooch's route back home. I begin to giggle. Marie joins me, laughing, as we stare at the jewel. Mueller still couldn't pay anything near what it's worth. Who cares? If he paid half its value we're ahead of the game. And it's ready to be pawned again. Our laughter escalates with an edge of relief colored with insanity.

Finally, tears roll down our cheeks. We grab each other, stand up and begin to dance to ward off cramping. We need a few moments of giddy freedom to rise above our clandestine lives.

1943

Chapter Ten

Sylvia

13 March 1943, Saturday

After many crossings, dreams, prayers, and hours in reflection over this dark winter of 1943, I divorce myself from daily routines and plunge into my Underground role with less fear. I trust my intuition to save me if danger arises in the midst of performing this odious Nazi théâtre. That instinctive sense seems to be wedded to my creative flair for drama. Dieter must have believed in me when he saw that on the riverbank in 1941. His confidence gives me resiliency now that Franz Mueller intrudes upon my life.

This Nazi's predictable crudeness becomes unbearable once his domination unfolds. His lascivious behavior drives me to visit my basement to justify servicing him. When I meet my Old Testament travelers face to face their gratitude confirms my sacrifice—and not a moment too soon.

Since September 1942, the Gestapo has encouraged Pierre Laval to pursue the French Underground. At the end of January 1943, Vichy officially ordained the French Paramilitary Police, the dreaded *Milice*, whose ranks swell with thugs and brutal mercenaries. Stories of Milicien savagery, infiltration and betrayal circulate amongst Résistance workers. Arrests almost always lead to torture. Increasingly, people disappear in the Vichy version of Hitler's *Nacht und Nebel*, Night and Fog, policy. Highly placed Underground leaders in Lyon and Paris go missing. I feel more alone and afraid in provincial Duchamps.

Sylvia Feinstein, a young Polish Jewish escapee, arrives from Germany in 1943. She helps me come to terms with living in a constant state of panic. Her needs embolden me to visit my basement, even when Mueller is in the neighborhood. Initially, handling the abrupt emotional change from upstairs to downstairs and vice-versa is a big challenge.

An enclosed staircase joins the street floor to the servants' floor below, and leads from there down to the basement. During the few moments I traverse the staircase alone, I learn to center myself and shift the gears of my persona up or down with each step. I descend with French on my lips and enter the basement speaking German or Yiddish. Then I ascend to French or German in the receiving salon. My language skills make communication with our lodgers much easier for Guy and Marie. I graduate from translating and writing notes.

When I finally juggle these opposite arenas with success, I scold myself for wasting almost two years crippled by fear. In moments when I am kinder to myself, it's clear that I'm a different woman now. This was no easy transition; possible only with love and support from everyone close to me, especially Dieter, whom I've abused dreadfully.

This evening Mueller is listening to recordings of his detestable German beer hall songs. The phonograph is turned up very loud and he drinks a lot of wine and brandy. Becoming sloppy, he dances all over my feet and wants sex. It's the wrong time of the month and I refuse him. He's annoyed, so I have to amuse him in other ways. He always disgusts me.

Then Marie knocks and calls through the door, "Madame, we have a major leak from the rain. Please come and look so we can get a roofer in the morning. It's very serious."

"Oh, I'm sorry, Obersturmführer. You'll have to leave now. I have household matters to attend to. Let me see you to the door, my dearest."

"What? Oh, yes. Curfew has begun. I need to get back. All right, mein Schatz," he belches coarsely in my face, "Excuse me, Schatz, it was a good dinner. When can I see you again?" His hand gropes my bosom as he pulls me to his mouth for a goodnight kiss. I give him my cheek.

"Oh, in a day or two. Off you go, dear."

He reeks of cigar mixed with sweat, garlic, and my liquor. I love to kick him out of my house.

✎

I have an uncomfortable feeling in the pit of my stomach when I look at the "leak."

Marie introduces me to Sylvia. She's in premature labor. Painfully thin from malnutrition, but a picture of the Aryan physique: blue eyes, blonde hair in thick braids, a good height and very clear skin underneath the pastiness of deficiency. I wouldn't have thought she was a Jewess. She's beautiful but very frail. Her abdomen is the only place with weight. She has given her very essence to her baby.

We have no choice but to move her upstairs to the kitchen area. It's warmer and closer to a bathroom and hot water. We install her in the large rear pantry. It was repainted just five years ago and there are cabinet doors on the shelving now so it's an organized, light, airy storage space. We fit a small bed under the high window with just enough room for a night table and Marta's old cradle.

Sylvia's contractions are coming every ten minutes so she's progressing well. One of the Jewish women volunteers to help but we need Amélie, the only midwife we can trust.

I send Guy to her house. He can show his Ausweis and say he's getting pills for Marta in case he's stopped. Amélie has medical permission to be out after curfew. She arrives a few minutes before Guy so they aren't seen together.

Then chaos ensues.

The front door bell rings, accompanied by loud banging, as soon as we move Sylvia one flight up from the basement. Her contractions are less than five minutes apart. I run to answer, so concerned for Sylvia I forget the ever-present possibility of a raid. I open the door without buzzing the basement first. A young Gestapo agent announces he's here to collect Mueller's gloves. I hand him the gloves lying on the hall table but he wants to linger. I'm afraid Sylvia is near the end. The baby's head will be crowning. Surely she'll scream.

My failure to use our front buzzer has put everyone at risk. Guy comes to the top of the stairs to see what's happening when he should have stayed in the basement. Making things worse, tonight I let Marta go to sleep early when I should have kept her awake to alert us on the water pipes when the SS are on river watch.

I struggle to put all the pressure out of my mind and speak to the Nazi cordially,

"Please Offizier, send my regrets to Obersturmführer Mueller. He forgot his gloves." He left them deliberately and sent this *Grünschnabel*, green beak, to catch us rejoicing with our human contraband. "Tell him I'll see him the day after tomorrow at our usual time. Excuse me, please, but I have many concerns. My daughter's very sick, in severe pain."

As luck would have it, Sylvia gives out a muffled shout.

"Oh dear, did you hear that? My daughter needs me. Gute Nacht, Offizier. I'm sure you understand I must tend to her immediately!"

"Ja, I'm sorry, Madame. Gute Nacht!"

The officer is young and naïve. I think speaking to him in German did the trick. I suppose he never heard a woman in childbirth or else he would have guessed what was really going on. As soon as the front door closes, I fly downstairs. Sylvia has delivered a tiny baby boy, just under two-and-one-half kilos.

Marie assists Amélie. Sylvia is exhausted. I'm fearful she won't survive. Guy immediately gets smelling salts and we work for the next few hours to make mother and newborn stable.

It's nearly midnight when Amélie leaves. Marie volunteers to sleep in a chair next to Sylvia and give her remedies throughout the night. Grateful to both women and extremely tired—with a banging migraine—I climb the stairs very slowly. My legs feel like stone pillars.

Then I stop and freeze in place. I hear Marta. She has risen from a nightmare and is walking in her sleep. She cries, trying to find me in the dark, and drags her left leg on the upstairs hallway carpets. I hear the uneven rhythm of her gait and rush to her before she falls down the stairs. Marta never sees herself crippled in her dreams. I'm terrified she will hurt herself when she sleepwalks.

"Marta. Wake up. Please, stop moving. I'm coming."

I burst with adrenalin and leap up the back stairs to the second floor hallway just in time to catch her. She's about to step into the protective gate across the rear upstairs landing. It's only as high as a table. She's so tall now she could catapult herself over it. I have to get a carpenter I can trust if Guy can't fix this.

I grasp her shoulders to rouse her to consciousness. She slurs her words, still not with me. All this since the direct hit to the side of her head from the accident. Dr. Duvette thinks perhaps she was so frightened by her father's tumble in front of her that she forgot where she was and hit the same tree full force. I battle to rouse her. Good, she comes around. Her color is back and she breathes deeper.

"Maman! Maman! Daddy's dead, *he's dead!*"

"Hush, my sweet, it's only a dream. It happened a long time ago," I kiss her and hold her close. She awakens cold and clammy.

"Where am I, Maman? Where's Papa?" Each time Marta's in this state, her small voice of three years ago wails until my baby fades away and my ten-year old re-emerges.

"I'm sorry, Maman. It happened again."

"It's all right, sweetie. I'm here. Let's wash your face and get you back to bed."

Marta's eyes suddenly become big as tea saucers. She looks at me in surprise. The distant cry of the new baby threads its way up the stairwell.

"Maman, what's that?"

"Not what, Marta. Who?" At a loss for words I have to tell her the truth. She's old enough to understand—but will she keep it confidential?

"Can you be a very big girl now, Marta? You know what I've told you about our downstairs guests?"

"Oui, Maman."

"Well, we have a young woman here and she just delivered her baby. We have to care for them for awhile."

"Oh Maman, how wonderful. May I meet them?"

She smiles with delight, anticipating new people in her drab lonely world. Unaware of the new danger, I have to be gentle but stern explaining our increased vulnerability. I put my arm around her and cover her with my sweater.

We sit together on the top step.

"I have to tell you more about the Nazis who come here and the young mother and her baby downstairs. We have to protect them and ourselves, Marta. Promise me you will never tell anyone about them. It will destroy our family and this young mother and her baby if the world outside our house ever finds out. It has to be our secret."

"So they are Jewish, right, Maman?"

Several days after delivery when Sylvia is comfortable nursing Pierre, I sit by her bedside in the pantry for a heart-to-heart talk. She's anemic but eats well and gains strength quickly.

Sylvia is a courageous young woman, although very rigid in her thinking. When she gets an idea, rather than bend to see how it plays out she wants to defend it and make everything else bend to it. In some ways this has kept her alive for the many months she's had to adapt to the rules for each new situation. Pierre's Bris is a perfect example.

"You see, Madame Fellner, usually by the eighth day after birth a Jewish baby boy has his Bris."

"His what?"

"His Bris. Excuse me, his circumcision."

"Ah, oui, I understand. Sylvia, do you need a doctor?"

"No, a special man performs the ritual, a mohel. We should find one."

"I'm not so sure that's possible, Sylvia. We have to ask in the Résistance community to see if anyone is shielding a mohel. Suppose we can't find one to perform this by the end of eight days? Is it a sin or something?"

"It's important to do it now, Madame. I don't want to wait until Pierre's older. The foreskin gets thicker. It will be frightening and hurt more. Please find someone."

"I'm not convinced this is a good idea, Sylvia. If Pierre is circumcised and. . . ."

"But lots of men are circumcised who aren't Jewish," she interrupts. She can't be convinced of the danger, "I have to insist he lives a normal life like any Jewish child. He has to have it. The Creator will protect him because the tradition has to be respected. Please, find me a mohel."

Sylvia is in shock, and denies the war and her loss of family. I can't reason with her. She can't believe her devotion to observing a Jewish way of life could lead to her death. Her attachment to ritual laws must continue. Even now, temporarily denied for safety's sake, I suppose she feels ripped away from the core of the life she has known.

I set about finding a mohel. Most of the Old Testaments hidden in town are in transit. They go to Switzerland or south to Italy and aren't here long enough to perform a ritual like this. I have Sylvia write a note in Yiddish for others to pass to their lodgers. Marie takes it to someone whose name is secret from me. That same day a reply comes and as luck would have it I find a mohel. Amazing! We have to bring the gentleman here from the countryside between curfew checks. We set up the time for that night. Sylvia is delighted and prepares little bandages. By then I'll have another group of Old Testaments to share the ceremony.

At 4:00 p.m. that afternoon Mueller arrives with two new Gestapo agents. Two short buzzes and a long one alert Marie and Guy, and everyone disappears into the hidden chambers. Marie takes mother and son down to the cellar from the larder. With three Nazis here, having Sylvia and Pierre only one floor below is too risky if the baby cries loudly.

The Germans have come for a light supper and to play cards into the early part of the evening. Usually Mueller wants to get drunk and have sex. Tonight he brings a rare treat of fresh coffee beans and asks us to brew them extra strong for him and his men. I'm surprised and happily accommodate him. I'll do anything not to have sex. Downstairs all is ready for the baby's Bris. The two worlds are ignorant of each other's existence. Then Marie calls me out of the receiving salon in the middle of their card game.

"Madame, the Underground has received word of a raid on the outer farms later tonight. Can you delay Mueller and his men? He's supposed to lead it."

"I'll try, Marie. Now I see why he wanted strong coffee."

"The farmers and Maquisards need another hour. The weather is turning very cold in the higher elevation. The muddy roads will show their tire tracks. Snow might fall. They'll have to go by foot into the hills. It won't be safe for the passeurs or the Jews."

"I'll try my best. Do you think Stefan will be one of the drivers, Marie?"

This sounds like another game of hours like the Christmas concert over a year ago.

"You'll think of something, Madame." I turn to the door but Marie hesitates.

"What's the matter, Marie?"

"It's Sylvia. She's very disappointed. She can't have the baby's Bris tonight. Her mohel went into the forest to be safe. He'll never come back. You need to talk with her."

"I can't leave these men now. They'll get suspicious. For goodness sake, Marie, tell her to be thankful I'm containing this poison in my parlor. Tell her to pray that I can do it a little longer, to save us all from arrest. Really, she's in another world that girl. Bring more coffee and sweets so I can lure them into staying longer."

I return to the parlor. Franz and his men are bored with their card game. I need to do something quickly to distract them.

"All right, my boys. Let's dance!"

"Mein Schatz! I thought you'd never ask," Mueller kisses me as he lifts me off my feet.

I put on some recordings to liven things up. Mueller grabs me around the waist and pinches my buttocks, then swings me side-to-side, crushing me against his porcine torso. I hate his vulgarity and would die of shame if not for saving people's lives. I have no choice but to give him a sexy look and reach toward the other two officers, whose jaws drop.

"Oh, my three sweethearts, you are all so strong. Please, gentlemen, follow me."

The music is the "Can-Can," but the Germans can only goose-step to it. I have to keep from laughing. I kick my legs high and raise my skirt slightly to reveal a little thigh. It keeps them interested. Mueller's very jealous so I'm careful to look only in his direction during this Moulin Rouge version of myself as Eurydice to his "Orpheus in Hell." Franz and his men are excited. When the music ends we're breathless. I root around in the rear of the old credenza and pull out a bottle of Pernod to celebrate.

"Oh, we shouldn't drink tonight, Schatz." Mueller puts his hand over the glass, as I'm about to pour.

"But why, dear, it's a great night to have fun, no?"

"Ja, but we have a little business tonight, mein Schatz, never you mind."

I give him a little bite on his hairy ear and blow into it.

"Too bad. I'm feeling so lonely," I whisper, "well, you don't mind if I have a little?"

Teasing him to join me usually works.

"Well, just a little," he pours us Pernod and toasts, "down the hatch."

About an hour later they're quite tipsy and happy. I've sipped sparingly to stay sober. Marie knocks on the door again. I leave my giddy Krauts. They struggle arm in arm to stay upright every time they kick their legs, dancing like drunken chorus girls.

"Yes, Marie, what is it?"

"Oh Madame, well done. The last refugees are safely hidden by now. If the Boches get out on the country roads they won't see tire tracks. The rain is freezing now, a blessing for us. It's time for them to leave. Are they drunk yet?"

"Getting there, Marie. I'll push them out. Guy should stay nearby in case there's trouble."

"Madame, can you get away and speak to Sylvia? She's overtired, not too rational."

"Yes, in a few minutes. Give her some chamomile tea."

Just then, the door opens and Mueller grabs me,

"Hey, Schatz, come on, just one more sexy dance before we leave, ja?"

"Coming, Franzie." I roll my eyes at Marie and slip back into the lion's den.

Mueller dances with me while the other two can barely stand. He carries his liquor well, even Pernod. It's expensive to inebriate him. At the end he pulls me into the bathroom and quickly drops his pants but is so drunk and excited he climaxes before getting to me. Thank goodness. Sweetly, I remind him there's always another time. He may have cost me in drink but his *Trunkenheit* makes him very pliable this evening. I hope in his drunken state he misses his appointment to raid the farmers.

I escort the Nazis to the front door. With a smile and kiss on the cheek for each man I send all three staggering out into a freezing cold drizzle. It takes them a few extra minutes to get their vehicle moving on the sleet. Quiet and reflective, I listen to them laugh and shout as they drive off.

Alone at last, a chill runs through me. These are grown men who dance like silly young schoolboys to music composed by one of their most famous German Jewish scapegoats. Jacques Offenbach's father was the cantor in the Cologne synagogue a hundred and twenty years ago.

How can they kick up their heels to his son's music and turn into mad dogs and kill today's Jews? How do we let Der Führer's maniacal craving for so-called racial purity rule us? These evil emissaries must suffer from the blindness of childhood indoctrination.

I would be living on my knees like the rest of France without the Résistance to channel my frustration over this tyranny. I scan the silent empty streets from the vestibule's narrow window. My eyes blink back tears. No one can blame the bystanders for their inaction. I'm grateful for their disbelief that someone like me does what they cannot. Still, the specter of their betrayal bites at my heels and the consequences frighten me to my core. I lock the front door, turn off the lights and go downstairs.

Sylvia is depressed and miserable. Her baby is oblivious to her tears and sleeps peacefully in his cradle. My eyes absorb her pain from the shock of running and hiding for the last nine months. I massage her thin shoulders with Maman's lavender lotion.

"Madame Ingrid, my baby's mohel has left. What can I do now?" She is so disappointed.

I've seen this in other escapees. They cling to the rituals that ground them even when those same celebrations make them vulnerable to lethal exposure. Dinnerware crockery on my table reminds them of cherished items like antique dishes and silver cutlery. My guests break down when the aroma of Marie's cooking collides with their memories of holiday meals with extended family.

For me the Bris isn't what troubles Sylvia. It's what it stands for. The ceremony welcomes the next generation and celebrates the continuation of a family line. She has no one left to rejoice with her. They're all dead. I can't say this. It would be rude and uncaring and she wouldn't hear me. Right now her baby is her only source of joy against her grief for his father and her family.

Sylvia is desperate. Destiny has dealt her a victim's course of extreme inhumanity. Grief grabbed her in solitary confinement when she hid for months before finding me. Her body won't release her agony until she is secure in the company of joy. Otherwise she won't go forward with her life and feel safe again. Pierre is the change that crowned her suffering with a safe delivery shared in love. In one short journey she has gained a new and different world beyond herself. The responsibility of her infant son demands she trust me, a goyishe stranger.

I sit down next to her and lean back against the pillows and tell her gently,

"Sylvia, you're exhausted and in shock. Marie explained the mohel had to escape into the hills to be safe because of the raid. You heard what she said, yes?"

"Yes, Madame Ingrid, I did."

"Good, stop worrying about the Bris. You're alive and so is Pierre. That's enough of a miracle for one day. You need your. . . ."

"But he needs his Bris," she interrupts, intent on making the illogical logical.

"Sylvia, why do you cling to your rituals? Because they give you sanity and purpose?"

"They are my way to show God I love him, Madame."

"Yes, you measure your faithfulness to His Covenant this way. I agree. As a Catholic, I too have rites and rituals. We've been taught we need these structures to approach the Almighty. I'm not sure they're necessary if God already lives in us."

This may reach her ears as anathema.

"What?" She responds incredulously. I must complete my thought.

"That's right. If God is Perfection He doesn't need rules. We do. And sometimes He takes away the rules to make us more aware so we listen more attentively."

"Why do that?"

"Because He has something else in mind and needs our attention. Why do you assume if you can't follow a ritual God will be angry or your child will be less worthy and not protected from harm? Maybe you need to see past it? Maybe he has another way to reach you?"

"So what are you saying?"

"If the mohel couldn't come tonight, remember God is in charge, not you. Wait and you'll get the answer. He'll speak through your heart, Sylvia. We don't worship the same way but please don't confuse the ritual for Yahweh's presence. You do believe Adonai lives and breathes through you and Pierre, yes?"

"Yes, I do."

"Well, if you allow Him into your being why risk killing Him by putting your son in harm's way?"

"I guess you're right but what's the reason I lost the mohel?" Around and around we go.

"I'm not certain, Sylvia, but it seems most important to have Pierre safe. God's priority sees what we cannot. The Bris isn't important now. Go to sleep and concentrate on your health. We can talk again later."

Because she's still in shock she asks again and again. We are strangers yet we speak candidly and share an easy affection—almost like sisters. I fluff her pillows and pour her fresh water. I bend over as she looks up at me with a shadow of pain covering her face. As I sit down she grabs my hands and leans her head against my shoulder. I stroke her cheek and rock her like a baby for a few moments. I feel so close to her. The emptiness of Sylvia's loss makes me kiss her good night on her forehead. She is so numb yet filled with new motherhood and cannot allow herself to cry. I'm old enough to be her mother and Pierre's grandmother. I sit at the foot of her cot, staring into space as she drifts off to sleep.

Sylvia's plight is bewildering. My little eddy of weeping looks insignificant against the turbulent undertow of her loss.

However much I care for her, Sylvia will have to leave my home.

Where do we put baby Pierre so his cries are not heard upstairs in the receiving salon when the Gestapo visits? He's not a colicky child, just hungry. Amélie finds a nursing wife of a trusted Résistance worker who's willing to share her breast milk until we increase Sylvia's milk with a few herbs.

When she naps, we take turns holding Pierre to keep him satisfied and close to our warm bodies. Sometimes he's wrapped in flannel inside Marie's old bib apron covered by her sweater, or over my heart in a blanket secured at my waist and shoulder. Guy wears him on his back in a blanket. We love to cuddle and sing to him. When everyone is busy, Pierre sleeps on top of the warming oven in an old metal breadbox lined with a piece of goose down comforter.

As Sylvia regains her strength, we make a safe private living area for her in the basement. She helps with laundry and food preparation for our guests. She comforts the refugees and begs me to find more for her to do. The full force of her loss has yet to hit her.

No one mentions the Bris if she doesn't.

As her emotional foundation begins to crack, she feels her losses one at a time. She shares her suffering over the death of her great-grandmother. I do my best to soothe her. Sylvia forces me to see my shortcomings and how spoiled I've been. Some nights I'm still afraid to face my Old Testaments and handle the Gestapo. Her confidence builds my perseverance when facing angry accusations from estranged friends like Germaine.

I must do everything to make Sylvia safe. She looks Aryan. With false identification papers she could almost go outside—but she's better off hidden as long as the Gestapo suspects me.

By mid-April of 1943, I decide to take Sylvia to meet Maman. I confess to an ulterior motive. I can't have little Pierre in our house any more. Mueller could overhear his increasingly powerful lungs. Hiding this risk behind the chores of daily living does not make it go away. Dieter, Marie, and Guy know we're on the edge of being discovered and denounced, and the special price I could pay: arrest, deportation or shot on the spot for deceiving an Obersturmführer. I don't want these good people to be afraid all the time. I have to protect Marta.

I hope Maman will welcome Sylvia and Pierre. They will be safer in the countryside. Maybe then we can get papers making them distant relatives.

⌒

We're on the short twenty-minute drive from town into the hilly terrain where my childhood home looks straight into the Swiss Jura. I love the trees along the country road. Maman doesn't bother to keep the estate as it once was. She has outlived many faithful attendants and gardeners.

Sylvia pulls me out of my thoughts unexpectedly. Actually, I'm sitting on top of her. She's hidden under my seat in a coffin-like box with a hinged side that opens into the trunk. When Heisler allowed me to keep Maman's ancient sedan, Guy made a hiding space for provisions.

This was after he constructed a rooftop coal burner with long tubes made from exhaust pipes that stretch like tentacles into the engine hood. He's the only one who drives our converted *gazogène* without the motor stalling. It takes thirty minutes for enough methane to rev the engine. Once we're up and running we can go about thirty kilometers before refueling.

Thankfully its noise and stench have not awakened Pierre, who's tucked inside Marie's old coat. Her shawl drapes loosely over his head and her shoulders. We time our crossing with Pierre's nap and hold our breath as we near the Gestapo checkpoint.

Just as we arrive a typical farm lorry approaches from around the bend—probably carrying early spring produce for the Wehrmacht plus a few hidden Jews. This isn't good. The longer we tarry here the greater the possibility little Pierre will awaken and cry and the gazogène will conk out and need restarting.

Luckily Guy knows the Gestapo. They are confused. They do not know if I'm his employer or my mother is. Assuming it's me, and assuming I worry about my old mother, my chauffeur's frequency on the road is believable. Guy brings Maman provisions from town and I send him to make repairs and do daily chores at her home.

In town it was raining but in the hills the weather is nasty. An unpredictable spring shower of sleet coats the high roads. At the checkpoint midway the Nazi death squad is warm and dry playing cards in their big sedan. They recognize Guy and wave us on from their open window to avoid getting wet. Everyone smiles sweetly. We begin to pull out when that lorry with two men in the cab pulls directly in front of us. Our brakes squeal as we skid toward the lorry.

Pierre rouses for a second and turns inside his cocoon against Marie's chest. We can't move now. The road is too narrow and there's a large puddle of sleety mud edging into the middle of it. We watch anxiously as the Boches curse the weather and come out of their lair to inspect the truck's papers. We pray for Pierre to go back to sleep. He's restless until Marie fidgets and sucks in her breath.

"What is it, Marie?"

"Ay, Madame, his canal overfloweth its banks. We'll have to change my blouse and his bottom when we get to Madame Mathilde's," she turns and winks at Marta, "Apparently, my understudy needs more experience restraining the floodwaters."

Guy chuckles under his breath.

I'm still smiling at Marie's humor when I feel someone staring and glance up at the driver's face in the lorry. Oh no, it's Stefan. I haven't seen him in months. If he knew the risk I take this very moment. No doubt he's also carrying Jews since he's not alone. The cruel irony unnerves me. I can't look away and search his face for mercy.

He turns to look straight ahead while the Gestapo checks his papers and hails him forward. So few young men move about freely. I worry because Stefan is young and healthy-looking. The Boches must wonder why he hasn't been sent away as one of their Führer's laborers. Guy backs up slowly to give him room. As he passes, I smile and wave but my beau-fils revs his engine and looks away, disgusted.

Our old enmities reignite. If everyone protects my stepson to avoid arousing his temper, how will he ever grow beyond it? I'm ashamed not to have cultivated more love in our relationship. I wish he knew that I'm in the Résistance and that this collaboration is a shield to help men like him do his job safely.

If not for Dieter's insistence on concealing my role in this war I would have told Stefan the truth at the scene of Heisler's murder. If Marta were not in this car I'd break down in tears. Instead, so tired from the strain of this double life I doze for a few minutes to escape it. As we crawl up the higher elevation, I'm grateful to be supported by my trusted butler and housekeeper.

We round the bend. The road narrows as we enter the gravel lane to the house. Guy stops abruptly just before making a left turn into the main horseshoe drive. The car loses traction in the freezing slush and skids. I'm thrown forward, out of dozing into a chilling anxiety.

"My God, what's the matter, Guy?"

"Madame, your mother has company. Look, Fritzies!" He hands me a telescope.

"Ah oui. I don't know anyone else with a Mercedes. Is anyone in the car?" I scan the yard peering through the scope. "I see the lightning strike symbols on the black pennants when the wind blows. They're not easily visible from the rear. I don't see anyone inside it, Guy, do you?"

"No, Madame."

"Where did you get this little telescope, Guy? It's German. I've seen it before."

"Yes, it's a souvenir from a dead Doryphore."

"Do you think anyone has seen us from the house, Guy?"

"No, Madame. The evergreens are too thick with sleet."

"Och, Mon Dieu, this thing belonged to Heisler, didn't it?"

Guy nods and instantly I return the scope to the glove compartment. Handling it made me uneasy. We stare at the imposing vehicle. I rethink my strategy,

"Perhaps, Guy, since no one has seen us, we should back up slowly to the side drive to the greenhouses and the well house."

At the secluded fork in the lane about two hundred meters from the front entrance Marie gets out with the baby and Marta. Sylvia is lifted out of the hiding space under the back seat.

"You have the spare key to the well house, Marie?"

"Yes, Madame, and the keys to the greenhouses, too."

"We'll send for you when it's safe." I kiss all three and caress sleepy Pierre.

"Be careful. There's wood in the well room but avoid using it. The wind is blowing toward the house and smoke would give away your presence. We'll send for you as soon as it's safe. Watch your footing in the wetness." The two women and Marta set off in the slush.

"All right, Guy, let's go."

He turns to me in a rare moment of disagreement and asks tactfully, "Madame, are you certain you want to go in?"

"I have to divert them, Guy. Who could it be except Mueller and his men?"

"Yes, but we don't know why they're here."

"Well, I have to take that risk."

"Madame, with all due respect, your mother is quite capable of getting rid of Mueller herself. Pardon me for saying this, but aren't we bringing the greatest risk to her safety with Sylvia and the baby? Don't you think we should avoid the Gestapo right now?"

"Yes, yes, you're right. We can't see them from here. Let me look from the trees."

I pull my scarf around my head and exit the car, walking gingerly to the edge of the tree-lined wall about thirty meters away. The tall cypresses sway. The shrubs raise their bare limbs like wailing supplicants before the sleety wind. Tangles of wisteria vines cower against the building's façade and reach to its second story balconies. The stucco is soft grey from age. Old columns on either side support the portico. A few steps lead to the regal entrance and carved wooden door. Ivy and spring bulbs blooming in the planters soften its austerity.

Today it's miserable, cold and wet. I marvel how the stately exterior disguises Maman's haven of activity in her rear greenhouses. I wonder if the food Guy brings me for my Old Testaments is from her sheltered gardens?

Our vehicle is well hidden from the front by the trees and evergreen hedges on the side lane. I see a figure move from the house to the Mercedes. No, two figures. I recognize Mueller's swagger and the lanky build of one of his drivers. They leave, moving slowly down the other side of the horseshoe driveway and out of sight. Hopefully not coming back in our direction. I return to our vehicle, breathless.

"Guy, we're safe now but shouldn't park in front. If they return and see a lot of footprints and tire tracks it will look suspicious. Go around to the horse barn and put the car inside. Then get Sylvia and Pierre to the house through the servants' entrance."

⤛⤜

I wonder if bringing Sylvia here was a good idea. Guy makes me think I'm too reckless.

I proceed to Maman's study, bringing Sylvia with little Pierre. We knock lightly. Ivan, the old Great Dane, answers with a loud deep bark and

Midgette, the Papillon, utters a light growl. I haven't talked seriously to Maman since Christmas. I've been afraid to extend myself beyond casual hellos at informal visits since I started my Underground work again.

Maman is wise and kind, though usually not openly affectionate. She's strict with herself, yet not judgmental toward others. She married late for position and not love when women had few choices. Independence was not an option in her time unless a woman was a spinster heiress or a widow with her own money. She is a strong believer that an education is a woman's only way to survive being restricted as a housewife, or *femme au foyer*. Maman's intellect is broad and sharp.

Most of her friends and family have passed on. A few are still alive in Louveciennes, Neuchâtel, Limoges, Luxembourg and the Patois region of La Petite Pierre outside of Strasbourg. When I was a child, she ran our home with an iron fist. Papa said he did as he pleased but he deferred to her superior business acumen. This they discussed discreetly in their bedroom-boardroom, as was customary for couples of their day.

She lives very modestly and spends more money on her greenhouses than on clothes, socializing, household baubles and fancy finery. She supplies Dr. Duvette and Amélie with herbs for their tinctures. Maman is a horticulturist who enjoys getting her hands dirty, unlike other wealthy growers. She sold her Montbéliarde cows to her neighbors before the war when she declared her old age wouldn't be spent overseeing farms. Instead, she rents out her pasturage.

After papa's death, she moved his study into the family library and opened the southwest corner of the house for a makeshift propagation area in her cozy, cluttered, monastic cell. Her horticultural texts are scattered in disarray on every flat surface. Seeds sprout in pots and jars meticulously labeled in Latin. They crowd the large metal planters, along with African violets, on the windowsills around the sunny corner.

Two old chairs upholstered with nondescript floral tapestry patterns are adorned with tatted doilies. They face her rocker that is covered with crocheted throws. A small footstool bears impressions from fifty years of slippers pressing into the cushioned top. Its edges are ragged from Midgette's teeth marks.

The room smells strongest of soil and burning wood in the fireplace and the lavender oil Maman uses on her hands. Today, add a hint of wet dog fur from Ivan's recent romp outdoors when Mueller pulled up.

A pot of soothing hot chocolate rests nearby. Her chocolate is a portion of my payment for services rendered to the Reich, which I hope she knows nothing about. The starkly modern, rolling, Bauhaus end table holding it attests to her practicality to keep life's necessities within reach. She catches its metal leg with her cane and reels it in close for a sip of cocoa from a porcelain mug.

A few framed examples of Marta's drawings made just before her accident, and a large photo of my wedding, hang on either side of the fireplace. Only family enters this private space. This hermitage is tightly locked when the Gestapo calls. Since the Occupation, its secret (and only) entry is obscured by a false wall, in the rear of a hall closet.

"Who is it, Michelle? I just got settled in here," Maman calls, thinking she hears her maid.

"It's me, Maman, Ingrid. May I come in?"

"Come, come, child, I have lots to tell you." She looks up from her herb album as Sylvia and I enter. She sits in her favorite rocker with her feet double-socked on the footstool. Glasses sit at half-mast. I kiss her soft wrinkled cheeks and rub her bony shoulders. I love her dearly.

"And who is this bébé with you? Come closer, my dear," Pierre intrigues her.

"This is Sylvia Feinstein, Mother. She and her infant son are guests of our basement."

"Oh my, what a tiny fellow he is. What is your name, my lovely?" She pokes her finger gently at his tummy and makes a funny face. Pierre smiles and gives her a deep, dry burp. We laugh at his timing.

"His name's Pierre, Madame," replies Sylvia, at ease with my dowager mother.

"You had him before you came through my daughter's basement?" Maman asks. Sylvia waits for me to answer.

"No, Maman. Pierre was born in the kitchen larder three hours after Sylvia arrived."

"My goodness. Ingrid, you take big risks these days. Are you all right, dear?"

If you only knew, I think. Maman's concerned, naturally, but always supportive.

"I'm a little tired, Maman. We hoped to rest a day or so here with you."

"Well, you just missed your paramour, my daughter. That crass Mueller was on his rounds of the country estates. He comes in for a free brandy and never searches anyone. He knows you too well, I think."

"Yes, I suppose."

I have no idea what she knows about my relationship with him. I've told her absolutely nothing. Did he tell her? Or did her cook, Michelle? Or maybe she's heard it from the local langues de vipères. I hope Sylvia didn't hear Maman refer to him as my paramour.

"Maman, is it safe here? Can we spend the night without Mueller coming back?"

"Oui, certainment, mon Chou. He's only doing his monthly visit. He dislikes me because I'm too old and not afraid of him, and tease him terribly in German. Put your car in one of the old rear barns. Be safe. Don't create any suspicion. Actually, I need help harvesting the rear greenhouses for "guests" in town. The sudden cold will kill off my early vegetables. Fuel can't be wasted heating them tonight. Guy can transport them."

"I'd be honored," Sylvia volunteers, "that way Madame Ingrid can rest and be with you."

I listen, stunned to learn that my mother has been growing food for escapees and the families who shield them—not only for me. She never told me. She didn't share that two Novembers ago when I brought Marta here the week before the bodies landed on the riverbank. Hmph, my own Maman keeps secrets. Well, me too. It's the war.

"Well, my dear, you have a loyal companion indeed," Maman smiles.

Little Pierre complains. Sylvia retires to feed and change him while Maman and I have a long tête-à-tête. I sense worry underneath her light-heartedness. As soon as we're alone she begins, "Ingrid, you're getting a very ugly reputation. I hope it's what you need to protect your work, but are you safe?"

"Maman, no one is safe. I live from one minute to the next with barely a second to think. At first I was terrified of every situation. Barely ate anything for weeks. Then I got used to it. Over a year has passed and I'm holding up better under the strain."

"But your old acquaintances have distanced themselves, dearest."

"I don't care. What I've discovered about them makes me sad. Their world is so lifeless. I'm happier now, despite my constant anxiety. I'm doing what feels right, and the more I do the more I see strength in myself and Marta."

"Oh, mon chou, how I wish I could also take Jews in here. I am so old it's all I can do to stay alive these days."

"Oui, but Maman, apparently you're doing a great service growing food."

"Oui, chou, and by the tone in your voice you're surprised and a little peeved that I haven't told you. Forgive me, but it was forbidden."

"And now it isn't?"

"I made a decision the moment I saw Sylvia and Pierre. It's reckless, chou, but I had to share my secret with you and Sylvia. We'll have to cover each other's backs now."

"I understand. Local farmers have open fields and could never hide extra crops. Your contribution is vital. You need someone to help you."

"You mean Sylvia, don't you?"

"Well, yes." She always sees through me. I wasn't sure she'd agree to take her and Pierre.

"She's so blonde. Does she have papers?"

"Not yet. I need to speak with you before we decide if she's to be related to us. Maman, it's up to you. I'm very fond of her but can't risk the baby crying in the house."

"Yes, I know. For me it's a pleasure to hear that little voice. When the war is over, she'll be free to reclaim her life. We'll help her in every way. She must have some family to go to, no?" My eyes say no.

"Oh dear. Well, the papers are just to protect her and us."

"Don't worry, Maman, she understands. She'll miss the basement lodgers and I'll miss her company, but we all have to be safe."

"Oui, certainment, mon chou."

Later I speak with Sylvia about staying at Maman's home. She confesses she loves the contact with refugees and agrees Pierre is a problem. She needs sunshine outdoors to convalesce from malnutrition and childbirth. Dieter will procure identification papers so Maman's agricultural workers here will be quiet. We're fortunate the Luftwaffe doesn't fly surveillance over this area. It's the only way the Boches could detect Maman's "agricultural Résistance," unless someone who worked in her greenhouses denounced her.

Toward eleven at night, Maman and I sit in front of the fireplace. Everyone's asleep. Old Michelle has the night off so I've come to take her up to bed.

"What is it?" I lean over to reposition the logs in the fireplace.

"You know, Ingrid, Stefan was here earlier today to get provisions for a crossing."

"Yes, we passed him at the checkpoint."

"We were alone out in the greenhouses and when I mentioned your name he became so indignant."

"Good. He thinks I'm a traitor."

"What? Ach, how can he? Anyone with any sense would not think that."

"Stefan and I have a long and complicated history. When Emil died, no one would tell me what Stefan held against me. Now he despises me. I'm a whore for Hitler. I've been told it's good for the Résistance. It reinforces my position with the SS but it hurts, Maman."

"Oui, mon chou, but your life with Stefan will endure beyond this war. I'm sorry he condemns you without knowing the truth. These things often work themselves out with only our intention for love to guide us to the answers. Be patient, Ingrid. He'll figure it out. If he's held onto his pain this long, it has less to do with who you are personally and more to do with what he thinks you represent."

"I don't follow you, Maman."

"Yes, I'm sure you don't. A quirk of human nature you need time to understand, Ingrid."

Maman smiles and grips the arms of her rocker. Before I can ask her for more clarity she commands her flesh,

"Rise, old carcass, before you freeze into this chair permanently," making light of her pain as I cringe, "Sorry, daughter, the old bones are talking back too loudly this evening."

I marvel at how she lords her powerful spirit over her body's tenuous attachment to this earth. I can't fathom her humor and wisdom.

I hope Sylvia and little Pierre will be safe here.

Chapter Eleven

Forethought for Foreskin

14 August 1943, Saturday

Our spring and summer crossings proceed smoothly despite the death of Jean Moulin, leader and hero of the Résistance. He died on a train after he was tortured in Lyon. There, Underground life is more perilous with Klaus Barbie running the local Gestapo.

In Besançon, the Préfecture of the Doubs, sixteen-year-old Résistant, Henri Fertet, a member of a Maquis escaping the STO (*Service du Travail Obligatoire*), awaits death by a firing squad at La Citadelle. Marie revealed it when I found her crying in the kitchen. She refused to say who told her because it was too dangerous for me to know.

Dieter has to worry about infiltrators in our ranks. The youthful Résistants who secretly harvest Maman's crops are closed-mouthed but still vulnerable to sly questioning that can lead to betrayal. To be safe, Maman fills out official paperwork to state she sells her food to the Wehrmacht. Her broker in agricultural distribution is a Résistant who covers her operation. I force Dieter to tell me that man's name since I'm so nervous about Sylvia's safety in the mountains. I am grateful for these precautions to make her appear legitimate because Mueller's surprise visits are actually covert raids. On one such occasion, we almost lose Sylvia and Pierre.

～

Behind Maman's house is a yard sixty by eighty meters, bordered by a stucco stone wall over two meters high. Inside the yard, she grows vegetables for her kitchen and leaves the greenhouses across the unpaved driveway in deliberate disrepair. Buildings for chickens, horses, and hay have no animals or farm equipment to attract attention.

Madame de Vochard is so old no one expects her to do anything more than breathe.

On a sultry August afternoon, I wake from a nap with a migraine. Holding onto a chair, I yawn and stare out a window in the cool servants' basement kitchen. Sylvia and Marie are nearby, weeding and harvesting in the enclosed garden. Pierre pulls up to creep on all fours and rocks unsteadily on a blanket covering the shaded cobblestone entry. Madame Mathilde is upstairs taking her sieste. Marta does school work upstairs.

Despite this peaceful ambiance, one's ear always listens for trouble. Marie raises her head at the unfamiliar sound of an approaching vehicle. She locks eyes with Sylvia and holds her breath. In a few seconds, the back gate to the stonewall enclosure rattles and a stern official voice hollers, "Achtung! Open up immediately!"

Franz Mueller's shrill voice cuts through my head like a knife. Sylvia freezes. The sun is too painful on my eyes. I dare not go out. I hear Marie call, "One moment, bitte."

She runs to Sylvia and asks in a low voice, "You have the papers for you and Pierre, oui?"

Our young Jewess stares into space, hands limp at her sides. Mueller's sharp authoritarian tone has catapulted Sylvia back to her nightmare at Dachau. Marie gently jostles her, "Sylvia, answer me."

"Oh, ah, ja, Marie. I do have them. I'm safe then, oui?"

"Oui, but how are you related?"

"Open up. What's taking so long? Machen Sie schnell!" The Krauts are impatient.

"Einen Moment bitte, I'm coming." Marie calls again loudly, anxious to placate Mueller with her attempt at German. Sylvia has trouble remembering her imaginary lineage, hearing enemy language from Marie's French lips.

"I'm her grandniece by marriage in her Alsatian family, Mathilde's brother-in-law's son's daughter, Sophie Liesse. Are we safe, Marie?" she watches Pierre babble at a butterfly.

"That's good, Sylvia. I have to let them in now. Be calm. I'll do the talking."

More banging sends fear down their spines and mine. Marie unlocks the gate to Franz Mueller and two henchmen behind him with a ferocious-looking Alsatian on a leash.

"Who are you? Och, you're the servant of Madame Ingrid, ja?"

"Oui, oh, ah ja, Obersturmführer. And this is my employer's grandniece, Sophie. How can we help you?" Mueller stares at Sophie. Then he points to Pierre.

"Und das kind?"

"He's my baby, Pierre, Obersturmführer," Sylvia smiles sweetly.

Franz Mueller is quite intrigued with this "Sophie." He moves closer to inspect her. Sylvia swallows and stares straight ahead at Marie who sends her a silent prayer to be passive with this Nazi beast.

"Mmm, ja, you look heavenly."

He's enraptured by her blonde braids, wrapped around her ears like a typical German schoolgirl and salivates over her blue eyes, creamy skin and fine full nursing bosom. She's the image of Aryan supremacy: clean, beautiful and irresistible.

"Let me see you up close, mein Schatz. Hmm, why hasn't Frau Fellner told me about you?"

Mueller stands too close to Sylvia's back. He fondles her waist with his right hand and grazes the edge of her breast with his fingertips. A streak of lust rises in his loins as he moves even closer. I can see the Obersturmführer is on fire with the fragrance of her hair.

He stands only three meters from the open window. I hear him speak into her ear. His lips brush the outer curve of its lobe, "Verdammt, little Fräulein, if not for that old biddy servant and my men I'd take you into the barn."

Beads of sweat dot his upper lip. His heart beats wildly but he pulls himself back to the moment. Sylvia struggles to suppress her terror. Her dress clings to her as streams of perspiration run down her torso. My God, it's always the same with him.

"Uh, why haven't I seen you before, Fräulein? Are you new here?"

"Oui, Obersturmführer, I'm visiting my great aunt for a few weeks."

Sylvia is revolted by his advances but manages to hide it. Mueller looks down over her shoulder at baby Pierre as his hand still strokes her hip. He's delighted by her discomfort.

"Ah hah! Well, let me see your baby." Suspicious once again, he regains his harsh SS demeanor.

Sylvia's heart must be pounding. I know the feeling when his eyes undress you with your every movement. She quickly leans over to lift Pierre who's curious about the big dog the men restrain across the yard. She holds her son out to Mueller who backs away. He doesn't want to touch the baby.

"Damn it! Remove his diaper!" he shouts.

Sylvia jumps back, startled, and asks, "*Pourquoi?* Why, Wha-what for?"

This infuriates Mueller who bellows again, "Remove his diaper, Fräulein! This instant!"

Her hands tremble. Mueller takes her nervousness as a sign he shall have his climax. He's so impatient, he grabs her hand and rips off the diaper, pressing her index finger into the sharp pin just as she opens it.

"Aye," she cries out and puts it into her mouth to stem the bleeding. Poor little Pierre is anchored to her bosom. Her left arm is across his chest and under his right armpit. Mueller's anticipation at discovering a Jewish baby is suddenly deflated like a balloon. The child is not circumcised.

"Oh, I'm sorry, Fräulein," he says, surprised, "I didn't mean to intrude. He's a cute little boy with blue eyes like yours."

Sylvia bows her head and murmurs, "Merci, Obersturmführer."

The finger throbs in her mouth. Mueller stands there motionless consuming her with his eyes. Blood stains her lower lip. The sadist in him enjoys her flicker of pain. It arouses him to concoct a fresh fantasy of violent conquest. He wets his lips and mops his sweaty brow. His eyes look inward and project a vile intimacy with this beautiful young victim who quivers before the ominous bulge in his trousers. Oh God, I know that look. He's not done with her. He's searching for a way to justify getting her alone outside of the yard.

Will he drag her into a barn and rape her? I pray the perspiration pooling at her feet doesn't give her identity away despite Pierre's intact foreskin.

The two junior SS standing at the gate look uneasy with Mueller's brothel-bound behavior.

Sweltering heat from the blistering afternoon sun appears to paralyze the five adults. The soldiers are head to foot in itchy wool. The women's bare arms and legs are moist. Their scalloped bodices hide breasts and torsos covered in clinging, threadbare cotton.

Marie and Sylvia are powerless, petrified with fear. Mueller is their authority. He will do as he pleases and get away with it. For the first time I realize how my allure absorbs Franz's lust and why Dieter asked me to join the Résistance. My aristocratic arrogance has been mistaken for a kind of sadistic control. Mueller has misinterpreted the coldness that masks my fear as casual disinterest. It has become a stimulus that excites him to sexual violence.

Mueller's desire appears to grow even more intense. He's figuring how he can justify what he wants from Sylvia. If she's worth the risk, he will ruin her. Marie hardens her jaw. I know that look too. She is calling on her Lord for mercy. The situation is hopeless.

Marie and Sylvia breathe heavily through their mouths, like stricken animals suppressing their bowels. We need a miracle.

Then a blessing floats down out of thin air. Our saving grace comes with the innocent counterattack of our six-month-old baby boy. Warm, new, and alone in his purity, little Pierre hangs limply from his mother's

embrace. Oblivious to the adults, he bends his tiny knees as a cool afternoon breeze tickles his naked genitalia. He waves his little arms, gurgles
with impending relief and suddenly empties a huge stream of urine
directly onto Mueller's boots.

"*Gott verdammt*!" Mueller howls at his youthful opponent.

Pierre squeals with delight as his vanquished foe fumes under his
breath. His Nazi target leaps backward to avoid further precipitation.
Mueller's face twists in rage as his carnal fantasy is halted. Sylvia is
frightened by the Obersturmführer's anger and takes a step backward
covering Pierre's genitals with her dress and shushing him to be silent.
Marie and Sylvia are ramrod stiff with terror—not knowing what will
happen next.

In the pause, Mueller overhears his SS juniors stifle sudden laughter,
doubled over pretending to cough. Aiming his frustration at them,
Mueller turns about-face on his pee-laden boots, curses through clenched
teeth and marches swiftly down the path. He slows every few steps and
adjusts his left pant leg to accommodate his mislaid arousal.

The two SS step back, cowering, as their irate Kommandant approaches.
In a vain attempt to garner decorum, the underlings click their heels and
salute him with a weak "Heil Hitler."

The Nazi bully stands with his legs apart and fists on his hips. He
scowls and flares his nostrils, berating the two for smarting his pride. But
his humiliation isn't over.

Fritz, their fierce canine companion, catches a whiff of Pierre's urine
wafting upward from Mueller's boots. In a wink, obedient to his own
territorial imperative, the dog lifts his hind leg and spritzes Mueller's
pants.

This time the two young officers burst out laughing. He orders them
to the Mercedes, hissing like a poisonous reptile, "Out with you, idiots.
Raus! Idioten!"

They back out of the yard, dragging poor Fritz away, to stop him
from licking his master's boots. The dog is frantic; he's discovered the
human spoor and rushes repeatedly at his commanding officer. His neck
strains on the choke as he slobbers with determined focus. Mueller can't

navigate around the huge dog. Fritz's claws dig up clods of dry soil as he blocks the entry, whipping his broad muscular body from side to side.

Poor Fritz is so agitated, Mueller trips over him on his way out and falls head-first through the entrance. His Nazi bulk slides forward on the parched gravel. Mueller barks profanities at his men, but his hoarse voice peters out in a hacking cough. He's swallowed dust kicked loose by the roll of his fatted girth. The men and dog rush into the car.

The gate slams shut in a noisy spasm, and the dark comedy is over.

Once the Mercedes' engine starts, Marie whoops with laughter. The muscles of her rib cage convulse in a cramp. She can barely stand up to catch her breath. Tears of relief roll down her cheeks as she leans against the garden wall. At first Sylvia stares at her, too numbed and overwrought to react.

After a minute, Marie composes herself and apologizes for her explosion of pent up nerves, "Forgive me, dear girl, but I couldn't control myself any longer. I thought I'd be the only person your little prince would ever baptize! Are you all right? Here, let me take the boy."

Marie cuddles Pierre and whirls him around in a circle. She plants a flurry of kisses on his neck. He giggles with delight.

"Ah, thank you, Holy Mary, Mother of God! Today you blessed our little champion." She coos to the victorious Pierre. Sylvia smiles as she picks up his dry diaper and pins.

A southwest corner window opens and Mathilde calls down. Marta is by her side.

"Och, Marie, don't you wish my Ingrid could have seen that little drama?"

The two old women look at each other with giddy relief. Sylvia waves the white diaper in mock surrender and Marie holds Pierre up high above her shoulders, answering,

"Yes, I do, especially their dog licking Pierre's piss from his master's boots. Surely it means we'll conquer the Doryphores in the end."

She transfers the naked little prince to his mother's waiting arms, and leans over him, tickling his tummy. He babbles as he flails his arms and kicks his feet with utter joy.

"Let's hope so, Marie. Watch out. Better not excite that scrappy little fountain of youth or he'll let loose again," Mathilde calls down in mock seriousness.

Sylvia carries Pierre inside the cool basement to change him and coos in her son's ear,

"Your Mama must get your little derriere out of the sun before it burns."

She nuzzles his neck and chest with triumphant kisses. Pierre grabs her hair and squeals with delight. Sylvia runs her fingers over his tummy. I overhear her tease him as she rinses him in the big sink inside the cool mudroom. Her voice lilts, "Pierre, my little pisser. What did you do, today? You saved your poor mama."

In the lull she says, "I have to wash you, *mein kleine gelibter.* My little beloved, Pierre, do you know what just happened? Your tantie Ingrid also saved *you* today—only she really did it six months ago."

At that admission I move closer to catch sight of them through the doorjamb. The door is slightly ajar. Sylvia washes Pierre while he splashes the water in the metal washbasin. Poor Sylvia gets a bath too.

I remember those wonderful, innocent moments when my Marta was Pierre's age. Thank God these two can share their love. I shake, remembering the Underground tracts that tell of Warsaw Ghetto babies impaled on SS bayonets. I hid them from Sylvia—even though it's likely she already saw such atrocities firsthand.

Oh no! Pierre insists on tasting the bar of soap.

"*Nein, mein zin, bitte.* No, my son, please give it to mama. Pierre, please, give the soap to mama." She holds out her hand. He pauses to look at her and drops the bar of soap.

Sylvia's happy voice immediately descends into an anguished cry. She holds her dripping son at shoulder height, looks up at the ceiling and calls out, "Oy Gottenyu, Mama, *die seife,* the soap, oh mama, where are you? *Vie bist du?* Look! Here is your little grandson. Can you see him, mama? I didn't mean to leave you for a bar of soap, mama. I didn't know it would separate us forever! *Aye,* forgive me, please, mama. Let mein zin be your *nakhes,* your pride and joy, from here to you above."

She swallows deep sobs and rubs her face into her little boy's neck. Not wanting to upset him, she fights to control her heaving shoulders and hides her moans in the sound of running water. She kisses Pierre's bare chest and ends her grief abruptly with a few deep breaths as she turns off the faucet. Sylvia wipes her eyes and nestles Pierre in a towel. Again the proud young mother adores the flesh of her flesh. Her husky voice chokes back another wave of sorrow,

"Today, you pleased the Heavens, mein kleine gelibter, from your mouth into God's ears. May you be healthy, mon fils. Pierre, *mein zin, zayt gezunt!*"

Chapter Twelve

Plumbing for Murder

20 September 1943, Monday

Sylvia comes to town with Guy when he brings food from Maman's greenhouses to distribute to the Underground. It's a bold move to leave the safety of Maman's home but sometimes it can't be avoided.

Tonight Guy leaves Sylvia alone to help the guests in my basement. He forgets to tell me there's an emergency. He must take Marie to assist Amélie *immediately* at an unexpected birth elsewhere in town. Sylvia has brought Pierre, who sleeps in his old cradle hidden at the far side of the room.

After two years of crossings, my home's plumbing is kaput and is being repaired. Sewage pipes have been replaced. The system is being enlarged. Our existing sewer was terribly strained. My beautiful yard had to be dug for new lines. For a time this forced us to empty all the putrilage into the garden and the compost piles.

A trustworthy Résistant, who is an old WWI veteran and also a town plumber, took on the work. It's cumbersome because he has no assistant at night except when Guy is available. The old man is connecting the new sewer line to commodes and sinks in the basement. He has placed two new toilettes in closets, one on either side of the wall of cabinets concealing our guests, but has not finished the installation. He keeps a temporary patch over the old refuse pipe that leads into the main drain. It's a decoy to make me feel less exposed, in case of an emergency, or questions about the "fragrance."

It turns out the plumbing isn't as big a problem as the old plumber, himself. He's almost deaf, as Marie calls him *"le presque sourd."* Against my better judgment, Guy gives him a key to let himself in the back gate after dark, between curfew checks. Guy should let him in every time, but often there are SS guests in the house. Marie has to serve the basement and leave me alone with Mueller upstairs when Guy is away at night. I consent to this arrangement reluctantly.

Tonight I put Marta on duty to monitor the old plumber's movements. I'm in the small street floor rear bathroom when I hear her wielding the heavy wrench and banging a warning furiously on the upstairs kitchen pipes. The sound is distant but clear to me in this small space below. I look out at the yard from the tiny bathroom window and realize the plumber left the rear gate swinging open in the breeze. Damn him. Where is he? I can't wait and watch any more. I have to get back to Franz or risk igniting his suspicions. Mueller can only hear the servants' toilet below the receiving salon.

Then I hear the servants' toilet flush as I enter the salon. Perhaps Sylvia rushed upstairs to dump refuse into it. If it were Marie, she would usually knock on the salon door afterward to see if I'm all right. But tonight, Sylvia did it. If she heard Mueller's voice in here after the incident in August when Pierre pissed on him, she would not risk interrupting us.

But I hear . . . wait . . . it's *Marta* outside in the corridor. Why is she downstairs?

"Excuse me, Franz, I hear my daughter. Let me deal with her and send her upstairs so we can have our privacy, ja, Liebster?" I raise my eyebrows seductively to keep him rooted on the divan with his pants open and slide out the door to the hall.

"What is it, Marta?"

"Ssshh, Maman, listen. The plumber made a mistake. He's brought trouble onto us. Please get rid of Mueller, *tout de suite*!" She stares, freezes and says nothing more. She's agitated and squirms like a small child. Seconds pass. Is she . . . afraid?

"I can't get rid of him, Marta. Why should I? What's happening, child?" With Mueller left alone, I can't wait. I order her, "If you can't tell me, young lady, go upstairs and wait at your post." She's hurt and astonished by my short temper. Her mouth pulls to one side. I'm too upset about the open backyard gate, and close the door to the receiving salon in her face.

Reentering, I see Mueller has unbuttoned his shirt as well as his pants. He paws at me as I fake moans of arousal. My mind runs in circles, trying to guess what is going on in the rest of the house. Suddenly there's a terrible tumbling noise coming from the stairs in the vestibule area.

"Stop, Franz! I heard something fall. Oh no, my daughter is crying!"

With super-human strength I push him away and run into the hall, zipping up my skirt and clutching my open blouse. I hear him curse hysterical French women.

I lean over my baby lying on the floor. She's surrounded by the ornate metal plant stand on its side, an uprooted philodendron with torn leaves, and soil flung all over the vestibule hallway at the bottom of the stairs.

Before I can apologize, mon ange shushes me and whispers, "Maman, I'm fine. I jumped down the stairs with both feet skipping two steps at a time. Near the bottom I tripped over my left foot. I screamed to get your attention! So be attentive, Maman, pretend I'm hurt."

Like a good actress, I improvise and lean over my baby to examine her for injuries.

"Marta, my angel, you've fallen. Where does it hurt?"

Marta puts her finger to my lips, "Louder, Maman, get Obersturmführer Mueller's attention—and get him out of here *right now*! We have 'neighbors in need across the way' in the basement. You know, 'unwanted company.'"

That part of her message doesn't register. I'm too embarrassed, rushing to dress in front of her. My fingers are shaky, dull and clumsy, my heart shamed. I skip the top button on my blouse. I hear Mueller's heavy footsteps in the hall and pretend concern for Marta,

"Oh, ah, my poor darling. Are you all right?"

Mueller passes me as I bend over her. She moans and rolls her eyes when she sees him. My voice is strained, "Oh, Obersturmführer, I'm so sorry. I think she's only scraped, thank goodness."

"I'm leaving, Frau Fellner." He's frustrated; I've destroyed his amorous mood.

I heave a sigh of relief. Tonight he's just annoyed and goes quickly, rather than make a scene. His future unannounced visits will continue to torture me with this game of to-raid or not-to-raid. Is he convinced I'm telling the truth? I'm not certain.

It's Monday evening. I must speak with the plumber. I have to go downstairs. But now Marta behaves like a soldier holding a live grenade. As soon as Mueller's gone she grabs my arm, "Maman, *quickly. Go to the basement.*"

"Yes, well, I am. Why the rush?"

"The plumber has arrived and a Nazi followed him into the basement, Maman! Sylvia is alone with the two men. Oh God, Maman, *get down there!*"

Her balance weakens and her breathing shallows from her agitation when she stands. As she reaches to steady herself, her fingertips ripple across the books on the hallway shelves and tip over a hidden box. At first glance it appears to be a set of encyclopedias of ancient music. Ignoring her I turn toward the rear of the corridor to the back stairs.

I'm opening the door when I hear from behind,

"Oooh, daddy's gun! Maman wait. *Look! Take this! Papa's pistol with its silencer!* I hit the hinged cover and it just spilled out. You must take it!"

Marta hands the gun to me. Her poise astonishes me. How did she find it?

"Be careful, it's loaded, Maman."

"Yes, I know, Marta, I loaded it." My ten-year-old is more alert than her mother. "You knew it was there all along. I can tell by your face. What have you been doing with it when I'm out of the house?"

"Maman, please don't be angry. *Use it.* Otherwise that Nazi will send us to the death camps. Sylvia told me all about them. We have twenty people down there, Maman. Please don't let that Gestapo send Sylvia and little Pierre and everyone away."

"But, I ah, I . . . what Nazi? He just left. Mueller, that's who you mean, right?"

"*No*, Maman! There's *another* one, *a new one* in the basement. Get down there now, please, before it's too late. What's the matter with you? *Go right now. Vas tout de suite!*"

Finally her words penetrate and I quiver with fear. She practically pushes me through the door. I must not let her follow. Cold terror begins at my feet and works its way up to my neck. I have to keep her away and safe before my mind goes blank.

"All right, go upstairs and look out the front balcony so you can tell me whether lights come on at any of the neighbors if shots are fired."

I hide the gun in my sweater and proceed down the stairway. This is happening too fast. My body trembles.

At the bottom of the stairs I overhear the plumber and a young SS arguing through the stairwell door.

"*Achtung! Was machen Sie?* Attention! What are you doing?" the officer demands.

"Merde," the plumber curses under his breath, "Offizier, c'est une urgence."

The SS sounds liquored and annoyed at the old Frenchman's slurred Patois.

The irritated plumber repeats loudly, "I said it's *ein Notfall!* Jesus! An emergency and I'm a plumber. Here's my Ausweis from your hierarchy." He shows his permit card to be out after curfew. The SS frowns as he steps into the main room and the foul odor greets him.

The plumber explains the sewage backup is from the main refuse pipe. "I told you before, it's an emergency. For God's sake, take a whiff," he says, annoyed. I hear him exaggerate an inhalation and then say in surprisingly accurate German, "*Das ist Scheisse, richtig?*" he asks, and continues without waiting for a response, "Do you understand, Offizier? That is shit, right? I'm out at night because during the day I have too many other jobs I have to do alone because my apprentices are in your labor camps in Deutschland."

The SS doesn't believe him and refuses to smell the pipe's covering. Now that they stand in the main room I gently open the door under the cover of the dark basement corridor.

Inside I see Sylvia's shock that the plumber has burst into the main room, snarling in vulgar French with the young Nazi behind him. Both men stop arguing when they see her.

The young SS smiles lewdly at Sylvia who holds her breath as he pokes under lids of pickle crocks and opens cupboards looking for incriminating evidence to impress his superiors.

Sylvia sounds frustrated, "*C'est une urgence*, Offizier, an emergency, please let the man do his job. The sewer pipe has burst. Last winter we saw a crack in it. Now it's worse. We have to repair it."

"Why are you doing the work at night then, Fräulein? Why not in the day?"

"He told you he's our only plumber. He works day and night for the town."

"I don't believe you, Fraulein. You're Résistance. There are people in here. It stinks like fresh shit. Jewish shit."

Oh God, when I hear his threats I can barely breathe and check my gun again.

He has pulled out his weapon. Sylvia tries to maintain a calm demeanor and not arouse suspicion, but I can tell she's terrified.

I'm still standing just inside the door that connects the stairwell and pitch-black cellar hallway. My door is ajar but the light is off. I hear Guy and Marie enter the basement from outside. They pass right by me, over-hearing the SS's loud, slurred voice. The Nazi must have turned around to aim his gun at them as they entered the large room because Marie stifles a gasp and leaves the vestibule door wide open.

"*Guten Abend*, Good evening, Offizier. How can we help you? We're law-abiding French citizens." Thank God Guy's voice is firm and patient.

"He's right," Marie confirms, "we're minding our own business, Offizier. The poor plumber has too many jobs and works all day and all night to serve everyone in this town. Please don't act rashly."

"You are in violation of the curfew. It's midnight."

"Bitte, Offizier, here are our identification cards." Guy produces their Ausweise and satisfies the SS—but he's still suspicious beyond the plumber's evening appearance, "All right, so you need him. He's not a Yid anyway but what about you, Fräulein? Where are your papers?"

Now he aims at Sylvia. The plumber slides in front to shield her. The liquored Nazi is arrogant and bold, bent on terrorizing us inferior French. He doesn't give Sylvia a chance to show her papers. He snickers, aroused by his power to force everyone to put up their hands. Without warning he fires a shot at the plumber's feet. Sylvia and Marie twitch and Pierre screams from the sound of gunshot in his tiny ears. Unfortunately, the Old Testament lodgers muffle fearful groans behind the cabinet paneling.

"Aha! I hear them!" The SS delights at the voices of frightened Jews behind the doors.

"Bring them out now! *Schnell!*" he orders, but no one moves.

The SS fires again and this time grazes Guy's leg as he steps forward. Guy cries out and falters, leaning on his good leg. Marie grabs his arms to steady him. I must act now.

The second gunshot and Pierre's cries have absorbed the creak of the stairway door opening wide. I enter the pitch-dark hall and stand five meters behind the officer.

I take aim and wait, so afraid my hand shakes violently. My mind is empty and my heart pounds. In a split second my humanity has been sucked into a vacuum tunnel. I'm a cornered animal with no time to think. It's him or us. I slink into the dark hallway, holding my breath.

No one moves. No one knows I'm there. I can't let him see my guests. I'm so afraid the Old Testaments will open the revolving false wall. This SS is crazy and drunk. He tastes blood. He'll shoot everyone right now.

"I said bring them out! Move! Schnell! Or I'll shoot!" he howls again, aiming chest high.

"No, you get out!" I hear myself shout back.

He whirls around to fire but falters for just a second. He can't see me in the darkness. I take advantage of his confusion and fire once—hitting him in the chest. As he falls, I move cautiously to his side. The plumber kicks his gun away. I look down, ready to fire again.

"Damn, you silly boy. Bought by evil." My fingers feel for a pulse in his neck. I begin to shake violently, "Oh God, he's dead. Get him out of here before he bleeds all over us."

Marie lifts me up and places me in a chair before bandaging Guy's leg. Without warning I spew a stream of vomit over the Nazi's blood and look at her helplessly, like a penitent child.

"It's over, we're safe, Madame." Marie calls to the door enclosing the Jews, "Please, someone, come out and help us with the baby!" A Jewish mother takes Pierre from Sylvia. Sylvia hands me a handkerchief and a glass of water. She and the plumber strip the corpse of weapons, ammo, and money. They wrap him in an old bed sheet.

Guy is bandaged and given a brandy. The plumber is ready, "Guy, can you walk on that leg? Guy nods yes, and the plumber says, "Let's take this SS to the edge of town in my boat. No one will see us if we go now."

They remove the body quickly. My stomach chews on itself. The room rotates before my eyes and I continue to jerk violently, retching dryly a few more times. I can't collect myself. Sylvia gives me a brandy and wraps me in a blanket. Marie notices movement in the dark hallway as she cleans the floor.

"It's safe, sweetie, come here," she calls. Marta peeks at us with tear-rimmed eyes.

"Maman, Maman. Are you all right?" she approaches cautiously.

"No, Marta."

"Where is he, the Nazi? You saved us, Maman."

"I took his life, Marta," I answer slowly. Shock grips me despite the liquor. Marta stares as I look at her through a new layer of grief. I lower my head to cry but no tears come. My poor daughter caresses my face and embraces my quaking body. My numbing hands are cold as ice. She fixes her question mark eyes on mine, and worries, "Your blouse is buttoned wrong, Maman. It's crooked."

My confusion and fear frighten her. She struggles to suppress the downturned waver of her lower lip as I slur my words, "I'm sorry, mon ange, for everything that hurts you."

Sylvia tries to distract Marta from my unresponsive stupor, "Marta, Madame's gun has a silencer, but the German's didn't and he shot twice. Do you think the neighbors heard?"

"I didn't see any lights, go on but I started downstairs after the first shot," she answers.

"Then please go back upstairs and look out at the street again. See if any lights came on."

Marta trundles dutifully upstairs to look out under the heavy dark drapes. She returns quickly, unable to stop looking at me trembling, dull-eyed, and staring into space.

"If they heard they haven't roused. There are no lights. Maybe the wind dispersed our commotion into the night, eh, Maman?"

When I don't respond, Marta sits next to me on the long bench with her arm around me, her eyes fixed on my sadness. Marie reassures our lodgers it's safe to come out. I look at their faces and hear myself speak slowly in German, "Bitte, I'm sorry I had to do this. I don't care what side he was on."

A middle-aged man wearing a prayer shawl, Ben Judah Regenstein, steps forward and kneels at my side. His eyes shine and emanate great kindness, absorbing my pain as he takes my hand gently, and says tenderly, "Madame, for your courage to defend us, we are so grateful."

"He must have been the age of my stepson, Rabbi. I took him from this life. I'm linked to him forever."

"Madame, God knows your heart bends toward love. We'll say prayers to rest your soul. Perhaps to you they will bring *Menuchas Ha'Nefesh*, acceptance, solace, and serenity."

Quietly, men and adolescent boys stand in a circle and recite King David's psalms of comfort and peace. The ebb and flow of their voices in unison wash over the room. Sylvia puts her arms around me, and Marta. We three sway tenderly to her translation of the Hebrew and

Aramaic. I ask myself in despair: where am I? Am I with the Almighty somewhere? My soul is dormant, arid: transparent like a naked tree in winter.

The soft ancient words calm me a little. I attempt to keep my mind clear of the clutter of timings, crossings, enemies, deceptions, betrayals, fornication, and now this murder. I thank the men and hug the women and children. For one moment our human family is safe again.

How can I look into their eyes and see God and do the same with the enemy officer whose life I just stole? A compassionate spirit is trapped inside each enemy—even those who kill as I did just now. No one is totally evil.

An hour later I chill at the thought: what if Mueller sent this young agent to spy on me? What will happen when he doesn't return? Have I brought more suspicion onto this house?

I hardly sleep, sick with worry. The next day Dieter and I have a few minutes alone after Marta's piano lesson. I ask him,

"If Mueller sent this Nazi to raid us, what will he do when the young officer doesn't return?" Dieter reassures me, one step ahead as always.

"Don't worry, Ingrid. Devoir will fix the time of death before Mueller came to you that evening. The body will be found where the Huns have been forbidden to go. When the SS hierarchy questions families of the Résistance in that area, they will claim they saw this man drunk and rowdy on his way out of town. They'll place the time of their sighting to confirm the coroner's time of death. Devoir will save you. The Nazis won't suspect you."

"But they might kill someone in a family who confirms the sighting. If they fear a reprisal, people won't say anything to protect us."

"That's not likely. The town has been too good to the Doryphores. It's the farmers the SS distrust since Heisler's murder, not the local merchants."

"I was afraid to shoot him in the back because it would imply no fight. Oh Dieter, he was barely older than my Stefan."

"You were right to wait until he turned around."

"How can you say it was right, Dieter? I murdered a man!"

He moves closer and puts his arm around my shoulder, "I'm sorry, Ingrid."

"I never thought this would happen," my voice is hoarse and spent. "I feel so empty, Dieter, like I shed my own body. I shot myself when I killed that young man."

The drain on my nerves leaves me needy for his counsel and gentleness. I'm afraid this tempts him. The soothing of his strong warm hands reassures me. His eyes tell me my listlessness worries him more than my usual anxiety.

I must keep him oblivious to my deeper feelings. I haven't thought of Emil much lately, but now that my heroic "mission" has become lethal as well as degrading, I dream of his embrace and crave the comfort of physical intimacy from any male.

"The war takes its toll on all of us, but for you, Ingrid, it's harder. I'll ask Amélie for a tonic to strengthen you. A little more experience and you will be able to handle all of this."

Immediately peeved, I rise from my self-indulgent torpor and answer sarcastically, "My goodness, Dieter, you must be kidding. What will that take? Another murder? My inner core is very strong, thank you very much, Monsieur Van der Kreuzier. I'm not afraid to express my feelings—which you interpret as neediness."

"I'm sorry, I didn't mean to insult or hurt you, Ingrid."

"Forget it, Dieter, it's just my nerves. I'm tired."

His Amélie must be a saint, certainly above my lack of reserve. Why does he treat me this way? Is it because I'm a talker, more intelligent than he thought, but alas, not a man?

I can't argue, still too distraught by what happened. It's enough to be grateful for his kindness. I smile sweetly as he hands me a brandy. He's reluctant now. The more I struggle to play my role and need his support, the more difficult it is for him. When I'm ready to leave, he looks down at my wan face. Usually he cups it in his hands to kiss my forehead, but not today.

"Get some sleep. I'll send Maquisards to guard your home. No more lodgers for a while. Rest at your mother's. Mueller will be out of town for a few days."

>ᴛ⌒

I lay in bed that night, thinking. Dieter affects me like Emil did except he pushes me to get past myself. His confidence inspires me. Strange, I never knew Dieter's power as long as Emil was alive. I haven't known any man like Dieter. My Emil was sweet but kept me under lock and key like my father. No, I let him do that. I welcomed it, and allowed myself to be cowed by *mon père* and my sweet husband.

Was I so passive because I had no dream to nurture? Nothing that would make me seek independence? No, that's not true. I had a dream to live in Paris and be an opera singer and harpsichord soloist, but I lost it . . . deferring so easily to everyone's criticism. Dieter always encourages me but leaves me alone to solve my problems. I behave so badly. Still, I feel comfortable being myself with him even when I must apologize later. He accepts it. Maybe it's because we're only friends. Why do I want to trust men more than women?

Why have I allowed Mueller to abuse me for a worthy cause? I am a good actress but there is some part of me that acts like a slut with that scum. Pure outside, but inside, my head swims with a need to control Mueller and all portals of evil. There is no satisfaction in this dangerous game if I am losing myself.

I grew up hoping to be a person of peace. Instead horrendous violence overtakes me. In a split second murder changes my life forever. Today it numbs me but I fear one day the need for forgiveness will consume me. I have saddled myself with a huge debt to pay back.

>ᴛ⌒

We go to Maman's for a brief respite before Christmas and decide to stay until the following Monday. The backyard's winter-steeped gardens appear drab and lifeless.

Inside, colorful, oversized yellow and lavender flowers dance on the walls, left over from Maman's early adventures in hearty Italian wallpaper designs from the twenties. It's a quiet afternoon. We're making a simple dinner.

I sit at the large table in the servants' kitchen peeling potatoes while Marie shells hard-boiled eggs. The aroma of freshly baked loaves of dark wheat fills the room. Bread made entirely of wheat—smuggled from some place Guy won't say—is a rare treat. No tasteless filler for once. Fruit tarts from dried peaches and pears cool on the oven's warming shelf and diffuse their aroma upstairs. Maman, with the dogs at her feet, her maid Michelle, Sylvia and Pierre, Marta, and Guy will join us in a few minutes.

We talk a little as we work. Marie watches me carefully these days. I feel her motherly concern. I'm not the same since that night in the basement. Part of me doesn't pay attention to myself or anyone else. Lately, I drag my legs when I walk like I'm carrying a heavy load—a sorrow I can't pull out of my heart.

"Madame, please don't think me out of place for saying this."

"Yes, Marie, what is it?" My eyes glance up at her.

"I, ah, well, I thought it was the shooting but it's something different. You're still very hurt about Stefan since that day at the checkpoint, aren't you?"

"Yes, I am. You know why. Images of him transporting refugees to the frontier haunt me. This deception to save myself from Nazi suspicion deepens the loss of his love. Now I've taken a life to protect Old Testaments he probably transported after they left us. He's made too many mistakes in judgment and can't afford to now. Stefan needs someone to look after him."

"Madame, please let him grow up."

"Yes, Marie, except I know what no one else does. He has that vein of Fellner self-hatred. He blames himself for everything that went wrong in his childhood. I know how to help him face that fear and guilt about his mother's death."

"Please, Madame," trying to console me in a sweet voice at first, she ends annoyed, "you can't be responsible for what happened in his life before you entered it."

With firm conviction she taps a hard-boiled egg too crisply. Both shell and egg break in half. I swallow hard and look down, reminded of a few unpleasant instances in front of Marie when Stefan was only eight years old, right after Emil and I were married.

"Marie, you remember how inconsolable he was when he made a mistake. The simplest errors in his schoolwork or small social blunders with friends made him excessively self-critical. I tried calming him but he usually rejected me."

"He loves you, Madame, and has held you in high esteem from the very beginning, even though you are his belle-mère."

"Yes, but to my face, privately, Marie, he was cruel at times. If he carries that sentiment forward and mixes it with angry feelings about my collaboration, I'll never regain his respect when this war's over."

Marie stops and pushes the bowl of eggs to one side. She reaches over and grabs my hand across the table. I look up into her clear blue eyes.

"Madame, you push me to reveal a confession Stefan made to me twelve years ago, when he had many nightmares. He blamed himself for his mother's drowning and was terrified he would kill you, too."

"What? Really?" I'm aghast.

"Oui. Do you remember, Madame, how much Monsieur Emil loved water sports? He always took the two of you to Lake Geneva or the Côte d'Azur. Even years after Hélène drowned, poor Stefan refused to go. He was terrified and guilt ridden. He was afraid it would happen again with you."

"I remember, Marie. Emil was terribly stubborn the last time we argued. He wanted to leave Stefan at home. I was angered at his insensitivity and refused to go. Emil had a blind spot where Stefan's trauma was concerned. Perhaps he didn't want to accept responsibility for Hélène's death. He put the life vests in the boat but didn't insist they wear them. He knew she couldn't swim. He just wasn't thinking." (My marriage wasn't always so pleasant.)

"Oui, Madame, delaying that emergency appendectomy made a mess. Emil thought Stefan complained to avoid the water. The poor boy's painful adhesions, the weeks draining the poison and the inoperable hernia must have convinced Stefan of his guilt."

I cannot say to her how blame is a cheap way out, akin to lying. You run the maze of human error and always return to the starting point, yourself. Is it possible to go back to the scene of a childhood crime to make sense of your feelings and succeed with your integrity? Be reborn with love?

I'm reminded what Maman said to me months ago about Stefan holding onto his pain.

"Marie, what do you think it means when people hold onto their anger for a very long time and make you the object of their disgust?"

"Perhaps, Madame, if they won't talk about it they're confusing you with their fear and maybe blaming you because they can't face something. And they know intuitively you could help and they are ashamed to ask. If you're speaking about Stefan, don't take it personally."

"You're saying I have to leave him alone?"

"Yes, Madame. Perhaps his mission in the Résistance will give him a clearer sense of his value as a human being."

"He's a good soul. If he only knew how proud I am of his sacrifice for others."

"Madame, just trust it will work out like the brooch that came back to you."

"I'm afraid to be that optimistic, Marie, but I'm grateful we are safe this Christmas."

Marie gives me peace. I find myself relying on her wisdom to be in this world but not of it. So much easier said than done. I would have mourned Stefan's absence from Maman's table today except for her wise insight.

We continue to peel our eggs and potatoes in silence for a minute when she says,

"About Sylvia, Madame, you know how intelligent she is. . . ."

I nod and smile.

"She hopes to continue her schooling after the war despite caring for Pierre."

I listen carefully now. Marie loves those two like a grandmother. Then, surprising me, she leans across the table and whispers, "It would be wonderful, Madame, if that happens. It's so hard to raise a child out of wedlock."

"Oui, you're right, Marie. I do love Sylvia and Pierre. They are like family since Emil is gone." Marie is encouraging me to extend my generosity to help Sylvia finish her schooling.

"Madame Ingrid, before Guy came into my life, I had a baby boy during the first war, but he died three days after birth. My first love never came back from the front. My infant son died the same day his father was shot." She bites her lip remembering it.

"I'm so sorry I didn't know, Marie. I recall Maman telling me you had been ill when I came home from Swiss boarding school and you weren't in the house. But she didn't tell me what happened." I place my hand over hers, "A double dose of loss, how sad it must have been for you."

I wondered why Marie worked so diligently to comfort Sylvia when Pierre was born. Sylvia reawakened Marie's history. I'm honored by her confidence. Only our shared work in the Résistance would make her reveal such a personal secret.

Sylvia is a healing presence in both our lives.

Chapter Thirteen

Confession

27 December 1943, Monday

I return to town after Christmas. My visit with Sylvia and Pierre was the first peaceful respite in many months. I never realized I could enjoy such contentment before the war ends.

Lately, siding with Hitler is less appetizing to the French palette. The Russians are beating the Fritzies, which makes my reputation as a collaboratrice more notorious. The anxiety about my concubinage bites at my back as soon as I cross the threshold of my front door.

Dieter meets me this first evening home with news of future crossings.

"And what excitement do you have in store for me this time?" I tease him tonight.

He looks at me from a face drawn and tired and apparently wonders why I'm sarcastic— but says nothing. We sit together on the small divan drinking a brandy. He's pensive and fearful about my safety, but will never divulge what he knows.

"I have to ask you to do something difficult, Ingrid." Instantly I bristle.

"Oh really? There's some other humiliation I have yet to perform?" I take aim at his heart and watch him react, unaware how much my emotional excesses hurt us.

"Well, is there, Dieter?" I reiterate, regretting my bitterness.

Ingrid, you fool, he didn't come here to listen to self-pitying rage. But he knows you can't let it out with anyone else.

At first he's patient. Then he interrupts my whining stance to announce tersely, "Ingrid, you need to make a confession. . . ."

I stop him and almost choke on my brandy, laughing scornfully, "Hah, oh Dieter, you must be kidding. To whom do I confess, and what sins, pray tell, am I confessing?"

"Cut it out, Ingrid. Be serious. It's important. You have to go to Fr. Beauverger."

His mention of the Church sobers my mind to a halt.

"Dieter, I haven't been to daily Mass since Emil died. Almost four years. To do it pulls me back to his death. Why is it necessary? I go on Christmas and Easter for Marta's sake."

"Do you blame God for your loss?"

"No, I don't blame God for Emil's death, my daughter's paralysis, my field mattress servitude, the murder I committed or my unhappiness in general. I just can't quite grasp why all these things have happened or what they mean, Monsieur Kreuzier."

I raise my eyebrows, jerk out another ingrown self-mocking sniggle and sigh.

How do I tell him I lost trust in the organized Church, as did many of my generation? Gunshots from the First World War rattled our complacency. I don't believe religion can soothe the savagery of this present landscape. Man has to take responsibility for his actions. I listen patiently to priestly advice and find my own answers.

"I don't blame anyone, Dieter. I'm dead inside and don't care. God must hide His face from shameful creatures like me. Being angry serves no purpose."

Thankfully, he moves on to a more rational, impersonal approach, "Ingrid, people you know here do business with the German war machine. These people must see you as sympathetic to their 'unfortunate plight' as middlemen in the rape of French industry.

"You and your mother are respected members of the land-owning associations in this area. If anyone suspects you're Résistance, it would be to their advantage to denounce you. If they cheat on their dealings with Berlin, you two would be the perfect scapegoats to prove their loyalty. You must confess to the priest. He'll shield you."

"How? He'd have to go against God to reveal my confession and to what? Being a lonely, pathetic, stupid widow who doesn't care about war, only to be content in the strong arms of dashing Nazi scum? Oh Dieter, who would believe that?" My laughter is brittle.

"Fr. Beauverger will, Ingrid. He has the ear of other clerics in this area. His support will silence their suspicions and the fascist élite hiding behind their gentleman farms. Please protect our operation for yourself and Marta, if not the Jews."

I wonder who the fascist élite are? But, I don't want to know. I've seen so few moneyed acquaintances since Emil's death. This scheme makes me queasy.

"I can't do it, Dieter. I dislike that priest. He has a long tongue like those in my old social set he still panders to. For a confession to be useful he must have the ear of the Milice and not know it. You want them to think I'm having an affair with the SS?"

"Yes, exactly, Ingrid. That's why you need to use him this way."

"And what happens if I give him this confession and don't go to Mass?"

"But you will go to Mass, Ingrid. You must turn over a new leaf. Be contrite."

"Dieter, I'd do it in a minute if I could get rid of Mueller, but I won't be able to stop servicing him just because I go to confession. Mueller won't laugh if I suddenly refuse him because I confess our affair to the priest. He'll beat me."

"Why does he have to know?"

"Dieter, the Church spies will see him come and go from my home. It will get back to the priest's ears. No, you're asking too much. Besides, everyone in town knows I don't like Beauverger. When Fr. Schlemmer left after Emil died, I lost my anchor to the Church. Schlemmer was a Franciscan, mystic and bold. This one's a diocesan tattletale, swayed by friends who abandoned me. He was too cowardly to read Archbishop Saliège's message about 'Les Juifs' from the pulpit."

"Ingrid, I realize you don't like him. All right, you *detest* him, but we need to use him to our advantage. He'd like to believe you're passive and swayed by loneliness. He thinks the worst of all females. You'll have no trouble convincing him in the confessional. Go to early Mass to avoid the people you know. Please Ingrid, you don't realize how much influence he has with the Milice right now."

I hear that word "Milice" and feel uneasy.

"Tell him you're tortured, and can't take Communion because even if God forgives you, it will be years before you forgive yourself. Say anything to convince him, but Ingrid, I'm not suggesting this move. I'm telling you for your own safety and ours too. You must do it. We have to stop the speculation."

"You're a hard taskmaster, Dieter. To you this is just another act for me to pull off. I've rejected myself so completely God can't get near me. I don't know how to pray anymore." I shudder and pull my sweater tighter as a cold draft blows through my bones.

"Ingrid, please. . . ."

"Please what, Dieter? When this war is over will I be forsaken like a Jesus? Ostracized, alone, with no one to support my good intentions, all disappeared or dead?"

Dieter looks at me with his warm paternal smile that usually melts me, but not tonight.

"You're wonderful, Ingrid. I know you'll convince him. Trust me, please. I want you and Marta to be safe. I wouldn't ask if it weren't necessary."

"Yes, fine Dieter, consider it done." With a grudging answer I purse my lips and rub my temples. My inner response is hopelessness. Outwardly, I show a twinge of irritation. He rises to leave and I escort him to the front vestibule. I'm so tired. Home only a few hours and this subterfuge already on the agenda.

I feel as negative as two years ago. He senses it. I want to punish him tonight for disturbing my peace of mind after a quiet week in the country, where I walked outdoors in relative freedom, even in the winter cold. To think I almost chose to move there the very week before the bodies appeared on my shoreline two years ago. I might never have seen them. And now, because of them, I stand here trapped like a small mammal about to be devoured by wolves.

Dieter turns to me before leaving to show a spark of his own need,

"Please, dear woman, don't hurt us this way. I can't change what's done. You simply have to find a way to work with the situation. I'm not God and can't do the impossible. Stop punishing me. I have enough on my shoulders. From you I need cooperation, not criticism. I'm not a spittoon for your Gestapo poison, Ingrid. Good night."

I lunge forward to grab his hand as he reaches for the door latch. His resentment, so justified, hits me between the eyes. He wishes to leave and I want the last word. Do I? What do I want? Him? How can I still think he's a knight in shining armor who rescues the little girl in me, when his eyes grind pity and disgust into my shallow soul?

My voice wavers, "Please, Dieter, you have no idea what it's like to be the town pariah. Mueller is such a bully. Forgive me. Don't leave like this." I break down and cry, worried about my encounter with the priest. I can't tell Dieter what I fear, but his reserve cracks. He embraces me, caresses my hair and whispers, "No more tears, my sweet, no more tears."

Almost three weeks later I enter the old church very early on a bitter Friday morning in January. I rehearsed this unpleasant vignette before my vanity mirror every day, until I could no longer delay the inevitable. I trust Dieter, yet a foreboding haunts this plan to fling myself at the feet of the real collaborators. Why do I feel this could backfire? Far from quieting their tongues, it might bring me to the brink of exposure much sooner. Is it my woman's intuition or just plain terror that tells me this plan is flawed?

It's very cold inside the Church today. No one else is in here. I tread softly down the side aisle not to awaken the Romanesque gargoyles asleep above the confessionals. The old nuns always warned us tiny children to tell the truth or the fantastic creatures would come back to life, leap down, and attack the liars among us.

My position in the Résistance forces me into silence. I can't confess the most heinous crime of my life, not fornication with the enemy, but murder. I resent the power and intrusion of this ancient theological darkness. Yet I shall be obedient to the form of its sacrament this one last time. I kneel down inside the chamber, clear my throat and begin,

"Ignosce mihi, pater, quia peccavi." Then I pause and decide to say, "Forgive me, Father, for I have sinned. . . .

Fr. Beauverger interrupts, "Madame Fellner, is that you? Pardon me, it's been so long."

"Yes . . . I ah . . . I know Father. This is very hard for me."

The priest turns on his patronizing charm, hearing my feminine remorse. His change of attitude withers my womanly prerogative, as does his personal acknowledgment. I haven't done this for five years. Amazing how the rote form of childhood memory spits out the ritual Latin phrases so mindlessly.

He remembers me, the stupid inept little woman from five years ago, just as Dieter said. Perhaps he thinks I'm going to ask forgiveness for my décolletage at the Christmas concert. I have forgotten how this man of the cloth fears women. I begin meekly to reach for his sympathy and forgiveness,

"Oh Father, I've suffered for five years without my dear husband. Life has been so difficult and lonely. I'm too weak, used to having someone to lean on. I made a tragic mistake and it hurts. Please help me, Father," I sob.

"My child, do not judge yourself so harshly. What could you have done that's so evil in the eyes of God, my little one?"

He's probably smiling now. Getting to the juicy part he already knows. He eats at Germaine's table every week. I ready myself for my reply and almost choke on it,

"I, uh, I uh . . . fell in love, Father."

"So what is wrong, my child? Human love is essential to God's Plan. Your late husband has been gone for several years now. You're still young."

His script is rote. Perhaps I shouldn't be so harsh and judgmental.

"Yes, I know, but it's wartime and this man was a German in the military and. . . ."

He interrupts. "So, you were in bed with the enemy, is that it?"

I hear the condemnation in his voice. Sobbing didn't work. Now he'll pressure me for details. I was right before not to trust him and now feel light-headed and confined in this infernal box.

"Well, yes, Father, but I didn't know how awful it was going to be. I'm tortured knowing he was a Gestapo agent."

The priest hasn't realized it's Heisler, and I will continue to speak of the rape as a past sin.

"How did it start, my child?" He presses for details.

"Uh, it began with that awful time the two bodies washed ashore on my riverbank. You remember, a little over two years ago?"

"Yes, I was told. They were Jews, oui?"

"Oui, Father. This Gestapo agent came to my house. I signed papers for Nazi records and gave testimony. It was strange. I knew this person. He was in business before the war and knew my late husband. It was quite innocent. I didn't realize the Occupation would preclude a simple friendship. I've had no experience of the war except what we hear across the borders, what goes on up north, and rationing. I haven't traveled since my Emil died."

"And you had relations with this man?"

He wets his lips and takes a sharp breath. Must I forgive him now that lewdness peeks through his priestly pose?

"It was gradual. He was very nice and brought me little gifts. We talked about our lives before the war and listened to music together. He was kind and it just sort of happened. I'm so ashamed, Father. All these years pass and I turned to someone like that? How could I have done it? I hate myself."

I sob again and blow my nose, but despite my performance, listen intently. Did I capture this priest's compassion? Calling his pity compassion when his ego bursts with paternal superiority makes me ill.

"Now, now child. You're a grown woman. This man . . . was he . . . ah, married?"

"Oh no, Father. I could never do that, be an adulteress? Oh no."

"You said you 'fell in love.' Did you love this man?"

"Ah, well, it never actually progressed that way."

Why does he want to know?

"I see. Was it purely a physical intimacy?" I don't think that's relevant.

"It soothed my loneliness."

I don't like this. Does he think I had some tempestuous affair? I decide to be more passive and break down in a flood of anguish. He pauses and can't get any more out of me,

"All right, my child, calm yourself."

Good. I have to take the upper hand now to end this. I'm not sure he knows I've talked about Heisler and not Mueller.

"Please, Father, how could I love a Nazi? I'm so ashamed. I feel people's scorn and suspicion behind my back, to my face, on the street, where I shop. I have to send my maid to do the errands now. I'm never sure who I'll meet and what cruel judgment I will encounter."

He listens as I keep crying. He wants more.

"Is there anyone, ah anything else you wish to confess to God in the anonymity of this confessional, my child? Anything about the nature of your sexual encounters for which you must seek further forgiveness?"

He must be wondering about Mueller. SS men are known to be sodomists. But how dare he push me like this? I have to stay calm, and strain to emote embarrassment when he stokes my anger.

"I'm struggling to be vigilant not to commit this sin again, Father."

"Excellent, my daughter, that is very noble. What else?"

"Nothing more, Father. Thank you for your encouragement."

I take a deep breath not to choke. If I let him he would turn a voluntary confession into an interrogation. I want to shout before God's altar that of course Jesus knows I'm an adulteress and certainly adulterated goods. The pain of rape makes hot tears trickle down my cheeks. So angry, I can't permit myself to care. This confession is politically motivated. Not personal.

"My child, it behooves you to seek the protection of Almighty God to stay temptation, especially in these times when judgment can be short-sighted, harsh and unfeeling. You have made a full confession, my daughter?"

"Yes, Father."

"For the sake of your eternal soul you would do well not to wait to confess sexual temptation. The longer it continues the more difficult it is to see the redemptive light of God in your life. It can become an evil habit, my child."

"Yes, you're right, Father," and I recite the act of contrition to end this charade.

"Oh my God, I am heartily sorry for having offended Thee, and I detest all my sins because of Thy just punishments. . . ."

My thoughts running parallel to this recitation are: my dear Jesus, I know this punishment is worth it because it comes from my hand, my heart, and my decisions. Why would I ask you to intervene to protect me from my lowly lessons in this life when I am my own victim? How can I seek holiness if I don't claim responsibility for the pain my imperfect ability to love causes me? This is my cross and I must carry it alone, as you did yours. I can't be overwhelmed by life. I must be aware and take action in dangerous situations to survive every day.

Fr. Beauverger gives me absolution and a small penance of Hail Marys and daily rosaries for a week. He tells me to avoid the temptation of sin. His penance doesn't fit my crime. In fact, the only error I confessed was sex without marriage. French society declares my lover the enemy. That's the real sin. I can't change the town's politics or its perception of my behavior.

I listen and am pleased with my impact despite this being a meaningless exercise. What could I have expected from this priest? That he would be a member of the Underground, an enlightened and courageous cleric? But he's not. His voyeuristic nature pulled him into my story. If I had volunteered more details he would have let me go on. I hope he's convinced of my sincerity. He encourages attendance at daily Mass.

I thank him and leave. Facing the altar, I genuflect, adjust my hat, cover my neck with my scarf, raise my collar, bless myself with holy water, put on my gloves, and slide out the side door. Amen.

I walk down the empty side street, increasingly embittered. To cross people to safety I will continue to sin. And what of adultery with Mueller? How does one weigh that sinfulness against deportation of innocent Jewish children and adults? My fornication protects them while Mueller and his ilk condemn them. Not enough civilian sinners risk their own crucifixions to save others. I hate sounding arrogant and self-righteous, but Beauverger behaved like a sex-hungry gossip.

Either human existence has become too complex in the last nineteen hundred years or some large piece of its spiritual puzzle eludes me. I cannot judge the evil of my fornication with a simplistic catechism swallowed as a child. My life is a continuous recitation of sorrowful mysteries. My weird repetitive dreams are soaked in bloody violence. They make me think absolution lies in a karmic conjunction I don't yet understand. A moral tie exists between a distant past of actions I can't grasp in this life because my church's theology will not admit to it.

Maybe it's a hook from the past? The paradox is: if I go beyond judging the good or evil of my actions in black and white terms, it feels like I'm cleaning both slates at the same time. If sin is a way to learn holiness, then my supine service is not without spiritual purpose. It condemns me for adulterous intentions I never had—yet somehow I need both experiences.

May I live to find the conjunction that ties the two lessons together because this confession has prompted more questions and given me no answers.

1944

Chapter Fourteen

A Mauling From Mueller

29 February 1944, Tuesday

Gradually, 1944 unfolds. A slow, plodding January passing refugees gives way to hints of a wild acceleration. It begins when a few local leaders in the Résistance in nearby regions who could verify my status in the Underground are deported to the Struthof-Natzweiler camp in Alsace.

Dieter knows them and only Dieter remains free.

Others have been killed or hide in the heavily forested frontier. In the end each Résistant will be on his or her own. I also agreed to it and now, dependent on these people, I worry for my safety. They know the truth behind my reputation. Under interrogation and torture they could talk.

My position is more involved than I realize. Refugees coming to Duchamps move through secret lines of travel and communication several towns north of us weeks before they show up at my basement. What "Madame Henri" does affects the whole line of weary escapees and those who shield them. Rescuers form a silent train of herders and lodgers.

When I entered this drama, my pride in an altruistic mission blinded me to the necessity of being safe. I didn't see the consequences this role might exact. I began this escapade with the mistaken idea that aristocratic status would make me immune to suffering. I was living in the past. The ghost of my rigid alcoholic father's guilt, fighting himself to obey his family's Victorian rules of etiquette, has also ruled me. Enjoying a lifetime of privilege has left me unprepared, just floating along without the tools to survive. I had no idea what kind of world I would create by taking action on my own as a woman.

Now I'm in the midst of a hell from which I may not flee alive. A dead Jewish couple, my mother, Dieter, my house servants, the escaping victims, my innocent daughter and an unseen God I rarely call upon for help know my secret sacrifice. I can't shake the weight of my murder. Still, Old Testament guests appear: poor, humble, and grateful. After two years only stragglers come to my cellar door. If what the Underground tracts report is true, tens of thousands of Jews in France have already perished in eastern death camps.

>∞∞

I go down to the basement lodgers one Tuesday evening, at my lowest ebb after nearly a year of Mueller ripping at my nerves through my womb. This despite the ever-present possibility the Obersturmführer will call on me tonight.

I have been visiting the basement quite often since Sylvia's arrival. Then the shooting in September made me more careful. But it's leap year and today is our extra day of February and the war. I hope for an auspicious evening, peaceful and alone for a change.

I proceed downstairs to meet a middle-aged Polish-Jewish couple. They hid for several weeks with a farm family near the French-German border. I find them sitting with Guy, and eating a vegetable stew with slices of pickled fish.

I speak a Polish phrase I've only heard,

"Sit, please, oo-shown, prosh-eh." It must sound unclear against my French and German because the man stands, leaning on a cane, until I say, "S'il vous plait, s'asseoir. Bitte, sitzen."

He laughs sweetly, and to my relief, sits down, answering in flawless French and German,

"Very good Polish pronunciation, Madame, oui, really! Vraiment, très bien! Sehr gut, ja!"

I blush at his show of respect and clear my throat, hesitating to introduce myself, "I am Madame Henri, your hostess. Please, eat. You two need nourishment. In a few minutes you will have to go behind the cabinets. Sorry I cannot share my upstairs, but you understand this is the safest way I can help you."

Hearing embarrassment in my voice, the gentleman smiles.

"We are most grateful for your hospitality, and your courage, Madame Henri. I am Monsieur Jakub Kleinboren and this is my wife, Miriam. It's an honor to meet you."

"You are not afraid to do this, Madame?" his wife, Miriam, asks.

"I am terrified, Madame Kleinboren, but if I don't resist the Nazis, my daughter will inherit a worthless legacy of fear." I sit down to listen. Their faces reflect a shared respect.

"We never registered as Jews, Madame, but we were in the *Armia Krajowa*, the Polish Résistance. We escaped from our last concentration camp, Sobibór."

Their strong voices contrast their gaunt faces with dark-circled eyes and taut lips. Powerful, intelligent personalities emanate from bodies shrunken into a generic humanity from corpse-like emaciation. The incongruity is almost nauseating—so offensive to my sense of decency. I suddenly swallow a sliver of guilt for my SS murder months ago.

"Please, eat heartily. You two have been starved for a long time. You need your stamina. You will go to a safer house from here. Then, in the late spring, to a less comfortable, but even safer place, near the Swiss border. I will give you herbs for your ankle, Monsieur Jakub."

"Our last protectors were forced to let us go, Madame Henri. The Nazis raided nearby farm larders and uncovered hiding spaces of other refugees. In Alsace, escapees and their rescuing families were murdered in public squares." Monsieur Kleinboren touches his wife's hand as she looks down briefly. Looking up again, composed, she continues, "There was no food for us, Madame Henri. Every time we approached a hidden spot along the Austrian or German-Swiss borders to cross to asylum, the Gestapo had raided it first. We have moved in a strange circuitous route to end up here in your cellar, over a thousand kilometers from our home. We can't go back to Warsaw. We're nomads now."

I bite my lip, absorbing their anguish. They tell me their saga of Auschwitz and Sobibór. They have lost their children. My mind withdraws from their gratitude as I go back upstairs, but their story contaminates my emotions. I walk up slowly, trying to forget their faces with each step, so I can deal with whatever lunacy will pull me to my collaborating persona this evening.

The bell rings at the front door when I reach the top of the stairs. The stab of panic is unavoidable. What will tonight be like? Will I be reminded that submission to Mueller's sadistic appetite is dangerous? How much worse can it be? I see him through the window and quickly buzz the basement with two short buzzes and one long buzz to hide everyone before I let him in.

This is a raid, another one of his undeclared impromptu visits to catch me off guard.

Tonight I am filled with revulsion more than fear, and can't suppress it. I should not have spoken with the Jewish couple. I see Mueller into the front sitting room and excuse myself. I dislike giving him time alone in that space. I've divested it of personal things except what I want him to see. Marie enters to offer Mueller schnapps while I run to the bathroom and in three short minutes retch, prepare my womb, change clothes, and return to entertain him. Guy will join Marie when the lodgers are hidden. The three of us perform this scenario like a well-oiled machine. We've had so much practice.

Earlier today Guy took Marta to Grandmaman for three days. She adores little Pierre and Sylvia tutors her in German. I send her when the Gestapo bothers me for "socializing."

It's safer, especially when my state of mind sinks this low. Mueller's sexual virulence is devastating. Heisler was a human being with some gentility, but Mueller was born an abuser. When he demands relations, afterward it's painful to walk up stairs. The possibility of pregnancy terrifies me. I feel nauseous for weeks at a time. Is that fear or conception?

Some days, refugee gratitude barely compensates for this hell. If I need to perform for everyone else's safety, I could easily do away with myself. Take a pill or drain my blood. This life of usury could only be made worse by starving to death, and I saw what that looks like tonight.

I have to fight against the desire to want Mueller dead. He's never told when Marta is out of the house. If he thinks she's here, maybe he will control his lust and temper.

Usually, I'm icy cold—but obliging. Tonight I'm too imbued with moral outrage that can no longer hide its catharsis in my basement. A bitter taste of stomach acid seeps through my detached demeanor. I am passionate with anger and sick of the scenario with this man. Like a spent whore, I want it over with as quickly as possible.

I grab Mueller and tear open his pants, pull up my dress and squat over him. My body envelops his erection as I hit and bite him. I hate him. He's oblivious to my real feelings. While we ride this useless intimacy it seems so odd this power-hungry woman-hater likes his victim on top. I guess he mistakes my behavior for genuine passion when it's disgust.

Could I lose my tenderness doing this? Yes, that's the real risk. Whether I ever regain my reputation isn't important. What I fear most is losing my self-respect, the feeling of worth when a man touches me. I'm losing my boundaries. My intellect can race all it wants to justify my deeds but my poor body can't cease recording sickening memories of these men.

Which will be first to condemn me: my emotions, my intellect—or my wounded flesh? How will I exorcise these bitter residues, assuming another man of value will desire me? Forget it. Don't torture yourself with the future, you foolish girl. Your whoring collaboration is a blessing if only for the survival of truth and humanity. Do what is in front of you. Numb yourself if you must.

My mind can't deal with this personal plight in the context of war with any balance of sanity. The pressure is too great. There's no time to contemplate my life. No one else cares. Blowing up a bridge would be easier work than exposing my flesh in my home.

You're lucky, Ingrid. At least you had your great love before the war.

Now it's only this insignificant coupling. You're a tiny spline in the cog of a great wheel that grinds the gears of the Third Reich. You deaden yourself for the lives of others one gear revolution at a time.

The ride is over. I move away from Mueller. He's exhausted and reaches for me. I light a cigarette to give him something else to put in his mouth that isn't one of my body parts.

He's amazed and thrilled. I'm on the edge of dry heaves but must not show it. He would like me to surprise him with more. I manage excuses. Fatigued, now I must bathe. It's late and he has to leave.

Instead, he falls into a deep, snoring sleep for twenty minutes and awakens refreshed. He dresses and knocks softly at the bathroom door. Opening it a crack, he sees me wrapped in a towel, and lusts for me again so intensely he forces the door open. Shocked as he enters my private sanctuary, I lose my footing on the wet floor and fall backward. He's excited seeing my genitals exposed. His huge hairy hands grab me, rip off the towel and press me to the floor.

We struggle; he pulls open his pants and forces himself on me. This pain is excruciating. My God, he will pierce my bowel. If I scream he'll know I'm alone in the house and he'll unleash more violence. I plead with him to stop hurting me but he laughs in my ear. Finally I pull my arm free and reach back to grab his greasy hair and yank it hard. His neck makes a cracking sound. I hear it but ignore it and shout,

"Get off me, now. I have no strength for this. Please, respect me or I'll not let you near me again. You've gone too far!"

I move away, cowering by the tub with a towel over my torso, spotting the floor with blood and digging my fingers into my cheek.

His face is dark with anger, and his manhood still poised for animal aggression.

"Why you little tease! What was tonight's performance about then? Come here, *meine kleine Feldmatratze!*"

"You're too coarse, Franz. Out of my house. No one treats me this way, not even you!"

"I'll show you who's the boss, *meine kleine Hure!*"

He grabs my head in his fat paw-like hand and forces me to stand. Pinning my arms behind me, he presses his arousal against my buttocks, and commands me to look at him in the mirror. I'm naked, and he's dressed—except for his open pants.

"I have always wondered whose side you were on, my little whore! You know what I mean."

"*Aye*, nooo. Please don't!"

Again Mueller pushes me to the floor and kneels behind me. My womb and my colon are taut and dry with fear. He prefers me in panic. The act is vicious, abrupt, a dry staccato. His heavy panting as he climaxes sets an odd counterpoint to my cries of pain. He throws a towel over my bruised body and leaves me lying on the bathroom floor like a piece of trash.

"Don't worry, Ingrid dear," he sneers, hiking up his pants, "your secret is safe as long as you give me what I want. I won't let Ravensbrück waste your charms!"

He slams the bathroom door and goosesteps out of my house.

I freeze at the name of the dreaded camp. Emil flashes across my mind's eye. I sob and lift to my knees only to collapse back down onto the floor. I wrap myself in another large bath towel and fall into a dead, cocoon-like sleep, hoping I am transformed when I awake.

It's early the next morning, about 6:00 o'clock. I hear Marie knock gently at the street- floor bedchamber door. I'm in the bathroom, too groggy to respond loud enough for her ears. If she sniffs for the stench of Mueller's cigars, the odor will be vague by now. I hear, "Madame, are you in the bath?" Her voice outside the bathroom door sounds hopeful but is hesitant. Although awake, my body jerks with a startle, sore and cold from hours lying on the hard floor.

"Madame, are you awake? Are you all right?"

"Yes, Marie, what is it?"

"Madame, remember you asked to go with me to early Mass today. Are you almost ready?"

Oh my, I forgot. I have to act this part as well.

"In a few minutes. Please Marie, lay out my black dress with the dark sweater, and the woolen wrap and woven cloche. I'll be out shortly. Do we still have time to get there?"

"Yes, yes, but only if you eat afterward, Madame."

"Please, pour a small chicory coffee, Marie. Just a mouthful will do."

"You're certain you don't need help, Madame?"

"Oui, I can manage, thank you, Marie."

I sound very tired. Her voice tells me she senses my fragility and suspects a hard evening with the SS. She knows this "service obligatoire" is degrading, but trusts my dichotomous life will work out in the end. It's the nature of this war to take morally disagreeable action for the freedom of others.

She returns shortly, announcing through the door, "I laid your clothes out on the bed, Madame. I will get your coffee."

Slowly, I raise my drained, aching body, hardly able to stand. I draw a hot bath and sit in it for a few minutes and then shower in freezing water, rubbing face, arms and thighs harshly to awaken my bruised limbs. I feel a headache coming on. The bones in front of my ears are sore from Mueller's hands compressing and beating my head.

I leave the towel in the basin soaking the dried blood free in cold water until Marie and I return. I'm ready ten minutes later, my face almost entirely covered by the hat and scarf. We stand in the foyer by the front door. Reaching for my heavy overcoat, I comment,

"Marie, you haven't seen this dress since Emil's funeral. Today I go to church to pick up where I left off five years ago. I can't believe it. Marta is with Sylvia and grand-mère, oui?"

"As you instructed, Madame. She'll stay there for two days." Marie's expression tells me she wonders where my thoughts are since I arranged it all.

"Good. I'll need time for other activities I can't expose her to. Let's go."

I gulp a little hot chicory coffee from the hall table and we leave the house, walking arm-in-arm in the cold. Marie feels me lean on her. She senses the tightness in my hips as we walk. I know she prays for my health. Where would I be without her?

This dear woman is like a second mother. She never judges me. I feel so small compared to her. I blink back a few tears. Living with Marie's infinite grace—surrendering to every day—is holier than going to Church.

The wind is up, so I tuck the end of her scarf into her collar. I smile a thank you to the nobility and love in her eyes. We disappear down the muddy lane in the cold winter drizzle, just two women on their way to early Mass.

At the church I sit in the back near the door, hiding in the cavernous dark of the old medieval structure. I don't want Fr. Beauverger to see me. Marie goes up front to her usual pew. I admire her ability to forgive everyone, particularly Beauverger. He may wear the same cloth but is a cut far below the courageous Toulouse Archbishop Jules-Gérard Saliège. The Archbishop's pastoral letter two years ago denounced the immoral treatment of Les Juifs after the worst French pogrom, *Le Grand Rafle*, in the *Vélodrome d'Hiver* in Paris. On July 16 and 17, 1942 over 13,000 Jews, more than 4,000 of them children, mercilessly separated from their parents, were held prisoner for five days in blistering summer heat. They had no fresh air, water, sanitation or food before deportation to death camps in the east. Saliège's courage to call French conscience into account on Sunday, August 23, 1942, has been a guiding light for faithful Résistants like my Marie.

Priests in all churches in the Toulouse Archdiocese, except one, read his public protest:

"There is a Christian morality . . . that confers rights and imposes duties. These duties and these rights come from God. One can violate them. But no mortal has

the power to suppress them. Alas, it has been our destiny to witness the dreadful spectacle of women and children, fathers and mothers treated like cattle, members of a family separated from one another and dispatched to an unknown destination—it has been reserved for our own time to see such a sad spectacle. Why does the right of sanctuary no longer exist in our churches? Why are we defeated? . . . The Jews are real men and women. Foreigners are real men and women. They cannot be abused without limit. They are part of the human species. They are our brothers, like so many others. No Christian dares forget that!"

I read a copy of his letter each time Mueller abuses me. But Beauverger, the priest who heard my confession six weeks ago, has never read this pastoral protest to his flock. His housekeeper posted it inside the rectory kitchen, but he made no public reference to it.

It was even widely broadcast over Vatican radio—and Pope Pius XII praised Saliège. Fr. Beauverger's only political achievement since 1940 has been to convince SS hierarchy to suspend curfew for the annual Christmas Concert. He did that to appease the Protestants.

Marie read Saliège's letter because her friend the rectory housekeeper shared it with her. After that a succession of supplicants read it when they came bearing homemade foods they donated for baptisms, first holy communions, confirmations, weddings, and funerals. Parishioners with no francs to spare gave from their gardens and orchards. The priest's cook dispersed the food to parishioners hiding Jews. They spread the letter's word by living it.

The priest has mistaken their gratitude as a sign of religious devotion for his sacramental blessings. He has no idea Archbishop Saliège's fierce fidelity to God's law to respect all life has made his parishioners more loyal to the Underground he fears. A few like me have abandoned the Mass. I'm not holy like Marie. I admire her trust and forgiveness. She has a love I must work for. I'm weak compared to her, Guy, Marcel, Dieter, Amélie and others who never flinch from aiding and hiding our Jewish brethren.

I sigh, open my eyes and sit back in the pew. It's so early only the elderly worshippers are here. They sit in the same places, the same pews they have been worshiping in for decades. A few candles light the side altars. Fr. Beauverger drones on in Latin. We never see his face, even those who take Communion with closed eyes and open mouths, their folded hands hidden under the starched rail cloth.

I can't do this anymore. I barely last the entire service. My body bursts with spasmodic pain from twisted muscles. Every vertebra is on fire. My mind is awash with images from my happy past with Emil, Stefan, and Marta. I went to Mass often, never questioning the Crucifixion or how I placed my life within the Christian message.

And then everything changed.

My balance sheet of good deeds was so short it necessitated the end of good times. I had a need for truth beyond the dogma. Now I'm swept up in a madness of war that spills out an ugly cornucopia of lessons. Do I plan to end it in a vortex of inhumane violence? Is my life what God doles out or did I decide on it from somewhere else? Maybe we decided together? I can't know for certain, but it seems the part of me closest to God would act exactly as I am now—and not ask forgiveness for it.

If God lives in me and these are His lessons for me, He would proceed peacefully without my fuss and drivel. And blame, well, I have to save lives by sinning. It's the only way. Maybe that's wrong, but it feels right. Someday I'll find the answer. Certainly, I'm afraid to die but each day the fear is less gripping. All that's left is the emotional weakness that gives in to it against my will, even as I see more clearly. I'm thankful for Dieter's patience. He shows me to myself. I have behaved so poorly. I wish I were a better student.

I lift myself forward to sit on the edge of the pew. My hips radiate the painful submission of pride when I kneel too long. My eyes take in the dull dark church, the same one I sang in two years ago when the Résistance needed help at the eleventh hour. My mind wanders. I struggle to remain awake after last night. In the quiet reflection after Communion, my thoughts drift upward to meet the fragrance of incense.

Gradually I lose sensation in my extremities and hover toward sleep. My eyes are teary in the darkness. My sorrow magnifies through the refraction of those tears. There's a bluish-white light in front . . . no . . . it's all around me. My mind is transfixed. My body can't move. I don't feel attached to it. The light is opaque but not dense. I can't see anything. It's blinding, and makes me feel warmer than I have for years. My heart is free.

What's happening? No thoughts come. I'm cut off from my flesh and float like an essence. Before I can be afraid, I sigh deeply and the light is gone. I couldn't hold onto it and am sucked back into my aches and pains. Tears rise for the loss of a sensation I couldn't grasp. Please wait, I have to go back. Oh God, I felt loved. I was invincible. I recognized something in my heart that was so real, but now it's gone.

That blue-white light left me feeling centered. I saw another way to understand why things happen. But it left so suddenly. I can't remember what was learned, yet those moments imprinted something on my soul, as if a dear friend inside me yawned awake for a second and then went back to sleep for an eternity.

I sit up on the hard, unforgiving wood and rest my head on my arms against the pew in front of me. Inside I'm weak, cold, and aching.

My wellbeing spirals down a notch as mundane questions return. Will my secret status be revealed today? When I'm afraid, I can't gain perspective. I need a measure of detachment to view life unfolding from a higher place as though it's someone else's story. Strange, to think of this now. Those precious moments with that blue-white light confused me and rattled my sanity. Were they from God? Did I touch the hem of the Divine?

I take everything too personally, yet I have to feel to be alive. Dieter complains about this. Do I resent him because he never appears frightened—or because he expects too much of me? Why do I see Dieter as . . . wait, no, it's not Dieter's heart I'm digging at. It's mine: my grief, my widowhood, my Marta. They brought me to the dead Jewish couple and the blood dream, that frightening nightmare. Did I make a mistake interpreting it too literally?

The storm was raining blood. The evil smell of death was coming closer. I couldn't turn around to identify it. But I awoke suddenly, conscious that Marta needed me. My skin flew off to Emil and Marta brought it back to me. Was it about this war? Is this war a vehicle to change me? Why think of it now, today, in this Church? There's a significance I cannot fathom.

Something inside me is opening. A blinder is peeling off. If that dream was prophetic I'm still not sure how to interpret it, except that by healing my daughter I am healed. Perhaps waking up to this world is part of the dream's message to be more attentive. Two years ago I had that nightmare without stopping it. Before I dreamt it I lived it, on the riverbank with the dead Jewish couple. After that, it came of itself. I didn't think about it. Yet that cauchemar is part of everything happening now.

I spend my days paranoid and obsessed with questions. I torture myself worrying about every detail that could reveal what I do secretly and then give up because it's too much to carry. But this experience just now lifted me so easily and spontaneously. This must be part of the spiritual juxtaposition I'm searching for. It's so new. I watched it happen and can't place it anywhere.

Yet now I know the core of my soul looks at my human landscape with a wisdom and love beyond the reach of the suffering that would destroy it. It is eternal.

Did the Milice send the man I killed? Is Mueller part of a conspiracy?

He threatens me with Ravensbrück. He suspects me.

I need protection.

Do I have it and not recognize it?

Chapter Fifteen

Pierre's First Birthday

13 March 1944, Monday

Today presents a rare happiness: little Pierre's birthday. Our miracle boy has survived one whole year in the midst of Nazi hatred. We will celebrate with delightful sweets. I have provided most of their contents by my *service du travail obligatoire*.

I fear this happy occasion will prompt Sylvia to talk about her escape from Dachau. Every time she expects an event to happen, the rug is pulled out from under her, like the cancellation of Pierre's Bris. I have said nothing. There is a vast difference in the way we interpret reality, yet we feel so safe with each other. I guess you could say our closeness is a mystery of the Holy Spirit that hovers over all people, regardless of their religion.

I'm sitting alone on the brown leather sofa in Papa's old study thinking about this when I hear voices outside. I go to the window and smile down at Marie, Pierre, and Ivan as a late season snow shower covers the backyard garden. Marie harvests greens and roots from a cold frame while Pierre teases the dog. Our little tyke throws snow into the air, catches it on his tongue and rubs his mittens full of flakes into Ivan's fur.

On the surface the rest of the garden appears asleep. Underneath cold topsoil, the roots stretch and awaken from their winter slumber. I watch the three disappear from view and hear the heavy thud of the outer basement door. Just then Sylvia enters the study.

"Sylvia, my dear, you look a bit sad on this happy day. Come here. We haven't talked in a long time." She sits down next to me. The pain of her past reaches silently from her eyes, as I hold her cold hands in my warm ones. "Oh dear, you don't have to talk about it, Sylvia. At least you're safe."

She sits up abruptly. "Please, Madame Ingrid, I do have to talk about it. I must preserve my history for the day I tell Pierre and others I will love. My life was spared, an arbitrary choice that makes no sense, when they took my whole family away."

"Why is that, Sylvia?"

"Because my Aryan good looks saved me from death.

"The night we arrived at Dachau I was numb. I clung to my mother like a baby. When we first arrived, glaring lights surrounded us. We couldn't avoid smelling a noxious, sweet, fatty odor. An inmate built like a stick figure whispered it was burning flesh. The prisoners wore striped rags. They looked ghoulish. It took a moment to realize all of them were starving. They flitted to and fro like phantoms when the SS gave them orders.

"Before that, ghetto life was the worst nightmare. But that did not prepare me. I had no idea how to maneuver in the hostile environment of a camp. I had to have hope against death all around me. Nothing there was even *vaguely* familiar. It was the bottom of a *Gehenna*.

"I was in a daze when the three of us—my mother, grandmother and I—boarded the truck headed for Linz's gas chamber. The SS doctor had told me to go with the prisoners designated for forced labor. I ignored him and went with my family. It was a turn toward death but something made me do it.

"At Linz we undressed with the other women. I helped my old grandma disrobe. She was suspicious. They hadn't initiated us. Unlike some of the other Jews, we bypassed registration and head shaving.

"I will never forget my Bubbeh's eyes. She was old like Madame Mathilde. In the middle of folding her clothes I kissed her very casually, forcing back tears. Part of me believed we were going to take a shower and register afterward. The sign on the building even said *Brausebad*. I could not see that the three of us would be gaping corpses in twenty minutes.

"I was the last woman to enter the small, crowded chamber. I looked at the female SS matron by the door. She stared at my long blonde braids and dark blonde pubic hair. I was embarrassed. Then she motioned for me to follow her with a slight turn of her head.

"When I hesitated she barked, 'Seife! Come with me to get soap for the others.'"

"She left the door ajar and I walked out, naked. I was swallowed up in numbness. *I never looked back at my family.* I was just going to get them soap. I even felt a twinge of relief at that moment.

"As soon as I was outside, the guard thrust the door closed and bolted it. That harsh metal sound cut my life in half: the time *with* my family, and afterward, *without* them.

"Madame, that bolt goes through my heart every day. You have no idea how I feel when I hear a door slam shut, or worse, when I rub a bar of wet soap in my hands. Even now the hurt hits me without warning—so profound and unexpected, I stop breathing."

Sylvia pauses, takes a deep breath and lifts her head to force herself forward.

"That SS matron handed me an old coat and shoes from the pile and took me to a waiting car. As I got in she grabbed my shoulders and spit in anger as she spoke to me.

"You are not a Jewess. Remember that or be killed. Tell them you were caught on the street with the others. It was a mistake. Decide who you'll be. You're blonde. Give them an Aryan name. You understand? *Sie verstehen?* You have no papers. *Du hast keine Papiere.* Get new ones. You are free. *Du bist frei!*"

"A driver appeared and took me to a large villa an hour away. It was a beautiful, private estate that had been confiscated for an officers' brothel. No gates or barbed wire fences.

"Another SS matron was in charge. She kept me away from the women already in their stalls. She said they would initiate me the next morning, and took me to the servants' quarters on the first floor. I had a real bath, was given elegant clothes, and the first meal in two days. I was in another world, still numb. I followed instructions and nodded.

"While I was eating the matron guarding me fell asleep at the kitchen table. (She had finished an open bottle of the officers' brandy.) I ate the food that was out on the counters. When midnight came, I put on extra-warm leggings and more layers of clothes.

"The matron was still snoring at the table when I grabbed all the bread I could stuff into my pockets and tiptoed out without a sound.

"I ran to the woods and kept running for hours until I found a farmhouse and slept in the hayloft. I kept moving for days, until I came near the French border. Eventually I stayed with a French Patois family for six months and tutored their children. They secured forged papers for me. That's when I realized I was with child. I ate whatever I could, never cried, but thought about my family every day. I had to preserve my memory of them apart from our arrival at the camp. I began to delude myself, wondering when I'd hear from them.

"As months passed my kind protectors ran out of food and money. They lived on the charity of their neighbors who were suspicious of me. I had to leave so my rescuers would be safe. They introduced me to a chain of families in the Résistance who passed Jews to the French/Swiss border. Through this chain I was led to your basement."

She hesitates and continues, her voice much softer, "Pierre's birth convinced me I'd never see my family again. Please forgive me, Madame Ingrid. I have been rigid and ungrateful. When the numbness goes away, I feel terrified, even now. It never leaves me. Please, I'm sorry."

"You have no reason to apologize, Sylvia," I hug her, struggling to smile, "on the contrary, dear girl, you have taught me how to love again."

"Madame, if I had become a prostitute for Nazi officers my confinement would have led to the gas chamber, or worse, to medical experiments. Pierre never would have been born. Instead, today I celebrate his first birthday without his father. I don't even have a photo of my fiancé."

"Maybe he's still alive?" I ask gingerly.

"It's impossible. My future in-laws were arrested with my family. Upon our arrival at Dachau an inmate assisting the SS whispered to me that the men die on the 'hooks.'

"I gave my love a hug and kiss before they separated us, but my mother overheard and became hysterical. The inmate was afraid the guard would shoot him for divulging the truth, so he told me to slap her face and tell her she'd be shot if she didn't shut up.

"All the while an SS doctor leered because my hair was a lighter blonde than the Nazi matron next to him. I think he spared me when he saw me slap my mother. I felt so guilty.

"I saw my father, uncles, and my dear fiancé led away to the under-ground crematoria where the hooks were. I knew my family was destined to die, but still hoped we'd get a shower. I thought I would be a prisoner," she pauses and takes a deep breath, "At least I can tell the whole story now, but the wound won't heal. How do I stay sane without my family?"

I hold her tightly. Her strong young body goes limp and trembles with the loss.

"This is hard to say; they're gone from here, Sylvia, but they're in a beautiful place of infinite peace. Love them in your heart without driving yourself mad to have them with you. If you need to cry, just do it. We all have to learn to carry our sorrows, and live without the people who gave us life. Your will to live honors them and strengthens your son. That's what they would want."

"Yes, you're right," her face looks old beyond her years. "Madame Ingrid, last summer when Pierre's lack of circumcision saved his life, I understood something new about God and mercy I can't put into words."

"We learn every day, Sylvia. Me too. The unrelenting nature of this war pushes us to change."

"I was arrogant, thinking of my own needs, not of the risk you take to protect us."

She's curious since that lecher Mueller fondled her. I denied seeing the incident in the garden. I was too ashamed. Exhausted and nauseated from the migraine, I couldn't take charge that afternoon. I jeopardized everyone's lives. Apprehensive that Mueller would gain entry to Maman's house, I feared he would rape Sylvia and me with his officers holding us down.

Sylvia is too young to have all her illusions shattered. I can't tell her today. I can't share my pain with a mere child made old and desperate before her time, despite her motherhood. Her son Pierre is the first gift of intimacy she will hold forever sacred—with the memory of her dead fiancé.

"Madame Ingrid, I can never repay your kindness."

"That's because you're not supposed to. Come, I hear Pierre babbling."

We walk arm-in-arm to the dining room. Sylvia's little cherub sits, waiting impatiently, with a yellow paper crown on his head. Pierre's cheeks are still red from his foray in the snow. His eyes dance as he reaches out for his cake.

Everyone joins our royal celebrant at the antique bagua gate-leg instead of the large formal banquet table. We sit and hold hands while Maman says a little prayer of thanks for our liege. When we sing "Bonne Anniversaire," Sylvia slides the cake closer to Pierre so he can blow out the candle. The scene is charming and civilized. Pierre watches intently.

The wheels of his one-year-old brain seem to question whether this white stuff in front of him is like the snow outside? Immediately the thrill of male conquest goads our birthday boy to find out. He swipes at his cake and grabs handfuls of light, soft, creamy icing. With a surprised look he flails his tiny fists and utters shrill cries of delight as gobs of white goo splat onto our shoulders, laps, hair, floor, everywhere!

Ivan, the Great Dane, who's asleep under the table, awakens abruptly to his majesty's high-pitched squeals. Startled, his huge head rises up and bangs the underside of the tabletop, lifting the entire table off the floor as he stands. Antique porcelain teacups, saucers, dessert dishes, and cutlery fly into the air. Oblivious to our sudden disarray, Pierre conducts the scene by splattering icing all over us a second time. Sweet, buttery goop slips over Ivan's back and rump before Marie can pull our little prince's ammunition out of reach.

Maman laughs hysterically as Ivan's tail beats her chair in anticipation of his treat.

"Ach! Ivan, some protection you are," she coughs out between chuckles, smoothing the tablecloth with the heels of her hands to avoid using her sticky fingers.

"Thank God this table's legs lock when it's opened, or we'd be eating off the floor. Och, goodness, my royal prince, what a delicious mess you've made! And we mustn't waste a blob of it," Mathilde savors the frosting as she wipes it from her shoulders.

Ivan cocks his head at her facetious tone and stares at us humans licking our paws and scooping white stuff from each other. We reposition our place settings with our hands—limp from deep belly laughs.

Maman looks over her spectacles at her drooling comrade and teases, "Looking for your share of sweet stuff from me, mon grand bébé?"

Ivan smacks his lips, moaning his readiness for duty, but when a treat isn't forthcoming fast enough, he turns and looks eagerly at his triumphant little prince, eyeball to eyeball. As if on cue Pierre giggles and babbles an incoherent edict, leans forward to bless his canine subject, and stretches his tiny hands toward Ivan's large quivering pink tongue. The Dane obediently licks his majesty's sticky fingers, tickling them clean with noisy ceremonial slurps.

Maman shushes the Dane back under the table. After a brief pause Pierre squeals his delight once more to see if he can garner another round of canine and adult attention. Ivan's ears can't stand the shrillness. He groans and howls under the table.

Instantly Marie and I grab the gate-leg. Still laughing, Guy presses down on its two leaves to keep our sweets grounded.

"Oh God, not again!" Maman smiles.

Marta slides the cake a little further out of Pierre's range before he fingers it a third time. Sylvia smiles, cleaning the dog's slobber from her son's hands.

Marie passes kitchen towels to everyone and declares,

"He's royalty all right! Our little prince makes trouble everywhere he goes."

"Like pissing on the enemy," Sylvia snickers, winking at Madame Mathilde.

"He made a bull's eye at his first public target practice!" Mathilde shoots back.

"Pardon me, Grandmaman, but that was not our prince's royal début, but his climax. The first target in his sport of spritzing was Marie's chest at the Nazi checkpoint," Marta winks.

"Oh my God! He committed infant precipitation under SS scrutiny? Quite a risk, eh Marta?" Maman keeps the humor going without missing a beat.

"Indeed, Madame Mathilde, his canal overflowed its banks onto *moi*," Marie titters.

Mathilde, inspired by our merriment, announces, "Is that so! Well, such Olympic prowess requires a formal commendation. Ladies and Gentleman, attend your teacups!"

We refill with steaming hot chocolate and await her command.

"All rise!" she intones, with a mischievous grin. We obey, pouring love upon our birthday boy, who looks up adoringly. We raise our cups as Maman declares with regimental pride, "My fellow Résistants, today we ask God's forbearance as we enjoy a bit of humor in this dreadful war. And so we honor this royal bébé who fired his weapon and subdued our enemy with all he had, his fountain of youth! To Pierre!"

"To Pierre! Vive la France!' We echo, laughing between sips.

"En garde!" Guy finishes softly, for we must stay vigilant.

Chapter Sixteen

Mission at the Hotel LaFrance

10 May 1944, Wednesday

A t times Dieter gives me coded messages in public places. My instructions for future crossings are hidden in discussions about Marta's musicianship. We think no one who overhears us guesses their real content.

Today, on a beautiful Wednesday in May 1944, he meets me in the local music shop. We discuss my successful confession with Fr. Beauverger while we look through sheet music on the rear shelves, obscured from view of the cashier up front.

"She's playing quite well now. Her style is very convincing since she expresses herself more freely, n'est-ce pas?"

"Yes, indeed, Dieter, but it's been hard for her to achieve fluency. Practice makes perfect, they say. Although she still prefers quiet études to loud demonstrative works," which means my confession to Beauverger was a passable performance. Then I catch a serious tone in Dieter's voice as he announces a new bit of intrigue—despite being unhappy with my lack of enthusiasm.

"By the way, I have a new piece for her. She's earned this one."

"Oh, really? Should I get it now?" I'm curious.

"No, I've ordered it from out of town. It will arrive in three days' time. I'll have it by her next lesson but she'll need to learn it in less than two weeks. This new one will be most difficult to master. In the end it will require a flawless public recital in a new location."

"What? A *public* recital in a *new* location?" I grab his forearm. Anxiety freezes my thoughts and the word 'public' impales my solar plexus.

In a rush to interpret Dieter's words my eyes blur, scanning the alphabetical titles of sheet music under "R" for Requiem: Bach, Handel, and Mozart. The threat of a dreadful event walks me around a familiar corner to a dark passage ahead. Is this metaphor for death what Guy's "en garde" was referring to? But whose demise, Dieter's, or mine?

I want to crumble at his pronouncement and whisper,

"Please, Dieter, don't tell me something like this in public."

My hand still clutches his arm and begins the familiar shaking right here in the shop. Dieter sees the color drain from my face.

"Hold on, Ingrid. You need some air. Let me take you outside."

He must wonder why I go limp so suddenly. He's always escorting me to something. Last time it was on the muddy river. No, it was the cemetery at Emil's grave the afternoon we escaped detection in the car. I look down at my body, helpless to stop its trembling, and can't breathe deeply enough to control it. I start to hyperventilate.

Nodding quickly to the store clerk Dieter steers me outside around the corner to the quiet side alley.

"Ouch. Stop pinching me, Dieter. All right, thank you. I'm sorry, but when you say I have to go out in public with him . . . I fall apart. I need support, not a more dangerous ruse."

As I look up at his face Dieter pulses his own fear from his hand into my arm. Now he pretends to be calm, which really worries me. Finally I take a few long breaths to feel a little restored. He forces a nonchalant adieu, worried about people in the street watching us. He walks away briskly to his bicycle as I return to my car.

I subdue my avalanche of worry in the minutes it takes to drive to Dieter's door. I dig in my purse for lavender salts and take a whiff before entering. For Marta's sake, I must act poised in the Van der Kreuzier home. Dieter ushers me into their cozy parlor. Amélie has just taken Marta to the garden to pick early spring flowers. We talk alone.

At first we sit in forced silence. He smokes his pipe and I sip a small glass of kirsch. The afternoon sun is low. The evening air from the mountains begins to chill. The room fills with the rich deep cherry aroma of his tobacco and the essence of Amélie's herb-filled stew.

I feel lonely sitting here, envious of Dieter's marriage, the loving intimacy of his home life, his strength, self-confidence, and manly self-control. He makes me resentful of the comfortable ambiance he and Amélie share. It doesn't combine well with my lonely widow's urgency to protect myself.

My resolve is crushed and a gnawing reminder surfaces. I resisted serving the Underground once, and when I returned to follow orders, my dreaded concubinage became worse. Dieter's pensive mood rubs my nerves raw. He's taking too long to choose his words.

"Ingrid, you'll have to go out of your house with Mueller if he asks you."

"Why? What's going to happen?" I feel uneasy about Mueller's increasing sadism. I haven't confided my suspicion that Franz knows about the basement operation.

Dieter studies my reaction. Behind his stoic façade I know he wrestles with my jeopardy. Does it make him sick at heart to imagine the indignity? So demoralized by the affair I no longer care whether Mueller suspects me of double-dealing. Dieter understands, but apathy like mine has caused others in the Underground to lose vigilance and become careless. They make serious mistakes and ultimately are arrested and deported.

"Do you think they suspect Stefan because of me? Surely, they know who he is, Dieter." I rub my hands nervously.

"Sorry, Ingrid, are you feeling cold?"

"No, just anxious. What do you think about Stefan?"

"He's well hidden right now. Just concentrate on your own safety."

The truth passes through our minds. Rumor is the Nazis think Stefan finished off Heisler. They would love to arrest him. Germany is losing badly. The Russians are advancing, and the Allies are a few days from liberating Rome. The SS avoid detaining people now and simply ship them east where they disappear into thin air, more Nacht und Nebel. If they suspect Stefan—naturally, I'm next on their list.

Dieter has already hinted concern for Amélie. She's too jumpy lately; it's not like her. Something is brewing. She probably knows and won't tell him.

"Ingrid, no one's sure exactly what will happen—except the war is winding down. The Americans will arrive shortly. We've heard this from England. Once they land in France the Maquis will strengthen, and the Boches will retreat. De Gaulle will return to lead The Free French Forces and we will see more chaos. The Krauts will lash out with more reprisals at local groups and then run away to fight on the Rhine. The local Milice's power depends upon which Nazi is in charge. Mueller's our burden. We watch him day and night."

Dieter doesn't tell me, but I guess Berlin badgers Obersturmführer Mueller for being lazy. Jews and Maquisard saboteurs continue to escape through his territory. He may be arranging to catch me and lure our Underground connections into a trap to expose Dieter. A big show for Berlin would earn him a promotion. Mueller will sacrifice anyone to save his booty, even make a blood bath to win clout with his superiors. It's a possibility that can't be substantiated nor overlooked. As a rule, Dieter won't discuss rumors that would frighten me. When I've already heard them, his reluctance means they are true, making me twice as nervous.

"My sources say Mueller wants to meet you for a luncheon at the LaFrance."

"Oh no, Dieter." I stand as if to run away and spill the last few sips of kirsch.

He puts down his pipe and sits on the edge of the sofa. Poor man, he tries to deliver his instructions casually, but I begin to tremble again.

"Wait, Ingrid, please, be calm. Sit down, please."

"The Gestapo is setting me up to be arrested in public. Isn't that it, Dieter? They could have arrested me at any time. They just didn't do it in my house because it would raise French eyebrows. The Huns can't afford to mistreat us French. Our hatred toward Nazis will garner sympathy from our fellow Frenchmen, even for me, the town pariah."

"No, I don't think that's it, Ingrid. . . ."

"Tell me the truth, then, Dieter. I must prepare, be resigned to deportation, lose my child, my family, Maman. What will Mueller do? Ship me to Ravensbrück? Or all of us?"

I bite my lip to force back tears when I catch sight of Marta through the side parlor window. Would Dieter take the same risk if his sons were as young and vulnerable? Would he feel as I do, staring at my daughter, the flesh of my flesh, so innocent? Running away would solidify Nazi suspicion. He thinks I overreact. He can't feel my pain or see my scars.

I sit down again, composed. I know he can't answer for future risks. He continues with instructions and holds my cold hands. He feels my pulse race and can't look me in the eye. He has to believe I'll come through this alive.

"Ingrid, if he asks, you will do it."

"Oh no, Dieter. I'm afraid to be with him there. So many old acquaintances I don't trust. I'm afraid of everyone's anger. I thought we handled their speculation with the confession."

"So did I. I'm not sure if this plan comes from the Gestapo or the Milice. You'll be safe from public eyes because Mueller has a private dining room."

"Is that safer? Maybe it's better to be seen so the Résistance can be alerted to come to my aid." Dieter shakes his head at how fast I think on my feet. I'm disturbed that the thought didn't occur to him first.

"Yes, probably. We have people inside the hotel. We'll do our best, Ingrid. Eat outside if it's a warm day. Ingratiate yourself to any old friends who might be there. Take your pistol."

"I'll do anything to stay alive, Dieter. Should I let Mueller have sex?" He blushes.

"I don't know, Ingrid. Plan for every contingency. Be alert to act."

"Perhaps it would soften him if he plans to arrest me."

"Ingrid, arresting you in public makes you an example in front of others he also suspects. He will watch everyone's reaction. Being singled out in the midst of your social class will alienate you even more. It may be another of his nasty little tests."

Dieter's cheeks color more deeply and then pale as he looks away. I know he thinks about my future and hesitates to say anything when I must offer myself to Nazi scum. He sees how distraught I am and is unable to say the obvious, so I do.

"If I go, I'm courting death. If I don't, it's a clear admission I'm a spy, right Dieter?"

"Perhaps, Ingrid."

"*Perhaps?* Oh please, all the times the SS have been in my home and I thought I was in control, I've been kidding myself. I've had no protection. It was an illusion. The Nazis justify their association with me because I'm the wealthy widow of a former German national. To accuse Mueller of rape would stir up more scandal in a town that already stands against me. My scarred flesh is real only to me, not you, not anyone else!" I watch his expression to see if what I say penetrates his scheming.

"How will you provide protection if the SS surround the hotel? The Maquisards will be caught with me when they enter. If I leave in full view of enough patrons the SS won't touch me. But there's no path leading directly from la terrasse to the road. If I have to go back through the lobby to the parking area the Résistance has to protect me. I'll be alone."

He's listening but says nothing.

I plead now, "Dieter, I have to know if the Résistance in the hotel will be told I am one of them. They hate me everywhere I go. I'm as uneasy with them as I am with the Gestapo."

"Ingrid, go to this luncheon and triumph. You will be blessed with safekeeping."

"Not unless you guarantee it. Look, I'll do anything to stay alive for Marta's sake. It's because of her that I haven't. . . ."

"Haven't *what*, Ingrid?"

"Um, ah. . . ." I can't finish the sentence, and mumble into my lap, head down, voice quivering. His eyes widen as I look up and feel his guilt as he stares at me.

"My God, woman, I did not know you had even *thought* of taking your life."

He realizes how profoundly disturbed I am. Red in the face, I catch myself. I don't want to slip up any further.

"Ingrid, why are you thinking like this?" he asks cautiously.

"It's about the Maquisard failure at Glière, six weeks ago, Dieter. Maquis against Vichy, French against French. Finished off by a Wehrmacht reprisal. All dead. You say ignore reprisals. Focus on what happens in Duchamps or I'll defeat myself. I'm already defeated, Dieter."

"No you're not, Ingrid. That simply isn't true," but his voice holds doubt.

A tear drops. I stifle the other tears, and rise to call from the open window, hoping my voice isn't tremulous, "Marta, we're leaving, mon ange." She turns and waves, smiling.

Dieter walks me to the front door. I sense a shift in his heart. His thoughts are heavy. Marta appears in the hall as he leans over to whisper in my ear, "May God be with you, Ingrid, and La Bonne Jeanne protect you. Am I forgiven for how I have undone your life?"

"Sois sérieuse, mon ami! Are you asking me now in case I don't survive the next two weeks?" I whisper as he leans his ear to my lips and Marta skips ahead to the door.

I laugh to suppress my nerves. My eyes mirror his pensiveness in their hopeful, trusting gaze. I shouldn't pull more uncertainty from him because we are about to undergo a terrible test. We'll need to concentrate on the work ahead without our feelings in the way. He has become too fond of me, and I fear we will both make mistakes now.

Two weeks later Marta and I take a hike. It's a glorious spring morning except somewhere in the distance the war continues. We're oblivious, strolling in the rear fields of my mother's estate where it's quiet. Birdcalls and the "moos" of her lonely *vache*, Marianne, echo through the gentle mountain breeze. Maman kept Marianne, her favorite lead *cow*, when she voluntarily sold her cheese herd in 1941. Too many workers with dubious Pétainesque leanings were needed to keep a large herd pastured and milked, so she kept only a few Underground farmhands willing to switch jobs—and grow food—for the Maquis in her clandestine enterprise.

What will tomorrow bring? My baby may be an orphan after this luncheon at the LaFrance. The idea of losing her . . . cuts like a knife. God wouldn't do that. Too many years restoring her health have brought us so close. I put away such thoughts, but can't hide deep anxiety from my little scamp.

Marta walks so well now. Even on this uneven terrain she moves fairly quickly, hardly limping when relaxed. She chatters away about everything she sees. I listen to the music in her voice and engrave each word in my heart: "Maman, where are you? So far away . . . you aren't listening."

"Forgive me, Marta, sweet angel." I gather her in my arms and hug her, and twirl us both round and round. I drink in her fresh fragrant hair and kiss the smooth silken skin of her cheeks. The strong tight muscles in her thin arms flex as we embrace. I bury my face in her neck. Warm tears form in my eyes. My prayer, unspoken, "Please, God, don't let me lose my life and this child. I've lost so much already. Please, let me live past Tuesday." I cling to Marta spontaneously and force myself to release her. She senses it.

"What's wrong, Maman? You're sad. I feel it in your thoughts. You're afraid, aren't you? Why? Tell me, please, Maman. Let me help you."

I put her down and turn away for a second to brace myself, and come back from the future into present time, her time. "I'm fine, a little fatigued from the walk. Let's eat here."

We have carried a picnic basket with lentil paté, fresh strawberries and green salad from Maman's garden, cheese from the neighboring farmer, bread made from secretly grown mountain barley, a cup of Michelle's mirabelle plum jam and a thermos of hot chocolate, courtesy of the SS. This feast will reward our legs and stomachs. We're blessed to have local food. Parisians stand in ration lines for every mouthful.

We spread the blanket near a spot protected from the wind. Sunshine streams down onto nearby boulders to radiate warmth. Marta watches every move I make. I'm too silent. She knows something serious is about to happen. Perhaps she eavesdropped at the door last week when Mueller mentioned the luncheon? I can't bring myself to discuss the specifics.

We eat in silence for several minutes. Then she says, very tactfully, in a matter-of-fact way, "I know every time you send me to Grandmaman, you're doing something so dangerous you can't be sure you'll live through it. And you love me too much to tell me. It's all right. I've known from the beginning. I've already seen too much in the house with the Gestapo and the basement. I love you, Maman. Do what is right to help others, like you helped me wake up and walk. You'll be fine and so will I. Don't worry so much."

I put down my barley tartine and smile. Marta takes pride in outsmarting me. She reaches over and gives me a sweet mirabelle-jam kiss, and laughs. It's tempting to be like her, apparently without a care or a worry, but I don't trust her childish façade. I'm certain she cries herself to sleep some nights as I do. She's too mature for her age, made so by her father's sudden demise and her struggle to walk in a Nazi world infused with our imminent death. Damn this war for making her childhood so unnatural. We speak no more about tomorrow.

The rest of the afternoon we play and walk, examine late spring flowers, insects hatching, and flower buds opening on the fruit trees. I'm grateful our Jura landscape is still pristine when a few hundred kilometers north the terrain is uprooted and bloodied. We trek full circle, and rejoice in nature before we arrive back at the house. I bid her goodbye and send her off with Sylvia and Pierre.

Alone, I give my Maman a long, tearful embrace and then drive to town to face an uncertain future.

Chapter Seventeen

The Luncheon

23 May 1944, Tuesday

I dress for the occasion. If I'm going to be arrested why not be arrayed in my upper class finery? I wear a favorite dark-green, silk dress from the days Emil and I attended afternoon social events. I include the brooch Mueller returned. I hope I look attractive despite the loose drape of the dress. Marie critiques my choices as I pose in front of the armoire mirror.

"Use more make-up, Madame, lipstick and pancake. You're too pale," she fusses.

"It's enough decoration for this late date in the war, Marie."

"No it's not, Madame. Most people at the hotel haven't seen you in public for years."

She won't soft-pedal my war-weary look from hard evenings entertaining the SS.

"And what else does my couturier demand?" I say nervously, with a scalding laugh.

"This contrasting sash will let the dress gather at the waist and offset how much thinner you are now, Madame," Marie clucks, ignoring my resentment. I follow her directions; then slip into a lovely pair of heels I've not worn in years. Their lift revives my regal hauteur, but instantly I'm reprimanded.

"You can't wear those, Madame. They're not appropriate. Wear these lower heels."

"Marie, this is a luncheon at a hotel, not a hike on the road. Those are too matronly."

"But high heels will be useless walking through clods of fresh manure in the moonlight."

"What do you mean, Marie? That's ridiculous." But her intention is more real than mine.

"Madame, if you're taking a pistol, then utility will be more important than style. You have no idea what's going to happen. You must be prepared. Don't argue with me."

Despite our affection, we are bitchy and nervous when we part company—afraid to face the real possibility we may never meet again as free people.

With Guy it's worse. At the hotel he stands (with red-rimmed eyes) by my car door as I exit. He appears afraid for me. I speak with my head down.

"Go back to Madame Mathilde and wait, Guy. Bless you and Marie. Pray for me."

He takes my hand and squeezes it tenderly, wanting to kiss it. Such gentility would be unacceptable for a chauffeur discharging his mistress to her destination. "Good luck, Madame Henri," he says. "La Bonne Jeanne will protect you."

I swallow his blessing and steel myself to enter the lobby. Mueller is conferring with the front desk staff and is forced to acknowledge me. The concierge raises his eyebrows. Mueller quickly comes to my side and guides me out of earshot. He offers the private dining room—as Dieter said he would.

I decide to be gracious and innocent, "But it's a glorious sunny day for luncheon outdoors. *Bitte, Liebster*, please dearest?"

I touch his arm coyly and head down the open corridor without waiting for a response. He's uncomfortable demurring to an impetuous female. As we walk to the terrace entrance he stresses in a whisper, "Mein Schatz, it's better not to be seen together publicly."

I surprise him by flirting. "Oh Franz, you silly man. After all I've suffered from my foolish friends who ostracize me because of our association. Why not go public at this late hour? I've nothing to fear when I'm with you. You're my protector, oui?"

I look up at him and smile broadly, lying through my teeth. Maybe he'll forget about arresting me if I charm him with irresistible sensuality. He looks down and I sense the lust rise in his groin. The beast wants me here and now. His French coquette tortures him and he obeys her with public solemnity, "As you wish, my dear Ingrid."

I make my way around the wide veranda with my heart pounding in my chest. I'm hopeful I will survive this meal, safe as his mistress. I head for a table for two near a group of six diners at the far end. A businessman from the bank, a Préfecture bureaucrat, a head of the agricultural district and several winery merchants: they are all petty aristocrats who eat freely while they sell out Duchamps' dairy industry to the enemy. I recognize Germaine's husband, Édouard deVillement, Vice President of the bank holding my accounts. The others look familiar from the days when Emil was alive—but I'm too nervous and angry to remember their names. People sit at small tables around them. I point to a vacant one. Mueller is visibly distressed with this arrangement. I sense it and feel good about controlling the seating at least.

"How lovely to sit outdoors, don't you agree, Obersturmführer?"

I hide my panic perusing the menu, as deVillement encroaches on my thoughts.

"Good afternoon, Obersturmführer Mueller, and you, Madame Fellner, this is a rare pleasure." I look up at Édouard's leering eyes and immediately force myself to play the part.

"Édouard, so nice to see you. Regards to Germaine." DeVillement plants a wet kiss on my dutifully extended hand. He curdles my appetite as I recall our unsavory history.

"Yes, we hope to see you soon for a musical evening. It's been too long since we've had the pleasure of your beautiful voice, Ingrid. Au revoir you two, bon appetit!"

Édouard nods to Mueller as he turns to leave and murmurs to the Obersturmführer under his breath. That's odd. Mueller nods back without comment as though something known but not expressed passes between them. I realize how insulated I've been in my home, unable to observe the Nazi machine wield its power over rich Frenchmen, even bankers.

Meanwhile the crowd fills the surrounding tables. I'm desperate to see a familiar face. Germaine and Agnes enter just as I give up. They don't see me at first and sit only two tables away. Germaine's back is to Franz. Then Agnes recognizes me and rises instantly. Germaine turns to see where she's going. She's taken aback seeing me in public with Mueller. Her face gives her away but Agnes doesn't care. She greets us both cordially,

"Good afternoon, Obersturmführer, you look well, sir, and hello, dear Ingrid! It's so wonderful to see you out and about. How are you?"

"I'm fine, thank you, Agnes. A lovely day for a luncheon outdoors, don't you think?"

We engage in a brief conversation and Mueller joins in reluctantly. I hope it's worth it. Perhaps he'll call off his arrest. We're so polite and civilized. If I stay put until the end of this meal I might have a chance to get away unharmed.

The luncheon proceeds. We order, the food comes, and we're eating our dessert when Germaine finally passes by. It kills her to be civil, but apparently Agnes chewed her ear through their meal so she has no choice.

"You're looking quite well, Ingrid dear, and how is your darling little girl? You certainly have done wonders with her. She walks quite confidently these days. I see her negotiate curbs and cobblestones so easily. She twirls her cane more than she uses it."

"How nice of you to notice her progress, Germaine. We worked hard for three years to get her off crutches. By the way, have you met Obersturmführer Mueller?"

I introduce them. Germaine contains her enmity. After she departs I say,

"You see, Franz, they finally accept my choices and realize Germans are good people. I was married to a German before the war. German men are so strong and decisive."

Mueller squirms as he squints at the sun and picks his teeth nervously. I surrender my exhausted mind to the possibility that he's not in control anymore. He must have orders to expose me. His cat and mouse game has gone on too long. No arrests for weeks will force him to stir his pot for victims now. I hate myself for entertaining this idea when my nerves tell me to stay calm. Instead I make a fatal mistake and play my trump card when he excuses himself to use the men's toilette.

"I'll wait, darling," I demur. "Then we can find a private room for a sweeter dessert."

I give a sexy look, to arouse him. He's confused. When he leaves the terrace, I know he's up to no good. He walks ahead and quickly turns in the wrong direction for the men's room. Oh God, what have I done?

Do I stay—or leave through the garden and risk enraging him? I could be arrested if I stay. How stupid to suggest going upstairs. He's probably arranging to take me into custody in the bedchamber. They will remove me without anyone knowing. Either way it's hopeless. At least Marta's safe and I helped a few poor Jews find freedom. I take comfort in that if nothing else. Hopefully, when I am deported, someone will speak up for my daughter and me. Maman will stand behind Sylvia and Pierre.

I look up from second-guessing my future. Mueller stands before me again. My mind is mired in my lunch.

"Let's go upstairs, mein Schatz," he says eagerly.

He helps me from my chair and leads me out. We head for the elevator. I'm panicky but appear calm. We pass the bellboy, desk clerk, and concierge. I study their faces, hoping one of them will save me. They appear indifferent and ignorant of what is about to happen.

Franz is very excited and paws at me in the tiny, wire-screened *l'ascenseur*. I suppose he's called off his dogs for the moment or at least until we finish having sex. Ah yes, he'll take what he wishes first and then get rid of me. We enter the bedroom suite. It's large and elegant with beautiful drapes and matching bed linens, clean and wholesome, unlike the scenario about to unfold.

He closes the blinds and stares at me with his ugly, lascivious grin. His full wet lower lip curls outward in a low whistle. He laughs and mocks me as he unbuckles his belt and removes his pants. A tremor runs through me every time he demands I look at his naked genitalia. I must tread lightly. By now, I know what he likes. Perhaps if I play to him he'll get so excited I can distract him from hurting me—and just get on with it. There's nothing in this room he can use to hurt me. I perform my usual act and soon he's thrusting like a machine.

Then the door latch releases slowly. I hear it but say nothing. Someone slips in quietly. I don't know who it is or what side he's on. The doorway area is in shadow. I can't see a uniform. My head is propped up on a pillow. Between the heavings of Mueller's shoulders, I glimpse a piece of shiny metal across the room by the door. A small pistol, perhaps?

I don't keep up the pace. My mind runs in circles. Mueller turns me onto my stomach so my back is to the door. He strikes my buttocks with open hands and fists and turns me over to face him again, never detaching. The pain is frightening. If I don't fake moans of orgasm, he will be more violent, but if I let myself feel this disgrace, I will lose my self-control. If I push and beat on him, he'll consume me with greater brutality. My mind strays to images of loved ones as I await my payment: arrest or worse.

A single shot is fired and suddenly my ears fill with a dull sound of metal penetrating thick flesh. Franz collapses onto me. Blood oozes from his back. Thick droplets roll down onto my shoulders and the crisp white bed linens. His dead weight is crushing. I'm being buried alive and scream. Instantly a hand covers my mouth, and Mueller's body gets pushed to one side.

It's eerie to see him so still when moments ago he was at the height of animal energy. I close his eyelids with my fingertips at the nauseating sight of his corpse with its eyes wide open. Then I look away to heave what little lunch I did eat into his pooled blood.

I turn to see a gunman who tells me to shut up and aims his pistol at my temple. I dress hurriedly, unable to recognize the masked assassin—who is wearing a butcher's smock. What side is he on? What will happen next?

The killer shifts his glance back and forth from me to Mueller's body. I move toward the bathroom to wash out my sour mouth and scrub Mueller's blood from my shoulders and arms. The gunman follows with his pistol against my spine, and says gruffly, "You, whore, we'll deal with you quite differently."

He pinches my buttocks very hard. I cry out, "*Aye*. Who are you? Résistance?" His rude behavior is oddly disrespectful for a member of the Underground, even if he suspects I am a collaborator.

"You slept with the enemy, Madame, you're a traitor." Is he SS or Maquis? I take a risk.

"No, I'm not. I'm one of you but you don't understand, young man. You know Stefan, the red head?" His French has no Fritzie accent.

"Yes, so what?" He releases his hurtful grasp as I calm him. Now I think he's Résistance.

"I'm his belle-mère. He thinks I'm in collusion with the Gestapo but I'm not. This affair is a front to avoid suspicion. I hide Jews by day and they cross at night."

"You do *what?*"

I shouldn't have said anything. He's too surprised. He must be German.

"You heard me."

"You're lying."

He leans over and I see a military collar under his smock. He's a Boche? I've said too much. Did he mean to kill Mueller? There's no time. I'll lure him home. I still have my gun.

"Come with me and I'll show you. Let me go home to safety, please."

Am I speaking too fast for this young abductor? He sweats and is shaky. Maybe he'll be sick. The right hand that holds his pistol drops to his side. Who is his superior? Mueller, who's dead? Is he Milice—or did Berlin send a child to do the devil's work?

He fixes his eyes on Mueller's corpse. I clothe myself and speak with urgency, but to no avail. "Please, let's get out of here before they come to kill us, understand?" Then I grab his shoulders.

He's startled and says unconsciously, almost innocently, "I've been told to kill you because you're a traitor. You lay with the Obersturmführer."

"Well, maybe whoever told you is an infiltrator and the Nazis are out to get us both. Come on. Let's get out of here. Move, damn it!"

I've revealed my life and sealed my fate like an idiot. Despite that my head feels clear, though my throat is dry. I hurry to finish dressing.

The young murderer listens by the door and calls out, "Merde!"

"What is it?" I whisper.

"They're coming down the hall."

"Here, quick!" I rush toward the window, open it and motion to him. "Follow me and close the window!" I still don't know who this young man is but he's strangely obedient.

Feeling my way carefully, I step out onto the upper-story window ledge and reach for a trellis thick with wisteria and ivy. My dress is unbuttoned so my legs swing wide as I half-jump to the trellis. It sways and jerks violently but holds my weight. My purse is over my shoulder. There's neither time nor opportunity to use a gun. Quickly, I scramble down to the ground and drop behind a hedge. The young man follows.

"Did you close the window behind you? I didn't hear it." He looks so scared.

"No, why?"

"Never mind, it's too late now. Sshh, they're upstairs. Get under the bushes and don't move a muscle. Be sure they can't see you from above."

We slither under a large yew and wait. Gestapo voices fill the air above us.

"Do you see anything?"

"No, sir."

"Shoot the bushes."

"We've commandeered the hotel, sir. We have Vichy locals in here. It will attract attention."

"Do it!"

A volley of gunfire rains down into the shrubbery. The young man is hit and dies instantly. I can do nothing for him. He's covered in blood from wounds to the back and head. Suddenly it's very quiet. I bite my lip and strain to hear.

"We must have gotten them, sir. Shall we go down and get the bodies?"

"Yes, in a few minutes. First, we see to Mueller and the luncheon crowd."

All this for an arrest? I have to get out of here. There's no time to search his pockets. I'm so confused. Why did I reveal so much?

I scan the wall of barberry bushes with impenetrable thorns that will cut me to pieces, and look for an opening between them and the yews. Frantic for a way out, I have to crawl underneath the yews next to the wall. The old shrubs are so dense their low boughs catch my hair as I drag myself slowly. I perspire profusely, scared and claustrophobic, pushing aside the smaller under branches and breaking off dead twigs. My slip fills with dirt and dry yew needles scratch and tear my arms, shoulders and breasts.

Sheer terror wipes my mind blank as I drag myself alongside the building. I hear a tapping sound nearby and freeze. The corner of my eye catches a movement. Someone's watching me through a basement window. Startled, I stifle a cry of alarm before recognizing the face of Marie's friend Annette, the hotel baker and pastry chef.

She opens the window and reaches out to me, "Give me your hand. Maybe you can slip through. You're safe with me, Madame Henri. Come. Quickly."

I can't believe what's happening. I press my body against the hard window frame and reach for her hands. Kind words from this woman who barely knows me unravel my fright and desperation. My body goes limp like a lump of her dough. I sink into shock with my torso caught halfway through the window.

"Igor! Come here! Help me." I hear Annette call and feel huge hands on my shoulders. I'm dragged into the rising room. Between panic and the yeasty warmth I nearly pass out.

Igor brushes the earth outside of the open window with a broom and scatters a few leaves to make it look untouched. He bolts the window tightly and pulls down the shade. Annette douses my face with cold water, examines my wounds and the bloodstains on my dress.

"He's dead. The young man's dead. They'll find me next. You can't risk your lives. I must get out of here." Verging on hysteria, I recount what happened.

"You can't leave now, Madame. The hotel is crawling with Doryphores. We'll hide you." Annette turns to Igor. He's about to return to the main kitchen to check on the Germans.

Thinking on her feet she says, "Wait Igor, open the other window and break new growth from the yew that leads to the open garden. If they question us, we can say we heard a sound from over there. When they open that window and see the broken twigs in the garden they'll be convinced she escaped that way."

"Here," I offer, tearing off a piece of my dress and slip, "take these and place them on the lawn under the trees in a direct line from that shrubbery."

"Oh, and this too," says Annette.

"No, please, not the jewelry."

"Sorry, Madame, that's the best clue we can leave them. We must use it." I'm too upset not to give in to Annette's authoritarian tone. She hands Igor the brooch.

"Hurry Igor. We only have a few minutes."

I feel defeated and so numb I barely notice the bee stings on my arms from the wisteria. Annette offers me a sip of brandy. She rubs my shoulders and combs the hair from my face.

"Madame, you're safe here. We'll hide you. Think what's best for you now. If they go to your home you shouldn't be there until tomorrow. Will they go to your mother's in the country?"

"How do you know about my mother's estate?" I see her hesitate to answer. Maybe she can't tell me, but then she says, "Marie and Guy helped me cater large parties for your mother years ago. It's easier to get you inside her place. Gestapo and Milice will crawl all over your mansion to find you. Marie and Guy will handle them. Don't worry. Where's your daughter, Marta?"

"In the country with my mother. I told her I'd meet her later. I can get onto my mother's property from several entrances. Why are you asking all this?"

"We have to get you out of the hotel this evening. Don't worry. We'll transport you. But you'll have to be absolutely silent the whole time. Not a sound, you understand. If you sneeze or cough, you'll be discovered and all of us will be exposed."

"Oui, I understand. Annette, you're another link in the chain of crossings. This hotel and these grounds, right under their noses."

In my warmed state, the liquor has brought me back to earth. How cleverly Dieter created the intertwining of circles of Underground members so that no one knows the whole pathway.

Igor barges into the room out of breath. "Quickly Annette, I have to get her into the closet. They're coming down the stairs to the front kitchen."

The two of them move a huge old breakfront storing baking utensils and spices. Magically, it splits into three pieces to reveal a small doorway. Igor stoops down to clear his head and leads me through the portal. I follow him down a long, narrow passageway and a few more stairs. My fingertips guide me along the rough rock and plaster walls. My stomach turns, touching sticky old spider webs and entombed insect prey. Finally we enter a tiny, stagnant, nearly pitch-black room with dim light from a dirt-encrusted window.

"Why don't you have a lamp in here?" I ask, nervous that the dim light will disappear when the sun goes down in a few minutes.

"Can't risk the smell; kerosene would give you away, Madame. I don't have a battery torch." Igor takes me by the hand to feel the closet door.

"Here." He puts a knife and gun into my hands and guides me to a table next to the wall.

"Oh no. Where is my purse? My gun is in it."

"Don't worry, Madame. Annette has it. It's safe. We've done this before. Now, get into this closet." He guides my hands over the wooden door's latch.

"Watch your head; stay down low by this doorway. Pull the little table in front of it. Here, reach down and feel that old barrel under the table?

Take that old keg in there with you. Place it right inside the door. And please, don't stand on it.

"Then, open the upper slat that feels like a ceiling. It conceals an upper chamber. Hide inside there. They will stop looking for you before that but get into it to be safe. You'll stay there only a few minutes. Let us get rid of them. We'll come back to get you. Do not open the door for anyone. I'm sorry, I can't help you with the keg, I must return to Annette."

"Uh, oui, merci," I finally utter. I'm bewildered, concentrating on Igor's words to orient me in the increasing darkness.

"Please, be careful." He leaves abruptly.

Alone, I try to memorize the space in this black hole. I figure out where everything is in the semi-dark—the table, door, and keg. I'm fine, until crouching to get inside the closet elicits my claustrophobic fear. My throat closes. My brain goes blank. My flesh panics. I gulp air to swallow against the tightness. My body refuses to hide on the shelf inside the closet above the ceiling.

The reaction is uncontrollable. My nerves are on fire for air, light and space. They rush me back out of the room. I hobble down the narrow passage in my stockinged feet. My hands recoil from touching the sticky cobwebs again on either side of the rough plaster walls. Oh God, I can't exhale! I must get out of here, now!

Five meters from the passage exit I see the rising room light under the door. I stop. I'm safe. Annette pounds dough as she kneads her bread. Igor groans. He must be lifting the heavy flour sacks.

But then I hear a commotion. Two booted Gestapo agents enter the rear room.

"Halt! Achtung! Stop you two!"

I wince as Annette says flatly with an edge of sarcasm, "The hotel's bread can't stop rising, even for the Third Reich, gentlemen."

"Watch your tongue, old woman. And you there, what's in those sacks?"

Igor plays innocent, "Just flour for your bread, officers. What's the matter?"

"You tell us. Where is she?"

"Who is *she*? What do you mean?" Igor replies with disinterest.

"The woman, the owner of this." An SS must be holding something for them to look at.

Oh God, maybe it's my brooch?

"Sshh!" The other officer corrects him, "Make them talk. You can't trust these Jacquies, they're Underground, all of them."

"Ja! Let's see those sacks."

"Oh no, please don't. We can't waste it."

The SS must have spiked them with his bayonet. Annette sounds upset. I have to get out of here. Merde! I must return to my horror chamber but can't move. My body is so lifeless I can hardly feel myself in it.

Then a Nazi voice asks, "And this? What's in it?" In the silence he waits for an answer. I hear tapping fingernails run along the breakfront's seams, and squirm when he hollers, "Separate them!"

I force myself to turn around and muster enough strength to save myself.

I hear Igor say, nonchalantly, "It's an old building, officers. No one uses these spaces anymore."

"You will lead the way then, old man." The Nazi raises his voice. Oh no, I hear the sound of a hammer cocked—is the Nazi aiming at Igor?

I take deep breaths to hobble quickly back to my den. My stockings tear against the rough dirty floor. They will be cut to ribbons. I keep smacking into the walls on either side.

I grit my teeth not to cry out in pain when I hear a distant, "Ah hah. Ja, now we'll find her."

I close the door to my mausoleum, and grope blindly, remembering the tiny closet door. I hear a lot of movement. The Nazis march down the inner hallway, opening side doors and calling my name into other rooms. This progression of opened and closed doors grows louder as it comes closer. The SS are annoyed, and growl about the cobwebs and filth. Their voices become angry. My life is about to be undone.

They haven't found Madame Henri yet . . . but they'll find *me* passed out in this stifling chamber, choking on its musty, yeasty air. I grab the table leg and crawl backward into the small hole. I pull in the large keg and, desperate for air, leave the doorway open a crack. Inside the closet I'm covered in sweat, but well hidden. Then I hear closer footsteps.

Oh, no—wait. The knife and gun are on the table. I forgot them. And my shoes! Where the hell are my *shoes*?

I scramble back out and search frantically. It's pitch-black in here now. Daylight no longer penetrates the window. I move the keg, feel the two weapons and grab them off the table. But there are no shoes. It's too late. The SS are nearby in the hallway. I close the closet door, reposition the keg, and creep backward into my burrow. I grope around inside and trip over something in the corner. My shoes! I catch my breath.

I wait in the darkness and remember Igor's instructions to find the ceiling slat. I slide it open to the upper shelf; lay the shoes, gun and knife on it, and lift myself up into the narrow chamber just as I hear footsteps stop outside the entry to my tomb.

Igor is there outside the door. He mumbles a Patois curse. I hear metallic clinking sounds. Sorting through keys? To find the right one to open my chamber—that isn't locked?

I inhale deeply, seal myself from view and close the slatted ceiling boards. German voices push Igor to hurry.

I grit my teeth, terrified—I'm hiding like my Jews.

Curled on my side on the shelf, something near me feels foreign and silky soft. Fur? A rat—or a mouse? God, what did I touch? I put my hand across my mouth to muffle a scream in the darkness. It's too difficult to control my breathing.

The outer door opens.

"She must be in here. Look behind the table in that closet."

"Ach, she's not here. I told you she went into the woods. We have the evidence, the bushes, the torn dress and brooch. Let's go."

"No, we have to be thorough or risk losing our heads. Our superior has been murdered. We must do a complete search if only to satisfy the next idiot over us. Here, give me a hand."

One SS pushes the table aside and bangs on the closet. His partner is angry and kicks the door with such force it splinters into jagged pieces.

I'm holding my breath, petrified. His second kick tips the keg into the room and spills years of rancid pickle brine over both men's boots.

"Was ist das? Scheisse? Phwew. Stinkt das!" The angry one shouts. The other says,

"Verdammt! The stink is all over our boots. Let's get out of here." They turn to go.

I open the ceiling slat for air. The terrible acrid smell rises up to the closet ceiling and tickles my nose. I make an unsuccessful attempt to stifle a sneeze just as the men slam the door shut. They rush down the hallway never hearing me.

I hear another pair of footsteps join them. Is it Igor? Their footsteps fade away. I imagine how long the passageway is and if they are only a few meters from me or at the far end by the kitchen. My ears are on fire to pick up any sounds of movement. I'm so confused by now.

It's silent. I can't hear anything. Where are they? What are they doing?

Without warning I begin a convulsive set of sneezes I can't suppress. For a few seconds in between I hiccup and try to catch my breath. Merde, the footsteps begin again. Oh no, they did hear me and they're coming back! I jam my sleeve into my nostrils to curb more sneezes and hiccup so violently I taste stomach acid. More footsteps. The door to the outer room opens again.

"Madame. Are you there?"

Tears run down my cheeks at the sound of Igor's deep voice, gentle and worried. At first I can't answer, my throat is so dry and gritty. The roof of my mouth feels like sandpaper to my tongue. My words are encased in thick, rubbery mucus draining from my nose and sinuses. I splutter, "Oui, help!"

The burning brine strangles my throat. Feeling faint, my hands drop and I begin to fall as Igor clears the broken door to reach me. For a few seconds my eyes try to focus through the piercing light of his kerosene lamp. I see a glimmer of Igor on bended knee, half in the closet.

"*Aye!*" As I'm reviving, a shelf board snaps and reels me toward the pickle fermentation on the floor. Then I feel it again, that soft, silky sensation around my head and neck. I shriek and immediately Igor covers my mouth with his large hand. He delivers me from this tomb into the dimly lit space with one rough thrust. I pull at the fur coiling around my neck, wild with panic in the darkness.

"Forgive me, Madame," he says apologetically, slapping me—afraid I'll draw the enemy back. My eyelids flutter open at the lamp on the table. He looks at my crazed expression, half here and half somewhere else. Then I close down to him and the world, preferring my inner darkness a minute longer. My arms are frozen around his neck. I breathe more easily away from the fumes and cramped quarters of the closet.

He holds up the much-feared object he pulled from around my neck.

"Look Madame, you had nothing to worry about."

"They're gone? It's safe?" Wild-eyed, I'm in shock, not in present time.

"Yes, Madame. They left. You're safe."

Afraid to move, I remain in Igor's arms, eyes closed again for a few more seconds. My fingers idly touch the dreaded thing. He turns the lamp toward me and I recoil in surprise.

"Ah, the *tzitzoyt*, the knotted tassels. How did that prayer shawl get in here? And around my neck?"

"One of our Jewish men left it behind when passing through. It must have fallen as you moved your arm above your head to get onto the shelf."

"I see, so this hiding place is for them?"

"Well, yes, until today. We can't use it any longer since those two found it."

"Why did you let the Boches in the passageway?"

"Madame, it's easier to play along with the Krauts so they come to their own conclusions. We defend the best we can—but we cannot arouse suspicion. They would take the whole basement apart and bring in a dog if we resisted. I pretend to use keys for every door to delay them. By the time they reach the last room, they're in a rush to look elsewhere. We won't use this room anymore. We have others, don't worry."

"Is it safe to leave here now?"

"Yes, surely. Can you walk?"

"I don't know. I feel so undone."

"I can't carry you, Madame. The passage is too narrow and the ceiling is too low. Creep in front of me if you can't walk. I'll light your path. Annette will stay with you while I arrange to get you safely out of the hotel."

We come to the end of the hallway. I've crept the whole distance à quatre-pattes, on four paws, bruising my hands and knees. Too woozy, my head feels disconnected from my legs. Seeing the horizontal sliver of light under the door to the kitchen stops me dead in my tracks.

"I can't move, Igor. I'm afraid to go into the kitchen. This is crazy. Maybe they'll come back and surprise us."

"No, no Madame. You must trust us. We're on your side. You're protected."

"I can't believe it. I mean, I believe you, kind sir, but it's so hard to accept that you would risk your life for me. Forgive me, please. I'm losing my sanity."

Teary-eyed, shaking from fright, and claustrophobic exhaustion, I look up from my knees as Annette opens the door.

"Oh, my dear child," she reaches to lift me up, "Let me help you while my man goes out to alert the others. You're safe. The Doryphores have left. By now they're half way to your house. Don't worry, Madame. Guy and Marie already know."

"What will they do to them?"

"Why nothing, Madame. Servants don't matter. They'll question them. Guy and Marie are prepared. Don't think about it. Just breathe and take this."

She offers me another small brandy and a wet cloth to wipe my face and hands. I catch a glimpse of myself in a reflection in the glass panes of the door to another storage area.

"I can't go out like this. My dress and stockings are torn. I'm filthy," I tell her, and become more agitated.

Annette grabs my hand to calm me. Her gentle eyes reassure me. She assumes correctly that this is as close to death as I have come.

"Madame, you just had a taste of the lives you're protecting. The Jews who live in closets, caves, basements, attics, sewers, under compost piles and haylofts, are the lucky ones. You and I, we're part of a small effort that can save only a few. Take a deep breath, Madame. Let it all go, your fear and the last six hours or the last three years. Just think on what is in front of you now. Tell me you can do that."

"Yes, I'm sorry for being childish. Forgive me. Thank you for helping me gather my wits."

To my surprise Annette interrupts sharply and challenges my apology, "You beg forgiveness, for what? Being human? Don't grovel for what is your right, Madame. You just helped the Underground get rid of a monster. No one else could lure that bastard, Franz Mueller, out of his lair in the back room of this hotel. Had you agreed to eat with him in there you might be the corpse now and not him."

"Yes, but that young man who shot him?"

"He was an infiltrator, Madame. Not one of us."

"I don't understand? Why did he kill Mueller? Was I supposed to be arrested?"

I'm confused, trying to recall Dieter's words of warning. Wasn't I the bait for the Résistance? Things are so complicated. My head, dull from exertion spins with questions.

Annette sees the uncomprehending look on my face and tries to explain, "Forget it, please. Just concentrate on getting yourself to safety. It's not important what side he was on, Madame. He's dead and you're alive. We let the Boches play out their game. We figured Mueller was an inside target. Anything to disturb that could signal your death, not just an arrest. We hoped you wouldn't get hurt. If we did anything more to protect you, the SS or whoever is behind the murder could use it as an excuse to exact reprisals upon the Maquis. The Doryphores are losing now. This way the enemy can't blame you or us."

"Merci beaucoup," I say with gratitude, not fully understanding.

Annette behaves like a mother. I guess she sees a fearful little girl stuck in a woman's body. She wants to soothe her, but worries that the child might shatter like crystal if she does. Instead, she smiles, winks and makes light of my near disaster,

"Madame Henri, today you gave a brilliant performance. In the future, please don't wear jewelry that can be lost. We can't afford to leave expensive souvenirs with the enemy."

Chapter Eighteen

Seeking Safety

23 May 1944, Tuesday

I'm transported to the hotel dump at dusk, wrapped in an old laundry bag. There I'm transferred into a cramped compartment hidden in the rear of an old truck. Bushels of fresh greens and root vegetables obscure mon sépulcre.

The vehicle follows a lonely stretch of country road. An otherwise enchanting evening finds my nostrils pressed against a breathing hole in the rough wood wall of this vertical coffin. I stretch upward on my tiptoes. My nose and chin rub raw against the splintered planking as the lorry groans over bumps and swerves around ruts.

Then it stops. The world is silent. I ache to sit down. My muscles are tight from scaling the trellis, crawling on the ground and creeping in the narrow basement passageway. I hear a man whisper and a dog whine.

"Madame Henri, are you all right?"

"Yes. Why have you stopped? Is something wrong?"

He calls his dog and has her sniff my chamber while he explains, "Don't be frightened, Madame. My Bijou is trained to do this. It's for your protection. We're coming to a checkpoint near the border. They have a dog too, and Bijou will distract him.

"You must be very quiet. It's unavoidable. Once we pass it, I'll take a back road to the rear of a neighboring farm. You'll be a kilometer from your mother's estate. I'll give you a lamp. Find your way across her fields to the well house. You remember the way?"

"I hope so. It's been twenty years. What if Gestapo is waiting there?"

"You'll be safe. Don't worry."

"Thanks. You're so kind."

"Let's go Bijou. Come on, girl."

The door slams shut, the old engine revs and we crawl into the night. Five minutes later he stops again. I hear other car engines and German voices. Another dog barks, maybe an Alsatian. Bijou answers excitedly. Then there's laughter as the rear doors of the truck open.

I'm paralyzed with terror as I overhear, less than two meters away, "I never forget you, mein Sturmmann! *Voilà!* Your favorite brew." The driver's voice seems quite relaxed, even jovial. "Don't drink it all at once now. Ha, ha! It will take me another week to get more!"

The heavy doors slam shut and the vibration catches me by surprise. The back of my head slams against the wall and my nose absorbs the brunt in front. I can hardly raise my arm to feel if I'm bleeding. I'm packed too flat, like a tinned sardine. Meanwhile the German officers sing. Haven't they heard about Mueller's murder? Are they celebrating? Or is all well now that they have their beer?

The truck engine growls to life again. Bijou barks and the German Alsatian barks back. As we move past the checkpoint I'm relieved until the next hurdle. Another ten minutes and the lorry stops again. The driver delivers his goods, travels a bit further and stops once more. He opens the door to my hiding place. My body is so stiff and cramped my legs give out and I fall into his arms.

"Oh, pardon," I shake my head, yawning and rubbing my calves. I step down off the tailgate with the young farmer's help. He hands me a shawl and a lamp.

"*Pas de problème*, Madame Henri. These are for you. Try not to use this lamp. You're most fortunate it's a moonlit night. Remember, they may be looking for you at your mother's. Go only to the old well house. You'll be met there."

I search his youthful face, so kind, another of my rescuers this day. He speaks too well for a mere country farmer. I don't even know his name and mustn't ask. My young driver turns to go, but stops to look back. He must be repulsed at the sight of me standing there in the moonlight, hair disheveled, nose clotted with blood, dress torn, stockings ripped, filthy and full of tiny cuts and lumps of bee stings. With a hand over his heart and voice filled with deep emotion he salutes with manly pride, "Vive La France!"

His gesture stupefies me. I look around to see if there's a statue or a cross nearby to which he directs his patriotic declaration. I shrug my shoulders and lift my hand to wave and whisper "thank you" in a hoarse voice. His back is already turned and he doesn't appear to hear me. Yet as the truck pulls away he waves from the driver's window with a "V" for victory and shouts, "Pon pon pon ponnn!" I smile and bite my lip to suppress tears. The opening of Beethoven's Fifth Symphony is Morse code for the "V" of our French Victory. My young rescuer is telling me I am safe.

Left alone, I'm surrounded by the once familiar wheat fields of my youth. Their new sheaves gently sway in the soft evening air, weaving the cadence of my thoughts with the punctuation of spring crickets. A pity this crop will not end in a French belly.

I inhale the fresh evening breeze and wrap myself in the hand-crocheted shawl. It's beautiful. I stroke its soft mohair, the same colors as tall cedars and spring flowers, violets and lilac. It's so warm. In a silent prayer I give thanks to the person who made it.

"One day you'll have it back when freedom returns," and I hum Beethoven's "pon pon pon ponnn" before stumbling forward into the night.

Gratitude clarifies my thoughts while I survey the fields in the moonlight. I choose a freshly hewn path down the length of the closest field and plod toward my childhood home. The walk will take about forty minutes. I approach the outline of a favorite orchard from years ago on the edge of an old forested area. The fences are broken now.

My tired mind is suddenly alive with memories. My feet tread timidly along the path strewn with random clods of freshly plowed earth that conceal clumps of debris from last season. Marie's scolding voice echoes in my ears: fancy heels would be useless walking through clods of fresh manure. Taking a pistol meant utility was more important than style.

The irony is unsettling when I realize how much my life has changed since walking these fields as a young woman.

The luncheon at the hotel feels like it happened in another world. I cringe at the image of Mueller dead and bleeding. What reprisal will his death bring?

We heard recently of a Nazi massacre. Three hundred Italian men were murdered. Ten Italians for each German—because sixteen Italian partisans killed thirty German police. It happened on the Via Rasella in Rome in March. The Underground calls it the Fosse Ardeatine Massacre.

What will our local Huns do about Mueller's murder? Will our next SS leader be worse than Mueller?

Then I remember Édouard deVillement's lewd smile as I sat helplessly on the terrace. Which side is he on? What an ugly twist of fate that he was the only man to confront me. My eyes could have appealed for help from any other male, except Édouard.

Why does he walk into my thoughts now? Ah oui, it's this field. We were here, he and I, well over twenty years ago. The memory makes my stomach turn. I loved to stroll in the woods and fields each morning before my main midday meal and in the afternoons before the Angelus rang from the neighboring village church. It cleared my thoughts before going in to be with my parents at the close of day. I hiked to gain courage to deal with mon père.

These fields and woods were a private refuge in my struggle. I found my balance here within nature's grasp, in her patterns of fruition and death, fallowness and rebirth. Seasons mimicked my life and still do.

Decisions made yesterdays ago hold consequences for me today: especially harsh lessons for my female independence.

The challenge to create my own life was a dream bourgeois society would deem unnecessary. The world of men disrespected the call of my soul. A woman couldn't enjoy adventure or a career if her beauty secured her father's financial position amongst land owning élite. Like chattel, I was a high-caste sow in an exclusive pigpen.

I loved my father despite his rigid nature. At first, when I was little, I saw Édouard as being like him—at least from a distance. Édouard was six years older than me. We had grown up together because our fathers were business partners. Our families were in wines, dairy farms and Comté cheese. Édouard went to boarding school at ten when I was four. I saw him infrequently until he came back to work in his family's business when I was sixteen.

It was impossible to like him after he went away to school. He always had packs of dirty playing cards in his pocket when he came home. He showed my male cousins pictures of naked women being sexually molested in degrading positions. They laughed and dismissed the images, but he would spend hours staring at them. He tricked me into looking at them when I was only seven. I never told anyone. It wouldn't have bothered me so much except that later, Édouard's behavior was very peculiar.

I should have told Maman that one Easter when our families celebrated together. Édouard, then twelve, begged their cook to let him kill the six rabbits she was planning to prepare for dinner. I remember walking into the old barn near the hutches where Édouard sat in the hay with the poor dead animals neatly lined up at his feet.

Instinctively I hid from sight as he caressed them and told each one to feel safe. He assured each rabbit that it had to die. Not one of them was perfect. They had misbehaved and didn't deserve to be loved. The poor rabbits were fools for trusting him. I was terrified when he came near me after that.

My father, furious and full of liquor, forced me to eat a mouthful of rabbit at that Easter dinner. I ran from the dining room retching and have never eaten it since.

Late that same afternoon, Delphine, Édouard's mother, made a terrific scene in front of our families. She was always unpredictable. Sometimes she was sweet and charming, and then out of nowhere she would change to nasty and vicious. Young Édouard had to bear the brunt of her anger for no apparent reason, at least to my childish mind.

He'd cry from her slaps and leave the room in tears. He always returned in a few minutes struggling to be composed. Then she would demean him for stammering which only made it worse. Finally, filled with remorse, Delphine would grasp his head and smother him against her large bosom. He would resist her attempts to show affection. I suppose he succumbed to her twisted ways in the end.

When I was four, my Maman would take me aside to calm me during these episodes. I was too sensitive to Édouard's pain and automatically cried with him. For several years I was kept at home during holiday events with his family.

By age twelve Édouard had stopped defending himself from his mother's abuse. He would sit passively and endure as Delphine ranted, twisted his ears and slapped his head while she pulled his hair in front of everyone. My father commented on how grown up Édouard had become. I knew he had learned to bury his real feelings. Delphine's insane world made poor Édouard even more remote. His father was equally passive after a few drinks. This made me angry with all adults.

Years later I realized how alike Édouard and my father were. Both were rigid and precise in words and bitter and unfeeling in attitude. Over the next four years while Édouard was away at university I stopped thinking about him. Then our young kitchen maid said my father was arranging for Édouard to marry me. Father fired her because I wasn't supposed to know.

For weeks I didn't believe her. Then, at dinner one night he announced I would marry Édouard. How could I reveal what I knew about him? I thought the adults would laugh at me just as my cousins had laughed at him. The thought of Édouard touching me sent waves of fear and dry heaves from my stomach. I couldn't finish my meal. My destiny was to be decided without my agreement because our fathers were business associates. I cried and fought him right there at the table. Maman was silent but she was mortified. I could see it in her eyes whenever I brought up the subject.

So desperate, I did something I swore never to do. I spied on my parents in father's study. I looked through a peephole in an old closet. My cousins had made it by boring through the closet wall and wooden bookcase.

We inherited the house after my uncle died and my aunt moved her boys to Besançon. My cousins showed me the hidden passageway to the closet when we were children. I stood on their backs in its narrow space and watched our parents entertain friends when they thought we were asleep upstairs. We took crazy risks to find out what adult lives were like. What began as childhood fun fueled in me an almost perverse passion to know what people think, and the feelings they express in private but will not admit in public.

Years later, my parents had their worst arguments in that study. Father was smart but too weak to face reality without a drink. Maman could not help him and over time gave in to her fury about it. Mon père was afraid of her acerbic tongue. He was overprotective. They slept in separate rooms after he pressured her to agree to my arranged marriage. She had to survive his excesses. He was afraid of my beauty—a blend of her elegant nose, stunning complexion, and his handsome, chiseled face. My good looks were a female version of his.

I wanted to go to university in Paris but father said "non." I wanted to sing opera and dance in the théâtre and films. Father said a bigger, more emphatic "Non."

I begged Maman to free me from the specter of an unpleasant union with Édouard and secretly plotted to leave home.

Édouard accosted me one day as I was walking this same path. He ran up from behind, still in his town clothes from doing accounting work at the local bank. He was excited and sexually aroused. I was very frightened to see him invade my private world. He grabbed my arm to kiss me as if he already owned me, without respect for how I might feel.

My feminine self froze when I smelled liquor on him. Instantly an ancient warrior stepped out from my heart and slapped Édouard squarely across the mouth.

I took off running in the direction of adjacent fields spread with autumn manure to weaken over winter. I was wearing old riding clothes, boots, and gloves. The wind was low for the moment and the odor wasn't very noticeable. I wanted to get back at Édouard, afraid and revolted by him. I could hear his labored breathing and his long legged, slightly gimpy stride, trample the freshly tilled earth. He cursed me to the uneven rhythm of his footsteps. His dress shoes dug deeper into the moist mire. I ran like a hunted gazelle, zigging and zagging across the furrows.

A meadow of freshly laid manure awaited us. It was so easy, no fences to climb or gates to open. I slowed just enough so he could reach me if he ran faster, and led him into the middle of the field before stopping. I paused to pick up a clod of fresh cow dung and turned abruptly to face him. I held it out like a shield. He stopped short of grabbing me. We stood there, our lungs heaving, a predator and his prey. The thick air choked us with its warm stench. Moist and shrill, it burned our throats and nostrils.

I shouted in a high hoarse voice, "Édouard, I shall never marry you. Here's my dowry!"

I threw the rain-moistened cow pie and it splattered across the front of his suit jacket. Humiliated and deeply angered, he cursed and lunged at me. I knew he would and stepped aside quickly. He landed face down in the richly fertilized earth. I laughed and warned,

"Leave me alone, you beast. Don't pursue me anymore, Édouard, or I will reveal your secret depravity. Tell your father you will marry someone else, not me. Do you hear?"

When he looked up from the manure his eyes were wild and bloodshot. The left one was totally diverged to the outer corner. Then he spat at me and an ice-cold sensation trickled through my veins. I shook it off and ran home.

Six weeks later I met Emil and we were engaged only four months afterward. He was long absent from German soil. He had been married to a French woman for six years and was a recent widower. We had a long engagement because people talked. His late wife's drowning wagged their tongues. I didn't care. Emil protected me. I felt safe from Édouard. I never told Maman or Emil about Édouard's sickness. She never discussed him or any other arranged marriage after Emil met my father. She only smiled serenely. Emil came from money.

Father died from a stroke three months into my engagement. I was sad but relieved. His death closed the door on a painful segment of my youth. My dear Emil saved me from a terrible fate. And then he was gone too, and now I'm here, alone with our child, facing life in another war. Hunted by another enemy.

The memories finish flashing across the landscape just as I near the edge of the old well site. Please, God, let them fade away! Return me to the present, my sweet daughter, my Maman, Sylvia and Pierre.

Surprisingly, I feel the same strength now as if it were yesterday when Marta and I went hiking. I need to see her, hold her in my arms. Oh God, I want to be a decent maman for her. May she never discover this part of my life—I can't imagine how to tell her. The weight of my secret world deranges my mind. I've been alone too long, confined to burying human waste in my backyard. Alive in this open land I must make peace with my past and bury it like that other waste. If not, Marta's future won't be safe.

A blanket of fear lifts as I near the old well house. A figure walks slowly across my path in the clearing about fifty meters ahead. I gasp, and stand stark still like a deer, alert to see and smell with ears straining to listen. Who or what is it? Not an adult, too small of frame.

I walk cautiously up to the rear of the old well room measuring every step to be soft and silent. I haven't been in it for five years. Tangles of vines cover its walls. The old shutters are closed, but a small light shines along the cracks of the window ledges. I can't see inside and look all around but feel no one is outside here. Taking a deep breath I knock at the door.

"Yes, yes, just a second, coming," a young voice calls. Marta opens the door and beams at the sight of her poor bedraggled mother. "Ooh Maman!" barely containing amazement at my condition that quickly dissolves into delight. She pulls me into the stonewalled room. My defenses soften as mon ange throws herself at me with hugs and kisses. There is a fire lit in the old chimney. Marie is here with food—and hot water in the stone washbasin. I stare at her and ask if I'm truly safe here. She embraces me with tears welling in her old eyes. But for Marta's presence we would both cry. My little gamine is full of questions and frets over me like a mother hen as I wash the blood and dirt from my face and hands.

"Come, Maman, sit here and eat something. You must be starving. Your nose is so red and och, hey, you stink, Maman! What is that odor?"

"Oh, ah, it's a, I ah, spilled some old pickle juice." I force a wry smile in response to Marie's bemused expression, "Just part of today's adventure, Marie."

Marie places hot tea and a platter of cold supper before me, so delicious on my lips after hours of this harrowing ordeal. Actually, I'm surprised I'm hungry. I suppose it's because I feel safe. I tell Marie what transpired on the hotel terrace. Marta flutters all around me and then explodes with a tale of the Gestapo and Grandmaman. Marie tries to shush her to let me eat in peace but it's no use.

"Maman, you should have seen Grandmaman with the Nazis. It was wonderful. She was so terrible to them and they accepted it."

I'm never sure how my mother will react to the Boches. I know she can handle herself, even at eighty-six. Nothing has ever frightened her, unlike her cowardly daughter who only dreams of what she will say after the fact.

Smiling, I encourage Marta, "Tell me all, sweetheart."

"Well, they bang on the door after Grandmaman awakens from her afternoon nap. I never knew she disliked the SS so much. She receives them in the great hall as she did in the old days when I was younger and you and papa had friends for dinner.

"There she sits in her big chair with Ivan and Midgette at her feet. The Germans come in throwing their weight around, until the dogs growl when the SS are within two meters of Grandmaman. Ivan stands and bares his teeth. They see how huge he is. They jump a little when Grandmaman taps him across the rump with her cane and hollers '*Setz Dich!*' and he obeys and sits down right away. Midgette stays by her feet and snarls softly.

"Then Grandmaman says in German, 'To what do I owe this sudden intrusion of Nazi officers?'" Marta imitates Grandmaman's condescending tone of voice perfectly, to our amusement. She dances back and forth as she takes the part of each speaker. She tells us we should have seen the looks on their Nazi faces. They went pale.

"Then the young one in charge, says, 'Madame de Vochard, I have urgent business with your daughter, Ingrid Fellner.'"

"Yes, so what is it?" Grandmaman acts bored at this point.

"We believe she's hiding here on your estate."

"Hiding, out here? Whatever for? This is her home, not a hideout, Monsieur."

"Excuse me, Madame. Let me introduce myself. I am the new Obersturmführer, Wilhelm Roemler. Your daughter was with our former Obersturmführer, Franz Mueller, when he was murdered today at the Hotel LaFrance. She is missing. We need to find her.'"

"'Why, may I ask? She must have been an innocent bystander at such a dreadful incident and about to be a victim, herself, yes?'"

"'We have reason to believe, Madame, that she was involved in the death of the Obersturmführer Franz Mueller.'"

"At this Grandmaman becomes pale and her eyelids redden. She frowns, stamps her cane and raises herself from her chair, demanding in German and French,

"'*Warum lügst du?* How dare you? Why do you lie to me? My daughter was married to a German national for eighteen years and I'm half-German. In this household no one lowers themselves to political chicanery for either side in the stupidity of this ungodly war.'"

"'But Madame, you don't. . . .'"

"'Don't you interrupt me, Obersturmführer! You're all *Hohlkopfen*, empty heads! I am three times your age, you *Grünschnabel*, greenbeak!

So *grün hinter den Ohren*! Green behind the ears! Well, Obersturmführer Grünschnabel, this is the third war between France and Germany in my lifetime. And my stomach has no more patience for it. To accuse my daughter of collusion in the death of an offizier is insulting and ridiculous. How dare you denigrate a tragic widow and imply she's anything less than an aristocrat. Out of my house, Monsieur. You're not welcome here. *Raus*! Get out!'"

"'Then she shook her cane at the new Obersturmführer and said something else I've never heard in German. It was so terrible that he turned pale, and the Huns backed out of the room with their eyes on the dogs and hands on their guns. Later, when I asked her what she had said, she pursed her lips and shook her head 'no.'"

Marta is very proud of her recitation. I'm silent. Marie applauds and Marta takes a bow. "How did you overhear all this, child?"

"When the men entered the house, Grandmaman asked me to leave the room, but I hid behind her in the black wool bombing curtains. The dogs started growling and distracted her so much she probably forgot and thought I had obeyed."

At that moment a slight knock on the door pulls Marie and me back to the fearful present, but not Marta. She doesn't understand the danger I face. I hide behind the washstand. It's Guy and Sylvia. We sigh with relief. I come out and embrace them.

"Oh, Madame, it's good to see you safe," Guy is so relieved.

Sylvia is too choked up to say anything beyond giving me a big hug. Marie announces Marta's bedtime. She's disappointed but leaves dutifully with Sylvia. After the door closes, I ask with concern, "Marie, how could my old Maman have been so brazen with the Gestapo?"

"Oh Madame, you know she rarely shows her temper, but when she does, well, I can only assume this new Obersturmführer is young and decent or else she'd be a corpse by now. I didn't witness it. I was en route here after other SS came to the riverbank mansion looking for you."

"Tell me what happened in town. I have to hear from Dieter. He'll tell me what to do. He'll guide me, but I *must* know how the Gestapo behaved."

Marie looks very worried at the mention of Dieter's name. She tries not to show it, but I catch her downward glance. A chill blows across my shoulder blades . . . and my stomach contracts as though someone punched it. I look around this tiny room with its history of childhood hours spent playing innocent games, and suddenly feel like the lone player making all the moves myself.

Marie confirms my worst fear. "I'm so sorry to tell you, Madame, but Monsieur Dieter has disappeared. He destroyed a lot of papers and buried some in his garden. Then, this afternoon, the Gestapo came to his house and took him away. Amélie told me he left, but she didn't know where he went—or for how long. He didn't say anything, so it's very serious. Amélie doesn't know why he didn't leave before he was arrested. He could have saved himself."

I mumble, "He sacrificed himself for me and the others. I knew it would come to this." I'm on the edge of tears. Guy places his arm around my shoulder to steady me.

"But Madame, why would he do that?" Marie is heartsick.

"Dieter let himself be a decoy to distract the Gestapo, SS, the Milice—*alle Ratten*. The time all the rats take to interrogate him will allow everyone to get their refugees to safety and clean up their hiding places. If they're raided, the Doryphores won't find any evidence. They don't have enough men to investigate us, or to raid, deport, or locate refugees and still deal with Mueller's demise. If they begin a wave of reprisals because of people like me, it's to make us look guilty for Mueller's murder. The Boches want it to look like the Résistance did it. Will they torture Dieter? Do you know who denounced us?"

"We're not sure. Perhaps his arrest led to a simple interrogation and he'll be freed." Guy is hopeful.

"No, Guy, he ran all the circles. He knew everyone in this operation," Marie says sadly.

"Yes, Marie, he did, and if he doesn't reveal anything, they could send him to La Citadelle at Besançon, or deport him to a German labor or death camp. The Milice are few but strong in this town. I wouldn't be surprised if they make a martyr of him, as they did with Jean Moulin in Lyon. There's no way to find out if I stay here."

"You can't leave now, Madame. You're safer here with your mother. People won't denounce you because you ate with them in public at the hotel. That was a brilliant move."

"I don't understand, Marie."

"Madame," Guy interjects, "If the Vichy set thinks the Résistance murdered Mueller, now they will be afraid of the Underground's power. They will be convinced of your collaboration, which means you will not be suspected."

I can't reveal to these good souls my real reason for eating outside but am grateful that my move to be seen in public was a nudge to the positive.

"Perhaps you're right, except here I put Maman and Marta in danger, as well as Sylvia and Pierre. My decisions could bring dire consequences upon all of them. It's not fair."

"You're taking on too much of the burden, Madame," Guy's voice is solemn.

"Guy, I'm convinced if I were to be arrested today, it would be a well-deserved atonement for my basement murder—even if I go to Ravensbrück. I must face the future and my mortality, and the worrisome possibility of being unable to protect those innocents dependent on me."

I feel more centered speaking with resolve to the two people who share my deepest trust, "If Dieter is released and goes into hiding, I'll have no choice but to rely on my instincts, and perhaps face arrest and deportation alone."

"Wait Madame, you have to speak with Madame Mathilde first. Let her decide. We can take care of you, Marta, Pierre and Sylvia more easily here without any crossings for now."

"Is she awake?"

"Oui, bien sûr. She's reading. She rarely sleeps until midnight. Do you want to see her?"

"Let me wash up first, Marie. Does she know what 'entertaining' the Gestapo means?"

"I don't know. She's very close to Sylvia. She may know more than you think."

I take a welcome spot wash, apply ointment to the cuts and stings, and put on a clean dress and shoes. A quick comb through my hair, and Guy walks me to the main house. I knock lightly on Maman's study door.

"Maman, are you awake?" I tiptoe in quietly. She's dozing, reading glasses on her chest and a book open across her lap. A light stream of air whistles from her lips. She stirs instantly as the door closes.

"Daughter, Ingrid, come here," she beckons. I bend to hug her and grasp her firm, gnarled fingers. "Let me look at you. Sit here and tell me what's going on. Move those books and bring the stool closer."

I sit, waiting to be interrogated. My mind leaps back to childhood when she would give me a thorough once over after I fell out of the chestnut tree, or ran through a barbed wire fence to escape a steer, or ate her raspberries before Michelle made jam, and wolfed down a kilo of fresh figs and had diarrhea for days. She looks at me for what seems an eternity.

Smiling a little disapprovingly but lovingly she says, "Et bien, ma chérie, still waiting for me to begin after what you've been through, today?"

"What do you mean, Maman?"

"Oh, don't play with me, Ingrid. I'm your old Maman. I see right through you and now more than ever. Your life is too close to being taken from you. Tell me everything or I can't help you. Shall we begin with the saga of the last two plus years or your red nose and chin?"

I can't believe it. Did Sylvia tell her everything? Instinct says to protect myself—but from whom—my Maman? I must stop these feelings of unworthiness. Spit it all out and trust her.

"Maman, they came to see you, oui?"

"Yes, yes, the nasty little boys without blood in their veins who kill so obediently. And they accuse you of being a member of the Underground? Do you think they believe that or are they so unsure even at this late date?"

"If I tell you I'm afraid they'll torture you for information, or take Marta away."

"Nonsense. This new one's a baby, a Bohemian farm boy, old Czech or Austrian, anti-German at heart. He never wanted to serve. He's no Nazi. Tell me the truth, ma fille. You're operating on your own steam now and you're terrified. It's all right to be terrified. You learn best when alert. Don't look frightened, Ingrid. Life has to be lived. You paid a price to reach past yourself. The universe offered you a doorway, you walked through it . . . freed yourself."

Just like Dieter, she sees my disbelief and continues, "Ingrid, we're Patois, a family of German, French and old Swiss blood. We live many kilometers south of Alsace but we carry the scars of three wars between Germany and us. War is not about patriotism. War is about money, power, fear to love—and standing up for the truth. Mon chou, the more things change, the more they stay the same. Let's hope this is the last act of a very badly written tragedy. Now, tell me what you've done that's so awful?"

My mother's wisdom has such a purgative effect on my emotions that I blurt out, "I've slept with the enemy, Maman. I distracted two Obersturmführers to protect Jews who came through my basement and I murdered a German officer last September. And a few hours ago Mueller was shot when we were together. I think his murderer, a Nazi infiltrator, was supposed to kill me, too. The Germans shot him dead, lying right next to me under the hotel shrubbery. The hotel's Résistants helped me escape—and here I am."

My sentences run on like a young child's. I speak looking down, certain to receive a brow beating. Instead, Maman sucks in her breath with a rising "ah, oui" and smiles broadly, leans over and picks up my chin, "*Bien fait*, bravo, ma chérie! Finally you take a real position in this life based on love: for morals and decent living. *Formidable*, my little one."

"You approve?"

"What do you mean approve? Who cares what I think? It's your action that counts, not what anyone else thinks. Ingrid, your father's long dead. Stop acting like he stands between us to judge your every word and deed. Please, before I die I'd like our relationship freed from the ghost of his heartless rigidity."

"Sorry, Maman. I hear you but can't connect with what you're saying. I have, ah. . . ."

"What? Gotten your hands dirty in the fray? Chérie, stand up for what you've done. Stop behaving like your cowardly Papa. Don't be ruined by fear as he was. Life with him was so difficult. Everything in its place, remember? That was lack of confidence, not strength. Leave the past. Keep coming forward with me. Work at it; it's a new sensation, n'est-ce pas?"

She stares into my face with teary-eyes and a wry little smile. I'm dumbstruck.

"Why has this conversation waited so many years to happen, Maman?"

"Ach! Ingrid, you wouldn't hear me! I've told you this a thousand times, but it went in one ear and out the other. I've watched you since Emil died. I've seen the changes. You're learning to be stronger, to think and reserve your emotions. You're not a little girl so much anymore. Be careful of that strength. Don't show it to the wrong people. You're doing well keeping everyone uneasy. They're asking if you're a slick spy or a mindless rich whore."

"Yes, Maman, but I worry now. I could make a mistake without my mentor."

"What do you mean? Play out the drama you are creating to its end, and we'll hope the war will be over very soon."

"Oui, but I've lost the person in the Underground who gave me instructions. He told me how to handle myself. He gave himself up when Mueller was killed. He did it to protect all the rescuers in town like me. I feel so guilty."

"Guilty? You did nothing wrong, my child. Don't waste your time on guilt. Leave guilt to the Church. Your friend may have had his own private reasons for allowing himself to be detained. Don't waste your energy guessing someone else's motives. Save yourself."

"But I'm unsure what to do when the Gestapo catches up with me."

"You'll do exactly what a fine young woman should. Defend your honor and deny everything. They have no proof you protected Jews, do they? Well?"

"The basement is clean; there's no evidence there as far as I know. Yes, I had relations with Mueller, but I was supposed to be arrested."

I tell her the whole sordid story of the luncheon.

At the end, she says, "Ingrid, if what you say is accurate, they have no proof you were involved in any murder scheme. You don't even understand what happened, or why. You reacted to save your life, and ran from everyone in the hotel thinking the Underground would kill you for being a traitor, and the Nazis would think you were in the Résistance. You couldn't trust either side. You are a naïve lonely widow and Mueller used you. He knew about your relationship with Heisler. You two had an attraction and a history because of Emil. It's perfectly *raisonnable*, oui, ma fille?"

"It appears so when you say it, Maman."

"Och, Ingrid, believe it with all your heart and they'll let you go free."

"You make it sound so easy, Maman."

"The truth generally is. It's up to you, Ingrid, to make it complicated. For tonight, mon chou, forget it. Go upstairs and get some rest. Plan your strategy tomorrow after a good night's sleep. You're exhausted. Give me a kiss. Remember, we'll back up your story."

"Oh, thank you, Maman." I clasp her fingers and kiss both her cheeks. "I was so afraid you'd be ashamed of my promiscuity."

"Me, ashamed of you? Never. What you did was in the line of duty. It's easier to surrender the body when the ideals driving it are high and mighty. No one will blame you. Peoples' lives depended on you. Enough, to bed. Use lavender oil for that nose and chin. And your poor legs, my dear, you will need to wear dark stockings. Too many scabs, chou."

I bid her good night. She sits immersed in thought, awake and clear-headed, raising her hand to acknowledge me as I leave the door slightly ajar for the dogs. Halfway down the hall I stop to remove my slippers and pad back to her. Hesitating to ask to accompany her upstairs, my ear against her door hears her tough exterior give way.

I peek inside. She dabs her sharp eagle eyes, leans forward and lowers her head to pray,

"Forgive me, Lord, for being tough on her. She doesn't realize how lucky she is. She's passed by exposure and arrest so many times with your protection. She has much worse to fear. I know it's coming. I love her. Let an old woman live a little longer to see her child through her hell. If you would be so kind, Lord?"

Chapter Nineteen

The Confrontation

24 May 1944, Wednesday

The Gestapo returns the next morning. Maman insists on being present for their interrogation. She receives Obersturmführer Roemler in the great hall. The dogs growl softly at her feet.

"Why do you bother me again, Obersturmführer?" she asks, annoyed. The Nazi is cautious after yesterday's meeting and tones down his demeanor considerably.

"I'm sorry to disturb you, Madame, but I must speak with your daughter, Ingrid Fellner. I need whatever details she can give us relative to the death of our late Obersturmführer Mueller. It won't take long, if you please."

I overhear from behind the side door, ready to give my version to protect myself.

Ah oui, a very different tone today compared to the tale Marta recited last night. Maman has clipped his wings! Now, for my entrance, I wear a revealing dark red dress and my hair is loose at my shoulders. I cut a lean but curvaceous figure that moves gracefully with a measured sway from my hips. I sit by Maman. My poise unnerves Roemler. The strategy is to make him feel guilty for even remotely thinking I'm a threat to the Third Reich. I look sensuous and relaxed. Burying my nerves is hard work.

"Gut Morgen! Obersturmführer Roemler, what can I do for you?" My cordiality in German takes him off guard. My allure clarifies why his predecessors bedded me.

"Um, ja, yesterday afternoon, the twenty-third of May, Madame Fellner, can you tell me what you saw when Obersturmführer Mueller was shot?"

"I'm sorry, but the man who forced me down the trellis at gunpoint was the only person I saw. I didn't see him kill your superior officer. The shot came from the doorway as a complete surprise. Suddenly, Mueller was dead. Then this young man I never saw before threatened to kill me if I didn't leave with him.

"Naturally, I was terrified. You can understand, I'm sure. The sight of Franz, ah, the Obersturmführer dead in a bloody heap," I break down and cry.

Guy rushes in on cue with a glass of water. Roemler's embarrassed and waits patiently. I measure my impact as I wipe my eyes and blow my nose gently. Good, he falls for it.

"I'm sorry, excuse my tears, Obersturmführer. Where was I? Oh yes, when I hit the garden there was no way out through the barberry bushes. I had to stay close to the ground. I heard shots fired, but kept crawling until I found an opening in the shrubbery and then ran through the wooded gardens as fast as I could."

I take a sip of water. Roemler asks, "Madame, where did you go?"

"I came here."

"Why did you not come to us for protection?"

"I was confused. The man who shot Obersturmführer Mueller said he was going to kill me, too, because I was a collaborator. I had no idea how many more like him were on the grounds. I was afraid. Alone. I wasn't thinking clearly. I've never seen blood like that. I was in shock. Even now I shake at the memory. Forgive me, please."

"*Jawohl, kein Problem*, don't worry, Frau Fellner."

This new SS doesn't believe me entirely, however, there's no evidence to substantiate his suspicion. He knows if the assailant was placed in the Résistance or not.

I remain in the dark, unsettled by what took place at the LaFrance. Was the killer a Frenchman or a German spy? Why did I trust his SS uniform under the smock? I'm lucky he's dead. Did he infiltrate to get rid of Mueller? Did Mueller have enemies in the Gestapo and the Milice?

Roemler appears satisfied with my alibi. I've given him some detail. Even if it's not all true, he will leave me alone. My account of the escape must fit with his information. I keep guessing what that is. He stares, probably thinking how nicely I bloom under my knitted dress. My hair shines and skin is rosy and clear. My God, is he my next pursuer?

I interrupt his daydream, "Have you finished, Obersturmführer? I'm quite tired from this nightmare. I need to rest." I lift my hand to my forehead to tuck a stray wisp of hair behind my ear and watch him ogle my bosom.

"Yes, ah, one more thing. How well do you know Dieter Van der Kreuzier?"

Dieter's name on Roemler's lips is a death sentence in my ears. Unprepared for it, my mind clamps shut and heart flutters. I work hard not to show it. Maman was right and the absurdity is: here I am, desperate for this Nazi to believe a lie that is actually true.

"We're members of a Baroque ensemble here in town. Monsieur Van der Kreuzier is a violinist and teaches my daughter piano," I mumble matter-of-factly.

"And you see him socially?" He's digging. I narrow my eyes and pretend to be slightly insulted. The measured acidity in my upper caste hauteur will forgive his ignorance.

"Oh no, Obersturmführer. He isn't part of *my* social circle."

I dislike relying on class privilege to disenchant his sleuthing, but the role of a spoiled, leftover aristocrat, is so natural. He smiles briefly, raises his eyebrows and looks around. The room is worn yet opulent, lined with centuries of de Vochard antiques, oriental rugs and artifacts. He's seen Dieter's cozy modest petit bourgeois home. My snobbery is convincing.

"Yes, well, Madame, anyway, I believe you left this behind?" He gives me a small parcel from his breast-coat pocket. I look at it, curious. He nods for me to open it.

"Oh, my brooch. Thank you, Obersturmführer, thank you so much. I was dismayed that in the commotion it was lost. Where was it?"

"On the lawn at the LaFrance," he stares again. I must not give him reason to continue suspecting me. I have to distract this Nazi's attention while I have him aroused. I decide then and there to pin the jewel on my dress, too low, over the contour of my right breast. His eyes follow. I watch him stare as my bosom rises and I heave a coy sigh of contentment.

He paces and looks out the window, flustered by the seduction. I look at him with soft bovine complacency. I'll get him now. Undressing me with his eyes. They all do it on cue, like dogs. Now for a fetching female pose. My eyes beg Roemler to dismiss me, to lick my wounds like a spent whore he's just ravished. Oh mercy, the same game I've played with every man, including my beloved husband. Today the pattern is so clear I barely perform it with a straight face.

Life with these people is théâtre. Self-important little pegs. They can't tell whether I'm sincere or not. I picture the brave souls who saved me yesterday. They know my sacrifice and respect for life. Vive la difference! This one next to me, my dear Maman, has no need for me to perform. Why have I been so timid about being myself with her all these years?

Roemler is taken with me.

I ask again more sweetly, with an earthy, alluring undertone, "Please, Obersturmführer, may I be excused? I've told you all I know."

I put my right hand to my forehead in a gesture of fatigue. My left clasps Maman's arm, like a child. My pitiable dependency on her softens him. Now I pull at him with my *aufgeilen*, sexual cunning. Good, he's aroused and wants to continue our meeting. This is the moment to overpower him with my feminine prerogative.

"Yes, Madame Fellner. Thank you for your help in this matter. Ah, will you return to your town address soon?"

"I suppose so, but at the moment I'm not sure when. Why do you ask?"

"I'm concerned for your safety. If there's sentiment against you because of your association with the Reich, we can offer protection and nightly surveillance to reassure you."

He hands me a card with a private number at Gestapo headquarters. As I take it the deep side slit of my skirt falls back to reveal a length of leg he can't help but notice. I extend my hand and turn to face him. He looks down at my upturned eyes and drowns in my feminine wile. I lower my head and raise my eyes again, saying with a hint of my caste's authority, "Thank you. How kind of you, Obersturmführer. Guy will see you out. Good day."

"And ah, good day to you both." Roemler bows deeply, stunned but helpless. (His interviewee has dismissed *him*.) He takes one last glance. Is he staring at my red nose?

I must distract him. Still seated I part my legs ever so slightly. He reddens, turns on his heel and marches out.

The door closes and Maman says dryly, "At least he did us the honor of not saluting der Führer in our presence."

I turn to her and grin broadly, "Oh no, Maman, he was too busy saluting my lingerie, pardon . . . *meine Unterwäsche*."

The twinkle in her old eyes tells me I did a good job. I breathe a sigh of relief and raise my arms high, declaring, "I'm cured, Maman, *je suis guéri!*" and then whisper, "To think the remedy would mean treading such a dangerous path."

"Ah, oui! Mon chou, your old Maman is proud. Perhaps you have found your stage."

I awaken the next morning with my head groggy, as if pulled to the moment from a faraway place. My body has surrendered to healing sleep for two nights, relieved that Mueller is gone. I hear Marta calling at the bedroom door.

"Maman, are you awake? Can I come in, please?"

"Yes, surely, Marta. We'll cuddle."

Mon ange bounces onto the canopied bed. She regains her old energy and zest for life, imbued with Sylvia and Pierre's youth. She's beautiful, slowly turning from childhood to adolescence. I'm a little sad, but hopeful. I won't limit her future as my father did mine. I accepted so much nonsense, and never understood my mother until I took the initiative to grow up through this war. It has taken too many years to appreciate her wisdom.

Marta interrupts my thoughts, "Maman, what are we going to do now? Are we going back to town? I like it here better. Can't we stay here?"

"Wait, one question at a time, please. Perhaps you're not asking, but telling me what you want? Is that it?" I chuckle at her manipulation.

"Well, no, well, kind of." She gives me her impish smile.

"All right. You stay here. I need to see some people. Now, come here, princess," I reach over and grab her by the shoulders and we hug, tickle, and roll around in the down quilting. Suddenly there's a growl from the bed and a lump under the comforter shows its furry face.

"Midgette, you bad dog. You've escaped from Grandmaman's side. She'll be lost without you."

We both laugh as the little Papillon turns her head to the side coyly. Marta and Midgette jump off the bed and scurry out the door together. Marta is much happier here.

I turn over and look out the window. Now what do I do? Do I contact someone? I must talk with Marie and Guy and find out what happened to Dieter.

Later that evening, after dinner, I have another talk with Maman in the sitting room.

"Can you keep Marta here a little longer? I need to return to town and make some inquiries. She's safer here."

"Certainly, my child. She's a delight to my old bones. She gives my old piano a rough workout. That wretched instrument is like me: flat, with its tension too loose. Do you think that sweet gentleman in town could tune it? What's his name? It's been so long since he tuned it regularly. Isn't he the same man we met a while back at Le Petit Chat?"

"Yes, Maman, that was Dieter, my Underground connection."

"Oh no. You think he may be missing? How terrible. His wife was there that night, oui?"

"Yes, and he's my main reason for returning to town. Now that I've had my interview with the new SS, Roemler, I hope they'll leave me alone. What do you think?"

"Ingrid, you need to be very cautious now. Keep your counsel. People from each side could trap you into implicating yourself. You have to play everyone the way you did that Grünschnabel Obersturmführer. Especially members of your own Résistance."

"But now, Maman, I feel so sure of myself and free to see things differently."

"Yes, yes, I don't mean to question your self-assurance, but precisely at these times life pulls the rug out from under you."

"I don't know what you mean?"

"Daughter, despite struggling against your father's fear and guilt you absorbed his attitudes like a sponge. They were truth for you until you almost lost your life. Now you're growing past his limitations to be your own woman. You're powerful now, yes?"

"Yes, I am. So why the doubt?"

"Ingrid, sometimes the heavens keep our path open and easy. We may not think so at the time because the lessons are so difficult. Until we apply what we've learned we don't appreciate the leap forward. Use your wisdom now. Don't be careless and ungrateful."

"*Jamais*, never, Maman. How could I be?"

"Oh, very easily, my dear. You already have been. When you learn to call attention to yourself you use that power to tame and change people of lesser understanding and self-control. You seduced that young SS goat into such a state he will be at your doorstep yearning for you. Be careful what you ask for and how you go about getting what you want."

"But I feel so much more confident, Maman. How can you say that?"

"My dear, we share similar natures with different quirks. You've come forward in victory. Bravo! You're now especially vulnerable to the world and its machinations. You can embrace it instead of defending against it . . . while you hold onto yourself. You must do so with balance because you've entered a new arena in which to play your role. Don't let your ego blind you when the stakes are higher, my sweet. I know the world doesn't look the same to you.

"Now you'll pass by people who were friends. Your new strength will underscore their weakness. It can't be helped. You're different. They can't keep up with you. People aren't always honorable and nice. They resent you for growing past them. You make enemies without trying. See what I mean?"

"Yes, Maman. How do you know all this?"

"I've already lived it. I'm too old and had you so late in life. My only regret is I didn't fight your Papa to set you free when you were young enough to follow your dreams. I hurt you and myself. I'm thankful for these last days, Ingrid. This ordeal has allowed me to make amends and beg your forgiveness so I can depart this world with a clearer conscience."

"No, Maman, don't say that. I'm not ready to let go of you. Please don't leave Marta and me now. We've lost too much." I lean forward to embrace her with an uneven sigh of regret and exhaustion. She strokes my head gently as I suppress a sob.

"Stop being dramatic, Ingrid. I can't live forever. I just wanted to share my love and admiration. It takes integrity and compassion to help other people. Be on your guard when you leave here. Don't make these last days the only lessons of your life or the best ones either. If you reach for more, life will keep you busy. It's the only road to old age," she chuckles lightly, "how well I know."

I look up, smile and shake my head at her easy laughter and hug her again.

⌒

After talking with Maman, I'm ready to retire—when Guy summons me downstairs instead. Entering the kitchen, I recognize the young farmer from the Résistance who drove me here.

"Madame Henri, can we talk?"

"Please, yes. I never got your name and didn't thank you properly. I was too frightened."

"My name is Jean Claude and you needn't apologize." He kisses my hand and smiles respectfully.

"Please sit down, Jean Claude. May I offer you something to eat or drink?"

"Don't go to any trouble, Madame."

"Nonsense. Guy, bring us some good wine and a little leftover dinner. I'm hungry. So, Jean Claude, what have you to tell me?" Guy hesitates. Jean Claude's expression is serious.

"You may not wish to eat when you hear what I have to tell you, Madame. I'm sorry to inform you, Monsieur Van der Kreuzier is still missing."

I hear the news for the second time but still can't absorb it. Then it finally pummels through my fatigue and grinds my hunger to a halt. Guy leaves us alone.

"Who told you?"

"The one who fetches the men from police headquarters after their interrogations. He went for Dieter, but no one had any news of him. It's not a good sign, Madame. We must prepare for the worst."

"And the coroner knows nothing?" I ask, incredulous.

"Nothing as yet."

I sway momentarily, hearing this awful news. My young rescuer guides me to the table. In other parts of France, men who linger in interrogation for more than three days oftentimes do not come out alive. Without a corpse, their fellow Résistants are left to guess if they died after a torture or—were sent to a foreign labor camp. The *Nacht und Nebel* game.

"Well, if he were dead, the coroner would know, so that's a hopeful sign. But if he's still inside and they aren't done with him, what does that mean—torture or worse?" I ask.

Jean Claude picks his words carefully to speak of Dieter in present tense, but his hands tighten on his béret, "*If* the coroner knows, he probably can't tell us. We all miss Monsieur Dieter, Madame. He is a great human being."

I can't go on discussing Dieter.

I sit holding my head in my hands and hear myself ask, "What do you do for the Underground? And—what do I do now?"

"Madame, I'm only one of the farmers who crosses refugees to their next connection. I get them from your place and other basements and attics. I can't even tell you who else houses them. The system was set up to protect us from infiltrators, but despite it, a bad apple got into the cart, and you were almost killed. You need to be very careful. Mueller's own men killed the infiltrator. We're sure they don't think you're innocent. Someone is still after you."

"If what you say is true, then the people I have most to fear are my own acquaintances, and well, 'friends.'" After the last three years, the word "friends" sticks in my throat. Who, Germaine, or Agnes?

"First, let me tell you something. Your beau-fils, Stefan, worked with the infiltrator."

"What? Oh no. He hates me that much, Jean Claude?"

"No, no, Madame. Stefan was duped. He had no idea the man was a Nazi spy or that he would kill the Obersturmführer. Your beau-fils has no idea what you actually do. Well, to be honest, none of us did . . . until your life was threatened. We all believed you were a collaborator, even when Heisler was murdered. I can't tell Stefan you're one of us. It's forbidden. Guy and Marie never said a word to Igor and Annette until the day you went to eat at the LaFrance."

He hesitates to continue so I add the truth, "Maybe he was supposed to kill me, too, but why did he kill Mueller?"

I give up trying to concentrate and rub the sore knots between my eyebrows. It's complicated and I'm exhausted.

Jean Claude realizes I need an answer and breaks the rules, "We think Mueller blackmailed a rich local family. He discovered their house servants were Jews. He extorted money from them and hid it from the high command rather than deport them. He blackmailed everyone and never shared his booty. He had every officer in his unit over a barrel for something. They hated him, but were afraid to tell his superiors."

"They were not alone, Jean Claude. But why did Dieter expose himself to detainment?"

"Either the SS are keeping Mueller's killer a secret—or they don't know who did it. If it looks like *we* killed Mueller, Berlin could justify reprisals against us."

"And Dieter would be their prey?"

"Oui, Madame."

"Does my stepson know which side I'm on?"

"Except for the owners of Le Petit Chat, Yvonne and Yves, only those who helped you escape know your identity."

"So that's you, Annette and Igor, and whoever transported me in the garbage, oui?"

"Igor transported you, Madame. And yes, Stefan doesn't know."

"That's why Igor didn't speak when you two transferred me to your lorry in the laundry bag. How do you know all these details, Jean Claude? Someone has told you."

"Each of us has a piece of the puzzle, Madame. Only Dieter holds all the clues. I don't know how to help you except to say we must watch this new Gestapo chief very carefully."

"Who will guide the crossings now?"

"They're suspended for now. Most people have already crossed. Those stalled in basements or attics will stay put. Maquis whose units protected refugees en route are pursuing the Boches. Hitler is losing badly. The war has to end next year, maybe spring or summer. The rest of the Maquis units will join de Gaulle soon. He'll return to France after the Americans arrive."

I look at his rugged young face and open honest eyes and plead, "I hope you are right, Jean Claude, but for me that day is a mirage on the horizon. I need to know who my enemies are today and how to protect myself and my family."

"Mind your back with your social class, Madame Henri. Let them come to you. Don't trust them. Say nothing. We hear some are in collusion with Nazi munitions factories. They hate you and may be a greater threat to your safety than the Gestapo.

"This new guy, Roemler, is young and green. Who knows what he thinks when he hears the lies and rumors? The men who served under

Heisler and Mueller probably resent him. He's easy to control, I'm told, but say nothing. Move cautiously. I'd better go now, it's late."

"Thank you, Jean Claude. Oh wait, let me give you the shawl so you can return it. And please give that woman my thanks for her kind gesture."

"Oh no, Madame, she wanted you to keep it as a gift for your service. Her son is a member of the Résistance. He escaped from a forced-labor camp and passed through your basement some months ago en route to Aosta."

"Oh, well, yes, all right, but I don't expect gifts. To know he is safely through my leg of his journey is privilege enough." I look into this young man's steady gaze and wonder. He speaks too well for a farmer. "You come from a big city, don't you? Maybe Paris?"

Jean Claude smiles with a twinkle in his eye, and salutes me, "Vive La France!"

He opens the kitchen door and disappears into the night.

Chapter Twenty

The Eyes Have It

26 May 1944, Friday

The valley opens up to the town, clouded in wisps of early morning chimney smoke and low-lying moisture, as we round the bend. The old stone and stucco houses, a few with medieval wooden grid-like patterns typical of towns up north, look lively and beautiful against the heaviness in my heart. It's very early. No one stirs on the streets.

Guy turns into a back alley a few blocks from the mansion and I get out to walk. I'm wearing a trench coat. My head and shoulders are wrapped in the woolen shawl Jean Claude gave me. I enter by way of the river path to the side servants' door and climb the stairs to the petit receiving salon. The place is cold and damp. There's no Marie to fix the fire. She'll come back when Michelle returns to Maman tomorrow. I am preparing the hearth when Guy enters the room.

"Madame, let me do that please. I'll stand in the ration lines tomorrow. I have the dinner your mother sent for this evening, and I'll bring you some tea." Guy is being very efficient while I stare at the walls with a blank look and an empty heart.

"I'm not sure what I'm doing here, Guy." I feel adrift, looking out the balcony window at the riverbank below. My eyes search for the two dead Jews on my shoreline from two and a half years ago.

"Madame, are you not feeling well? Perhaps you shouldn't stay here. I can drive you back to Madame Mathilde's if you wish. Please, don't force yourself."

"It's all right, Guy. Please bring me something to drink, to eat and a hot tea." I hold myself in check not to take advantage of his kindness and patience.

A wave of nausea seeps through me as he closes the door. I have to deal with my feelings. These last days have been the most trying since I murdered that young Gestapo agent. I'm not the same woman inside. I knew it at Maman's, but it's more pronounced now I'm here. I can't identify with this place. It represents a cloying past I don't want any more.

I survey the petit salon with its family photos and old furnishings. Then I move through the adjoining rooms on this side of the street floor: the bath, the bedroom, and the side study, then return to warm myself by the fire. The memories of life before 1940 prevent me from entering the public side of the manor: the formal dining room, butler's kitchen and larger salon de réception.

I shake my head in disbelief and catch sight of my face in the mirror over the writing desk. I look old, worn and used up like this building. It's a paradox that only now as I stand here in the room of my infamy does my heart know its sacrifice is over with Mueller's death. My God, how did I survive it?

Guy enters with a cognac. He places it on the table and turns to leave.

"Guy, please, I need to ask you something."

"Yes, Madame."

"How can I arrange to speak with Dieter's wife without being seen? Maybe Amélie knows where Dieter is."

"Perhaps I can convince her to come here, Madame, but you know she never talks about personal things. He may have sworn her to secrecy to protect her if she knows something."

He's right. Amélie is quiet, sweet, and reserved. She intuits life. She had little secondary education and her work as a midwife is heroic. Like most of the town she's seen little of the world beyond Duchamps. If the SS have Dieter, they're watching her, too.

"I remember years ago, Guy, people called Dieter foolish when he 'married down.' They said Amélie was below his class, a simpleton and a fool."

"Madame, with all due respect, her father deprived her of an education. Her gift for prophecy threatened him. His people came from a long line of political clerics. She was punished for her 'second sight.' Monsieur Dieter believed in Amélie when her family mistreated her."

"Well, perhaps we can help her through this," I offer, a bit over-confidently.

"Madame, we can not presume she doesn't know what to do because she may not divulge any information. As I said, she's a private person and very vulnerable right now."

Guy won't say it, but he thinks Amélie is a great deal more knowing about life than I am. I'm too obsessed with clearing my name to let the subtle doubt behind his voice irk my ego.

I rub my finger over the glass of cognac and wonder why I'm drinking so early in the morning? Am I that distraught, losing my internal sense of time and rejecting practically all I see? I just arrived and already want to sleep and wake up somewhere else.

"I can't accept that he's missing, Guy. I have to find him. Can you help me?"

"Give me a little time, Madame. I'll see Amélie tomorrow at Mass. Will you be coming?"

"Oh no, I prefer to remain hidden until I know what is happening. And please, Guy, don't shop in town. I don't want anyone to know I'm back just yet. Park the car where people suspect you're here for Maman. We can eat well on what she sent—and the garden. Marie can bring more tomorrow."

"Very well, Madame."

I pass a very long and unhappy afternoon and evening, and my night is worse. Tossing and turning in bed, ugly scenes with Heisler and Mueller crowd my mind to chase me out of sleep. In the morning I awaken less sure about remaining in town.

At 9:00 a.m. Guy comes back from Mass and calls me to come downstairs to the main kitchen next to the servants' quarters.

Amélie sits at the table with her head lowered slightly, shoulders hunched, hands folded in her lap. Since Sylvia's delivery we've spoken only at Marta's piano lessons or when she came to get food to deliver to those shielding Old Testaments.

Her customary exuberance has evaporated. Her spirit is forcibly withered, like a late autumn blossom the lethal winter freeze cuts down. Her direct and trusting nature that consoled me at Le Petit Chat has surrendered to the downward pull of her mind.

As she stands to greet me, her grief and worry elicit the inflexible reserve of my upper class breeding. I must resist beyond its grip and soothe her pain before she locks herself back into calculating where her beloved could be.

"My dear, Amélie," I clasp her about the shoulders, embracing her, "I'm so sorry about Dieter's disappearance. Do you know anything?"

"No Ingrid. It's been very still in town since Mueller was killed. The Gestapo came to our house and questioned Dieter. He said nothing. When they left he opened his strong box and burned a lot of papers and buried others. He told me he might have to go into hiding, but he waited for the Nazis to return and went with them."

"Did he tell you his reasons for doing that?"

"He said he needed to protect everyone and he alone could distract the Gestapo. There were several dozen people crossing in the last big group—spread among many basements. I don't know where they took him. Usually when he goes away someone comes to tell me how long it will be. Three days have passed with no word. He's in hiding somewhere."

"Do you have any feeling about it?"

"I had a terrible dream the second night he was gone. I don't know if I should tell you."

"Please do, Amélie. Maybe it will shed some light on his whereabouts."

We take a chicory coffee and a tartine. I study my mentor's wife. Her long elegant fingers clutch the warm mug. They have an ethereal quality like the rest of her. She has lost weight and her usually rounded cheeks are haggard. She is tired and her voice is thin with worry,

"Ingrid, you know many people in this town think I'm a simpleton and a fool."

I choke and cough on my biscuit, embarrassed. She repeats the very words I spoke earlier to Guy. "They don't know you, Amélie, and they're probably envious."

"What I tell to you now, Ingrid, I've never told anyone except Dieter."

"Yes, Amélie. What is it?"

"Well, you know I see things. All my life I've done this. It's taken years to understand. When I was a young girl, many times I saw tragedy before it struck and made the mistake of telling the priests. They thought I was possessed and told my parents I was evil. My father wanted to disown me, but my mother threatened to leave him. He shut up in front of her, but privately intimidated me. My youth was a nightmare.

"Dieter married me when I was sixteen and he was twenty-one. He understood and was my loyal protector. I was a beautiful young woman. I sang well and played the violin. I was able to return to church after we married because the old priest who had made my life so miserable retired. A new one came who was kind. Do you remember Fr. Schlemmer?"

"Yes, I enjoyed a certain trust with Fr. Schlemmer, Amélie. In fact, I've not gone back regularly since he left."

"Well, he knew about my gift but never threatened me. I've sung in church ever since. Dieter helped me with my musical skills, playing flute and piano to accompany him on the violin. Our life has been short on money but long on love. I have no complaints. We survived the first war when many of our friends died. I had hoped we might survive this one too, but, maybe that's not to be."

She sighs and her eyes stray to the crucifix over the kitchen doorway.

"So is there some ominous sense you have about Dieter you wish to share, Amélie?"

"Um, well, yes, Ingrid, if you will listen impartially."

"Of course."

"I was terribly worried the first day after Dieter left with the Gestapo. In the middle of the night I awoke with a splitting headache. Then to my horror, I saw a pair of eyeballs watching me from the foot of the bed. They glowed. They sat on a plate framed by a flame."

"Do you know what they meant?" Gooseflesh crawls up and down my arms.

"The problem is they could mean so many things I'm not sure. I see things all the time, asleep or awake. It's normal for me. The image wasn't disturbing, but what I was feeling didn't go along with what eyes usually mean to me."

I am completely out of her league now. I know so little of the spiritual world, although I am well read on the lives of Catholic saints.

"Do your symbols relate to any of the saints, Amélie?"

"If you mean St. Lucy, I thought of her. My baptismal name is Lucille. I wondered if my Dieter was telling me he was still alive through the image of eyes."

"But Amélie, in the legend, St. Lucy tore out her eyes and sent them to a young suitor to show him how much courage she had in the face of her martyrdom. She wanted to relieve him of remorse for her impending death because he couldn't save her."

"I know. I thought of that, too, because if I interpret the image strictly I will be the dead one. And my beloved is telling me to have courage to face life and death without him. But, if, on the other hand, the eyes belong to Dieter then he'd be the one to die. Oh Ingrid, I'm so troubled by this."

Suddenly Amélie bursts into tears. I reach across the table and grasp her hands to console her. After a minute she wipes her eyes and blows her nose. We exchange the knowing look of women whose lives have been suspended by love's loss.

Gently, I ask, "Amélie, do your children know?"

"No, and they live so far away I think it's better not to say anything until I'm certain one way or the other. Let me tell you the rest.

"Ingrid, the strangest feeling comes over me whenever I see those eyes. I feel that my Dieter is alive. He's not far away but I can't find him.

My intuition tells me we should not look right now. I don't know what to do. Some moments I'm hopeful. Then I despair. To make matters worse I see those eyes every night. They follow me all over my dreams and haunt me until I can hardly sleep.

"I'm having difficulty teaching Dieter's violin students. Music is the only thing that helps me relax. The best of them put me to sleep when they play during their lessons. Many of the parents are rich clients who can't be trusted. They ask where my Dieter is and I'm so tired that I'm afraid I will make a slip and reveal something."

"What have you told them, Amélie?" I don't mean to interrupt, yet fear she might have already revealed something to a rich Nazi sympathizer.

"Oh, I tell them he went to visit his older brother, François, who has health problems and lives many kilometers to the south near Annecy. Dieter said it would work to say that."

"It's just like him to cover all the possibilities," I sigh, "but we need to know where he is. We have to hope Dieter is safe. He prepared so many details before he went away. Thank you, Amélie, for sharing your private thoughts. Look, it's late. Please stay and dine with us."

Amélie's face brightens into a sweet, girlish smile, "Oui, merci, I'm grateful not to eat alone, Ingrid."

She couldn't have imagined me eating a meal with Guy and Marie five years ago. I'm hardly worthy of her gratitude for finally living in accordance with my conscience; a lesson her noble husband taught me.

I will be left to tick off long, empty days without Dieter's counsel. No one will tell me if he's alive or dead. My reputation is in his hands. This town has branded me a traitorous whore. I'll be lost without his support from the Résistance. I catch Guy looking at me with a worried expression. Gradually I sense a conspiracy of silence brews within the Résistance. No one answers my questions. All I can do is wait.

Chapter Twenty-One

Dead Reckoning Conspiracy

28 May 1944, Sunday

A single bulb lights the coroner's examining table. The shades are drawn on a somber scene. Dr. Duvette applies various remedies. They should sting but alas, the patient doesn't respond. Jacques Devoir watches and questions his colleague. Duvette inspects the wounds and discards used bandages. The room is cold. Their patient is covered with black and blue welts, contusions, blisters, and bloody abrasions. His eyes are swollen shut.

"What'll we do now? He's almost dead. We've been at this for a few days with no improvement. Can you save him, Alain? His eyes, what did they do to them?"

"They put a substance into them. If he survives the beating and electrocution, I'm afraid he won't get his vision back. I can only use some basic remedies here until I find out what was done to him. He's a strong man. He's still here, he might survive, but I doubt it. The bastards really brutalized him."

"How much did it cost you to get him released?"

"Nothing."

"What do you mean, nothing?"

"I told Roemler's assistant his captive was dead. He didn't care to see the body to confirm it. I just took him out of the cell with one of the younger SS. We had a sheet over him and his breathing was so depressed the Nazi never noticed he wasn't dead."

"Then he's never lifted a corpse."

"That's for sure."

"This could be a long haul, Alain. What do we do now?"

"Be logical, mon ami. We have a funeral. . . ."

This logical conclusion Duvette speaks of so coldly is more than I can handle. I have listened through the door as these two good men talk without entering into the privacy of their bizarre conjuring. Their housekeeper, Patrice, will lose her trust in me for what I'm about to do, and Duvette will be very angry. . . .

I open the door and stand before them. Rightfully astonished at my presence, their conversation halts. Duvette's latest solution appears so extreme. It hangs ominously before me—and my small, selfish need to remain undercover—to be protected by the man lying on the table. My heart is transfixed on his bloated, barely recognizable face.

"How can you take him from us? Dieter is a husband, a father, a grand-father—the keel and rudder that directs us to ferry human cargo through moonless nights, snows, mountains, forests, across the Doubs. . . ."

"Ingrid, who let you in? You shouldn't be here. It's not safe. You can't know about this. You are. . . ."

"I am *what*, Alain? Your greatest asset? Meat for your trap, that's what I am!"

"Please, Ingrid, not now," the old Doctor demands, undone by me. Jacques looks upset.

"Not *now*? Are you kidding, Alain? I used to be a beautiful woman. Thanks to the Underground I've graduated . . . to become an alluring decoy, a distraction, a sexual tool to absorb Swastika lust! Well, all hail the Underground! Oui, bon, just accept your level of usury, s'il vous plaît, Madame Henri, and keep quiet."

"Please, Ingrid. . . ." His voice is tense as he glares at me.

"*Please?* How dare you dismiss me when my salvation lies here almost dead! And just when were you going to give me the good news? *Gott Verdammt!*"

My harsh voice hisses like a barroom hussy. I'm desperate, angry and scared to death.

"All these months and now mein Kreuz—oui, my cross, lies here dying. And you two argue about what to do and say for all of us who serve the cause. I should have known it was you, Alain, wielding the decisive influence over the chronic infection of this town's moral compass."

Jacques Devoir blushes deeply again and looks away. At least one male in this hierarchy has a conscience.

"She's right, old man," the coroner defends me, "You're not serious, are you, Alain? What about Amélie and the Underground that depends on him? You can't let people think he's dead."

Alain doesn't want to respond with me in the room, but I refuse to leave and he knows why. Marie has told him how ill I've been. Mueller finished me off, in my womb and in my heart. I stay and listen. Alain shakes his head and continues.

"We have no choice. If we don't bury him, the SS will suspect everyone in this town."

"But what about Amélie? You have to tell her he's alive, Alain."

"We can do that after the funeral, not before."

"You're being cruel and crazy, Duvette."

"Shut up, Devoir! Stop being a damned romantic idiot. Amélie will never convince anyone her grief is genuine if she knows her husband isn't dead. We can't take that chance. Whoever killed Mueller will blame the Underground. You know this town can't afford a murderous reprisal. We narrowly missed one when Heisler was killed. Do we risk ten Frenchmen killed for one Kraut? Merde, mon ami, we're too close to the war's end to play such odds.

"Besides, Jacques, we're the only ones who know that you, Ingrid, are one of us and in the most precarious position of all. We have no idea who's after you. We didn't think the SS was after Dieter either, at least not directly. Maybe the same person was after both of you. And damn it, woman, now that you know he's alive you are more vulnerable than ever and the whole town will be too, if anyone else finds out."

Alain Duvette is immovable and impatient. I disagree but inside know he's a true warrior under intense scrutiny from the town magistrates.

"You have no idea how complicated our situation is, Ingrid. And Jacques, you have to help me. You must see past everyone's neediness, including your own, to keep us safe. You're angry, Ingrid, at Dieter's sacrifice, and yours too. So, now get past it."

Alain pauses to control his frustration. But when he speaks again, his voice is no less strident.

"You've overstepped boundaries that were created to keep you safe, Ingrid. You're the one person who speaks to the SS constantly, in your own home for God's sake. You are now responsible for your own protection and everyone else's safety in this town, Jacques and me, and people you don't know. By coming here you have drawn the Gestapo to our morgue!"

"If you had told me something, Alain, *anything* . . . even a *lie* that sounded reasonable . . . I would not be here," I murmur, fearful, aware as he speaks of this new layer of suspicion.

"Ingrid, you're being watched day and night."

The old doctor's spitfire rationality silences Jacques and me. Alain looks over his half lenses at us and realizes his acrid delivery has been too shocking.

He is exhausted: "Sorry, you two. Forgive me. It's been a long war. So harden up for the next few months. It's almost over and can't get any worse than this."

"Yes, sure, I see your point, Alain. Only, how do we work this funeral with the priest? He will want an open casket and a viewing. And the widow may wish to see her husband's body before his funeral Mass." Jacques questions as he accepts the inevitable.

"The priest is easy. I will tell him Dieter looks so bad from the torture that the casket must be closed. Otherwise his wife will faint and we risk the entire town going into an uproar. The youth will challenge the Gestapo and there will be bloodshed in the streets. Even Beauverger will comprehend that," Alain looks up at Jacques while bandaging Dieter's arm. "But Amélie . . . well . . . I'll tell her something convincing. I know it'll be all right. Look, Jacques, just leave it to me. I'll worry for the two of us. Go find me a coffin, eighty kilos of rocks, and a pair of old-fashioned, one-piece long underwear."

"We can't move that many rocks ourselves without arousing the neighbors' suspicion."

"Hmm, you're right," Alain thinks, as he looks at me, "You know who can bring the material here. But hurry. We have to prepare the coffin right away and seal the lid before it goes to the church. Help me move Dieter upstairs before you go, Jacques."

Alain turns to me, "Ingrid, you wait downstairs. I need to talk with you."

I retreat to the front mourning parlor of the morgue and sit quietly in a daze, confused, feeling completely exposed . . . with no protection. Alain appears in a few minutes, stern and omnipotent.

"Ingrid, Dieter is so deeply bruised and concussed. He will have damage to his brain *if* he lives. It would be better if he didn't. Surviving his injuries would make any semblance of a normal life impossible. Jacques says he may have inner scar tissue. If it ever breaks loose, Dieter could die of a cerebral hemorrhage. Look, dear girl, we don't make the rules. We only know a little of how an injury plays out on the inside of the body, *capiche*? Jacques is the expert. I'm just a country doctor."

"You two must keep me informed, Alain."

"We will not tell anyone anything, Ingrid. Dieter was never here. And you are not to say one word to either Guy or Marie. We are each at risk of being questioned. Dieter said nothing and you saw what they did to him. We cannot afford a slip of the tongue. You have a long history of being abused by the SS. To get anything out of you—can you imagine what horrifying torture they would use on you? Are you prepared to die with the truth locked inside your heart? Like Dieter is or will? Well, what? Speak up, I can't hear you!"

"I'm not to tell anyone what I know. You will refuse to tell me whether Dieter lives or dies."

"Right. And you are forbidden to come near this morgue."

Duvette will tell Amélie that Dieter is dead. And I must never reveal that he isn't. Angered as I am, I will respect Duvette's decision because he has no choice. Apolitical, Duvette joined the Résistance out of a profound sense of moral indignation. He's a tough character; cuts to the quick in everything and says very little. Alain knows the ills and secret desires of this small town. He's the real pastor of Duchamps.

He birthed me and has been like a father and confessor. I adore the character in his wizened old face, and his wiry grey hair that's beyond taming. The deep bags under his sad grey-green eyes hold a reservoir of unshed tears that jump to attention when his thin cheeks lift in a smile, a rare occurrence these days. Today his face is haggard. His concave cheeks give him a ghostly air that matches the awful news he will give Amélie, our best midwife and his colleague of twenty-five years. Like me, she was one of Duvette's deliveries.

Does he reflect upon the deep trust in their friendship he's about to break with a blatant lie?

I slide out of the side alley on the old bicycle, sent home with my lips sealed.

><del>✦</del>

This evening, just before Amélie arrives, Guy tells me that everywhere she walked through Duchamps people approached her, squeezed her hand and looked at her with sympathy.

"The whole town knows Dieter's gone before she utters a word, Madame."

I catch a glimpse of Amélie from the small window on the landing between the stairs. She's here and uses the servants' side entrance to avoid being seen on the street.

"Guy, please greet Amélie for me. She's at the side door. I'm slipping into the corridor."

"But why do that, Madame?"

Without answering him I slip out of the servants' kitchen as she knocks. I hear them speak while standing in the hall steeling myself for this encounter because I will lie to her.

"You wish to see Madame Ingrid?"

"Yes, Guy . . . uh, do you know my Dieter is dead? Dr. Duvette told me this morning. He's arranged everything for the funeral. It's tomorrow morning. I have no family here now except my older sister, Claudine. Dieter's family is too far away to come. I don't even know exactly where our boys are. Please, could you and Marie come?"

"Oui, of course, Madame."

"And Madame Ingrid, too?"

By now Amélie is practiced in her delivery of the sad news.

"You'd best discuss it with her, Madame. Let me tell her you're here."

"You don't have to, Guy," I enter the kitchen, "Amélie, what do you have to tell me?"

I have drilled my mind for hours to control my tears and not voice what I know.

"Dieter's dead, Ingrid. Will you come to the funeral?"

"I . . . I think not, Amélie. I'm afraid to rub shoulders with so many people in public. Despite our musical interests, much of the town doesn't associate me with Dieter that way. It could be dangerous. I'm a pariah now and must not arouse any more suspicion. We don't know who killed Dieter and whether that same party is after me—or anyone else."

Letting my real concern slip out is a stupid mistake.

"But I thought it was the Gestapo, no? They're the ones who arrested Dieter and took him away. I don't understand, Ingrid."

"It's too confusing, Amélie. The Gestapo has informers. Dieter knew who they were. He wouldn't tell us."

I shouldn't have spoken so openly. Seeing her distress, I embrace her warmly.

"Amélie, I wish I could be more supportive at a time like this. Becoming a widow suddenly is painful indeed." We embrace and stand clasped together for a few long moments.

"I suppose the eyes were Dieter's," she whispers in my ear, too over-come to continue.

"So it would seem."

Thank goodness she accepts my evasive response. I must be more discreet. We sit down to talk at the kitchen table in the servants' quarters.

"Ingrid, I asked Alain if Dieter was in hiding. I thought that was what he would tell me. It seemed so logical."

"What did he tell you, Amélie?"

"He sounded so distant. He fell over his words, saying, 'I'm so sorry, my child, I love him so. We all do, ah . . . did.' It isn't like Alain to confuse tenses in his line of work. When a person comes into Jacques's morgue and Alain sees them, they're dead after all. I suppose he's worn out from the Occupation. I crumbled in his arms and now I'm floating and can't seem to get my feet on the ground. I'm *numb* as the grief settles in. It's unbelievable."

A few tears run from the corners of her eyes, but Amélie recovers her usually stoic composure.

I wait for her to continue, wondering if Dieter is still alive.

"You know, I asked when could I see Dieter since he was in the morgue. It was strange, Ingrid. Alain said it wasn't a good idea. That it was better to remember my husband as the handsome, valiant man we all knew. He was severely injured. It would only hurt me more deeply to see it."

The edge of disbelief fades in her voice when she adds, "I was afraid when they took him away this time, Ingrid. He made decisions and destroyed many papers the night before. He was so very tender that last evening. He looked longingly at me when he left . . . but to be dead? How do I tell our children? They can't come to a funeral now. Travel is unsafe with babies. The Underground is scattered up north and I'm not sure where my sons are located. Their wives are living under false names, too. It could take weeks to find them."

As the realization hardens she groans, "Mon Dieu, Claudine and I will have to bury him alone. François is too ill to come. He's the only brother left. Dieter's younger brother was killed at Verdun in 1918 with Étienne Beauchamp."

Amélie leaves a few minutes later. Unfortunately, her news of Dieter's death is all the more tragic against the enormous hope the Allies promise after the terrible lull in France. Our German overseers are bored, irritable, and nervous awaiting the Amis and Brits. Goebbel's rhetoric is so shrill only the most devoted anti-Semites still believe him. We will wait, silently, unable to go forward openly—until the Wehrmacht is in retreat. After four years, the atmosphere is thick with the anticipation of Victory.

I work hard to be convincing when I comfort Marta. She loved Dieter like a father after Emil died. My sprouting adolescent takes this loss very hard. She has bouts of crying all day and refuses to eat. Consoling her makes me relive Emil's death all over again, ashamed to admit it's almost as if Dieter had been a husband or a lover.

The funeral is on Monday, 29 May 1944, a beautiful spring day. Guy and Marie go and return with a detailed account. Guy feels uncomfortable discussing Dieter's life in the past tense. He has always been more spiritually attuned than Marie, despite her devotion.

But Marie tells me, "The church's stained glass windows dispersed the sun's rays into streams. They pierced the apse as vivid ribbons of color, Madame, and pulsed their refraction from the cut-glass chandelier and crystal candelabra onto the white altar cloth." Marie sighs, "such vivid energy against Monsieur Dieter's death was beautiful but *tragique*."

"Madame, the black drape over Dieter's coffin absorbed the rainbow colors. The dance of life trying one last time to revive him in that box . . . I, I'm . . . sorry, I can't accept that he's gone." Guy holds Marie's hand. Usually so quiet and unattached, he speaks more now than he has for months.

Marie continues, "Madame, Amélie couldn't bring herself to mourn openly."

"Marie, she's too connected with Dieter to accept the notion he's far from her side. I imagine her thinking she's the one lifted up, the one dying."

His presence must have felt that close, especially if he wasn't lying in that coffin.

"How did she bear up during the ceremony?"

"She was transparent like an angel. The priest droned on while her body stood, knelt, and sat as though it was disconnected from her thoughts. Claudine sat next to her and never touched her. Her own sister was afraid to disturb her. She seemed so far away from the proceedings. She's like that sometimes."

"Like what, Marie?" surprised to hear this from a starched Catholic. We never discuss issues of faith; they are always secretive or seem vaguely forbidden.

"Visionary, Madame. I remember Good Friday in March of 1940. She was in the Church, praying. I had finished my private devotions and was leaving. She was kneeling at the altar of Holy Mother Mary and her rosary chain had just broken at the beads of the 'Our Father.' I couldn't imagine why she was so upset. I knelt down next to her and whispered to ask if there was anything I could do to ease her pain. I never interrupt anyone in prayer and felt odd doing it . . . but something led me to her."

"What did she say, Marie?"

"Her voice was hoarse, Madame. The church was dark. Every statue was shrouded in black cloth. Her eyes shining in the flicker of the votive candles were fiery and sad as though they saw the future.

"She whispered, 'My beads broke as I recited deliver us from evil. Our Marianne will be so sick and parts of her will die.'"

"What did she mean, Marie?"

"Marianne being France, Madame, Amélie saw the war coming. She mumbled we would lose our freedom. Thousands of Frenchmen would die. The Huns would rape and scold us all over again. This time we would betray each other."

"Oh my God, Marie, the poor woman. Fr. Schlemmer left the parish at the beginning of Lent that year and Beauverger replaced him. She was so nervous. So was I. We had lost our confidant and had to tuck our spiritual intuition deep in our hearts. Amélie had to tell someone she trusted. You, Marie."

Marie wipes her eyes and sips her tea. Guy returns the conversation to the funeral. I'm grateful to drop my thoughts on how Amélie copes with her visions. Why, when I'm so fearful of all things mystical, do I try to interpret them? It's either hubris . . . or desperation.

"The conductor of the local choral society eulogized Dieter as a musician and teacher of thirty-five years. It was odd that he spoke at the gravesite, Madame. People assumed the Vichy-ites needed to downplay Dieter's influence on the town. The Milice feared civilian recrimination. They knew fewer mourners would attend the burial. Even there, nothing was said about Dieter's past mayoralty, his politics or the war. They only mentioned his service in the first war. There was no mention of how he died."

"*Mais, c'est typique*, Guy," I sneer, "Vichy forbids us to recount a man's political accomplishments publicly if he wasn't a fascist. Everything is censored. I'm sure Résistants, musicians, political cronies, Dieter's violin and piano students—and certainly his enemies—did better searching their own hearts in silence to remember him."

"There were a few in the pews spying for tidbits about Dieter's hidden life, Madame. Hundreds of people watched from the streets. Amélie was overwhelmed by their support. This funeral was a political protest. First the town lost your husband and now another former mayor," Guy frowns.

"Oui, our best men have been vulnerable. Strange, isn't it?" Marie questions, "Rumors were flying before the Mass began. Everyone wondered why his casket was closed at *la veillée*, the wake, the night before."

This surprises me until I recall what Alain said to Jacques about a closed casket.

"Mon Dieu, do you think he was disfigured, Marie?"

It kills me to hide what I saw. In the end I don't know if Dieter was in that coffin. I swallow hard as she answers, "Maybe when this hell is over Alain will tell us, Madame."

"Madame, did you see the procession?" Guy tries to pull me away from my sorrow.

"I watched the cortège from the balcony, Guy: the casket strewn with flowers on the open horse-drawn carriage and everyone in silence as the dirge played.

"I was surprised the Gestapo placed officers along the route to the cemetery. The Milice must have insisted on it," I stare at the tablecloth and blow my nose before adding, "Amélie looked fragile with Claudine and Dr. Duvette walking beside her.

"I saw you two in the second row of mourners. I inspected each person. The old political hacks from Dieter's mayoral days were in the rear. I saw Édouard, Emil's finance administrator. He was Dieter's magistrate before he left to head the bank. I hadn't seen him since the LaFrance luncheon."

"How did you see us in such detail, Madame?" Guy asks surprised.

"Last night when you returned from Maman's, I took Heisler's telescope out of the sedan. Sorry, I forgot to tell you, Guy. I'll return it."

"No, no, Madame. Perhaps you should keep it now that you don't go out so often."

Marie looks worried when he says this and tries to distract me, "Madame, did you hear Dieter's students playing with the band? Wasn't it beautiful to honor him that way? He had so much love and enthusiasm. His was a life to celebrate."

"I heard some of their tribute, Marie, but I retreated to the bedroom to check on Marta. She was asleep at last, poor angel. And the rest of the service afterward?"

"There was no reception," Guy says, suppressing his anger.

"Vraiment? That's incredible, Guy," I shake my head in disgust.

"Claudine took Amélie to her house and only immediate family and closest friends were invited. It was understood that no one from the Underground should visit. The SS and Milice were watching Amélie . . . hoping to finger anyone suspected of being Résistance. Obviously Dieter said nothing under torture, and by publicly avoiding our moral obligation to his widow in her hour of need the Milice are still guessing,"

Marie speaks softly until desperation breaks through her tightly controlled demeanor, "This loss, Madame, of a real Frenchman who stood for our values of free France is so humiliating! Hitler has us cornered by our own French fascists. It's shameful that only a hidden Résistance has had the courage to hold fast to our liberty. Now that the Boches are losing, everyone parades full of pride as though they've been Résistants since 1940. It's a disgrace when hypocrites try to be your friends. You have to acquiesce because they could still denounce you at the eleventh hour."

The loss of our champion so near the end of our bondage lays a heavy weight of grief and foreboding on us. Especially on me, since I know there's a slim chance Dieter may be alive.

Our effort to shield and ferry human beings to safety has been undone. We're adrift without a greater unifying purpose. The prospect of returning to a perfunctory life in which Guy and Marie serve me, and I treat them as my butler and housekeeper appears absurd, rude, and impossible. This hell has made us stronger than a family.

We sit hunched over the end of the kitchen table. A few candles light the room. My lip quivers and my eyes begin their slow climb to shed sorrow. Immediately, Guy and Marie place their hands over mine. I need to stand and cannot move.

Marie hesitates, "Madame, please, let us pray."

I nod yes and she clears her throat, "Dear God, as you watch over your mortals here, be most kind to one who is now at your gates of eternal life."

Guy and I recite with her, "Oh, most sublime soul, in peace to thy blessed home may ye go, to receive the full measure of love ye have in this life so graciously bestowed. Amen."

We bid each other good night with tired, red-rimmed eyes that mirror stalwart commitment.

I go upstairs and sit by my bedchamber window, looking down at the soft flow of the Doubs in the moonlight. My mind ponders what it means to "cover another's back." According to the Underground's discipline it's almost impossible to lie successfully to an enemy interrogator if you know the truth. Being kept ignorant of another's orders is a deliberate protection in case of arrest. If we know nothing, there's a slim chance we might be acquitted, eventually. The enemy has to find the one person who knows all the ranks and cells of activity. Only a few people carry that responsibility. Dieter is . . . was . . . one of them.

I'm the most ignorant member because I play both sides of the fence—a unique "privilege." Despised by the public *and* my Underground tribe, no one trusts me.

Two years ago Dieter held me in his arms when I was at my turning point. I had to let go of the trauma of Emil's demise and accept the bitter sexual indignity I paid for shielding refugees. I stepped forward with Dieter's support, and in 1939 and 1941 we stood together on the same ground that holds my beloved Emil. Today that earth received Kreuzier's body.

Maman says, "The more things change on the surface—the more they appear the same underneath."

The timing of Dieter's death so close to the finale of our Teutonic servitude is an even greater misfortune when the Normandy Invasion renews our hope. The Amis and British are on French soil in force now, in the north and south. All one hears is support for de Gaulle's Free French Forces. While this is a sign of hope, dark events remind us the war isn't over.

Telephone messages from Maman's friends near Limoges detail the increasing boldness of Résistance attacks and the Huns' vengeance against French civilians. People in the path of retreating Waffen SS are very nervous.

Maman's friends tell of a Nazi reprisal on June 10th at Oradour-sur-Glane. The whole town assassinated . . . 642 men, women and children burnt to a crisp, and only eight hours southwest of Besançon by car. It's beyond belief. The news of the massacre spreads first via witnesses, then through the Underground.

As the Allies push the Boches east to the Rhine, crossing France toward our border with Switzerland and Germany, my wretched collabo-ratrice status is a threat to my safety. Marie was right. Vichy-ites see how unpopular their stance is and switch allegiance overnight. No one has come through my basement for weeks. I'm a prisoner in my home like a fly trapped in a spider's web.

Against the growing anxiety, I receive a dinner invitation from Germaine for Saturday evening, on June 17th. I suppose it's to celebrate the Invasion, but still, I'm surprised. The last four years have been harsh, and even the rich in this largely sheltered area are feeling a pinch in the pantry. People spend hours growing what little seed they saved each year. They scour the forests and fish the Doubs to compensate for shortages and avoid shopping "au noir." Stands of trees are nearly clear of brush and dead wood used for fuel. Windowsills overflow with pots of greens and herbs. Cold cellars hold dwindling supplies of roots, beans, squash, onions, potatoes, dried fruits, and wheat in strong boxes beneath floorboards hiding a few Old Testaments.

The populace is quite lean, even in this less trampled corner of France. No one expected the war to endure for years. Stocks of smoked meat are gone and the pickled fish have been consumed. People have to avoid butchering the few chickens and hooved animals they were allowed to keep. Dried fruits and homemade jams are eaten sparingly.

I ponder this as I reread Germaine's invitation. The change in my attitude amazes me. Feeding unexpected lodgers has been a challenge that developed my frugality. It makes me aware how the poorest families struggle. Four years ago I lacked the charity to care.

Like many wealthy individuals, Édouard has access to imported foods traded "au noir" along the Mediterranean. I suppose Germaine can always serve champignons from the forest and fresh truites from the river. That's how we celebrate "basement soirées" in this house.

Still, I'm intrigued. People are nervous these days. Perhaps a party is a good idea. I mustn't judge. Germaine always chooses her public moments to impress her friends, but to invite me, of all people? I'm afraid to venture out of my home.

I made a practice of seeing her separately after she married Édouard. I still felt naked in his presence without another man's protection. I thought I buried those fears years ago in a field of fresh manure. I have tried to forgive him. But when Édouard was friendly at the bank after

Madame La Farge fainted, I left ill at ease. When he kissed my hand at the LaFrance luncheon I suddenly felt like a helpless, marked woman entangled in Mueller's web of betrayal.

At some point, every man in my life—including Dieter—has been my Judas. I brood over this, frustrated by the need to share my foreboding and gain perspective.

At dinner I ask Guy and Marie what they think about the invitation.

"I need your opinions," I announce apprehensively.

"Oui, Madame?"

"I received an invitation to a soirée at the deVillement's."

Immediately Marie is suspicious. "It's too soon for Germaine to make amends, Madame. The war isn't over. Roemler comes here for tea. Why would Édouard want to see you?"

"I don't know. I'm sure Germaine still sees me as a traitor. Unless she's inviting me for a public berating, I can't imagine what to say to her. I'm uncomfortable about going."

"Well, don't go then. Except you're curious, aren't you, Madame?" Marie knows her mistress well.

"All right, Guy," Marie gives him a wink, "let's see what we can uncover about Madame Germaine. Meanwhile, rethink your encounters with her, and anything others have told you that might shed light on her reason to invite you."

❧

Later that night, just before I retire, there's a knock on the side door entry to the servants' quarters. A dark figure is admitted as I watch from the window in my bedchamber. Surprised and curious, I tiptoe slowly down the back stairs to listen through the door. Inside the kitchen I hear Guy, Marie and their visitor.

"What can we do to help?"

"There are many who still need to be moved. Give a party for the Gestapo. It's the only way to do it safely. Entertain with music. Be festive with liquor and food so we can get the job done without detection. It should be the last group. Paris will be liberated after Bastille Day, a few weeks at the earliest and the end of August by the latest. The Allies will bomb Germany into oblivion. With luck and planning the Krauts will be squeezed dry between the Soviets and the Americans. Our refugees will be safer here if moved to more livable places."

"When do we do this?"

"In a few days. You'll be notified. We'll supply you with food, drink, and music. She needn't spend any of her money."

"Wait, she has to go to a soirée this Saturday evening. It can't be then."

"Who's giving this party?"

"The deVillements, Germaine and her husband."

"Édouard is dangerous. Your mistress has to be careful. Someone is after her."

"What do you mean?"

"Édouard deVillement is the reason many others are out of sight. You must say nothing about seeing me. I know she's innocent but after the Liberation it could be hard on her."

"Yes, we understand that."

"No, you have only a piece of the story, a fragment, believe me. DeVillement is a devil. He's powerful in the Milice. I'll arrange this party to cover the crossing for another evening, perhaps the next day, Sunday. We need to act fast. Please, take care of your mistress."

I can't identify that voice. It's familiar but deliberately husky. The chairs scrape the floor, and before the outer door creaks open I race upstairs to a window. The figure moves back into the night—too heavily cloaked to identify. Who is he?

And why are Guy and Marie so secretive when I risk everything for us? Who is this man who has as much knowledge of our Underground operation as Dieter?

✄

I sleep badly that night, and still feel resentful toward Guy and Marie the next morning. She knocks lightly at the sitting room door with tea and biscuits. I stop her as she leaves,

"Marie, I need to speak with you about last night."

"Oh, you mean about Germaine, Madame?"

"No, about the man who came here."

"Oh. I, uh, how did you know about that?"

"I listened through the door. I feel slighted, Marie. Why didn't you and Guy take me into your confidence? How could you operate behind my back?"

I let my fear and isolation out on my dear housekeeper. The last few weeks I've been stuck in this house have been awful without Dieter—and Old Testaments to cross. My mission behind this ugly collaborative persona has dried up. I'm tense like a cornered rat while the war crawls on. I finally master my role and the play is on hold.

Marie gives a respectful but cutting retort, "Madame, don't think all that circulates under your roof is your business or is even safe for you to know. We protect many by our silence, especially you. Please, don't press us for details."

"Why, I . . . I'm sorry," I'm speechless at Marie's directness. She quickly tries to smooth things over after realizing her harshness.

"Madame, please forgive me for being short of tongue, but Guy and I have run the crossings out of your home from the beginning. We know what a terrible toll this has been on your health. We've had meetings in your kitchen on details unknown and unimportant to you. Whatever we could tell you we did, but this time, you'll have to trust us. However, I will find out about Germaine soon."

My eyes redden again. I begin to cry like a small child, ashamed of eavesdropping and my lack of respect for Marie's loyalty. How I wish Dieter were here.

She puts her hands on my shoulders. "Madame, I know you're lonely here without Marta. You're exhausted from nerves. You must hate this place by now."

Through my sobs I manage, "Marie, forgive me for treating you badly and behaving like a child who feels left out of everyone's game."

"Madame, you were raised to feel superior to people like me. You're my employer, naturally, but please don't question my obedience and devotion. We must guard you. There's a higher cause that dictates."

"You're right, Marie. Say no more. Forgive me, please." Interrupting her, I retrieve my reserve again. She leans down to whisper in my ear, "There's nothing to forgive, Madame."

Just then the doorbell rings. We stiffen in anticipation. Our eyes lock us into our familiar defensive stance. Marie answers the door as I run to the bathroom to wash my face.

In a minute she knocks. "Madame, Obersturmführer Roemler is here to see you. Are you in?"

His presence shocks me back to reality. My adrenalin flows again. Quickly I reconstruct our last meeting.

"Wait Marie," I open the door as I wipe my face, "What do you think he wants?"

"I'm not sure, perhaps he's nervous about the Americans' landing, Madame."

"Oui, bien sûr." He must also listen to the BBC to find out what's going on. Maman wrote in a note he was overheard at the LaFrance saying Goebbels' harangues are ridiculous lies. "Let him wait in the front salon. I'll ring if we need schnapps and food."

I straighten my skirt, tighten my belt another notch and hike up my bra, leaving the top button of my cotton sweater undone. I pull my hair down from a matronly chignon to let it hang freely over my shoulders and dab on lipstick. "There," I look in the mirror, smiling, "Hah. That ought to arouse him to my way of thinking."

I stride into the room confidently. Roemler is looking at my wedding photo with Emil by the writing desk and turns quickly to greet me. He's my third taskmaster, and this time I don't extend my hand. Enough of ignorance and vulnerability. I just smile.

"Guten Morgen, Obersturmführer, an unexpected pleasure. Bitte, sit down. What can I do for you?" I search his young face for the reason he's here.

"Guten Tag, Madame Fellner. I ah, came here to ask a favor of you."

"Yes, go on."

"Ja, well, there's a dinner party this Saturday at the deVillements estate and I've been invited. I'm new here and wonder if you'd accompany me."

"Oh, well, strange you should ask. I too, have been invited and hesitate to go because I'm a widow with no escort and an outsider in this town."

I speak flatly of my dilemma. Roemler is pleased.

"Well, shall we go together, Madame? I shall call for you at what hour?"

"Oh, let's say about 7:00 p.m. By the way, Obersturmführer Roemler, how old are you?

"Madame, I am twenty-eight."

"Fine. Well, then, that's settled. Anything else?"

"Ah, no Madame. I shall be going. Until Saturday evening?"

He's too young for me to be seductive. I can see he's disappointed so I link my arm in his and press my breast against his bicep as I escort him to the door. He sighs and blushes. Oh no, a virgin, too? The thought of another affair wearies me. This war won't end soon enough.

The next morning the weather is predictably beautiful . . . in contrast to the precarious direction my life is taking. Today sunshine highlights the yellow, blue, and white late spring bouquet on the breakfast table in the servants' kitchen. The blooms burst from an antique Italian majolica vase surrounded with other hand-painted bowls on a soft, pastel green tablecloth. This arrangement against alternating off white panels and pale flowered wallpaper is contained by dark wood moldings. The room reminds me of the intimate Post-Impressionist interiors of both Vuillard and Bonnard. The feast of color settles my eye. I smile as Guy serves.

"Madame, a word with you please?"

"Yes, Guy, what is it?"

"You have decided to go to the deVillements on Saturday evening?"

"Yes. Roemler is escorting me. Why?"

"Please, be on your guard there. Don't let anyone take you away from the main rooms."

"What are you talking about? Stop all this mystery, Guy, get it out in the open."

I catch myself annoyed at how his urgency washes away my fleeting peace so early in the day. "Please excuse me, I didn't mean to be rude. Must we discuss this now?"

"Sorry, Madame, yes. We have to make preparations. Let me tell you what we've learned about Germaine's husband. He has had a secret affiliation with the Reich for the duration of the war. His family has had a major financial interest in German generator factories since the late thirties when the Reich converted them to airplane engine manu-facture. He's made a lot of money. His outward demeanor has been quiet because his wife is an ardent supporter of the Fighting French. He has used her opinionated anti-Vichy sentiments to hide traitorous business dealings. We think he has invited you to find out which side you're on."

"Oh God, a political test. But why me?"

"If the war goes against Édouard, his retribution may wreak serious consequences on innocent victims. Beyond that we can only speculate." Guy is pensive.

"Wait a minute. You mean someone is using me to find out what his intentions are?"

"We appreciate that this is risky, Madame, but. . . ."

"Oh my, I'm not so sure I should go at all," I interrupt.

Guy is very formal when apprehensive. Marie watches with pursed lips and a deadly serious expression.

"Please, Madame, you will be safe with an SS escort. It means the Boches trust you."

"Wunderbar! Sticking my neck out again to be both the fisherman and his bait? You realize if Édouard was intimate with that scum Mueller, he knows all about my private life. Sacrebleu, I don't mind risking every-thing for Old Testaments, they're innocent and honorable, but for the spoiled rich, my own French caste? Do you think Germaine will put up with me, a widow, for the sake of her husband? I'm a threat to every woman in this town with a shaky marriage. They're all on the threshold of old age with a waistless figure and a sagging face. She'll never leave me alone with him. I'm a slut and a traitor."

"That may appear to be true but with Roemler at your side it won't be a problem."

"I have to be really careful, Guy. Only Dieter would ask me to do such a dangerous thing. I can't imagine how my stomach will behave in Édouard's presence for an entire evening."

Guy and Marie are holding back a lot more details and again I'm annoyed.

"Who sent you this message? Guy, who was that man who came here the other night?"

"Oh no, Madame, no. Please don't ask. I can't say."

Guy knows the truth, but it's my body on the *bascule* and my head in the *lunette*.

"Anything else you can't tell me, Guy, before I lay down for *notre rasoir national*?" He catches the fear behind my guillotine sarcasm and almost answers.

"Well, yes, Madame. The person who came. . . ."

"Guy! Be quiet!" Marie rarely disagrees but turns away from the sink as Guy responds,

"Madame, please don't ask about visitors. He was a servant of the Résistance, all right?"

Guy defers to Marie's raised eyebrow. Concerned about my growing paranoia she adds, "Anyway, the visitor said you must have a party for the Germans within ten days."

"What? For all of them?" Stunned, I look at Guy. Surprise bleeds through my battle fatigue.

He answers patiently, "Yes, Madame, several crossings will disperse those in hiding closer to Italy. They're counting on you to distract the officers when they move people."

"We'll have guests here in the basement at the same time, Madame," Marie adds.

"Vraiment? I thought we were done with that," rubbing my left cheekbone to quell my head from exploding into a migraine, "Well, all right, but to have a party I'll need to invite other women. I won't have sufficient funds to cover food and drink until next month. The expense must be hidden from Stefan," and sigh as my fingers chill.

"Don't worry, Madame, food, drink and women will be supplied, even records and a gramophone, whatever you need," Guy explains.

"And this diversion will be on Sunday evening, the day after Germaine's party?"

"Oui, Madame. Will you send for Sylvia to help you and Marie prepare the rooms?"

"Yes, I hadn't thought of that. The Boches will get drunk and want sex. We'll have to open at least one side room with a day bed and use a screen for the other area. The dogs will simply have to wait their turns. Maybe the war will end while their pants are down!"

Guy snickers at my risqué humor before leaving the room. I stare out the window at the beautiful warm day and shake my head at the upcoming storm of events. Full of questions, now more distraught over my own party than Germaine's soirée, my work is even more dangerous and demoralizing. Its higher purpose shames the anger clinging to my nerves. I fight to digest today's petit déjeuner—soured by these new marching orders.

After the meal I ponder the jealousy Édouard felt, living in Emil's shadow. My spurning him was not the only thorn in his side. Emil was the other. Édouard never had Emil's charismatic energy or the rugged masculine presence of the men I admire. He was insecure and a sickly child, loveless and dull. He took life from the sidelines and never caught up with the other males. Who'd have thought he'd marry Germaine and become rich from his sleazy business acumen?

I must wend my way carefully through this maze. I go upstairs to select a dress for the dinner, musing on how strange life is when a Nazi escort gives me comfort.

Chapter Twenty-Two

Inimical Intrigue

17 June 1944, Saturday

Musicians are playing a Strauss waltz as Roemler and I enter the mansion. Here we are, a handsome Vichy couple. He looks so young in his uniform and I still feel elegant despite hints of age. The sixteen years between us don't show too greatly tonight.

My only problem is his Nazi affiliation. A pity he's caught in a web of moral heartlessness.

I worried about it in the car when I was seated next to him. My mind was spinning with the latest news of reprisal I don't dare discuss with Roemler.

I wonder what he'll say tonight about the massacre at Oradour-sur-Glane? The news still circulates across the country—there is more to it, and it's even worse now. Vichy Milice betrayed Résistants who nabbed a Waffen SS leader, a German battalion commander. An SS Sturmbannführer apparently ordered the *wrong town* destroyed. An arbitrary revenge on his part, the village of Oradour-sur-Vayres should have been their target.

Was this carnage for the loss of one Boche higher-up, or revenge for the Allies landing here in France to redeem us? It's a national disgrace. The Huns have become diabolical as never before. Such sadistic satisfaction has to have Hitler's stamp of indoctrination from a twisted childhood. Even a dog's brain must be inflamed for him to become rabid. And what of the rabidity of Vichy . . . to turn on other Frenchmen?

Roemler looks as out of place in this mansion as he did sitting in the Mercedes. He reminds me of my adolescent years during the Great War in 1914, when a Christmas truce was called on the Belgian battlefield. My uncle wrote to Maman that English and French Allies exchanged holiday greetings with the German enemy in a "no man's land" between their trenches.

Infantry from each side shared food from home. They gave each other haircuts. If the enemy and allied foot soldiers had had the choice, in those few hours their war would have been over. As it was, never more would opposing generals call for a Christmas truce. Charity and human kindness are dangerous weapons in the hearts of mere infantrymen.

Pulling back to the present I tell myself: "You're on duty, tonight. Your words must not echo sadness or anger. Put the ousting of the Boches aside for this soirée. You know nothing if asked and have no opinion. Replay this script with only trivia to discuss. Sashay your vapid mind and sexy terrain across Germaine's wooden inlaid floors on Roemler's arm."

Édouard greets us outside the large dining hall with its beautiful antiques and carpets. I've forgotten how impersonal the interior of this old château is. My Résistante persona squirms in this large, vacant space with drafty windows and enormous chandeliers. The irreplaceable cut glass pieces hang over Germaine's long dining table and corridors. To think she dragged them from her old home in Strasbourg. They hang today because her confidence in the Allies *not* to bomb the city before 1943 was matched by Édouard's conspicuous consumption.

Aye, Ingrid, watch your tongue. Your old aristocratic hauteur sounds just like your father. Have some discretion, woman. I chide myself until

I glance at my enemy escort—who has difficulty concealing his awe at the opulence I disdain.

Roemler, son of a farmer and ironworker, hasn't been privy to the lavish living and social masks of the rich. My casual handling of Édouard, glued to my face and salivating at my bosom, shocks his agrarian Austrian Catholic morality—yet a sidelong glance tells me SS Wilhelm is also aroused.

I'm quite chic tonight in a black silk and taffeta floor-length gown, with thin shoulder straps and low-cut back. It's not a new dress. I fashioned a black and white checkered bow and basted it to the right hip. Then I twisted a long red chiffon scarf from the bodice on the bias across the sarong type hip section. It ends at the bow. My hair, upswept to the left side of my temple in a deep wave, completes the attention to my war-torn torso. Elbow-length black kid gloves conceal my fingers, roughened from gardening.

I walk gracefully across the room. The guests appear breathless at my poised entrance. The men fantasize and the women contain their envy. Their social posturing in these overstated interiors feels like it's 1913.

Tonight I sit opposite old acquaintances who sold their integrity for Nazi profit. I knew these six couples informally before the war when Emil was alive. Goodness, I haven't seen them for almost five years. They moved south to the unoccupied zone in the early days. I suppose they now spend even more time abroad to recuperate from the war, "dahling."

Watching them I wonder how one can deny change when it will blossom in the near future. No one can escape it. I'm prepared to face detainment except for losing Marta, but at least I've done something to ease my conscience.

My nerves may be raw from the public's constant gossip but my soul is at peace. My Underground script has taught me to replace resentment with mercy. I accept those who can't be trusted and strain to make them comfortable, as much out of charity and pity as for self-preservation. They'd never guess what my secret sacrifice entails or what it means to me.

How did I escape their superficial world? Oh, don't be so arrogant, Ingrid. You made choices they didn't. Your experience is totally different. Smile sweetly at each introduction, old girl, and remember the names you once knew when you were ignorant and playful in 1938. But you wonder what this public attention from Édouard and Germaine means? You delayed your entrance thinking it wouldn't matter, and here they are, waiting for dinner on your account.

Embarrassed? Don't show it. Play these people from your position of superior aristocratic caste. Let them bow tonight while you hold court for those lacking courage to come near you. Interesting, Agnes and Charles Balfour are not here.

Germaine surprises me with kisses on both cheeks. Why does she fawn all over me?

"Good evening, Ingrid. You look lovely. A new dress, my dear?"

"Oh yes, thank you, Germaine."

This dress is new because I am. Will I ever have the inclination to shop again? She looks so wasted. Her face is over-painted and dwarfed by that ash-blonde wig. She's lost a lot of weight. Her clothes hang on her.

We're escorted to the dinner table with the other guests. Roemler and I are seated across from each other, with Édouard at the head of the table to Roemler's right and my left. Germaine sits next to Roemler. By custom, I would have expected her to sit at the other end, across from Édouard. Tonight, however, one of his bank cronies faces him with his wife on his left. The other couples sit alternately male and female on each side between us. This appears highly irregular, but I don't question it.

As the object of their pecking order, I'd expect my seat, as in medieval days, to be down wind and "down salt"—far from the bite of their malicious seasoning.

"Your table is elegant as usual, Germaine," I observe, "quite an achievement at this stage of the war." I get a good look at her and notice how wrinkled she is since the LaFrance luncheon. Why has she shrunken so? She must be terribly ill. Oh dear, her petulant lower lip protrudes, undone by my comment on her largesse. Germaine speaks only once to Roemler.

"Do you have a river for trout fishing near your family home, Obersturmführer?"

"Yes, Madame deVillement. We prepare the trout the same as you French do—but your trout paté is particularly fine."

"Thank you, Obersturmführer. You are most kind."

"Not at all. Your French cuisine is an occupier's greatest pleasure. Madame Fellner also serves a most delicious baked trout, as I guess you already know, Madame deVillement."

Germaine smiles dutifully at him and gives me a sour glance when he looks down at his plate. Naturally I entertain him just as she does.

Thus the dinner conversation commences with a light fishing expedition into my life, a massive waste of breath, really. Édouard knows well over sixty percent of my cheese feeds the Wehrmacht and the rest sells through rationing with a hefty percentage of profit taken off the top for Vichy. Still he casts his bait, "Your farms are producing nicely, aren't they, Ingrid?"

"I look forward to the day when I can own my herds and fromageries again," I reply stiffly and glare at my SS escort, "when this lethal folderol that steals my profits is finished."

The other guests swallow hard and stare at their plates. Good. Let them see that I can get away with insolence when they can't. That should convince them of my privileged status in the eyes of my local enemy escort. Roemler has no retort. I'm not sure whether that's because of good manners or his lack of information on the state of agricultural finance in beleaguered France. I don't care. My goal is to stop Édouard's conversation on any topic about my life.

"Well, ah, I'm sure you will agree that Vichy is wise to work out solutions to help both France and Germany with regard to food supplies, Madame," Édouard tries to smooth over my abruptness and impress his German guest.

"Germany should have known mowing down other countries in the Einsatzgruppen massacres would leave their Eastern larders empty. Obviously, the Russians preferred to eat the flour and water holding up their wallpaper and burn their fields rather than let an enemy have access to their delicious *sarrasin* (buckwheat). So sad to say this, but General Zhukov made certain Herr Hitler learned that lesson the hard way, did he not, Obersturmführer?"

I repeat in French what I say in German. Édouard almost chokes on his dinner when he hears this bilingual vitriol roll off my tongue. Roemler's cheeks turn a deep red. He murmurs a small "Ja" at his plate and raises his eyebrows, looking down at his trout.

"Really Édouard, haven't you seen enough at the bank? What's that phrase—Fritzie guest steals profits from Jacquie's nest?"

Dead silence reigns. Having disposed of Édouard's financial talk leaves only my mother and daughter on his conversational agenda. I suppose he's had enough fishing on my sour riverbank and doesn't inquire about my family. I quit talking for the duration of the dinner and let the other guests go on about their trips, furs, the price of coal for their gazogènes and diamonds—the usual flotsam and jetsam of insipid rich lives. Never once is Oradour-Sur-Glane mentioned. My God, these people are no longer French citizens.

Roemler has nothing to discuss about any of their topics except the relative merits of der deutsche Mercedes against *das französische* auto, der Citroën, und *das englische* Rolls Royce. I translate for him when the vocabulary strays from elementary automotive to technical mechanics.

The food is very rich, and as the meal progresses I eat and drink more than usual to avoid conversing. Germaine remains a curiosity; I am so intrigued by her role as Édouard's passive marionette.

Everyone rises for liqueurs, smokes, and more gossip after dessert. The genders retire to separate locations like Victorian English, except for our host. I catch Roemler's eye when Édouard sidles up to me. "My dear, shall we go outside on the balcony?" I remember Guy's warning to stay inside. Germaine overhears his invitation and immediately escorts Roemler to the other male guests.

"I'm quite cold, actually. Could we go into your study, please, Édouard?"

"Your wish is my command, my dear."

My dinner lurches in my stomach at Édouard's reply.

Once inside, he moves very close and runs his fingertips over my bare shoulder. I bristle at his forwardness. His devious eyes bore into my back as he moves behind me. I sense him misting over to concoct some bestial sodomy in his sick mind. He inhales my perfume sharply and brushes his hand against my taffeta dress.

Coming in here was a mistake. Even years later I still arouse a passion in him. He can't stand being so close, yet unable to subdue me.

"I compliment you on your beauty tonight, Ingrid."

"Thank you, Édouard." His cornered prey forces herself to be civil and waits, hoping he'll expose his political intentions once he gets past his carnal inflammation.

"The fragrance of your thick dark-reddish hair and that soft brunette fuzz moving in a vee down your spine, the idle curls at the nape of your neck, that wild violet scent. . . ."

Oh God, it's *worse* than years ago. Aye, Ingrid, you idiot, you dressed to impress and never considered how his reaction could infect you.

"I see you naked in the dark, outside, your hips firm as you prance, a succulent young doe. Your clean body quivers and short soft fur stands erect with fear. You surrender the essence of spring flowers from your warm underbelly. Your innocent flesh reclines, dew-kissed in the sweet young grasses. You're trapped in a black, directionless midnight only I control."

Édouard's eyes are fixed to a sadistic image. In his own darkness his sick appetite possesses him—as he fights to curb his lust. I'm appalled that his fantasy tugs at my stomach. It swells with the cloying bait of his extravagant dinner table. My digestion spins in acidic somersaults.

I say nothing, but move toward his desk. His hideous subliminal message makes me ill, like the wounded doe caught in his snare—about to be massaged into orgasmic surrender, seconds before her death.

He smiles at the effect of his verbal seduction and turns his back for a minute, nervously reaching into his tobacco pouch on the reading table. He prepares his pipe and searches clumsily for matches.

On his desk I catch sight of a document with Emil Fellner's name on it. I reach out gently to push the top paper aside. To my horror I see one of Emil's old securities with a forged signature and the deVillement seal at the bottom.

I startle when Édouard's voice breaks the tension of our lurid encounter in his head. His wicked fantasy has squeezed the life out of my feminine goodness. I feel weak and sedated, and hover—almost outside my flesh—as a final effort to remain in this room with him.

"So you have kept a running acquaintanceship with the SS these last years?" he begins, still standing with his back to me.

I can barely keep up the conversation. My eyes drift over the papers. How fortuitous to have decided to come in here after all. Their damning evidence is too good to be true.

"Yes," I answer coldly.

"And I suppose you realize the war is winding down, now?"

Where is this leading? I'm distracted by his lewd thoughts. He's driving fear into me to force me forward, but I have no idea where to go with this conversation. What is his plan? I have to stop this superficial repartee. I'm alert, nauseated, and anxious like a fleeing quarry. I feel undone and give up all tact after reading Emil's forged signature,

"Édouard, let's be frank. Why did you invite me and what do you think I can tell you? Your wife has disparaged me for the duration of this war—from the moment *she* decided what my political views were. So what is your interest?"

He laughs to cover his surprise but his tone is guarded, "Oh, Germaine is a card, she and her fighting French. She has nationalism like one struck down with a fatal disease. Why it's nothing, my dear, nothing. I ah, was just making small talk."

"Like hell you were, Édouard. We're both too wise to waste time on drivel."

He squirms, taken aback by my toughness. Quite different from the pre-war princess on Emil's arm who barely smiled and rarely talked. I still have no clear idea what he wants. I should keep my mouth shut, but my newfound courage makes digging at him irresistible.

"Well, I want to know what inside information you have on Berlin," he coughs out after the first pull on his pipe is bitter. Distracted avec moi, he didn't clean it well and packed it too tightly.

"Me? You have eyes in your head, Édouard. You think these wind-up toys they send here to harass us and deport Jews know anything about their future? They're hardly paid anymore. They send children like Wilhelm Roemler. You didn't invite me here for this."

"Oui. You're right, Ingrid. I want to ask you for a favor. I need you to pass some documents from abroad to Roemler and receive others for me."

"Do it yourself, Édouard. I'm not a courier service."

What's this about? Why should I pass documents? And what are these papers here with my departed husband's name on them?

"You'll be paid handsomely for your efforts, my dear."

Édouard doesn't know I suspect he plans to leave Europe. He's pilfered profits from German factories for years and will take large sums out of France. Perhaps they're already placed in a foreign bank for safekeeping. He must be looking for a way to involve me that will keep me quiet and blackmail me into collusion. Why else propose such a ridiculous scheme?

I feel sorry for Germaine. If this is what he's doing she won't be going with him. Actually, that would be a blessing for her. It's amusing that Édouard treats me like the collaborating prostitute everyone in town claims I am. I laugh out loud.

"What's so humorous, Ingrid, darling?" He tries again in a tone that begs to be genuine but sounds hollow and manipulative.

I feel threatened. Does Germaine know this is being dumped into my lap?

"Nothing of public interest, Édouard."

He stares—at a loss for words. He's been told I'm destitute, and he's certain of my imminent disgrace when the war ends. I'll be publicly humiliated and divested of my income. Apparently he thinks I'll accept his offer of money and jewels even if I manage to retain my fortune. Maybe he thinks I *want* more money. Just like everyone else at his dinner table. He's not sure how to proceed. My confidence has ruined his plans. What's he hiding? What would my being his accomplice do for him?

"Well, my dear, you're making a great mistake. I can make you a wealthy woman indeed," he adds when I skirt his question.

"I don't want more money, thank you, Édouard, dear. And thank you for the lovely dinner. I'm going home now."

"But, Ingrid, we haven't finished."

"No, sorry, Édouard, I must leave." I open the study door and walk straight into Germaine . . . who was eavesdropping.

"Oh, excuse me. I was just coming to find you, Ingrid. Please, let's go outside on the terrace to talk."

"I'm sorry Germaine, but I must leave. Where's Roemler?" I catch sight of Wilhelm crossing the entrance hall. I call in an authoritarian tone to mask my fear, "Obersturmführer, please escort me home now."

"With pleasure, Madame."

"But Ingrid, it's still early and we have a lot to catch up on. It's been many months."

"Germaine, if you have anything kind to say it will be news indeed, dear. Call on me at home if you must. Good evening."

"What did you say to offend her?" Germaine interrogates Édouard as Roemler places my wrap over my shoulders.

"Nothing!" He barks back aggravated and beaten, "She's as you have said, Germaine, a hardened slut for the enemy!"

As I whip past my host, Édouard leans toward me, and pouts, whispering, "Damn it, I wanted you and lost."

"So generous of you to admit it, Édouard," my pursed lips reply in defense of my bristling flesh, as we fly out the door to Roemler's waiting car and driver.

I have had no idea how obsessed Édouard has been with me. His presence now feels like a greater poison than Mueller's and Roemler's together. As we pull out, the car's headlamps reveal movement in the bushes to the left of the terrace, by the open doors. I strain my neck to look at the garden. Was someone waiting there? I look at Roemler's profile in the dark. Is he behind this tonight? Does he wish me dead? Is it Édouard, Germaine—all of them—or someone else?

Roemler is inebriated and obnoxious, behaving like a playful young bear feeling his power. He leans in my direction and plops his big paw on my thigh, leering. "Ingrid, dear, perhaps you will teach me some tricks tonight, like you did with Franzie? Eh, Schätzchen?"

"You're drunk! I don't entertain drunken men. Forget it!" I push him away.

Old revulsion surfaces when I hear "Schätzchen," Mueller's favorite term of endearment. So demeaning. I've been free of it for weeks.

Tonight this liquor-emboldened virgin bears down on me in the back seat and grabs my arms, "Don't forget who I am, Madame. It's my turn to occupy you. I bought you for the evening and the duration of the war, in fact. Hah!"

I see *his* ugly side and feel his holstered pistol press against my ribs.

"Let me alone or I'll retch all over you, Obersturmführer. I'm feeling quite ill from the heavy food and drink. I warn you, please, don't push me."

Will I have to surrender a third time to Nazi lust? I'm hopeful he'll keep his pants on in the car. He moves away. I begin coughing when we pull up to the house. Guy immediately comes out to escort me in. I practically throw myself into his arms. Shaking, I turn to my escort about to follow me inside, and put my hand up to stop him.

"No. Sorry, Obersturmführer, I'm nauseated." And I lurch toward the shrubbery to heave a bit of dinner very ungracefully. I lean on Guy's arm and bid Roemler goodnight as I wipe my mouth and end with, "Bitte, Obersturmführer; another time."

Guy guides me into the house. Roemler's disappointed and annoyed. He slams the Mercedes' door shut and the vehicle speeds into the night.

"Madame, are you feeling all right?" Guy closes the door and takes my wrap.

"Yes, fine, except I ate and drank too much. I had to leave. The air was too tense in there. I was scared but no one saw it. I had to get rid of that SS. If he calls in the morning, please say I had a sleepless night and can't see anyone until the evening soirée, as planned. I must figure things out."

A few minutes later, changed into my heavy silk robe, I join Guy and Marie in the kitchen. Marie has steeped a cup of peppermint tea.

"Everyone with money to hide has a use for me now," I'm sarcastic between sips. "I have to examine who my social set thinks *they* are and who they think *I* am to understand what's going on with les brahmanes of French society."

"Only one more crossing, Madame, and the pressure will be over for a while."

"For me it's only just begun. What could have happened tonight if I'd gone outside on their terrace, Guy? Who told you to advise me to be careful? You must tell me. After all, if my life is in real danger I deserve to know. This silence isn't fair."

Guy keeps me talking. He knows I'm tired from the strain of the soirée and hopes I will forget to hold him to revealing that name.

"Madame, first, what did you learn about Édouard?"

"He tried to lure me into handling documents and money from Germany. I told him I would not be his courier. Can you imagine? He must have thought I was stupid and didn't understand anything."

"Was there anything else unusual, Madame?" Guy asks cautiously.

"Oui. This was very odd. I saw an old securities folder on his desk with Emil's name on it. I don't think Édouard saw me looking at the papers. I never saw this kind of form in any of Emil's holdings. After his death, the lawyer and accountant made a painstaking review of his legacy. Something is wrong here, terribly wrong."

"What did he offer for your services, Madame?" Marie asks.

"Oh, money and jewels, the usual stuff a female collaborator would get. I refused."

"What do you think he wants from you, Madame?" Guy worries.

"Something evil, Guy. I think he would blackmail me and force me to go away with him. He'd use my alleged collaboration in court to steal my money. Recently he gained controlling interest in the bank holding my family's estate. Emil moved everything into that bank when we were married. I never understood why. I cared so little about financial matters back then.

"And now, Guy, I'm in a very bad position. If the Underground leaders don't come forward to support me, and I'm judged a Nazi sympathizer I could lose my inheritance and *never* recover my reputation. I could be incarcerated or forced to leave France. When Dieter died, I lost my only hope to be safe."

Marie and Guy listen intently. I approach the future realistically, dry-eyed, and trust they understand my plight.

"I cannot rely on testimony of people like you two when the time comes. I trust you both, you know that, but you have no power against the political machinations of our Milice-infested local government. Nor do the farmers or shop owners. If I believe testimony from the leadership in the Résistance is not forthcoming, I should leave now and get my money out while Maman is still alive. Only she can withdraw large sums without causing a scandal."

"Madame, would you leave Stefan without a chance to reconcile?" Marie asks.

"Yes, what about him? He hates me. If he learns I was in the Résistance all along he still may not support me. His word is of no help. I can't continue to play this game without some real security for Marta, and you two as well.

"We will have to leave this house. I have to think about how my actions hurt Maman and my daughter, not to mention Sylvia and Pierre. Stefan's safe financially with a third of Emil's money and all his property. He's a grown man and must live by his own decisions. Lord knows I was a kind belle-mère but failed him. I tried, you know I did, Marie, oui?"

"Oui, Madame, one thing at a time. Be calm, or you'll make yourself ill with worry."

Guy reaches across the table and touches my shaking hands. I sigh sadly and feel ashamed before these two angels. It's unfair to press Guy to reveal names.

"Yes, you're right. I need my rest. I'm exhausted with worry. I don't know who is after me, or if I face arrest, interrogation, deportation, or being murdered like Dieter." I bite my lip and my eyes swell with tears, "My needs are so minor in all this Underground business."

Marie volunteers, "We think it's the same person or group that was behind Mueller's death, Madame."

Guy interrupts her, "Perhaps that person is involved with the bank holding your accounts, Madame. It's impossible to keep Underground contacts inside local banks. The last one was betrayed when he discovered which Vichy-ites sold their estates to raise cash."

"Well, I suspect deVillement will leave when his money is out of France. Probably flee to Algeria or South America. He won't take Germaine. He can't stand her. They live in separate worlds. She had an urgent need to speak to me but I put her off. The house was too thick with intrigue to open a conversation. She'll call here. Whatever Édouard wants me to do means a lot to him. He's perplexed that I refused. He may try to persuade me again."

"Proceed with caution, Madame," Guy warns firmly.

"I will await instructions—wherever they come from," and I narrow my gaze at Guy. My faithful butler scours my mistrust and hardens his jaw the way Dieter once did. I see Dieter in my mind's eye. I wish he were alive. I can almost sense his presence in the room.

Chapter Twenty-Three

Amélie's Visit

18 June 1944, Sunday

"Amélie Van der Kreuzier is downstairs, Madame. Will you come?" Marie calls me away from Marta's schoolwork. I leave Marta to read her history lesson and promise she can visit with Amélie later.

My thoughts wander back over the last three weeks. Amélie sat in my kitchen, forlorn with the image of Dieter's eyes. So much has transpired since his funeral. Fear distracts me after the dinner party last night. Danger looms.

Mundane preoccupations make the day long and dull. Awaiting tonight's SS entertainment makes me behave like a curious animal that cautiously skirts a newly set trap.

Amélie turns to me as I open the receiving salon door. I'm not certain I can carry on a simple conversation anymore. I reach for compassion to share a widow's need for solace.

"Hello, my dear, what a pleasant surprise!" We embrace warmly. I expect to see mourning in her eyes today. Instead she looks otherworldly, not in pain, just distant. I can't push her to divulge her private woes so I try to be positive.

"Join me for a cup of tisane?"

"Yes, thank you, Ingrid. I stopped by to get the herbs your mother sent. I have people to see for Dr. Duvette, and births in the next weeks. I'm preparing tinctures. Do you need any?"

"Not really, thank you. We use my mother's concoctions." I can't maintain this jittery lightness and stop to look directly in her eyes, "Amélie, how are you holding up?"

"I manage, Ingrid," she sighs, "It's lonely without the children nearby. At least now they've been told. As soon as it's safe to travel I shall visit them. I can't make decisions of any importance right now. The pain is too new."

"Oui, I remember floating for months after Emil died. I can't imagine what I would have done without Marta. Her injury needed immediate attention. I thought of nothing else."

Marie has brought in a tray of herb tea and fresh berries. She observes the two of us for a moment then leaves without a sound. After a long pause while I pour, Amélie abruptly sits up very straight on the edge of the rocker and praises me,

"You're a wonderful mother, Ingrid. I don't think I ever told you. You have the gift of tenacity needed to be a healer. It's important to believe in your patient's recovery."

"Why thank you for the gracious compliment, Amélie."

Taken aback by her tone of voice I detect a twinge of sadness, perhaps related to Dieter. I keep looking at her. What is it? I am so attuned to fishing below the surface I can't accept what she says. Her words don't seem attached to whatever has prompted her visit.

"Promise me, Ingrid, if you're ever called upon to help someone else as hurt as your Marta was you'll respond with the same love and devotion. It's easy when it's your own flesh. Much harder when it's a stranger."

"I'll remember to do my best, Amélie."

Our words hang in the air. Their context is vague and unfinished. They disperse to memory as Marta knocks on the door. She enters with a big smile and gives Amélie a hug and kiss.

"My favorite almost-auntie. I love you, Madame Amélie!"

"And I you, young lady. How tall you are."

"How quickly they grow up. I can barely keep her in the same clothes. Becoming so sophisticated. She will soon shed her need for her old mother," I smile at my leggy lass.

"Ah oui, they all appear mature at this age but we must be more careful to protect them in these terrible times."

Another of Amélie's comments hangs in the air to gnaw at me. What is she saying? Speaking in parables today. It's best not to search too deep for meaning. She's been under a terrible strain. Marta enchants Amélie with her flute. They *are* like an aunt and a niece.

"Let me play a little Blavet for you, Amélie," Marta smiles proudly.

"Blavet? Already? How long have you been studying the flute, Marta?"

"Since my eleventh birthday."

"She wanted to surprise you, Amélie, when she knew enough to coax a little music from it. Coaching her keeps me busy. These days are quiet with so little action. Marta's playing staves off worry about the future."

As we listen I search Amélie's face from across the room. She stands next to Marta, reads the music, turns the pages and taps out the rhythm on her shoulder. Amélie is strangely protective of Marta today. Oh well, she's alone now. I suppose Dieter's old music students make her feel more connected to him.

Odd, how her color is back—despite her widowhood. She's at peace, but elusive, secretive, still in pain, yes, but I'm not sure it's about the past. Maybe she sees something. I can't ask. A wall surrounds her. I suppose only Dieter understood this part of her and she must feel lost without him.

Today she behaves like the calm before a storm.

Chapter Twenty-Four

Germaine's Visit

2 July 1944, Sunday

Marie and I scour our "diversion chamber," the large dining room opposite the sitting salon that held the Sunday evening "service." Oh, pardon, "soirée," for the Gestapo. We work together taking down the heavy woolen bombing drapes. They shut out my whoring obligation from the neighbors' eyes as they strolled on the riverside esplanade for the last three years. Removing the curtains is a natural climax to an exorcistic housecleaning.

The crossing went smoothly. We had only four refugees in the basement, three adults and one child from the twenty-four who came through Duchamps. Roemler was strangely respectful toward me that evening, but his carousing officers and hired women poisoned my home with lust and liquor.

I have pondered my behavior at the deVillement dinner party and my little "diversion" for Nazi officers the following evening. I'm preoccupied with my uncertain future after refusing Édouard's proposition.

In the midst of musing I have an unexpected visitor. Marie answers the door and returns a bit bewildered.

"Madame, it's Germaine deVillement. Are you in?"

"What? Oh, yes. My word, I'm a mess." More respectable in old cleaning clothes than sexy lingerie, sipping coffee and eating bonbons from the Boches as she might expect.

"Show her in here, Marie, please, not the petit salon."

I expected this visit after her shameful behavior toward me. Her apology is late by two and a half years. I'm unprepared and annoyed. Her request that I go outside with her on the balcony the night of her dinner party still eats at me. I can't trust her. Why would she agree with Édouard to put me in danger? She had to know what she was doing.

My vengeful need to question her dissolves into pity when she enters the room appearing frail and meek.

"Good morning, Ingrid. I'm sorry. I should have called first. I didn't realize you would be so busy on a Sunday."

"Oh, nonsense, dear, come in. The day is beautiful. I couldn't stand these depressing curtains any longer. I'm helping Marie to take them down."

My nerves were so on edge at her soirée I wasn't sensitive to the extent of her physical deterioration. She's lost even more weight. In daylight I see how much worse she looks than two weeks ago.

"Do you think it's wise, Ingrid?" She's timid and almost contrite, yet surprisingly—I still want an apology. My answer is rather snippy.

"Yes, the war will be over soon. Hitler hasn't much Luftwaffe left and what little he does certainly won't be wasted on this corner of Europe. Sit down, please, Germaine."

I study her carefully. She's in pain. I put my drapery down and sit across from her, knees to knees. She looks pathetic and alone. Whatever is wrong has also tainted our friendship, yet it's not coming from her heart or she wouldn't be here. I see death all around her, imminent death—perhaps her own?

"Germaine, tell me, what is it? Why are you here?"

"I, uh, I'm so sorry for the way I berated you, Ingrid. I avoided you and publicly scorned you for the whole war. Other people like Agnes snubbed me because of it. She warned me not to ostracize you from our circle. I have been so headstrong and opinionated and. . . ."

"And revolted by my seamy collaborative behavior. Yes, I agree with you, Germaine."

Her face shows astonishment at how easily I finish her thought. Lucky me. I have the "good fortune" to take myself less seriously these days. Her judgments don't hurt any more. The cynic she can't see in my eyes knows my end justifies her meanness.

"My dear, I forgive you and everyone who's agreed with you. Don't worry, please. But what is wrong with you?"

"I, . . . I . . . ah, I am . . . uh, . . . oh, Ingrid," Germaine suddenly cries, covering her face with her hands and lowering her head. I move beside her on the small divan to cradle her in my arms. In over thirty years I've never seen her so out of control.

"Dear friend, what's wrong? You can trust me, Germaine. You always could when we were young. Please, let's put this ugly war behind us and be caring friends again."

A minute passes. Germaine sits up and wipes her eyes.

She can't look at me when she says, "I'm dying, Ingrid. I've had cirrhosis for some years. It's part of my anger. All my life I've had the same quick temper as my father. My liver is extremely weak. I get every illness passing around and have no energy. I don't want to eat and get bilious at meals. My body's on fire; yet my hands are freezing cold and my head feels so heavy. I'm dizzy, anxious and dull. My skin peels and I have sores that won't heal."

"When did this become so serious, Germaine?"

"Before the soirée. The doctors have little hope. I've pushed myself too far already. They think it's liver cancer. I wanted to tell you privately that evening before you left so suddenly."

"Germaine, I'm sorry but something was pushing me out of your house."

She doesn't appear to hear me. She keeps right on talking. "I wanted to apologize for everything, Ingrid. I know Édouard is a coward. He's used me all this time. I've found out dreadful things about him. Please, I must ask you this question. It's about your affiliations."

I know what she thinks.

"No, Germaine, I'm not a slut for the Nazis. And if I told you what I've been doing these past years I'd put you and many others in danger."

Oh damn, I've said too much. It's been a secret from her for so long and she looks so near death, the poor woman.

"You're a member of the Résistance, aren't you?" Her spirits soar instantly.

"Infer what you like, Germaine."

"Oh Ingrid, Agnes always believed in you when I didn't. She defended you all the time. How did she know? Did you tell her?"

"You and Agnes and everyone else in this town can infer what you like. No one, especially you, knows anything from my mouth." I grab her by the shoulders and speak with great solemnity, "Germaine, you have to be serious now. You can't go out of my house and blab this conversation all over town unless you want me deported to a Nazi death camp! And you can't tell Édouard, of all people."

"I won't. I promise."

She's sick and too pliable. I'm afraid she won't resist her husband's grilling. She could slip and tell him of her visit here today.

"Ingrid, tell me what you have learned about Édouard."

"What do you mean, Germaine? What should I have learned and when?"

"When you were in his study." She's so eager, I dislike the direction of this conversation but something in me allows it to continue. I have to find out what she wants.

"Oh no, Germaine, you first. You tell me; then I'll either confirm or deny it."

"Right. About two months ago I discovered some documents disclosing his family's holdings in Germany. You know he inherited his father's business many years ago and invested heavily in electronic things and engines of all sorts. He's amassed a fortune there. No one realizes how much of his wealth comes from this because his French heritage is all wines and agriculture. To people here he's just a wealthy upper class gentleman landowner who dabbles in politics and banking. The rest was hidden from me until recently."

"I hope you haven't confronted him about it."

"Well, you know me, I did. It was tactless but my temper got the best of me and I asked a lot of leading questions. He became cautious although I never admitted to searching or finding anything. He must have figured I did because he moved all his papers."

"Do you know what he's planning?"

"No. But I'm sure it's evil. I think he's tried to poison me."

"What? How so?"

"When the doctors tested me they said something had weakened my liver very quickly, in one to two months. They took hair, urine and blood samples to evaluate."

"How did they know to do that?"

"I told them to check for arsenic, mercury, or whatever else Édouard could use."

"You trust doctors here in this town?" I conclude she didn't go to Duvette.

"Oh no. I went out of town far away. I told Édouard I was going to visit my sister in Annecy, so he never questioned it. It was a torturous trip. I was sick all the way and only when I started back home did I notice I felt a little better. That's when I was sure he was putting something in my food."

"Germaine, what are you doing about it?"

"I have stopped eating with Édouard. I thought I could avoid the poison if I ate earlier or later and the food was prepared fresh. Mostly I eat alone because he isn't home."

"And are you still feeling sick?"

"Yes. I think someone in our kitchen is being paid to do it. I don't think they know it is poison. I suspect he said it was medicine. I'm terrified, Ingrid. Someone in my kitchen is killing me."

"Shall we put it to the test, then?"

"What do you mean?"

"Germaine, you're right about Édouard's investments. I think he's planning to get away to South America with your money, but not with you. He asked me to pass documents for him to and from German hands but I refused. He thinks I'm a Nazi slut. You've encouraged him with all your bitching behind my back for the last two and a half years. No, don't look downhearted. You did your job as I had hoped. Do not change your attitude when you get home today. We never had this talk, understand? You still hate me. He must believe I'm no good."

"But why?"

"Look, Germaine, you know the wild sentiments about women sleeping with Nazis. I could be tried as an enemy of the Republic. I could lose everything I own and worse."

She lowers her head. "Yes, I'm ashamed to have been part of that sentiment."

"Yes, well, hang onto it a little longer. Édouard has a lot of power in this town. He'll speak out against me publicly and privately arrange to have me exiled."

"But how would he do that, Ingrid?"

"Using me to pass papers—he could blackmail me into going abroad with him."

"Oh, the bastard, he'd do that. He's been obsessed with you since you were children."

I can't trust Germaine when she stokes her anger and wastes her energy on that misogynist.

I grab her hand to quell her darkening mood. "For goodness sake, let go of it, please. Your relationship with him has been over for years. But you still must play the part of a self-righteous loud mouth for a while longer. Are you well enough to handle such deception?"

"I'll have to be, right?" she laughs, "For now I will eat somewhere else."

"Right, then invite me to your house again."

"Why? You just said you were afraid there."

"I was afraid with Édouard there."

"Why do you want to come?"

"To see if we can locate the documents while he's out of the house."

I won't tell Germaine what I'm looking for. Édouard or maybe Roemler hired someone to follow me to that soirée. Or were Résistants hiding in the bushes to protect me? The reasons are as clouded as Mueller's murder. I feel more like the "catch of the day," than the fisherman or the bait. She interrupts my distraction.

"Ingrid, at the party I told Édouard it was too cold to open the balcony doors. He was strangely insistent. When you didn't go out he feared I'd be envious and eavesdrop if he took you to his study. You were stunning. I struggled with ill will toward you."

Germaine astonishes me. Either she's not very coherent today or she *is* being poisoned.

"So why did you ask me to go out on the balcony as well? You did ask me, remember?"

"Yes, Ingrid, I'm sorry. I asked you outside to have some privacy from the other guests. I feel bilious these days and crave fresh air. That's all."

"Germaine, when I left with Roemler I saw movement in the bushes."

"You poor dear. All this time everyone has hounded you. I hope one day you can share the whole story with me. You can count on my support and my silence. But now I'm tired. I want to go home and find out who's giving me the lethal remedy."

She's only interested in herself. Why not? She looks so poorly. I'm convinced she's another of Édouard's victims.

"You must proceed with caution, Germaine."

"Yes, you're right. Can I call you?"

Her innocence undoes my trust. She doesn't realize the danger we're in and still thinks she's safe in her mansion. She hasn't heard a word I said.

"No, Germaine. Send a note with your driver or someone you can trust or come by and give me a message. Or call from a public phone box. It's too risky. You don't know who's hurting you. Look Germaine, you're safe here. Why not stay and have lunch with us? Marie, Guy, and I eat together in this house. I hate eating alone when Marta's in the country. I've abandoned a lot of old formalities. I hope you don't mind."

"Mind? Oh no, I'm relieved. Thank you for your kindness, Ingrid." She grabs my hand and kisses my cheek.

"Mind? Oh no, I'm relieved. Thank you for your kindness, Ingrid," she grabs my hand and kisses my cheek. My intuition tells me to avoid her conniving husband.

Chapter Twenty-Five

Amélie's Sacrifice

5 July 1944, Wednesday

Marta is like a flower bud on a bent stem. If she can bloom despite the bending, who in this world owns the right to discard her blossom before its time? Better to prune her stem above the bend—so others won't know her past. Her flower will give its beauty and fragrance the same as the others.

She thinks she's normal when she's especially vulnerable now that our French culture is infected with a "super race" mentality. I've tried to protect her from vicious tongues. Her love is so genuine and courageous. People could crush her spirit and make her ashamed of her flesh. It sickens me to limit her trust in humanity when I explain how her slight paralysis might frighten or disgust others. I don't want their ignorance to stigmatize my daughter. But it's too late to stop that.

Her mother, their curb-sniffing bitch, has gotten what she deserves for whoring with Nazis. That's why her daughter is physically hurt, *une infirmité*. They have forgotten Marta's accident happened in 1939, *before* the war.

My increasing paranoia makes me insist that one of us escorts Marta to and from her lessons, and the homes of friends. But once, against my maternal instinct, in a rare moment of ambivalence, I give in to her constant childish nagging for a measure of independence. I will never forgive myself for this mistake—even if the hand of Heaven is upon it.

Marta wants to walk home alone from her girl friend's house despite being told not to. We argue about it, and I give in.

Two hours later I telephone to have Marta wait to walk home until I get there. I'm told she's already gone. Usually Marie or Guy escorts her since being in public is not safe for me. But they're not here.

I rush out of the house and ride one of our old bicycles toward the center of town, hoping to find her on the street. I stash the bike behind a building in a familiar alley not far from Philippe's apothecary.

She should be walking in this direction at any minute. This narrow section of alley is empty at this time of day. I head toward the upper end, feeling very exposed but more worried for my daughter than myself.

Suddenly a hand comes from behind to cover my mouth. Fingers dig into my liver. A man drags me into a yard with a high fence. I try to get free, "*Aye*, mon Dieu! No, let go of me! What are you doing! Ach, stop! *Help!*"

I jerk my head around to see a face on this attacker—but he's wearing a bandana. He stinks of Gauloises, cheap liquor and sweat. He wears old, dirty clothes and has gummy, oily hands with blackened nails. He forces his knee into my tailbone and presses me up against a wood-slatted fence, grunting in street slang,

"Here you are, bitch. Have a front row seat."

A sidekick helps him press me against the rough wood while he pushes my face to a hole just large enough for my right eye to see the alley. I'm shaking like a leaf. My throat dries up. He grabs the back of my head and forces me to be still.

"Don't fight me, honey, or I'll splinter your pretty skin."

Right. Be passive. Whatever is coming, survive for Marta's sake, and breathe.

And then I see her. But at the very moment I would shout to alert her, a hand covers my mouth and another presses against my throat so hard I can't scream.

The ugliness starts with that same little street urchin from three years ago who is now at least twelve-years-old. Other street urchins accompany him.

His family is from Lyon. His father is a Milice informer, a former underling for Klaus Barbie, a street dog who ran errands and defaced property. Sacrebleu! My attacker must be his father. Who does he work for now, here in Duchamps? His adolescent son carries on the family tradition by taunting defectives.

Oh, here comes my sweet girl turning into this alley. How did they know she would?

As she comes closer, I struggle to scream. Only hoarse grunts come out. My assailant presses his hand harder against my throat. Then I cough vigorously. Marta hesitates, hearing the coughing, but can't localize the direction it comes from. Tears cascade down my cheeks. For a few seconds I struggle to free myself, but my attacker holds my head tighter. Again and again, he smashes my face into the rough wooden fence.

The little monsters surround Marta, the defective daughter of Duchamps' "la Courtisane." They tease her and incite older boys in the alley to join in taunting her:

"Little traitor who peepees,

Your mother's a whore for the Nazis,

All the night you suck her nipple!

Dance for us you little cripple. . . .

They run from behind and encircle her, limping and flapping their hands, imitating Marta at her worst.

The older kids shout, "Voilà, see our little défectueux, danse, pour nous!"

They tease her, but Marta stands her ground and ignores them at first. (She's heard it all before and never tells me unless I insist.)

The kids mock her with the same ugly rhyme she's repeated to me in the past, but now it's in vulgar street slang:

"La petite traîtresse qui fait pipi,

Ta mère est une pute pour les Nazis.

Suce ta tetine toute la nuit!

Danse, pour nous, vous petite boiteuse!"

They begin to push her and lift up her skirt. Marta sways, and trips trying to balance herself.

"No. Get away! Leave me alone. I haven't done anything to you!"

She tries to dart away from them but drags her left leg and hyperventilates, terrified. A few pick up sticks. They jeer and scream at her:

Her leg is bad. It's just a cramp.

Slice her up in the camps!"

A few of the bullies close in on her. She lifts her cane to protect herself. One of them grabs its end and pulls. Marta loses her balance. Another closes in and pummels her with his fists. Marta screams at the top of her lungs.

They've backed her into a metal fence with barbed wire at the top.

I cannot stand watching this. I'm hysterical, driven to help my child. I try to bite the hand of my attacker when he repositions it against my jaw. I catch his pinky in my mouth and bite down hard. He shouts in pain and smashes the back of my head. I scream, and for a moment the scream is heard in the alley. The kids whip their heads around. They're silent for a few seconds.

I grunt as loud as I can before I'm gagged so tightly my lips separate and my tongue tastes a nasty combination of old liquor and petrol.

Even though she has no idea who it is, it seems Marta hears me. Even if I only sound like another victim she doesn't know, please dear Jesus, let her know in her heart it's me, her maman, she hears. Her maman!

Salty tears cloud my vision and refract the horror unfolding in front of me. I become shocky and my head feels disconnected. Gross forms attack her, she cries out as stones hit the ground. Then I blink hard to clear my eyes so her face is sharper.

Older brats have managed to pull her cane away from her and one strikes her with it. She covers her face and tries to get away but is chased back into the fence every few meters. I can see people across the alley stare out their back doors and windows. No one in this neighborhood who recognizes my child will rescue her because they hate her mother.

Then I catch a glimpse of Amélie a quarter of the way down the alley from the direction of the apothecary. She's been shopping. Her basket is heavy so she turns this way for a shortcut home.

The rise and fall of children's shrill, angry voices and clustering of footsteps don't catch her attention at first, but when she gets closer, she hears the ugly rhyme and walks faster, recognizing Marta's screams:

"Sa jambe est folle

C'est juste une crampe

Découpons-la dans les camps!"

She sees the backs of children attacking Marta like wild dogs, and drops her groceries and bandages, calling out as she enters the fray,

"Hey, stop that. Leave her alone!"

Horrified, she sees blood dripping from Marta's face. She screams, approaching the young boys cheering the older ones, "Stop this! You're not a pack of wild animals!"

She reaches for a timid runt, maybe six-years-old, who followed his older brother and grabs him by the back of the collar. Pulling him aside, she yells, "Go home, you little brat!"

He's frightened and runs away. Amélie rushes into the mob again. She shrieks until her voice is hoarse, grabbing the younger boys by the hair. With a powerful grip, she thrusts them aside and raises her fists at them. She pulls and twists their ears. They reel, some fall, but one by one they run away until the hardened bullies remain.

"Stop! Stop hurting her! Go home, the police are coming. Get away you brutes!"

She pushes and shoves her way against the bodies of the older bullies. They ignore her and pull at Marta, who clings to the fence. If she falls to the ground they will stomp her to death.

I watch helplessly, praying for the gendarmes to arrive.

Amélie shrieks again, "Stop! Stop! You're hurting her! Marta, I'm here, love."

Now almost in tears herself she finally pushes her body between Marta and her adolescent attackers. Marta looks up at Amélie through her tears, her face frozen in terror. Amélie embraces her to take the blows. In the midst of the pummeling she shouts for help realizing these thugs are out of control. I can't see her face now, but she is shielding my baby.

Amélie shouts to reassure Marta, in a pause between the taunts, "I'm here angel, you're not alone, help will. . . ."

Her unfinished sentence hangs in the air as . . . aye, God, no! A brick flies out of nowhere and with *enormous* force, smashes into her temple.

The attackers stop, step back—and freeze in place as the brick pounds Amélie's head into the fence post. She falls over onto Marta, forcing her to the ground. Marta struggles to get out from under her. Amélie lies in the dirt, bleeding and losing consciousness. Her face goes white. She gasps and grabs Marta's sleeve to pull her close, mumbling something barely coherent. Marta puts her ear next to Amélie's mouth to listen, but I can't hear what Amélie says. I look down through the peephole as her breath escapes slowly . . . in a long, foaming wheeze.

Marta screams. Amélie is mortally wounded, verging on lifelessness.

Marta senses her almost auntie's end is near and goes into shock witnessing another death—another profound loss. Mon Dieu, her body reacts with a jerking seizure right here in public. She's peeing on herself. I squirm again to get free of these bastards. They only push me harder. The fence shakes with my frustration—to get my hands on my daughter and help her—*now!*

The adolescent rowdies stare at Amélie's bloodied face and Marta's convulsing body with urine running down her legs and into her shoes. A vague awareness of guilt covers their malevolence, and stills their aggression. Startled by Marta's uncontrolled eyes and her mouth that pulls to the left side, they turn and run wild through the alley until they disappear.

Jeanne darts from the bakery after a few boys run past her. Philippe, the pharmacist, meets her from the opposite end of the alley. A few shoppers follow them and search the immediate area for the culprits.

Window curtains part and one or two back gates along this alley open cautiously, but no one ventures out to help.

Amélie is unresponsive. Philippe gives Jeanne instructions to check for her pulse, as he holds Marta in his arms. He knows dear Amélie's life will be over in a matter of seconds. Blood trickles slowly from her ear and nose, until it coagulates with no pulse to move it.

The two Samaritans suck in their rapidly rising grief and revive Marta to wild-eyed hysteria. Still blue around the lips, trembling and out of breath, she's stunned and stammers, looking down at her dress. Shame replaces her fright. She knows she has lost control of her bladder in public.

Then silently, with beseeching eyes, Marta insists on lifting Jeanne's apron that covers Amélie's face. She stares at her almost-auntie in disbelief and wails in Philippe's arms.

At the sound of the Gendarmerie siren, people on the main street peel away from ration lines and spill out of their shops and homes. A crowd gathers just before the van arrives.

After they pull me away from the fence, my attackers wrap me in a huge blanket to immobilize me. I try, unsuccessfully, to call out to everyone above the din, but they have covered my head.

I'm lifted up and carried to a vehicle, a lorry of some sort by the sound of the doors closing and the odor inside. Odd, but it isn't a gazogène. It leaves immediately, and within two minutes carries and deposits me at my basement entrance. Abandoned there to unwrap myself, I must steal into my empty house, alone.

Caught in a daze about where I am and what to do, I realize my arms and legs are terribly weak. When I move, my mind cannot coordinate my body . . . it's resistant and slow. I still contain in my chest the images of love I sent Marta in that alley. My mother's heart is wounded for my angel once more. Marta becomes Ingrid and Ingrid becomes Marta. My breath holds hers. Her lessons are my lessons. We feel two traumas of pain: today's, and that of five years ago, when she lay bleeding and unconscious in the snow.

Suddenly limp, I lean into the inside basement wall to get to the toilette. Tears trickle into my wounds. My God, my face looks worse than it did after that vertical coffin in Jean Claude's lorry. My hands aren't still enough to remove the splinters in my cheeks. The pain is so severe I can only splash water lightly onto my face. I unwrap a new toothbrush reserved for fleeing refugees and brush my teeth to wash out the vile taste and texture of cigarettes, liquor and petrol. The images of Marta, alone, victimized, and then shattered by Amélie's death, replay over and over in my mind.

I can't go back to that alley. I *must* trust that Philippe and Jeanne will protect Marta. I have to wait here. My job now is to be patient and think of a suitable story for my facial swelling, bruises and bloody clots. What if I said I had tripped in the backyard and fallen on the newly cut evergreen boughs and their hard, piercing needles? It's ridiculous to hide this, yet my heart is too weak to muster anger at my enemies—or myself. My choice of excuse harbors my guilt. But I cannot lose the trust of those I hold most dear. I'm trapped. If I appear weak and tell her, Marta will be even more frightened. I have already acted once against my mother's intuition to let her walk home independently, and cannot make any more mistakes.

I search the medicine cabinet for Maman's precious little bottle of homemade rose hips oil to apply to my face.

><~~

Later I sit in the receiving salon with a cognac in my trembling hands and stare at a huge bouquet of flowers from Amélie's garden. The fireplace across the room explodes with their color and fragrance. She gave them to me only two days ago. It's too much loss. Twice my poor angel has been an eyewitness and a victim. First Emil; now Amélie. I wait, uneasy, wishing for Marta's quick return.

Guy looks worried as he enters the salon. At first I think it's concern for me. He says cautiously, "Madame, I was in town. I saw Marie with Marta in a police van. They will arrive shortly. Please, sit still and collect yourself. I can bring anything you need."

The front doorbell rings and Guy answers. I've done my best to clean my wounds and fix my hair, but it's obvious I've had an accident—or an incident I don't wish to discuss. Later I will tell Guy the story about falling into the evergreens.

He returns to tell me SS-Obersturmführer Roemler is here for tea. For a few seconds, it doesn't register that the Nazi is on my doorstep. My body starts to feel encased in ice, as if in shock. My heart sinks to my knees. Guy asks very formally, as my butler, "Madame, are you in?" As if to remind me what's next on the roster of today's tragedies. I cannot handle this. Dieter is probably dead and now his wife is too, and I saw her die with my own eyes only a few minutes ago.

France is supposed to be an Occupied nation, not a civilian battlefield.

I had forgotten Roemler was coming. I've resisted his clumsy advances but am annoyed at his tactics. He doesn't seem overtly suspicious but deliberately provokes me, and abuses his power by showing up unannounced like his predecessors.

"Yes, I'll see him, but wait please, Guy. First, tell me more about what happened."

"Madame, Marie called from the Police station. She was on her way to bring Marta home when she heard the siren and saw people run down the side street to the alley. When she rushed to Marta's side the officers wouldn't let her take Marta away. They were awaiting the arrival of the coroner to examine Amélie's body at the scene. Marie tried to avert Marta's eyes but our little soldier commanded the gendarme to lift the cloth over Amélie's face for Marie to see. They are safe, Madame, as I've said, and will arrive here soon."

I give Guy a horrified look and nod. He returns to the foyer and leads Roemler in. He brings a tray of tisane and biscuits. I sit there, immovable—an uncommunicative carcass.

"Guten Tag, Madame Fellner," Wilhelm begins, "Oh my, what happened to you? Is something wrong?"

Thankfully, before I open my mouth to say something grossly caustic that might put me before a firing squad at La Citadelle, Marie interrupts and speaks urgently,

"Madame, come quickly, there's been some trouble."

"I have to attend to this matter; excuse me." I don't give Roemler an explanation. As I reach for the door latch, Marta shoots past Marie and rushes in, twitching, sobbing, frantic.

Her mouth pulls to one side as her words jerk out, barely clear, "Maman, Maman, Auntie Amélie's dead! She saved me but she doesn't know she did. She was bleeding and white and still and, oh God, Maman, she said to me, "Dieter, I'm co . . . mi . . . ng," and then she died. What did I do to her? Maman, she's gone! She left me just like Papa did, right in front of me. What have I done? *Je suis une malédiction!* A curse! I bring the darkness."

My baby rushes to me and buries her head in my skirt crying uncontrollably. Stricken by her tumultuous entrance, I examine her quickly. Her hair is disheveled. She reeks of urine. Her dress is torn, stained with mud and blood. Her tense little body is covered with bruises, cuts on her legs and arms, and one on her left cheek. Most of the blood is Amélie's and not Marta's. I suck in my breath and tears, and lead her to the divan.

The meaning of Amélie's message is garbled but the rest of Marta's tale penetrates deeply. My daughter believes she caused these two deaths. The realization makes my heart want to burst. Quite possibly now that the town has seen her seize, she can add self-hatred and shame to her onus of self-deprecation before she arrives at puberty!

I want to say so much to comfort her but Roemler sits here unmoved. He doesn't recognize a human tragedy and my need for privacy. Is he so dehumanized, or is this just bad breeding? I'm furious.

He's the perfect target for my maternal indignation. I dare not let him have it. I'm sure he thinks Marta's a cripple. Evil Aryan arrogance is responsible for this, but I pull my anger in and speak with restraint, "Bitte, Obersturmführer, you have to leave. You see I have a problem with my daughter. We've had a terrible loss in our lives. Leave us alone."

Why doesn't he go? What a self-centered man. I've had enough, so I attempt to exit the room with Marta still crying and tugging on my skirt for support.

"Marie!" I shout into the hall, "Please, escort the Obersturmführer out."

I turn to Roemler and look him up and down once more and insist, "I can't cater to you right now. I'm a mother first. You must go. Raus!"

"*Ja, ja. Entschuldigen.* Excuse me," he mutters in German and rises to let himself out.

I nod and ignore him to gather Marta into my arms and lay her down on the divan with her head in my lap. She sobs quietly as I stroke her.

I happen to look up and see that Roemler's face has changed profoundly. In a switch, after sitting here hard as a rock, he appears softened and thoughtful, perhaps finally . . . humanized?

Am I witnessing the birth of a genuine conscience in a specimen of the super race? Possibly, but at what cost? Dear God, when will the butchery end?

He leaves when Marie appears at the door.

Now I need to focus on my poor child. I must speak carefully. My sweet girl must not blame herself. She needs to talk. I raise her to a sitting position and ask for the whole story. I promise not to weave my emotions into the ugly images. She has to make sense out of this bad dream or it will haunt her forever.

"How did it begin, Marta?"

"Wait, Maman, what happened to your face? You've been cut and scraped, and you are swelling and turning black and blue. When did this happen, Maman?"

"I'm all right, Marta. I had a fall out back a little while ago. I tripped. I hit my face and my head. Please tell me what happened to you, mon ange." I hope she accepts my story.

"Eh bien, ah some kids teased me about being crippled. They chanted horrible things Maman, like 'your mother's a whore for a Nazi.' You don't allow me to use such crude words but I know what they mean. They don't know you, Maman. I couldn't let them say such bad things about you, so I fought back. They pushed and kicked me and tore my hair and dress and beat me with my cane. Madame Amélie heard me scream and came to save me. Then someone threw a brick and it hit her head instead of mine. She fell over on me."

My daughter's beautiful clear eyes stare into the horrible scene. Her voice is ragged with disbelief, "Maman, she bled all over me and never woke up."

"Marta, you had nothing to do with Amélie's death. You were in trouble and she saved you. She came to help you. Never blame yourself for losing a person if they're responding to your need. If anyone is to blame it's me for allowing you to be alone on the street."

I can barely hear myself say this. I am overcome with grief and worry. How will she get past this tragedy? She's already sustained too much pain in her young life.

In fact, I'm relieved when she hits me with a barrage of questions.

"Will she be happy where she is now? How can she be? Maman, before her breathing stopped, she called Dieter's name. Is she going to see him in heaven, Maman? Is that what she meant?"

"I have no idea, mon ange. She passed very quickly and that's a blessing. She died living her life as an angel of God. She was a saint, Marta. You must always remember her kindness and love and cherish your friendship with her. She'd be very unhappy if you blamed yourself for anything that happened today. Do you understand?"

The irony hits hard. My mind wanders through the infestation of guilt silently consuming me. Marta stops shaking now but her face is ashen. The spiritual purity of her questions reveals my inadequacy to answer them.

"Yes, Maman. My need caused her to appear. But why did she have to die? And why shouldn't I blame myself? No one else was there with her. We needed more help."

"Angel, you can't assume your encounter or your need caused her death. It was just her time."

"Time to die? Why? You just said that Auntie Amélie led a blameless life, no? It doesn't make sense, does it?"

"Well, ah, I think maybe for you it can't."

"Maman, when people blame you for collaborating with the Nazis they spread dreadful lies. They never ask you for the truth or look you in the eye. You accept their behavior and tell me to do the same? After this, I need a better reason why I should."

"Marta, to be fair and loving is hard, very hard. Mostly you just keep going forward to do the next work in front of you. You have to let God show you how to live with the things that hurt and lead you to the people who can help you heal."

"So, Maman, what does it mean when most of those people end up dead?"

Her eyes reflect deep disappointment. Marta wants a spiritual explanation for worldly affairs I can't give her. My reasoning smacks of *papist pabulum* that irritated my mother so much she left the church when I was a child.

Thankfully, my baby doesn't wait for an answer. She falls asleep, exhausted. My arms cradle her head in my lap. Marie, who waited outside the salon, enters to help me remove Marta's muddy, blood-stiffened dress and put a large bath towel under her. Together we gently wash her with warm water and apply ointment to her abrasions. We bandage them, lifting her left hand and leg, so oddly loose and relaxed in sleep. We comb out her braids, wash away the blood, and dress her in a nightgown. Then Marie covers her with my favorite shawl. Our eyes lock in sorrow before she leaves to prepare a light supper.

I stare into space—so lonely and empty, my heart aches to tell Marie the truth about Amélie and Dieter, what their deaths mean to me, and my daughter. I dreamed of celebrating the end of this war with them.

I can't imagine Alain Duvette's grief when he receives Amélie's body. Guy and Marie now share knowledge of her death with me. God bless them for their charity and fidelity to love my little girl. I wish I deserved these two angels.

This incredible tragedy pushes me to go to the morgue once more. I disguise myself—wearing pants, a belted taupe-colored trench coat and slouched béret to obscure my swelling features. I slip out of the house on Marie's bicycle. Taking back streets I arrive at the morgue and knock at the kitchen-side delivery door. Patrice opens the door and leads me to the empty viewing room. I grab her arm and beg her to let me announce myself.

She looks at my stoic face, wrinkling from scraped tissue, grimacing to hold back pain and another round of tears, and puts her fingers to her pursed lips. She nods her head in the direction of the inner entry to the autopsy room. Her lips mouth for me to follow. We both stop when we hear voices on the other side of the door.

She admonishes in a whisper, "You can't interrupt this time, Madame. Please, just listen. Let me open the window in the hall by the door so you hear what's said outside in the yard. Please, be prudent. If they see you here a second time I will lose my job and my head. 'Zut!' she exclaims, running her thumb horizontally across her neck in a guillotining motion.

Sufficiently warned, I overhear Jacques say, "She must have been on her way here. We can't be concerned about it. We have to meet our connection, Alain."

"Sshh, Jacques," Alain whispers, "Keep your voice down. Patrice will hear us."

"So what if she does, Alain? It's too late to worry now. You arranged this meeting."

"Yes, yes, I know, Jacques. I dragged my feet but finally couldn't stand to see her so downcast. I felt bad. I finally offer her a chance for peace of mind and fate intervenes."

"I hope the truth is easier for her to accept from where she hovers now, old man."

Oh no, Dieter must be dead. What else could Alain mean? He was buried once. It never occurred to me that Dieter's funeral at the end of May really was a fake. But he has died since and now they must be taking his body someplace else to bury it secretly. And when the war is over they'll tell us the truth. *Aye*, Mon Dieu, my heart collapses as the reality sinks in.

"You have to meet Jean Claude. You can't be late, Jacques. Grab the coffin's identification papers for the checkpoint. Have you started the bin, yet?"

Alain refers to the gazogène hearse. I can't stand this hiding and eaves-dropping when I already know what happened. They left me hanging to discover what they decided to keep secret. I turn my head to look out the window at the backyard driveway.

Then I hear Jacques say, after a pause, "Here we are in this little nothing of a town with no gunfire at our heels." Deep sadness overtakes his voice: "And no serious privation like other parts of France. We're just a small effort to get a few people to safety. We did it so well in the beginning, and now, my God, what's happening?"

As he says this, I spy a pair of cardinals, male and female, sitting on the fence near the lilac edging the alleyway. A cat darts up from the morgue's enclosure and startles the couple. They fly off in opposite directions. What could that mean? The deep anguish in Devoir's tone confirms that Dieter is dead. Everything points to it. I wipe my eyes.

Patrice returns and touches my shoulder before leaving the room and whispers,

"Whatever you do, Madame Henri, make these men honor you. Make them protect you in the coming days. Bless you for your sacrifice. When you leave, if you need me to check the alley to be sure there are no spies, tap lightly on the kitchen door. Night is coming on to protect you." She smiles.

I nod and mouth, "merci," then overhear Alain calling, "Hey, give me a hand, here, Jacques before the police van arrives."

"Coming," Jacques's heavy footsteps move swiftly, automatically. Duvette's breathing is suddenly raspy and rapid, as though unable to keep pace with an exertion. I look out the side window again and watch the two men maneuver a coffin carefully into the hearse from the wheeled gurney. Alain leans over with his head down near the side of the casket for a few seconds and then straightens up again.

"I have enough time to make it past the checkpoint to Jean Claude. Don't worry, Alain. The worst of the public part is over—doing my job with the whole town watching."

"That's for sure." Alain's voice has a note of distraction, "Hey, don't forget this," and he places some small cloth-like parcel into Jacques's hand.

Jacques remarks oddly, "If they stop me, and smell this, the Boches will be suspicious. Take it back."

"No," Alain insists, "Put it inside. Jean Claude's vehicle will probably stink like sheep and goats."

The two medics force themselves to laugh. They're edgy but I can't tell why. Their humor is unnecessary since the situation is hopeless. Their mood is very sad, yet Jacques makes a heroic effort at being cheerful as he drives a few screws into the coffin's lid. That doesn't make sense.

Alain asks him, "Do you think the cops were suspicious because you didn't do a big forensic search of the scene before you came back here? What did you tell the Prefect to get away so fast?"

"Our young gendarme is checking the area carefully for evidence, and I left an apology about having to come back here. He knows what to look for. I left my kit with him. It's normal procedure, Alain. I've done it before when we've had multiple medical emergencies at the same time and the two of us were on call. People weren't surprised I left so quickly. You'll recognize the young cop driving in. He'll be here shortly."

I have no context for what Jacques says next.

"Remember, the hole is on the left side."

I'm missing half of a conversation. Very little I have overheard makes sense. Coming here wasn't worth the effort when I can't confront these men.

I'm about to leave the building when another vehicle approaches. I return quickly through the side door to the anteroom of the receiving salon, afraid it will be Milice or Nazi hierarchy. Where to hide inside here? I tap on the housekeeper's door. Patrice comes out quickly and looks out the side window.

"Ssshhh!" she whispers, "Look Madame, the local police van is bringing a body. You can't leave now. One of the good docs will have to stay behind. Probably Dr. Alain."

Jacques backs up to the side of the building to make a space for the police van. Alain greets it. Jacques says something before he exits the hearse, but he's probably just cursing aloud. Alain waits at the rear of the van. The gendarme speaks loudly as he gets out.

"Hey, Duvette, another stiff for you and Devoir. Sorry sirs. Looks like I caught you just in time. Going to the church, eh Jacques?"

"Apparently, not yet," Jacques replies, distracted. Climbing out of the hearse he leaves the engine running and the door wide open. The two doctors join the gendarme to lift the new body wrapped in a blanket, Duvette at the head and Devoir at the feet.

"It's a woman, that midwife Amélie Van der Kreuzier," the cop bellows.

The two médecins freeze momentarily with their hands cradling Amélie's lifeless body. They glance at the open hearse door. Alain's eyes fill with tears as he stares at Jacques who bites his lip. Watching Alain and Jacques react to Amélie dead in their arms fills my heart with sorrow, as if the tragedy is fresh news—when they were both at the scene a few minutes ago. It's overwhelming. Wherever Dieter is, thankfully he's dead to this dreadful scene.

"Come with us, please," Alain calls quickly to the cop, "You need to sign papers inside."

The policeman responds to the brittle urgency in the old doctor's voice. Jacques quickly returns to the van and slams the door shut.

He took too long and the van stalls. "Merde! Damn coal bin!" (In the rush he forgot to add more coal to keep the gazogène running.) Jacques adds the fuel and sits behind the wheel waiting for enough power to build for the vehicle to move. I see him watching the male cardinal alight on the fence post alone. I guess he also wonders, what does it all mean?

Patrice returns to me, takes my hand and leads me into a closet that is right near the door to the autopsy room. She puts her finger to her mouth, indicates I should get inside and hands me a water glass to put against the wall and listen.

From inside the autopsy room, I hear Alain gasp and groan. He must have pulled back the blanket and seen Amélie's large, dark, blood-filled contusion. I remember her shattered cheekbone and indented skull. The right side of her face was a massive clotted cavity, and the imprint of the barbed-wire fence was etched into the left side of her head. Bits of brick and dirt lined her wounds.

I hear conversation with the gendarme about official papers.

"Sign here, Doc. Sorry, This must be quite a shock for you."

"Yes, it is."

I hear the door close as the gendarme leaves. Then it sounds like Alain must be positioning a chair next to Amélie's body, but I also hear footsteps and the rear door opens. Quickly, I leave the closet and stand by the window in the hallway to eavesdrop on the policeman speaking loudly with Jacques.

"Sorry, Doc. It's a pity. We're so close to liberation. It hurts to see more people die."

"Oui, one hopes everyone lives long enough to see the damn war end."

The gendarme continues casually, "She was killed under very strange circumstances—taking a brick for that young cripple. You know, the rich hussy's kid, that widow who sleeps with the SS. What a waste. I'll see you again, Devoir, hopefully under better circumstances."

A rich hussy, oui. I'm exactly what he and the town think. I return to the closet when the hearse's engine belches back to life and Jacques departs. Alain calls out to the gendarme,

"Hey, where's the coroner's evidence bag? Did you bring it?"

"Ah, not yet, sir. The younger cop has the brick but was checking for more evidence."

"Oui, d'accord," Alain replies. Closing the rear door he mutters, "Goddamn this war."

I hear a chair scrape the floor again. There's a pause and then his phlegmy chest heaves with deep sobs. Oh God, I haven't heard Alain cry since Jacques brought my Emil to the morgue from the ski slope five years ago. His raspy voice tells me Amélie's death wrings the blood from his heart.

"My Amélie, my little angel, you guided so many souls to their first breath of life in this world. Why are you taken from us now? And like this?"

Hidden in his closet, I hear his footsteps pass me in the hallway.

"Patrice!" he hollers authoritatively, "Join me in the morgue, right now!"

"Oui, Monsieur le docteur! Tout de suite!" Patrice calls back in an obedient voice, like a military foot soldier. In less than a minute I hear them next to Amélie's corpse.

"Madame Patrice, your brandy," Duvette sounds surprisingly gentle toward her.

"Merci, Alain," she replies softly like a lover, not a housekeeper.

I hear him utter a deep sigh and together their voices salute Amélie's departed soul with a toast, "Vive La France, mon amie!"

As they down their brandies Alain's voice wavers, "My sweet, innocent Amélie, we argued about your faith in a God I cannot accept. I trusted you with my lack of belief precisely because you paid so dear a price for yours. You honored my secret atheism in front of this town. You know I don't pray, Amélie, my dove. I can't understand why darkness must reign in this world, and when I do, the answer I find will be different from organized religion. But for you, dear girl, this is the one prayer I can utter with my love behind it, because Amélie, you and Patrice here, have taught me charity."

The good Doc and my secret ally recite the prayer warmed with cognac, "Oh, most sublime soul, in peace to thy blessed home may ye go, to receive the full measure of love ye have in this life so graciously bestowed. Amen."

I can't attend Amélie's funeral. Claudine, sole survivor of her immediate family understands why. I send Marta to my Maman to be with Sylvia and Pierre. The town blames me, especially the uninformed Résistants. Guy stays with me for protection. Marie goes to the funeral alone. For her safety, she stands apart from Claudine. When she returns she reports every detail.

"Madame Amélie's ceremony was dignified but the town's frustration was clear. Her Madonna-like face was half-destroyed by the brick. I saw it in the alley when her flesh was still warm, but to see it when it was, ah . . . never mind, there's no need to describe it. Sorry." She dabs her eyes.

"Everyone must have been upset, Marie." I haven't told either Marie or Guy what I saw.

"People were horrified. You could feel her disfigurement boil their sentiments, Madame. Only the most hardened souls could swallow communion at Mass. The rest were sick recalling the sight of her and, like me, chewed their wafer with a dry mouth of rage. I don't know who decided on an open casket at her viewing. If her Dieter looked worse than she did he must have been barely recognizable as a human being."

"I suppose the coffin was open to remind the good citizens of Duchamps that the killer was one of their own, a Milice informer, not a Boche. What do you think, Guy?" I'm curious about what he will say.

"No one will tell me anything, Madame, but rumors say this was no accident and the SS had nothing to do with it. It's strange—no suspects and no arrests."

"Then that brick was well paid for. The question is where did the money come from to pay the lowlife who threw it? Only an adult would have the strength to pitch it with enough force to kill someone."

"Oui, Madame, but who would do it? Everyone knew Amélie. She birthed many of Duchamp's children over the past twenty-five years. Who would hurt *her*?"

"Maybe Guy, it was Marta they wanted to hurt? Amélie saved my daughter's life, but was she in the wrong place at the wrong time?"

This evening we go to bed with heavy hearts. Again, Guy locks the window shutters as well as the doors. The house is like a fortress now and we are its prisoners.

>᠆᠆

My emptiness is heightened barely a week later. Today is the fourteenth of July, Bastille Day. This year our national holiday of Independence is shrouded in anticipation. For the second time in twenty-six years American Allies galvanize us ailing French to rid ourselves of a German scourge.

Amélie's purity and candor were balm for my splintered soul.

When my loss settles, Guy drives me to Claudine's farm to pay my respects. She gives me extra sets of keys to the Kreuzier home for the few music students I take over for Dieter.

>᠆᠆

I have little cause to celebrate. I'm now the music coach for Georges, Agnes's son, who is . . . oh God, . . . *was* Dieter's best student. An eerie succession passes this honor from Dieter to Amélie to me.

I unlock their front door and immediately a vague aroma of Dieter's favorite pipe tobacco pulls me to the afternoon in early May when he told me about meeting Mueller at the LaFrance. The house is stifling with memories. Being here is a mistake. Is someone watching us? Did a neighbor betray him? I catch myself being afraid and fight it. No one is home on either side. The town is celebrating in basement cafés.

I open the side windows to air out the front parlor and rear music room. Amélie's presence emanates from their wedding photo on the mantel. Even as a young bride her expression dissolved into that far-away look where she saw the future, shared what she deemed appropriate and held back the pain. Marie was right. Her face glowed like a Renaissance Madonna. Dieter's dearest love faced life with equanimity but her eternal nature was a mystery.

In this modest home everything about her permeated her husband's world: her beauty, music, and feminine touches like the lavender sachets basted onto the pillow shams on the divan. Amélie gave Dieter every comfort. Did he ever pierce that private place from which she perceived the world?

I sit in Dieter's chair and stare out the window at the back garden, still in rich bloom in spite of recent weeds. A lump of sadness clings to my throat. A thought crosses my mind—the sachet, could that be what Alain gave to Jacques by the hearse? I bury the idea, can't bear to think about it.

Agnes and Georges will arrive shortly for his lesson. My eyes swell up with the pressure of tears as I set out the accompanist's score on the piano and dust the keys. Georges is very talented and prepares for an audition at the Paris Conservatory. Life goes on despite Hitler. The doorbell rings.

"Good afternoon, Madame Fellner, thank you for helping me today." Georges has a strong, warm handshake.

I manage to smile into his lovely blue-grey eyes, his face framed by the slight redness of his deep sandy curls, a little like Agnes. He reminds me of Stefan when he was younger. Georges is a sweet boy, his arms and legs are caught in a gangly adolescence he coordinates when he plays his violin.

Agnes greets me. "Ingrid, it's so good of you to help Georges, but I'm sorry to have brought you here. This house is so lonely with both of them gone. It's hard to believe, n'est-ce pas?" She comes close and embraces me tenderly, seeing the heaviness in my face.

"Oui, Agnes." But to myself I'm saying, "Chin up, Ingrid."

"All right, Georges, let's get these pieces down perfectly. Auditions at this level separate mere players from real interpreters, first chairs from future soloists. Let's begin, shall we?"

Agnes sits in Dieter's chair. I'm at the piano. Georges tunes to my "A" and warms up a little. We review difficult passages for thirty minutes with pointers for emphasis I learned from Dieter when we played in the Baroque ensemble. Then Georges nods to me and opens the first movement of the third *Bach Partita*.

I let him play without interruption and make mental notes, remembering what Dieter used to say, "Give the student a chance to warm to his task. The violin must be absorbed into the musician's very flesh to best express his melodic voice." Dieter cultivated a rare talent in Georges. One can feel the young virtuoso's love for the music.

I'm honored and saddened being here, standing in for two lives lost, two dear people who came bearing beautiful gifts to this miserable world. George's music shreds my soul with memories. I can barely concentrate. Somehow I get through the lesson and critique. We applaud him wholeheartedly. He needs to polish only a few places.

When the lesson's over he goes out to pick flowers for us. Agnes and I close up the house. She touches me on the shoulder as I stare at Amélie's garden.

"Ingrid, are you all right?"

I can't answer. We haven't talked seriously for almost three years, but today Marie told me Agnes always believed I was a Résistante. I'm grateful for Marie's confidence because I trust Agnes. I never understood why she became very discreet and stopped talking to me, except she was also silent with my detractors. What does she fear?

"What can I do, Agnes? I'm trapped. I have to ride the tides now. We all do. Little by little the best Résistants disappear. Now so many picturesque hamlets in France have Nazis executing young Maquisards, our latest martyrs, like what happened at the fortress at Mont-Valérien in Paris."

"Ingrid, war has made us very restrained and afraid to talk honestly. If we don't serve the Résistance our passivity serves the Reich. I love you despite my distance for these last two years. My Charles decided it was safer to stay away from our old acquaintances. We don't agree with their politics and I. . . ."

"Don't worry, Agnes, I understand. It's so good to see you. Thanks for coming today."

She's agitated about something else, not the war. Her older son is safe in England with his wife and their little boy. What does she want to tell me?

"Ingrid, Germaine's been more than rude, calling you a traitor. It wouldn't surprise me if you didn't want to hear her name anymore, but she's very ill. She scares me. She's lost her strident nature. It's uncharacteristic of her to be passive. Have you seen her lately?"

I listen and it all falls into place. I understand why Agnes wasn't at the dinner party. Those guests were Édouard's cronies. Agnes and her Charles wouldn't fit in. I say nothing. A moment ago I was on the verge of tears. Now I'm grounded in a pervasive fear. Its cause eludes me.

"Well, I'm sure the war is getting to her, Agnes. She has quite opposite views from her husband. No doubt it's driven a wedge between them."

I can't disclose Germaine's confidence. My own fate somehow seems linked to the deVillements. Agnes knows I'm hiding something, but doesn't press for details.

"Please, Agnes, let's get out of here. It's airless now that we've closed the windows."

We walk outside, arms linked. Georges greets us with stunning bouquets. We depart, strengthened in friendship, with no idea when we'll meet again.

At home I place my blooms in a large vase in the salon by my writing table and distribute smaller bouquets to Marie, Marta and my upstairs nightstand. They absorb my sorrows whenever I look at them.

That night I dream of Dieter and Amélie at Le Petit Chat celebrating their wedding anniversary two years ago this past February. What purpose did Amélie's death serve? Who sanctioned her murder? Someone in this town was convinced that her life was not as precious as his. A lesson of this war, maybe. We act recklessly then deny we must pay for our evil choices. Me too. I intruded on the sanctity of the Van der Kreuziers' marriage.

I awake drenched in perspiration and wonder if I'm mad with guilt, or just too alone with the burden of having murdered a human being now that my two dear friends have been murdered.

><m

The flowers' purity wilts, signaling my return to duty. I receive an urgent message. I must give yet another small dinner for the Gestapo less than a month after what I thought was my last event. Guy tells me this directive is a plea from outlying farmers to move refugees since they've lost protection from Maquis now sabotaging Nazi rail lines, as the Allies get closer.

The evening of the party Roemler is well behaved but I ply him with my best liquor to detain him as long as possible. Like a Madam in a brothel I can't ignore the two local prostitutes who cater to the other SS. I once bestowed sexual favors as they do this evening. The spectacle of usury revolts me. I entertain the men like an automaton, encased in icy grief for Amélie. Afterward I order Marie to throw out the old divan covers. The final rendezvous was worthwhile; a sizable number of Old Testaments were moved to safer locations.

These last weeks compel me to plan for a future that appears cloudy at best. I ask Maman to take her financial holdings, along with mine, out of the deVillement bank and deposit them elsewhere. She understands my caution without having to discuss my fear of Édouard. She closes my accounts into her name and moves them to another bank under the guise of remaking her will. To thwart her accountant's suspicion Maman implies she's near death. Her timing is excellent. Édouard's businesses have called him out of town. We act swiftly in his absence.

Dieter's death haunts me. Sometimes at night I hear his deep resonant voice talking in low tones as he did when he gave me information for crossings. How cleverly he handled me when I was upset. I miss his embrace. Amélie would still be here if I had protected Marta. How did the brick-throwing assassin know to enter the alley at that precise moment? Who was lurking in the shadows at the deVillements? I can't investigate these mysterious events.

Roemler has stopped pursuing me since Amélie's death. It seems coincidental that he stopped when the crossings did. Did he know?

Chapter Twenty-Six

A Trip to the Cemetery

20 July 1944, Thursday

Marta is not well. Amélie's death pulls on her other losses to overwhelm her. I watch my daughter withdraw into silence as her sweet, loving heart shuts down. She's moody, irritable and too sad for a young girl. She must blame her ill fortune on someone. Her life is lonely without siblings. She has to blame someone who loves her.

What do I say to calm her anxiety? That the world doesn't revolve around her? I must allow her childish vengeance to have its day and at the same time lead her to a sense of mature responsibility. Marta must accept what she uncovers of life and build upon it with hope and love. She's old enough to own her thoughts and actions. Her reality has been so negative. How does a war weary widow make such a harsh truth palatable to her daughter's young mind? It weighs on me like the first saddle on a yearling's back.

Then, Marta asks for a trip to the cemetery to plant flowers at Amélie's grave to remember her. We go on a warm summer afternoon.

We emerge from the car and she runs ahead. When I catch up she's glassy-eyed, staring at Amélie's headstone, lost in thought until her questions spill out.

"Maman, why did she have to die? What did I have to do with it? Why didn't I die with her? Why didn't I die with Papa? Why am I here and they're gone? Where are they? Are they together wherever they are, in heaven or what? Tell me what you know. Don't hide it. I have to know. I have to understand why I'm losing everyone I love in this life, one by one."

Before I can answer she adds with a dark mature expression, "And will you go next?"

"Oh no, my dove." I embrace her, feeling the tension in her bony, pubescent frame.

She talks faster and faster. I can't interrupt her.

Her voice raises a quartertone in urgency, "Maman, please don't ever leave me. Please, please stay near me, always!"

Tears begin as her body jerks into a stream of spasms cascading unevenly down her left side. I'm afraid she'll have a seizure. I kneel and gently lower her to my lap, sitting back on the edge of the low rock wall at the side of the graves. I rub her back and shoulders as she heaves years of suffering into long, painful sobs.

"Hush, my angel. Breathe deeply. Amélie and Dieter and Papa had to go. It was their time. We love them and miss them but their leaving this world had nothing to do with us. Except you could say being with Amélie was a great blessing. If you must leave the world it's best when someone who loves you is nearby. It makes your departure easier."

I don't know why I say that. How the hell do I know? What a terrible piece of adult arrogance. In an instant I realize what a dreadful mistake it was. Marta stops crying and looks at me eyeball to eyeball.

"No, no, Maman. He ran from me. He did not want to leave then. I made him go."

"Who are you talking about, Marta?"

It's then I see how truly obsessed she is with these deaths. Her demeanor of the last few weeks since Dieter and Amélie died reflects some awful childish fabrication to make sense out of adult senselessness. What have I done to her?

Finally the explosion comes. Before I can get her to explain her feelings she jumps to her feet and rushes off, zigzagging through the graves. Rage builds and colors her face at every step, and ironically, her body gallops more evenly with each leap forward.

"Marta! Come back! Where are you going, child?"

I run after her. By now she's already deep among the older gravestones. She heads for Emil's plot, a hundred meters from Amélie and Dieter. I can't see her. Maybe she's fallen. I catch up to her, out of breath.

"*Aye*! Marta. What are you doing, child?"

She's a maniac, bent over her father's grave, ripping up flowers and throwing handfuls of dirt at his headstone. I chill to the sound of her anger.

"I'm going to wake him up and scream at him! I need to tell him how angry I am that he left me. He didn't listen. Damn you, Papa! You had no right to leave me alone. And now you're taking everyone else I love with you!"

"Marta, stop this. He can't hear you. Control yourself."

I kneel next to her and grasp her shoulders. She glares at me, her hair, wind-loosened, in tangles, her face smudged with dirt and pools of tears.

"I know he can't hear me. Sacrebleu! Maman, what does it matter? It doesn't change how I feel. I begged and screamed for him not to go ahead and he never answered me."

"What do you mean, Marta?"

"He was full of his own thoughts just like you have been for the last three years. You were more excited to be with Dieter than me and now he's gone. At least when he was in your life you treated me better. You're never with me now unless I'm sick! You've made me *want* to be sick. Yes! *To be dying* to have you near me! I hate you and Papa and Dieter. You're all so selfish. You make me live like a prisoner. I have to 'stop crying, little one,' for you to manage your calm exterior—or be sent away to Grandmaman. And now Amélie's gone, too!"

She mimics my voice with bitter sarcasm. I sit back on my heels speechless, cut to the quick by her outburst. Her face is rigid. Her voice is clear. I see my part in her fury and a tear rolls down my cheek. I can't touch her. Nor can I force her to accept endless adult justification for what happens in her world.

She's strong and I'm defeated. She has the power of youth and I'm empty. Her virgin womanhood is fresh upon her while my femininity bears a continuous cycle of grief. She's willing to confront and I'm tired of hiding.

What am I doing caving into the whims of my angry child? Her behavior almost pushes me to feel openly as she does. She forces me to face the awful prison of other people's notions about who I am. I want to be free to join her in throwing dirt. But to follow her erroneous thinking that Emil and I moved too fast for her? How could she be so presumptuous and assume herself our equal? What does she mean?

"Did Amélie run too fast for you, Marta?" I ask, seeking clarification.

"At least she cared enough to try to save me," is her flat answer.

She understands what she's saying but I can't break her code. Her rage is spent now and I haven't given her any satisfying answers. She hasn't pressed me for any. I'm not surprised. She knows they're mostly lies to cover adult cowardice and ignorance.

How dreadful that my duplicity has layered my daughter's life with doubt. When she expects wise answers I'm mute. I can see both sides and understand that people are judging me according to their fear and not what they would do in my place. At least now I don't take their criticism so personally—but with Marta my life plays out like a piece of bad théâtre. Am I the director or another actor? Is God the author of my tragic drama and Duchamps, my audience? All my questions sit with my Marta on the front row.

On days like this when my darling child is in deep pain—what prevents me from giving her a reasonable explanation? Is it my confusion, helplessness, and fear of her rejection—or my lack of stability?

Only five months ago in Church I had a moment of lucidity, when what I was doing made sense. Was it acceptable then *only* because everyone was still alive?

Marta's breathing calms down and she stands up like a toy soldier. We leave Emil's grave askew and return to Amélie's plot to plant our seedlings in silence.

As we drive home she's quiet, cleansed of a small portion of anger. She ignores me to look out the car window. I will return later with fresh blooms for her father's plot, and perhaps make her replant it with me.

No wonder she hates me. I've had to keep her separate from the most courageous work I will ever do. I thought she would learn how honorable it is to risk dying on one's feet rather than living on one's knees. Perhaps my inverse pride to serve humanity has been too sharp an axe to her sapling—cutting her out of my world. The only world I permitted her to have. Her cruel but righteous judgment is my payment. I fear it will it be worse later when she's older and more eloquent.

Chapter Twenty-Seven

Unveiling a Nemesis

24 July 1944, Monday

Since my troubled afternoon at the cemetery with Marta, I surrender to the consequences of dealing with Germaine. Days later I receive her handwritten message to come to her house, please. I arrive in the afternoon. She receives me in her sunroom. I'm uneasy that she's lost even more weight.

"Germaine, I must be honest; I still don't feel comfortable with you."

"Why not? What's changed since our tête-à-tête in your home weeks ago? Not to mention our luncheon together? I don't understand, Ingrid."

"Nothing has changed. That's the problem, Germaine. When I came to your dinner you asked me out on the balcony because you wanted privacy. Why didn't you just take me into one of your smaller sitting rooms away from the other guests? You overheard me tell Édouard I was cold. I don't doubt you're ill and hate your husband, but. . . ."

"You don't trust me. You already said it."

She's insulted. I dislike being so callous but I'm still ambivalent toward her and Édouard. My fear is so great I don't care about her excuses to be desperate for fresh air all the time. It's hard to separate her from him when now I can't trust anyone, anymore. Suddenly the atmosphere in her house is too disconcerting, and I'm sorry I came.

Germaine plunges into a new subject before I can leave.

"My food was poisoned. The testing revealed it. I located the vials in the kitchen. It was arsenic. I've stopped it and am trying to clean it out of me before I die from it."

Curiosity rivets me. My forearms dance with gooseflesh at the irony of coincidence. Not only from the past, but maybe for the future. . . .

"Does Édouard know you suspect him?"

"No, not yet. I haven't told him but I keep a pistol in my nightstand drawer. I've sworn the maid to secrecy."

"You trust your maid? Are you kidding me, Germaine? How long do you think that will last once Édouard is home again? He'll come here to gather his ill gotten gain and go abroad, never to return. He'll leave you destitute, without a sou. You have funds to count on, yes?"

"Nothing, I have nothing. He took over my investments and my cousins bought out my shares in the family business years ago."

"Right, and which maid is guilty? The youngest one he hired last year?"

"Why yes, how did you know about her?"

"Never mind. She's not loyal to you. He's giving her money on the side and probably having sex with her. Germaine, how can you be so blind?"

"Dear Ingrid. To think you have to be the one to tell me these things. What an idiot I've been. That bastard will pay!"

There she goes, angry again, cranking up the same venom that drains the life out of her when she should be calculating her security.

"Please, Germaine, don't allow your temper to eat up your energy. Don't do anything rash. Let good will triumph as always. You still have many valuable objets d'art to sell."

I try to deflect her anger but she turns on me to speak with the characteristic scorn of her healthier days, "Oh, yes, and I should live so long with this war and a rotten marriage. Well, thank you, Ingrid Fellner, for enlightening me. You've learned a lot serving the Gestapo on your back."

She finishes her snide remarks—almost reveling in my shock, "What a clever girl in the end. Yes, I know who you are. My Édouard told me how you seduced him."

"Germaine, *what are you saying?* I've never had any interest in Édouard. Quite the contrary! When did he tell you such nonsense and how could you swallow it?"

I'm aghast. Her mind shifts. It flutters from one bit of untruth to another to shore up her dead marriage. She won't learn until he walks out on her. So much emotion and it runs out of her like a diarrhea: down, dispersed and weakening. She doesn't want to admit the truth and flits from anger to desperation.

"He told me when I came home from your house that afternoon. He was quite graphic about it. I believed him. I, uh, I wanted to believe him."

"All right, Germaine. That's enough. You're on your own. Thanks for your friendship." I don't bother telling her Édouard never came to see me.

"Ingrid, don't go. I'm sorry. It was another one of his lies."

"Right, Germaine, but you chose to believe it and try it out on me. You're losing your mind. You're a greater danger than your husband. I'm sorry for your illness but I must go."

I head for the door and as luck would have it, Édouard enters—pretending to be innocent.

"Well. My two doves; how are you?"

First I'm sorry I didn't get away and then think: let me see what he's up to.

"Oh darling, it's so good to have you home again." Germaine grasps Édouard's arms and looks up at him adoringly. He doesn't reciprocate. No kiss, no outward affection. He leers a smile at me Germaine misses as she inclines her head toward his chest.

"Nice to see you again, Édouard. I was just leaving," I make a curt formal adieu.

Och, Édouard deVillement is so twisted. Germaine debases herself living with him. I shudder. Their life is none of my business. I walk out and close the door on them for good.

My war seems to intensify after I leave the deVillements. The pace of events quickens, compressing my options minute by minute. My feet are no longer grounded. Home not more than an hour, there's a knock at my door.

I look through the narrow glass window and see Édouard. I'm alone in the house. Something deep inside me says to resist. Don't invite him in. But my prying nature overtakes my better judgment.

"I don't think we have anything to say, Édouard."

"Oh, but we do, Ingrid. You must let me in."

"Why?"

"Because I have news that will change your life."

"What could that be?"

"Your collaboration with the Nazis will have to be paid for, my dear. And I alone can help you avoid the consequences."

I must hear him out. I know I'll face physical torture or exile or both if the right people in town don't support me. It will take a public hearing with a miracle of evidence to prove my noble intentions. Édouard could use his influence on the court to convince everyone I was a collaborator. I'm not sure how much he despises me or if he's the lethal boil from my past that's about to come to a head.

"Come in and deliver your message, then kindly leave."

I lead him into the front salon. The rest of the house is in boxes but this room is untouched to avoid Roemler's suspicion, although his visits are scarce lately. Édouard neatly folds his jacket over the back of the rocker and sits down. I perch uneasily on the divan.

This was a big mistake. He's been drinking.

"Ingrid, let's be frank. There's ample proof you've played with the Gestapo over these last years. Everyone in town thinks of you as a fallen woman. Do you know what they'll do the very moment the war is over in these parts?"

To anyone else he'd be acting strangely, but for me he's typically Édouardian, a spider savoring the victim in his web with words that paralyze like venom. I'd be bored with him except alcohol has loosened his boundaries.

"Yes, I have an idea."

"Well, I have a plan. You'll need money. I have plenty. You'll need to take your family out of France. I can arrange that. You'll need p-passports and b-bookings and. . . ."

His stammer from the past interrupts my sarcastic laughter. My heart recoils as his old perversity surfaces too rapidly.

"What? Go with you? Where? To North Africa or South America? Blackmailed? Chained to you and a life of pornographic sex? Oh, I think not, Édouard." What I hear threatens me to my core.

"Oh, m-my dear, I am, ah, would, ah, b-be doing you a g-great favor. I would be sa-saving your reputation and guaranteeing your free-freedom, Ingrid. You c-cannot stay here."

He wrings his hands anxiously, thoroughly convinced of his scheme. The dimensions of his deluded state are clear. It never enters his mind that I'd refuse. I hear it in his voice. His mind is a covert arena of adult lunacy I had not envisioned. He could affect both my freedom and my reputation. I cut him off bluntly.

"I'll take my chances with the truth, thanks, Édouard."

He's not satisfied with my response. Angry, his voice becomes strident. Emboldened, he speaks without stammering.

"Ingrid, you need protection. The war in France will be over in a matter of two, maybe three weeks, certainly by the end of August. If you don't take my offer. . . ."

Oh God, intimidation by ultimatum, but I'm too incensed to realize how I inflame his fantasy to own me body and soul.

I leap at him, releasing years of pent-up angst, "*What?* You bully me because Germaine told me about her poisoning? You'll make sure I suffer, lose my daughter and my money. You'll smear me publicly. Och, Édouard, what a beast you are. I'm not as afraid as you think. You don't own me. Now get out!"

I point to the door, more enraged than afraid. I've been sickened with worry over someone's traitorous influence. Now I know for certain Édouard is my nemesis.

He stands, shakes, wags his finger in my face and utters a stunningly cryptic threat that opens my eyes completely, "Not so fast Ingrid, or you'll end up like your late husband and the Van der Kreuziers."

"What? What do you mean? What are you saying? What possible connection is there between Emil, and Dieter and Amélie?"

I can't believe my ears. His self-incriminating threat clears my muddled brain. Is it his henchmen who have been stalking my daughter and me? I thought it was the Gestapo. My mind fills with images, each one races over the other—filling in the blanks between the three deaths.

"*You* were behind Emil's death? But, it was . . . an accident." It takes a few seconds to realize Emil's demise was premeditated murder.

Outraged, I go after Édouard shouting hoarsely, "You murdering bastard! You made it look like an accident. But why kill Dieter and Amélie? Why?"

"Your thoughts are running wild, my dear. I don't know what you're talking about. I can tell you a few things perhaps. Naturally, you'll have to pay for the information, my sweet."

"Never. I shall see you guillotined first, you scum!"

Calm again, he doesn't sense my anger but toys with me like I'm one of his dead rabbits.

"Oh, come now, Ingrid, let's not be unfriendly. All's fair in love and war."

He makes light of his threat but it's too late. He backs away, condemned by the fatal slip of his own tongue. He's demented. There's no reasoning with him.

Yet, I think aloud, "You sick little man. What have you been hiding all these years? I never loved you. How could you be so covetous? Stealing from Emil and his children. I saw the papers on your desk. Now you blackmail me because I won't play your game? What little honor I have left will be protected against a worm like you, Édouard deVillement."

"I doubt it, mein kleine Feldmatratze. I will arrange to have you undressed in public and dragged naked through the streets of Duchamps, my sweet. The day is coming for women like you. One word from my lips to my friends, my darling Ingrid, and your soft, perfectly formed flesh will be rubbed into the dirt in front of all the men in this town!"

When he realizes I'm unmoved by his threats I see the crack in his armor. He's oblivious to my revulsion and consumed with his sadistic need to dominate. He hates me and despises honorable men like Emil and Dieter. He knows only to conquer, to use.

My silence triggers another bizarre change in his tactics. Édouard holds out his arms to lure me, purring with his lecherous imagination, "My sweet, come, sit on your Édouard's lap. Let's play while we plan how to save you."

He sneers, thinks he's won and believes I'll cooperate with his scheme. The sixteen-year-old Ingrid in his salacious dreams is still a stupid sexual adornment.

"You'll never touch me. Now get out."

He becomes very edgy and sours at my resistance. I've spoken too harshly. His face is flushed. He moves toward me. His mood turns ugly, dark, seething. His head twists to the side, and his eyes redden as the left one diverges.

My body tingles with terror when he reaches to strike me. I pick up a lamp and hurl it. It narrowly misses his face and crashes against the wall. He keeps coming toward me. His features transform him into a lecherous ogre. His hands shake.

Salivating like a monster, his voice pulses between a guttural growl and a vibrating bellow, "Come here, you bitch. You lousy rotten whoring little bitch!"

He lunges and tears open the front of my dress. I scream and fight back, scratching and biting his arm. He has one hand around my throat and begins to squeeze. I'm terrified he'll strangle me. I have to give in as he pushes me down onto the divan. With his left hand he immobilizes my pelvis and bends his right knee into it, then raises my skirt. He fondles my thigh and relaxes his grip on my neck as he sprouts an erection.

I twist and squirm to get free of him. The more I move, the more aroused he becomes. Sheer animal instinct grabs my intuition. My only hope is to weaken him with seduction and then hurt him. I shake my exposed bosom and fake moans of arousal. He can't stand the excitement. He makes a mistake and reaches for my breast. In his blind lust he loses his balance standing on his good leg and leans into the weak one bent against me.

In a flash of superhuman strength a blood-curdling mammalian grunt bursts from my throat and I thrust my hip free, kicking Édouard in the groin so forcefully he catapults backward over the rocker. Blinded by searing pain, he screams like a mortally wounded animal and collapses to the floor in a writhing heap.

I'm free, my heart pounds and I shake at the sound of his pained voice. I grab the heavy iron shovel in the fireplace ash bucket. While he writhes in agony I search his jacket pockets. I find a sheathed knife and take it. In the midst of my numbing terror the front doorbell rings. I stumble toward the vigorous banging and open the door, oblivious to my state of undress. It's Roemler!

The Obersturmführer sees me holding the knife and wielding the shovel, dress torn and breasts bared, mumbling and crying incoherently. He reads my frenzied eyes and pulls out his revolver as I grab his arm to lead him into the receiving salon.

Édouard whimpers, curled in a fetal position on the floor. I show the SS the scratch marks on my neck and gesture to show him the stranglehold. I can't stand any longer and fall onto the divan to recover my breathing from the onset of hysterical sobs. I point to Édouard and drop the shovel. Between breaths, my voice cracks in German and French—before my mind blanks with shock: "*Raus mit ihm*! Out with him, Wilhelm! Please, save me! *Bitte, retten Sie mich!*"

I cover myself clumsily with an old sweater, trying to button it with hands like clay and eyes riveted on Édouard's pale face, aghast at what I've done. Roemler grabs him and tries to pull him to his feet but he can't stand. He's still doubled over. He retches and pants for air. . . .

Roemler has yet to recognize my attacker's face. "Why would you molest this woman?" Then he turns to me, "Are you all right, Madame Fellner?"

I nod and whisper, "Yes, oh yes, thank you for hearing my screams."

"Madame, You'll excuse me while I take this man to jail."

Édouard is speechless, twitching as he tries to lift himself on his own. I can't believe what has happened. As I calm down, the odd twist of the situation isn't lost on me. Here I am, protected by the Gestapo, my alias, Madame Henri, one of the most notorious Résistants in town, *really* Madame Fellner, its wealthiest collaborator. And then to my great sadness and astonishment, like the worm he truly is, Édouard wriggles out of his arrest.

"Obersturmführer," he says, voice cracking, "this was just a lover's spat. You had no right to interrupt us. You know how these mistresses can be when promiscuous. One has to discipline them every so often, no?"

Roemler locks the salon door while Édouard tries to convince him that he's exercising his manly duty to keep me in line. The German is confused because Édouard only recently shaved off his mustache and goatee. He doesn't realize deVillement is my attacker until he hears him speak. This monster is the very man whose extravagance Roemler envied at his soirée a few weeks ago. The Nazi frowns as the lie settles into his ears.

"A lovers spat? But you sir, Monsieur deVillement, that's your name, correct? You are a married man." Innocent as he is Roemler doesn't believe Édouard. He looks at me. It's the second time I sense this human being behind a Swastika.

"Sir, it looks like you attacked this woman, pure and simple. You want something she's not willing to give. You deceived her and your wife."

Édouard is desperate to save himself and pulls one last card. He speaks in German to Roemler about his contacts in the Gestapo hierarchy. Édouard forgets I can understand what he says, so I play dumb and listen.

"You have no power over me, Obersturmführer. I own the Milice in this town."

"Are you threatening an Offizier of the Reich, sir?" Roemler takes aim, cocking the hammer of his gun.

"Me? No never, Obersturmführer, just testing your loyalties. I, ah, assume you haven't been paid lately?" Édouard fishes to see if Roemler is corruptible.

"How much, deVillement?" Roemler answers, immediately anticipating a bribe.

"Fi-five thousand Francs for your lips to remain sealed. You ne-never came here to-today."

"Ten thousand will be fine." Roemler narrows his eyes and flashes a conqueror's smile.

"Yes, all right."

"I'll meet you at your bank in one hour to get the money, deVillement, but I'll hold your wallet and papers and return them only after I receive it."

Édouard is relieved that Roemler accepts. He's paying him too much but for once he's fearful. Behaving mawkishly, Édouard places his wallet and papers in Roemler's outstretched hand and backs toward the door, bent in pain.

Roemler keeps his gun aimed and warns, "You're a lucky bastard. She should have neutered you when she had the chance. Go home and stay away from her. I'll post guards to protect her from vermin like you. If you threaten her again I'll hunt you down personally. Now get out."

Roemler's Teuton chivalry is impressive but I'm saddened he gives in so easily. I assume he wants money because the Nazi war machine is on its knees. I can't be surprised. Still, I sense Roemler dislikes Édouard for some other reason.

Édouard coughs, reaches weakly for his jacket and shuffles stiffly to the door. His hands cover his manhood. He departs like a ghost, face white, shrunken and wet with perspiration. I overhear Roemler tell his driver to escort Édouard to the Gestapo office for thirty minutes and then take him to his bank. The junior SS is to keep him under watch at all times. He orders Édouard's driver to go home. I take a deep shaky breath when my SS hero returns and bows,

"Is there anything else I can do, Madame Fellner, before I leave?"

"No, thank you. Well, maybe, sit with me, please."

Then I think, you could have shot Édouard as an intruder and been done with him. Now he could return or worse, one day in my garden or in the street I could be hit with a brick like Amélie was. Immediately I bite my lip in remorse for ill will . . . even against my nemesis.

The memory of Édouard's childhood sickness stabs my heart. I've known him forever. My mind returns to the present. I resist voicing disgust at Roemler's decision. He's in charge. It's martial law. I'm grateful for his presence. Perhaps the God of self-mockery has smiled on me today to shut my mouth.

"Join me with a schnapps, please?" I point to the decanter on the table. The irony of needing a drink after Édouard's Trunkenheit gets my attention but doesn't stop me.

I rearrange my clothing and hair, calmer though my flesh still quakes. Finally I've come face to face with another act in Édouard's evil puppetry. I will have to think long and hard about Emil, Dieter and Amélie.

Roemler pours our drinks and sits opposite me. I sip slowly.

"You know, Obersturmführer, when this war ends I hope you'll go home in one piece to pick up your life where you left it. If you fail in the war it's only in the context of the whole of Germany failing. You will have done your best. Me, I haven't failed and yet after the war is over I'll be treated as a traitor. I'll lose my reputation and be severely dishonored. I may have to leave France and go away empty-handed to save my life. Can you understand what that means?"

His reply amazes me, "I'm sorry, Madame. I think we've all lost our humanity in this madness. French, German, it doesn't matter any more. The longer it goes on, the worse it is. Please do not think me disrespectful of my Vaterland," he pauses to sip, "You have been most kind, Madame, despite my unhealthy desire to use you when we first met. You are an honorable person. Even if I discover you are a spy I will not turn you in. I know almost everyone in this town has a low opinion of you. But your goodness is too clear in your face. You only want to save life. I hope you will not suffer at the end, Madame. I know you will honor my confidence when I tell you there has been entirely too much death in these last years. Europe stinks of it."

Roemler's remarks are genuine. Perhaps he was forced to serve because of the Austrian Anschluss. Yet something else must have happened to change his attitude that terrible day he witnessed Marta's grief when Amélie was killed. I was bitter then. Now I wish I could ask his forgiveness for my nasty judgment of his "piddling" Aryan conscience.

"I want to believe you are telling me a truth from your heart, Obersturmführer. I'm tired of dealing with men who use nationalism, politics, religion, race, money and sex to exercise power over others, over me. They're paranoid, envious and defensive. Their xenophobic fear feeds on a scapegoat, a tribal bulwark for their greed against honest people. Seduced and depraved by power, they have no compassion. I don't care what side anyone is on. When personal evil becomes a national obsession souls are lost and civilization is damned."

My bitter disillusionment causes Roemler to reveal a surprising postscript, "Madame Fellner, you're disappointed because I let deVillement go free just now. He needs to think I can be bought. He's very dangerous and controls many people. He helps the SS but uses us to get revenge with vicious criminal vendettas he set up before the war. He's another demagogue who has betrayed French and German industry. I need time to uncover his underworld connections and complete my investigation.

"When the war is over deVillement and his cronies will be arrested. I assure you the evidence will go into the right hands before I leave France. In the meantime while Germans are still on French soil I will do my best to protect you. I'm very sorry for your indignity."

I smile helplessly at Roemler. At least he endeavors to be fair.

Minutes have passed and the full impact of the attack loosened by the alcohol transforms me into a dead weight. I look at him through a veil of blurred vision and shiver.

"Please, bitte, excuse me for yawning, Obersturmführer."

Our rendezvous is suddenly so intimate. Alone in my home, I am an injured, vulnerable female forced to recline against pillows to be upright. Broken glass, ashes from the fireplace, my torn dress, rising welts on my neck—my head is spinning, and I can't care about any of it. And yet, staring into space, I work hard to suppress a sudden swelling of emotion, realizing what just took place here, and what could have occurred if Roemler had not appeared. My body jerks in relief, as if to acknowledge its safety.

Without asking me, the young Austrian picks up my favorite handmade wrap sitting on the end table. The one made by the mother of the escaped Résistance worker. His fingertips caress its soft mohair wool.

"Bitteschön, if you please, let me help you, Madame Fellner."

He covers me with it. If only Wilhelm could hold in his heart the sentiments she crocheted into this shawl.

"It's a beautiful piece of work, Madame. My grandmother used to crochet a similar pattern."

Did I dream this or is it happening? My mouth drops, and I nod a 'yes,' smiling at him. His eyes catch mine briefly. Self-conscious, he looks away. We have been too human with each other, for once the rescuer and the rescued, instead of predator and prey.

He leaves quietly, locking the door behind him, and I fall into a deep sleep on the divan.

Chapter Twenty-Eight

Gathering Forces

20 August 1944, Sunday

Marie watches me deteriorate for weeks and worries as I sink into terrible hopelessness. I see it in her eyes. Long days of apprehension deepen her frown lines. The erosion of my confidence began with Dieter's near death . . . or bogus death . . . or maybe now his *real* death? Then seeing Amélie die—climaxed by Marta's outburst at the cemetery, Germaine's poisoning and finally Édouard's attack. I suppose there is a just God, but lately moi, a little spit of His creation, has regressed to her self-pitying prima donna status of 1941.

Marie watches me vacillate between groundless optimism and certain despair. She shares the intense pressure, and fears the coming liberation will crush me. I see a constant query in her eyes. Is her mistress's detachment normal or is her survival instinct dulling as her world diminishes?

I struggle alone; hoping the dearest people in ma famille de la Résistance will devise a plan to help me. I did not burden Guy and Marie with the details of Édouard's attack. If I could have hidden it entirely I would have, but the room was a shambles I could not clean up alone.

After the incident with Édouard, no one says anything. I have days of nervous exhaustion; I'm unable to eat, and must keep Marta at a distance. Then, one afternoon, Sylvia visits me unexpectedly without Pierre. Her sweet toddler is a balm for my weary heart, but he and Marta stay with Grandmaman. Sylvia is preoccupied until she settles on the divan after Guy and Marie leave the house.

She explains why cautiously, "Madame, there will be a meeting tonight of a few local Résistants. I'm going to smuggle you into the building to eavesdrop. It's all worked out. You must agree to do it, of course."

"Agree? Mon Dieu! How do you know about such a meeting, Sylvia?"

"I can't tell you, just bring old clothes you can throw out afterward. Cover your head with something you can pitch to the trash."

"When do I dress like this and how do I keep it secret from Marie and Guy?"

"You will change at the location. We'll get you inside to hear what will be discussed."

"I love my Underground family, Sylvia, but the ones in charge have been ruthless."

"Oui, Madame, but the effects of the Liberation could be most grave on you. You must know how to handle yourself. Not everyone agrees about keeping you ignorant. You must be vigilant and stay silent tonight, no matter what you see or hear. I don't have to tell you that after all we've been through together. Trust me, please. I wish I could do more for you," and her eyes look so sad, "You saved me, and my Pierre, Madame. Now that we are so close to freedom, I can barely breathe. Once the war is over, I'm afraid to discover all that I have lost."

"My dear girl," I embrace Sylvia and rock her in my arms like I did those first nights she and Pierre slept in my pantry.

⤛⤜

Guy, Marie, Sylvia and a few others break the rules to meet in the basement of the old morgue. I'm amazed the location is right here in town, but can't be surprised if Patrice had anything to do with it. That tough old bird is Alain Duvette's equal . . . if not his superior . . . in guile and subterfuge.

A narrow basement corridor leads to a dingy space crowded with discarded furniture and piles of temporary viewing coffins. I'm standing in the coal bin wearing old clothes, boots, and a scarf over my head. The door from the bin to the room is heavy, metal lined on the inner side. I've stood in this dirty crowded space for thirty minutes. I could sit, and get coal dust on my derriere. I may have to before long. Sylvia and Patrice suggested I sit, but at shoulder level there's a sliding cover that opens a 10 by 14 centimeter rectangular window used to check the bin's level of coal. Patrice opened it to a narrow slit so I see the table only six meters away.

One by one I watch other rescuers arrive after Sylvia, Marie and Guy. They sit around the old table dimly lit by candles. Finally everyone assembles, except the two doctors upstairs in the morgue. I gather they are the uninvited when Patrice locks the cellar door, sits and announces, "I asked you to come tonight for a very special person. We're breaking the rules to tell you who she is. We have to help her now before Paris is liberated."

"Who is it?" Stefan asks casually. Patrice hesitates and looks at Marie.

Marie gingerly says, "Madame Henri, your belle-mère, Stefan," and awaits his indignant response.

"What do you mean?" he explodes in a loud whisper, "my stepmother slept with every Obersturmführer for the last three years. She's one of them. I found a brooch my father had given her on Heisler's body. She had his family crest and initials rubbed off and pawned it behind my back."

I bite my tongue listening to his rage. Stefan really didn't catch on that Heisler was cursing me just before his murder. Thank God Marie reprimands him.

"Exactly. And she gave the money to us. The same Madame Henri who passed dozens of refugees to farmers—the Jews you drove to the border came from her basement, Stefan. Be quiet and listen. You'll learn something."

The old pawnbroker continues less gruffly, "Sonny, your belle-mère played this town for a pack of gossips with nothing better to do than think the worst of her. That brooch was pawned twice and brought money to forge papers, feed Jews and the Maquis."

"Wait, please, excuse me for interrupting," touching the pawnbroker's arm, Sylvia addresses Stefan. The candles highlight her poised features and golden hair. She speaks with a measured voice, "You've had quite a shock just now, Monsieur. I'm sorry you think the worst of your step-mother but she's had to conceal her position from everyone."

Sylvia senses old personal issues cloud Stefan's relationship with me. Her tenderness disarms him.

"Who are you? I've never seen you before, Mademoiselle."

"My name is Sylvia Feinstein. Your belle-mère and her Maman have hidden my little son and me for seventeen months. My son was born prematurely in Madame Ingrid's house. She, Guy and Marie here saved my life. Please open your heart to understand. Madame Ingrid is an extraordinary woman. So is her mother."

Sylvia's eyes grip Stefan's attention and disperse his anger with the force of her gratitude. I stand here crying silently, grateful and hopeful that no matter the violence ahead—these people will help me. All I have done and suffered has been worth the pain, if only to have their respect.

Marie grasps Sylvia's hand, adding credence to what she has said, "Oui, Stefan, we delivered her son on the same night Mueller was upstairs. Madame has sacrificed more than any of us. She adored your father. She buried him all over again to pawn her brooch. She couldn't ask your accountant for more money. She was afraid to break her silence to protect you. The brooch came back to her anyway."

"Please, Monsieur, we need your help." Sylvia's appeal softens his face.

Stefan's impulsiveness and negativity were expected. My dear beau-fils shields his eyes with his hands and stares at the table, ashamed.

Then Guy tells him the worst, "Stefan, last year in September Ingrid shot and killed a junior SS in her basement to protect her Jews. Our people shielded her from suspicion to offset any reprisal."

"Jean Claude, you never told me anything," Stefan's voice withers with embarrassment. He continues to look down at his hands.

"He was not permitted to, Stefan. Your belle-mère has also been in the dark about everything," old Marcel interjects.

Jean Claude nods, adding, "We have no idea of the suffering that elegant lady will bear for the rest of her days."

All present could be trusted save Stefan. It makes me sick to see him so upset. He sat like this when Emil berated him as a child. And now Dieter's insistence has done this to him. The decision to keep Stefan in the dark about my position Underground might have seemed correct, but given our uneven history the risk would have been worth taking. Dieter and Alain have been cruel to me, and my beau-fils.

The old farmer Marcel Beauchamp continues, "Do you recall the note you tucked into your documents on that day with Heisler? It didn't matter that Madame Ingrid signed her nom de guerre. Heisler recognized her handwriting from the SS death notice she signed after the Jews washed up on her shore. I had to kill him to save you and Ingrid." Marcel watches Stefan's face cave in to grief.

"Dieter sent her shreds of your scarf that Jean Claude here, pulled from Heisler's fingers. Jean Claude saved your hide, too. Dieter never knew Ingrid witnessed that murder. And your belle-mère burned the evidence in her fireplace minutes before Mueller came to interrogate her. If she hadn't, you and Ingrid would be starving in Struhof or Ravensbrück, or Mueller would have had the two of you executed in the town square. Reprisals like that happen all over France now. People hate us for fighting Nazis and Vichy. They're too eager to betray us. They're afraid to stand up to the evil bastards and pay the consequences."

The room is locked in silence. No one knew this much of my story until now.

"Enough. Save your stepmother from being labeled a traitorous whore, eh Stefan? Or she'll lose her money, land and reputation," Philippe wants to press on with a solution.

Stefan replies meekly, "I was convinced of her treachery and never thought she was the 'bitch' Heisler referred to. No wonder he tried to kill me! What I said to others about her while she was saving. . . ." Stefan rubs his chin and squints back tears, "I'm relieved she sided with Free

France. Her collusion protected me but it feels odd that I couldn't be trusted. My worst behavior was used against a woman who loves me as if I were her own child."

Old Marcel is gentler now. "Don't beat yourself too badly, sonny. You need to get out of your past. Dieter used that weakness to our advantage. You have helped him build a very convincing image of your stepmother as a slut for the Third Reich."

"Oui, bien sûr, she needed your public hatred to save Jews," the pawnbroker adds.

"We don't have much time," Philippe continues, "Ingrid needs support to confirm her position in the Résistance. She's especially vulnerable since most households in the Underground do not know she plays both sides to protect us. When the Germans flee the Milice will smear her to guard their interests. They're certain she knows their dirty secrets from her intimacy with Boche hierarchy. The Vichy power mongers controlling this town will ruin her. In court they'll rule our evidence insufficient and unsubstantiated."

"We need testimony from someone important to validate her duplicity," the pawnbroker interjects, "Jewish refugees or someone in a high position like Dieter was."

"What about Sylvia, here?" Stefan asks, searching her face.

Sylvia is glum, "I can't help her. I have no written proof of German citizenship nor was I registered in Dachau. My story is compelling but at this moment it cannot be officially substantiated."

"Unfortunately, we have no refugees in our area whose testimony would be irrefutable. They've crossed to Switzerland or Italy. Who knows if they're even alive," Guy concludes.

"So what do we do?" Stefan voices defeat. The situation appears hopeless.

"We take a chance. It's all we have," Beauchamp declares, "A Jewish couple came through Ingrid's six months ago. I took them to the edge of your land, Stefan, where Maquis led them to an old cabin."

"The one used by groundskeepers years ago," Stefan interrupts, "about six kilometers inside the forest. I remember it," Stefan's attitude brightens, he's curious.

"Yes, that's the one," Beauchamp is encouraged, "they were to stay there until the weather was warm and then go to Switzerland. The man's leg was so lame he could barely walk. We gave him herbs for it. Surely he can walk by now."

"Even so," Jean Claude says, "it's a very long journey to the Swiss frontier, another eight kilometers in the mountains. They couldn't go alone. If they're waiting for a passeur to guide them across we might find them before they leave."

"What does this have to do with Ingrid?" Stefan asks.

"They're Polish Jews. They crossed through Ingrid's basement. She talked with them. They could clear her name," Marcel answers.

"How? Who will believe them? They could be any old villagers."

"No, Stefan, they were in the Polish Resistance in the camps. Few escape alive and besides, they speak fluent French, German, Polish, even English," Sylvia adds.

"We need to bring them back here to testify," Marcel agrees, knowing Stefan can find the cabin.

"But what if they won't come? Why should they? The war's not over yet. They could be deported if they return," Stefan's shame for years of hostility colors his optimism.

"I'm sure they'll come if we protect them," Sylvia is hopeful.

"What about contacting people as high up as Dieter was in the Underground?" Igor asks, "Even if they don't know Ingrid personally her position affects the movement of refugees all over this valley."

The others watch as Jean Claude stares anxiously at Beauchamp. The two men seem to share knowledge they discuss only with their eyes. The old farmer shakes his head in disapproval and waves his hand slowly in a "no."

But Jean Claude reveals their secret with cautious optimism. "You might find Dieter alive with the Jews."

Hearing these words I shove my hand across my mouth, not to utter a sound, and almost faint. Too much information makes my head dizzy and heart skip a beat. Working for years on the same side yet cut off from my compatriots' knowledge: Alain, Dieter, Amélie, Guy, Marie, and

Marcel were attentive and made me feel secure in my widowhood, but in the Underground they have treated me like a deaf-mute, denying me the truth under the necessary guise of . . . secrecy?

"What! He's alive?" Marie stares at Jean Claude, incredulous, as if he has personally deceived her.

Guy grabs his wife's hand. I can feel his heart leap for joy.

Quickly, Jean Claude adds, "I don't know, Madame Marie. No one knows. He was frail when we moved him. He could have died from exposure in the forest. We lost touch with the Maquis who looked after him. They went southwest to fight in the Rhône. We haven't heard from them. We can't know if he's alive without going into the forest ourselves. We think he didn't make it or we would have been contacted to supply more medicine for him."

"And his funeral in May?" Marie is stuck in disbelief, "We, his own Résistants searched all over France for him. He didn't want us to know the truth, did he?" Her temper rises against the old veteran, "Damn it, Marcel, *you* knew there'd be no record of him in any detention center or work camp. *You* knew he was alive from the beginning, oui?"

"Even if he is, Marie, we won't know for sure until the war's over. By then it will be too late for Ingrid," Stefan agonizes bitterly.

Marie ignores Stefan and aims her barbs at the old farmer. "Holy Mother of God, Marcel, do you have any idea how much my mistress stands to lose? How dare you keep this information from us?" her eyes brim, "And from *me*, of all people."

She clenches her jaw at him. The two face off for a few seconds until Marcel looks away. A flash of remorse crosses his face. Marie shakes her head in a no and wipes her cheeks.

I never thought, but maybe it's true—Marcel adored Marie but his twin brother was her lover. Étienne was the father of her baby? Amélie reminded me about him before she died.

"I will beg the good doctor Duvette to tell me if you won't," Marie threatens.

"Marie, calm down, please," Philippe insists, "No one was supposed to know."

"Dieter was very close to death. Duvette and Devoir had no choice. Don't be angry with Marcel. He and Jean Claude only transported Dieter a few kilometers. They couldn't reveal anything," the old pawnbroker explains.

Marie stares at the apothecary, gritting her teeth, "But, Philippe, this silence among ourselves has gone on for too long. Madame can't go outside on the street. She's not safe. Marta has to stay away from her or the child becomes morose. She and Madame almost died in that alley when Amélie was murdered. I can barely get Madame to eat," Marie's thin lips twitch from long suppressed fear for my future.

I love her dearly. But I never told Marie I was in that alley. I wonder who did.

"I have to agree with my wife," Guy shakes his head sadly. Guy is precious.

Sylvia puts her arm around Marie and pleads with Philippe and Marcel, "Oh sirs, if Madame knew there was even a glimmer of hope she would have the strength to bear up against the public scorn that will be inevitable."

There's an uneasy pause as the terrible portent of future days settles on their humble shoulders. They can feel a little of my fear now. Something has to be said.

Beauchamp warns both women sternly and addresses Marie directly: "You can't say a word to your mistress as long as we don't know if he's alive or dead."

Marie wipes her eyes and blows her nose. Some unspoken hurt passes between her and Marcel again that causes Guy to reach around Sylvia and put his hand on his wife's shoulder.

She squeezes it and takes a deep breath until she's composed enough to ask, "Oui, bon, we're agreed to find the Jewish couple. Who searches for them?"

"Stefan," Philippe and the old farmer say simultaneously looking at the young redhead.

"Why me? I need to go to Ingrid and beg her forgiveness for my dreadful arrogance. Send Jean Claude," Stefan insists, smarting at de Voisin's privilege to know the truth.

"No, Stefan," Beauchamp responds, "we must move very quickly. Without the Kleinborens' testimony we have only our own stories. To hope corrupt judges and a prosecutor bought off by rich bankers will believe us is foolish when they can crucify an easy mark like a reviled rich widow. Besides, think what it would mean to Ingrid if you are the one to bring the evidence that clears her name."

Beauchamp sweetens the remainder of his delivery with genuine love for my Stefan, because he has driven hundreds of innocents to safety. "You know the path through the forest, Stefan. We must prepare at once. Come with me, son. I'll give you tools and food."

Stefan rises and walks around the table to Sylvia. He smiles, taken with her beauty, dignity and kindness. He kisses her fingers and murmurs a sincere "thank you." She blushes, bowing her head. He freezes for a moment then reluctantly releases her hand.

Joining Beauchamp at the door he turns to bid her a silent 'au revoir' before the two men depart. "I should leave right away," Stefan says to Marcel, pausing to thank old Patrice.

"No, no, sonny, it's too dangerous in there at night. You go by daylight."

"How many days do I have to get back here?"

"Oh, I guess about three or four. Our liberation is a week away at the earliest. When that happens events will move very swiftly, Stefan. We have to be ready with whatever defense we can muster for Madame."

When the meeting is over and everyone leaves, Patrice hurries me out to a waiting gazogène hearse, its engine humming to an occasional belch.

"Quick, Madame, get in. It took me forever to get this wood sucker burning. I must return before the good médecins come home."

She slams the doors closed and races down the alley, glancing at my trembling hands,

"Did you leave the clothes in the bin, Madame Ingrid?"

"Oui, Patrice. How did you keep this meeting secret from Duvette?" I'm impressed with her swift timing, mechanical skill to start a gazogène and drive like the wind on rural streets.

"The two doctors were busy tonight at the edge of town helping a family deliver twins. When they arrived, the farmer's mare was in labor too. I know. I took the phone message this morning." She smiles and lifts her arched eyebrows.

"Did you tell Marie that I saw Amélie murdered in the alley, Patrice?"

"Oui, Madame. I had to explain why I sent her that special ointment from Dr. Alain for your face. He would have given it to you if he had known."

"I see. You would have made sure of that, I suppose?"

"Oui, bon, Madame."

"Well, thank you, Patrice. I didn't know you drove more than a mechanical vehicle, eh?"

She smiles, blushes, and laughs. This woman amazes me. She drops me by my side servant's entrance, turns and says, with a hint of mischief in her eyes,

"I'm just a farm girl who learned early, Madame, the eldest of eight. My maman had two sets of twins. My uncle was the engineer and his brother, my papa, was the farmer; so we had a steam tractor from the 1880s. I learned to drive it when I was nine after papa broke his arm.

"I sat on his lap on a feedbag stuffed full of hay. When papa clutched, he shouted and I shifted the valve controlling the steam pressure. By the Grace of God we moved forward. It was a noisy, smelly mechanical dinosaur. Horses on a plow are a lot smarter, Madame. But you know, men are dreamers, and today, well, their machines are more sophisticated, even if they haven't changed." We laugh heartily at her droll assessment when I ask,

"I suppose working for Alain reinforces that opinion, n'est-ce pas?"

Patrice eyes me grinning,

"Oui, Madame. Women's lives are about being grateful for courage and ingenuity to solve the problems we can see *and* the surprises that find us along the way."

Chapter Twenty-Nine

Disgraced

8 September 1944, Friday

Paris is liberated on August 25th, after six days of fighting. Pockets of resistance remain in our area of eastern France. The war is far from over for Eastern Europe, but for the French, it's safe to begin rejoicing. The Allies with the First French Army converge in the Rhône Valley southwest of Duchamps and push the Boches north to Besançon. The few remaining Jews are safely sequestered in barns and basements awaiting liberation.

Roemler and his officers flee our area to join the Wehrmacht retreating to the Vosges. The rich who sided secretly with the Führer's economy collect their dwindling finances and leave France.

My world since Édouard's attack a month ago has become deathly still. I planned to hide far away, on Saturday the 9th—designated the day of Duchamps' Liberation—but by today, Friday the 8th, it appears I am running out of time. . . .

The air in town seethes with an odd mix of burgeoning exhilaration and dark foreboding. Euphoria erupts with a seamy underbelly to this first "meting"—no, it's more accurate to say "meating, m-e-a-t-i-n-g" of peace. Duchamps is crazed with freedom and rife with retribution. A wild purge or "*l'épuration sauvage*" infects our civility and reduces us to a tribal Gallic community.

It begins when several mobs of drunken celebrants become violent on this sunny afternoon. They tear down Nazi Swastikas and German street posters. They burn them in a huge bonfire in the main square of the old municipal building.

We see the flames as Guy drives us home from Maman's estate in the gazogène lorry. I'm inside the cab. Marie sits in the back of the wooden side-paneled open bed, next to the pot-bellied burner. I'm not happy with this arrangement but she and Guy insisted.

Then we see a small group of men spot a prostitute who catered to well-paying German officers crossing a street. First they leer at her. However, in a flash a mob chases down the poor woman and corners her like a wounded quarry.

"Guy, look! What are they doing?" A sharp pain sears from the pit of my stomach under my sternum as I cry out to him.

Marie bangs on the back window—gesturing wildly for Guy to get off this street. It leads directly into the mêlée in the square. The prostitute's screams pierce the air as the commotion of men's bodies swarms over her. They gesticulate lewdly and growl with a primordial vengefulness that would slay the weak.

I am riddled with fear and can't take my eyes off this public spectacle when we overhear, "Get that whore up there, Guillaume, and undress her. Marc has the paint. Hurry."

"Madame Ingrid, put your head down. Don't let them see you." Guy's voice is hoarse. He's petrified. The mob gets larger, while smaller packs of men break away and roam the streets with sadistic hunger.

"Merde, Madame, get down! The insanity has come a day early! Down, please, *now!*"

I barely hear him as he negotiates the lorry around the noisy mob. With all the people beginning to gather there's no way to turn the truck around.

"Oh Guy. They're pulling off her blouse!"

Their raw sadism has me transfixed. They drag her by the hair, half-naked, down the street. I scarcely feel Guy's right hand forcing me down onto the floor of the truck. His full weight presses on my left shoulder. All around us the rabble foment their sour witch-hunt, spitting and cursing.

The stuffy darkness of the lorry's floor immediately ignites a claustrophobic memory of the closet in the basement of the Hotel LaFrance. Coughing and gasping, I bob back up to the dashboard and cannot help but look.

"No, please, Guy, I . . . I must see this!" I cry out, stung with horror.

The prostitute stands on a makeshift platform. The men pull her skirt up. They call her foul names and hold her down to paint black Swastikas on her bare breasts. Then they release her—but won't let her off the platform. The poor soul cowers, cries, and crosses her arms over her chest. Her head is down. Her long hair hides her shame. A few men leading the crowd taunt her and throw garbage at her. I'm terrified they'll lynch her!

Another group of rowdies races to a nearby boarding house. They drag out a younger woman who has an illegitimate child by a German soldier.

"Get down, Madame, please. Remember Amélie and your Marta. *They must not see you!*" Guy's voice is stern, and his eyes are wild with fear.

By a miracle he slips the lorry past the mob—and has just two narrow blocks more before he reaches the wider avenue along the river. We'll be safe then.

But just as he turns onto the small street, men from the first group of drunks jump onto the back of the lorry to grab Marie. Guy and I look back as she screams. Guy stops the vehicle to go to her aid.

One of the men races around to my side of the truck. Before I can lock Guy's door and roll up my window another reaches in and grabs my shoulder. I roll the window up against his arm and make him scream in pain before his crony pulls me from the van, grabbing me from Guy's side.

"I've got the high-class bitch, the one who slept with the Doryphores' leadership. Here we are boys! Let's have her. She's the *real find* of the day."

Marie and Guy fight off the men. Marie swings an old table leg and Guy a large wrench. Guy is hit on the head and bleeding, but on his feet. Marie is disheveled and scratched—but   not hurt. I manage to break loose by kicking my assailant in the shins. I run down the narrow street, screaming at the top of my lungs, *"Help! Please!"*

Two men run after me. Two others nurse wounds from Marie's table leg and Guy's wrench . . . while the last one leaves to get reinforcements. Windows and doorways open on either side of the street as neighbors hear the clamor. I want to shout my history of the last three years to anyone who'll listen, but my mouth is dry and my mind is blank. I'm running so fast and breathing so hard, I can't shout.

A man in a doorway fires two shots into the air in quick succession! Two drunks behind me stop in their tracks. I look up, panting, as my mother's accountant takes aim at them. I nod my head to acknowledge his help and disappear down his alleyway toward the wide tree-lined street along the river—hoping Guy and Marie will meet me there. But I can't see their lorry.

Hysterical, I trip here, rush there, forward, sideways . . . anywhere I see no men to grab me. More come toward me at the end of the alley. I turn to run down the other block but there's another man at that corner. I'm out of breath: my legs cramp; my heart races. Resisting is useless.

Then they pounce, with their hands all over me, and press in to bruise to the bone. I stiffen at their grip. My instinct has no voice, but deep inside me, I know not to speak or they'll rape me here in this public alley. They drag me by my hair. Men and women curse and carouse behind me. Others spit and throw trash from their balconies. My town hungers for a public orgy of sexual humiliation, and now revels—they have captured their favorite target.

My attackers lead me to the open square. One of them points to the first woman, still half-naked on the crude platform. She crouches in front of us, pelted, and dripping with garbage.

"Too bad, Antoine, we made a mistake. This is the one we were told to expose."

"Forget it, Paul, we've got the money. It's enough work for one day. Better enjoy her on the march, like this." He rubs his left hand across my bosom, laughing as he pinches my nipples.

"You mean like this, eh, boss?" his comrade shouts back as he slaps my buttocks while they pull me along.

"Yeah, merde, they've seen us. That's all you can have of her. It's too late. We can't take her away and get at her before he does."

"Are you sure he won't know we have the wrong one?"

"Shut up, Paul. Get this bitch up there with the rest. They'll all look alike from a distance when his barber is finished."

I hear this and go limp with no more strength. My voice is mute like my mind. The terror of being publicly abused forces me out of my flesh. Time suspends. People's faces and bodies blur into a whirr of moving shapes, sounds, colors, and body odors. The men drag me, digging their fingernails into my armpits. My shins scrape the cobblestones.

Pain throbs in waves and pushes me in and out of shock. Intuition tells me the less I fight, the better my chance to come out of this alive. I listen for the lorry's belching engine. Guy and Marie follow, and honk to reassure me I'm not alone.

The mob parades me into the main square. I join the other women. We six are forced upon a crude platform where a brute wields a pair of heavy tailor's scissors. He cuts each woman's hair—then hands her to the local barber to be sheared to total baldness. Men reach up to pinch, pull and grab us. We shield the half-naked one to protect her and ourselves. One prostitute removes her cardigan to cover the naked girl, just before her hair is cut off. The other women are undressed down to their undergarments. Their breasts and genital areas are smeared with mud. I expect I will be treated the same before it's over. A huge hulk of a man holding a bucket waits on the platform. He squeezes the mud oozing through his paws.

I'm on my hands and knees, light-headed, trembling and in tears, covered in other women's shorn hair. I must stand to avoid the groping hands that reach across the platform. Two women help me to my feet. My shins bleed through my torn pants. I totter and reach out to the nearest woman for balance. Oh no, she's the twenty-two-year-old who came to my dinner party weeks ago. I look into her frightened eyes and gaze back over the sea of crazed humans.

We are victims in our own mad world. A few women have family members and friends in the crowd who plead with gendarmes along the periphery to stop this insanity. The mob's faces rapidly dissolve into a hissing, salivating haze like wild jackals about to feast on a territorial invader. Who is the real enemy here?

I stare up into the face of the barber who cut my Emil's hair and coifs Duchamps' rich clientele, and plead, "Gilles, how can you do this? We're not the enemy. Stop this madness; you know I hid Jews." I search for a hint of sympathy. Then I see a tear run down his cheek when he recognizes me. My reproach has cut into his mind like his razor. His breath tells me he's been liquored to accomplish his task.

I faint dead away at his feet when it's his turn to skin me. The same men who grabbed me on the street sit me down in the chair. I come to as Gilles resists, arguing with Antoine, who orders him to shave me at knifepoint.

I'm thankful to be wearing pants and not a skirt they could lift to advertise my feminine wares, as they did with the other women. Antoine is annoyed by this and orders two henchmen to spread my legs as he slithers his knife along my genitals and threatens to cut off my work pants down the crotch seam. The crowd foams at his lewdness.

Poor Gilles is distraught. His hands shake as he works his razor, and mutters an apology under his breath. Long red lines of blood drip slowly down my face, cheeks and neck. What more will they do to us? Make us raise our arms in a Nazi salute?

I'm the last one shorn. Guy and Marie force their way to the front of the mob on foot, shouting and swinging their weapons, fearing the aroused men will lose all self-control. The police decide the rabble has had enough "recreation." They push forward to arrest us women and disperse the crowd. By some stroke of luck I leave the platform still dressed and not muddied.

Guy, tall and imposing, cradles me in his arms, while Marie curses the rowdies and everyone else in her path, wielding her table leg as we proceed to the truck.

"You animals don't know your saints when you see them. Bastards! Out of our way! Move! Go home and dry out, you scum!" Her years of silent forbearance break wide open,

"Cowardly swine! You should have died on battlefields as respectable Maquisards instead of idling about in cafés drinking and playing cards."

She marches in front of Guy with her head held high. Tears stream down her cheeks and bloodied chin. Clutching a rosary and a table leg, she reaches into her pocket and hands Guy smelling salts to revive me. By the time we return to the lorry I'm awake, but unable to walk unsupported. My head is a mess of cuts and clotted blood and my extremities are covered with scratches, bruises and spit.

Then an old gendarme bars Guy and Marie from placing me in the truck to take me home, "She has to come with me."

"Why? She's done nothing wrong," Marie is indignant.

"She's an enemy of the Republic. The war is over and she collaborated."

"She did not! She was a member of the Underground and diverted the Gestapo to help Jews escape out of her basement and everyone else's." Marie is adamant.

"Yes, Madame. All the same she's under arrest."

He doesn't believe Marie. She scowls at him fearlessly refusing to budge until he softens,

"Look, if it's true, she'll have a chance to prove her claim in court at 9:00 a.m. tomorrow morning. For tonight, she stays in my hotel, Madame."

"And where is that exactly?" Marie senses something amiss with this public servant. The old Gendarme hesitates before saying "municipal jail." I wonder why?

Guy uses a fatherly tone to intercede for his wife, whose patience is thinning. "Madame can barely walk, officer. Please let us bring her medicine, food and clothing to the jail."

Marie gets a closer look. "Eh bien, we know you. You're officer LeBrun. You patrol around the Fellner mansion along the riverbank, no?"

"Oui, Madame."

"We've exchanged greetings over the years, haven't we?" She has Lebrun cornered.

Guy takes over in a rare moment of authority, knowing where Marie's inquiry is headed,

"Officer, you know this is Ingrid Fellner, the rich philanthropist who donates money to the hospital and orphanage. Her late husband was Emil Fellner, our former mayor," Guy is uneasy informing Lebrun unnecessarily, and waits for the gendarme's slow, perfunctory nod.

"Well, I'm her butler, Guy, and this is my wife, Marie, her housekeeper."

Now I speak up in a small dry voice, "Thank you, Guy; I'll go with this gentleman."

I look up at the gendarme and attempt to hold my full aristocratic stance. I speak in a conciliatory voice, too exhausted to argue. He must have an unsavory connection with Antoine I can't risk pursuing.

Wait, aha, I remember how I know this policeman. Years ago I arranged a successful job introduction at the orphanage for his son. The memory pushes me to take over the situation with the upper class hauteur he heard from me in the past. Let's see if it works today, uttered from my disgraced personhood.

"Officer LeBrun, allow my house staff to bring me in the truck. You're on foot, no?"

"Oui, Madame Fellner." Oui, indeed, he's embarrassed now and remembers my good deed for his family.

"Well, please sit next to me in the truck and direct Guy to the entrance and let them return with food. Let my housekeeper stay with me, please. I need medical attention. You don't want me to be ill at your jail, do you?"

"At the jail? Ah, no, certainly not, Madame. We can summon you a doctor," he sounds relieved, but hesitates, confused, as if the jail was not my original destination.

"Could I summon my own doctor and lawyer?"

"If you wish, Madame."

Guy and I sense the gendarme's awkwardness. He's edgy—as if he had other orders to follow—and looks nervously around the street. He seemed oddly guilt-struck when I said "jail." Where else would he have taken me? Who else owns his allegiance today besides Le Préfet de Police?

✎

I spend the night in one of three tiny, airless cells upstairs behind police headquarters. The jail is a nondescript grey masonry fortress a few blocks from the public square. An ornate pattern of metal bars on its windows and large wooden doors of Napoleonic proportions distinguish it as a public building. A conforming elegance on the outside is contrasted inside with sparse, rough, whitewashed plaster walls that meet low curving ceilings. Floor tile the color of dried blood repels my feet. This interior has absorbed the pain and confusion of men's moral undoing for over a hundred years.

My breeding would never entertain this humiliating confinement, except in defense of my nation's honor, in my service to the Résistance.

Inside the cell Marie, my guardian angel, carefully cuts off my blood-soaked pants and cleans my wounds. We rig up a blanket for privacy. She helps me bathe in a bucket, dress for sleep, and wrap my clotted, bald head in a towel. Later Guy will bring me food and remedies. Marie will sleep sitting outside the door.

I am relieved this first leg of my "liberation" is over and grateful Marta and Maman did not witness the street violence. I'm safer in jail and too exhausted to deal with a lawyer until tomorrow. I have no idea what will happen but trust that my good intention will triumph.

The night is long and hard. Marie prays while my mind runs amuck with a thousand thoughts, just as it did after sex with the SS. I lie here . . . imprisoned in darkness . . . seeing my daughter's sweet smile . . . and Maman's soft wrinkled face. I reach for their love past my hot head, besieged by throbbing pain that brings me to tears. I never realized how taking my destiny in hand would affect their lives.

I search up and down the scale of today's deeds for some peaceful note upon which to sleep. Instead I plunge into a cauchemar. A high wall, embedded with glass, surrounds me. A soldier—perhaps me—wears red and blue. Another soldier dressed in Prussian military garb points a bayonet at my throat. The person I am pleads for his life on his knees. The two faces are shrouded in a murky mist and the silhouette of a guillotine looms behind us. I can't place this past, yet somehow it connects with my life today.

At dawn I rouse with a dull mind. My head spins as numerous people dance and whirl in front of me. I feel like I've been on my knees in supplication all night. A thin stream of sunlight passes through the high window over the coarse blue blanket that covers me.

I raise my finger to twirl a tress of hair before realizing my clotted head has none to offer. A chill runs through me. I sit up suddenly. Am I here for the murder I committed in my cellar? Wait, I've skipped over yesterday's trauma. My God, where have I been?

The nightmare took me far away. I struggle to identify the jail cell's crude surroundings. A curtain of exhaustion falls on my mind as it surveys this foreign stage.

I put my head down and rub my face with bony, aching hands. My back and legs are stiff from running in the streets. The hard scabs below my knees pull my parchment-like skin when I bend. Spasms of pain shock me into the present when I try to stand. Every movement is an effort. My flesh pulls me back to the days of Mueller's abuse.

Fully awake—I'm practically helpless. Then I realize Marie had another cot moved into this cell after I fell into my torpor last night. She dozes peacefully, leaning into the iron bars separating us from the free world. I force back tears at her devotion. I can't bear to wake her but I have no choice. I whisper hoarsely at first and then raise my voice,

"Marie! Please, help me. Marie, I need the toilette and my calves are cramping. I don't think I can stand—or walk."

Chapter Thirty

My Defense

9 September 1944, Saturday

This morning we six women are herded into the old courthouse. Our stark features and covered heads stand out against the severe dark paneling and dull ochre walls outside the judicial chambers. We grow nervous waiting to enter the courtroom. I feel the other women's pain and fear, especially the girl with a half-German baby boy. They look young and vulnerable, not hardened—as one might think.

Last night Marie cleaned and dressed the wounds of those without caring kin. I gave them scarves and decent clothes, and reminded each one not to be intimidated by the proceedings, although we have no idea what will transpire.

Marie tries to compensate for my bruised, exhausted body. She clothes me in a conservative dark blue dress with a hem well below the knees to hide my scabbed shins. Its delicate lace collar softens the strain in my pale face. Then we argue over a wig.

"Please Madame, wear this. I am lucky to have found it."

"You didn't find this, Marie. Germaine gave it to you. Isn't that the truth?"

"Madame, please, she is desolate, and gravely ill. Édouard is her jailer. She loves you and needs to know you don't hate her. Please, wear this today as a sign of forgiveness."

I relent, too worried about the next hours to argue. Marie makes a chignon out of it. I wince, placing the wig over my wounds. Marie secures it very tenderly. Wisps of bangs and a few tendrils of curls show from under a light blue paisley silk scarf. She ties it into the bun at the back of my neck to secure it over my clotted head.

I wear one piece of jewelry, my infamous brooch, as an act of defiance. Its mysterious passage reinforces a message of support for me for what I've done to protect innocent people.

The jailer appears and we six are marched to the courtroom. Despite the help Marie and I have given to the other young women they still seem to resent me. I haven't told them that I passed Jews through my basement.

When my story comes out in the public courtroom I may garner support from Duchamps but the best these women can hope for is pity. Strange, isn't it? No one bothered when they catered to local Frenchmen. But in 1940, when Nazis paid for the same service, overnight it was called *collaboration horizontale*, and these women became "political property" of all Duchamps' males. I wonder if having the right to vote someday will change that male prerogative in the boudoir?

I search the walls for a distraction to stop my mind from chewing on my nerves while we're waiting to enter the courtroom. I see a dusty bucolic painting done sixty years ago by a local amateur. The landscape boasts dizzying color daubed with Impressionist flourish at the edges, but its figures freeze front and center in Davidian/Ingres neo-classical rigidity. The artist painted a confusion of the two styles.

One could conclude this work aims to please everyone—when more likely the artist was struggling to understand what he could not make his own. Playing with surface but not yet in union with his paint, he compromised himself by exhibiting this picture. I can identify with his effort: imperfect, uneven—but very human.

The avant-garde Impressionists were forced to placate the French Academy or starve. The Academy accused them of dilettantism and refused to exhibit their open, bold and colorful canvases. The artists were after an essence beyond the surface of realism. French culture lagged behind their free spirit, still fractured between monarchy and democracy, suppression and expression. The artists endured. The Salon Des Refusés took up their new wave of genius that today's world honors as French Impressionism.

Human nature changes so slowly, it appears never to change. Enlightened members of a society must co-exist with its rigid reactionaries.

What chance do I have against the corrupted Judiciary inside?

I am a refusé judged by an oppressive enemy. My plight is not a matter of taste and style, but Liberté, Égalité et Fraternité—my freedom.

The reactionary vipers on the bench secretly protest an alliance with de Gaulle, who at this moment frees France of Allemande bondage. Self-serving Vichy-ites sit comfortably while the dirty, fuzzy mold of public opinion from 1894 crawls up the walls from the courthouse floor. *Nothing has changed.* Today's stale judicial leftovers hail from the same treasonous French anti-Semitism that falsely accused and imprisoned Alfred Dreyfus. Paternalism and political fascism still rule France.

I didn't align with my fickle political culture. I sought enlightenment in my conscience. Shielding Jews out of humanitarian love nearly drowned me in a vortex of moral and social backwardness. What seemed noble and logical exploded into a political witch-hunt to destroy me. I hope this Occupation is the death rattle of a national infestation that hides under the guise of collaboration. We let fear rule against our human dignity. But we each had a choice.

When the chatter in my head stops, my arms harrow with moist, cold gooseflesh. Yet it's a warm September morning. Some might think it's better to cry, worry and tremble than to defend against my fear with metaphor. But a philosophical apologia is my only way to make sense of yesterday's vicious street attack. I'm numb with exhaustion. Numb for *three years* anticipating this public moment. I gave in to it long enough to sleep—but not long enough to forget my humanity. I may never be safe enough to release the pent up grief from the violence committed against my flesh, but I can't let that terror destroy me—certainly not today.

I remember listening to my Old Testament travelers speak of the horror they were living through. I wept when their flat voices told me, "Madame, to cry in a camp was to die in a camp." I wonder, has Duchamps been my inferno?

I scan the courtroom and see Édouard and Germaine sitting with the prosecution. The judges' money-grubbing backgrounds make them fickle like Édouard and yesterday's mob. They covet power as they huddle like Daumier caricatures in a cartoon on the Inquisition. I'm certain Édouard has convinced his judicial cronies of my traitorous collaboration.

DeVillement leers with a disgusting little smile; he's sure of my fate. He stares at my brooch. My blood runs cold—but at least my finances are safely out of his hands. My family, including Sylvia and Pierre, will be cared for if I'm sent to prison.

I wish I knew what he has embezzled. Who were his other victims? I remember his feeble encounter with Roemler, and try to be impervious to his unsavory ogling. Observing Germaine makes me wonder once again how she lives with him. She averts her eyes from everyone by burying her face under the enormous brim of a woven summer hat. She doesn't look at me when I'm wearing her wig. A shudder runs through me. Will she be Édouard's next quarry?

Germaine and Agnes are usually inseparable but today Agnes Balfour and her husband, Charles, sit with the Underground bakers, Jeanne and Mirek.

The room is abuzz with all political persuasions: undeclared Milice; old Vichy-ites who made German money; overnight Gaullists; rabble do-nothings whose politics blow in the breeze; the ardent local Underground; socialists; wounded Maquisards; angry farmers; stale Catholic monarchists; diehard anti-Semites; a sprinkle of communists;

and a few callous merchants from the black market—all sitting among the Résistants. Here we are, the ingredients in a distinctly French recipe for political and social instability we call a coalition.

The only hope I have to be exonerated from this charade is the Underground's commitment to honor my conscience and my contribution. The bona fide Résistance was a small group whose dedication changed Duchamps. They exposed her materialists and anti-Semites who justified their bystander allegiance with Vichy. The Underground has a slim opportunity to force this court to throw out the charges. Could it happen? It depends how many were Résistants in heart *and* deed.

I'm the only defendant with a lawyer. Old man Leclerc is here at Maman's request, I suppose. No one has informed me of anything. He's younger than she is and a great friend, always happy to help. He's come out of retirement to represent me. He is a fearless man and Résistant in spirit. No one challenges his opinions. He's jolly, but bald like the "tondue" he defends and is homely, with huge ears. When his mouth opens you automatically trust his intense scholarship and welcome his courtroom theatrics. Today his dramatic flair must subdue the hatred stacked against me.

Maman arrives. Our eyes meet. I feel love and support from my feisty old mother and smile to reassure her, worried that these proceedings will strain her old heart. Despite my fluttery stomach I feel morally strong, only a little indignant facing the town in here.

There's little cause for hope without Dieter. A few members of my Underground family can testify: Drs. Duvette and Devoir; Jeanne and Mirek, the bakers; Marcel Beauchamp; the apothecary, Philippe; and men who transported and shielded Jews after they left my home. The townspeople respect them, but their mission, like mine, was a small contribution to a beautiful silent network that Dieter organized. I know Leclerc will do his best without Kreuzier.

Oh no, Marta, my little scamp, is in the front row of the balcony, hiding. I catch sight of her ragged hair. Did she sleep in her clothes? She's not sitting with my Maman. She probably hid under the seat, slid in with the crowd and begged Sylvia to let her stay in here. She'll hear awful accusations. Her love makes me self-conscious. I can't stop looking at her.

The proceeding is called to order. Poor, ignorant, manipulated by their poverty—and without support—the prostitutes, and the young mother of a German-French child, stand straight. Their disgrace should be forgiven.

One has her shorn head uncovered. Overcome with nerves, she forgot her scarf. I signal to Marie and she passes her one of the worn silk extras. Discreetly, spectators hand the scarf from person to person across the room toward the young accused. It passes to the angry old woman who threatened me in the street eighteen months ago. She was upset at my cleavage at the notorious Christmas concert. She sits forward with the threadbare scarf daintily suspended between the same gnarled arthritic thumb and forefinger she has wagged in my face. Scowling, she tears the silk in two with a loud ripping sound, smiles and stuffs the pieces into her pocket.

The poor young woman mouths a "thank you anyway," and shrugs her shoulders. The morning wears on as the court prosecutes the women. They're declared guilty and sentenced to jail where, no doubt, they will fend against ugly solicitations from their French jailers.

When it's my turn, the courtroom becomes very quiet.

"In the case of the Provisional Government of the Republic of France against Ingrid de Vochard Fellner, how do you plead to the charges of traitorous collaboration with the Nazi enemy?" the main judge asks, raising his eyebrows in Édouard's direction.

"Not guilty to all charges," replies my advocate Leclerc.

The room explodes with heckling and angry sentiments. The judge has trouble securing order. The crowd tosses foul epithets at me. My lawyer is handed a note during a pause. In a surprise move, he leaves the courtroom momentarily, and returns with three people. The gallery hushes.

Everyone recognizes the old farmer Beauchamp but not the two strangers.

Leclerc announces, "I call Monsieur Jakub Kleinboren, your honors. He will testify to Madame Fellner's position in the Résistance."

The crowd murmurs briefly; all eyes on the witness. Monsieur Kleinboren comes forward, clean-shaven and dressed in a borrowed suit. He leans on a cane as he enters the witness box. I remember this couple. Their grim testimony will be unbelievable to the bystanders who did nothing to stop the Boches and are ignorant of the heinous civilian Holocaust outside of France.

"Monsieur Kleinboren, you were an inmate in two death camps, were you not?"

"Yes sir, first in Auschwitz and then in Sobibór, both in Poland."

"Describe to the court what you told the defendant, Ingrid Fellner, about these camps."

"Objection, your Honors. This is not relevant to the court's judgment of the defendant," argues the prosecution. Leclerc nods his head and says respectfully, edging toward boredom,

"Your Honors, the defendant is accused of treason. It is pertinent therefore, that the court learns with whom this alleged traitor was consorting and why."

"Proceed, counsel." The judge knows the prosecution is eager to avoid direct testimony, but the tension in here fast erodes Vichy control.

The witness begins, "My wife and I were separated at our capture in April of 1943. When I arrived at Auschwitz I didn't know she was alive. I passed the 'selection' and. . . ."

"Excuse me for interrupting, Monsieur, tell the court what a 'selection' is."

"That's a camp doctor's inspection. When you arrive he decides if you are fit for hard labor or should be gassed immediately. If you are to go to the gas, they say you're going to a group shower. The showerheads put out insecticide. In just a few minutes, it asphyxiates everyone. Then they cremate piles of naked bodies after they remove their hair and gold teeth."

Spectators suddenly sit on the edge of their seats. The room is deadly quiet. Most people in here are ignorant by choice. Few French ears heard

BBC radio reports of Nazi atrocities at Majdenak, after the Soviets liberated the death camp on July 24th. They're concerned. Vichy sent a number of Duchamps' men to work in Germany, and no one has heard from them.

"Please continue, Monsieur."

"They placed me in the Sonderkommando or worker unit. They branded me. They shaved my head. I lived with lice in unheated barracks. We had no showers. The latrines were filthy. No fresh drinking water and no change of clothes. You stank of fecal matter if you couldn't find a piece of cloth. Inmates were issued only one set of light cotton clothes to wear and a pair of wooden clogs. I had one ration of bread a day, sometimes margarine, rarely a piece of sausage, two bowls of turnip and potato water they called soup, and a ladle of ersatz coffee for breakfast. By September, I was starving and cold. I had lost almost fifteen kilos. Conditions were deliberately designed to cause death."

"Was there no way to protect yourself from death inside the camp?"

"At risk of torture we stole food and clothes we collected from suitcases of those who went to the gas. Their belongings were left behind on the train ramp. Thousands of Jews, old people—and mothers with young children—were sent to die as soon as they arrived. My first job was to sort their valuables. Later someone told me my wife was alive. She weighed gold extracted from their teeth. We lived in separate barracks and occasionally heard news of each other. Our primary concern was to barter for enough scraps of extra food each day to stay alive."

"What was the goal of the Nazi overseers?"

"Extermination. Jewish and non-Jewish workers in the gas chambers were murdered every six months to prevent anyone from smuggling information about camp atrocities outside the walls. We never knew when we'd die or how. Our Kapos routinely beat us."

"Please define what a Kapo is, Monsieur Kleinboren."

"The Kapos were other prisoners in charge of us along with SS guards whose vicious dogs watched our every move. We worked twelve to fourteen hours a day. I was caught stealing food for other prisoners I hadn't shared with my Kapo first. I was tortured and demoted to more demoralizing work: throwing corpses into open pits where they burned in mass burials."

Suddenly, Monsieur Kleinboren's controlled monotone voice gives way in his emotional appeal to the spectator gallery, "The Nazis couldn't cremate large numbers of Jews, Poles, Gypsies, whoever they were killing, fast enough. They're still doing it, today. Right now! They keep the truth of their butchery hidden from the world—but its time will come. As I speak, they gas and burn Hungarian Jews in Auschwitz. Tens of thousands! Women and children!"

"Objection! The witness is making an unqualified conclusion."

Leclerc is ready for this. "Your honor. I have here copies of photos from French Underground news tracts showing piles of corpses. May it please the court to admit them as corroborating evidence."

Leclerc hands the evidence to the main judge, who's repulsed by the images and mutters,

"You may continue."

Jakub Kleinboren stares at this uninformed, complacent French farm community, realizing the death grip that bound his life to ashes is gone. His years of silent reserve begin to unravel.

He points to me, "Believe it, ladies and gentlemen! As she did! I told her I found my young nephew Piotr, naked, in a pile of rotting children. I recognized a scar on his right thigh from a childhood accident before I saw his emaciated face. A guard had a gun at my temple ready to shoot me if I winced or cried."

"How had the child died, Monsieur Kleinboren?"

"Starved and gassed. His body . . . oh sir, it hasn't stopped! The war isn't over! Madame Henri knows. She heard the cries of our hearts. How can you do this to her?"

The gallery holding Résistants hears the witness speak of me as Madame Henri. This ignites murmuring among them until the gavel calls for silence.

Monsieur Jakub continues, "The Nazis have gassed millions—tens of thousands since June! You will see it in cinema newsreels when the war is over and these camps are liberated. The Allies have sold out the Hungarian Jews, over four hundred thousand human beings!"

The witness pauses, stunned, at the silent, wide-eyed townspeople. Leclerc blows his nose loudly and wipes his eyes. Coughs are muffled into handkerchiefs. The listeners barely breathe; the testimony is too grisly. The tense faces of the prosecutor and judicial bench are pinched, and silent.

The old lawyer, patient and plodding, concentrates on dissolving the prosecution's case.

"Tell the court why you risked your life to escape, Monsieur Kleinboren."

"Life in there would be a meaningless death. We were powerless to raise our voices to tell the world. My wife and I were in the *Armia Krajowa*, the AK, Polish Underground. We learned to document crimes we saw every day on scraps of paper. Others took photos secretly. We had to smuggle our evidence out of the camp to alert the Allies to bomb the camps and move faster to liberate us. We hoped the war would end sooner, if the world knew the magnitude of Nazi genocide."

Leclerc interjects, "Your reason is compelling, sir. What about the risk?"

"My six months in the Sonderkommando were ending. I was old for a camp worker. They would kill me anyway. I stayed alive fueled by hatred for my oppressors. I speak four languages. Once on the outside I had a good chance of not being caught. The Underground decided I should escape.

"I hadn't heard from Miriam for weeks and thought she was dead. When people died, lines of communication were lost. Had either of us escaped, the Nazis would have killed the remaining partner and all family members. If there were none, they killed those living in the same barracks with the escapee as a group reprisal."

"Tell the court please, sir, how did you escape?"

"A strange twist of fate forced our group of workers to be moved out of Auschwitz. In 1943 the Nazis were constructing new barracks to increase their killing machine. Slave labor moved from one site to another. It didn't matter where you died along the way. At Sobibór, a smaller camp, I met Leon Feldhendler and members of my original Armia Krajowa unit. They were planning an escape and had support of a Russian, Sasha Pechersky, and his group of Soviet military prisoners. They chose me and another inmate to smuggle documentation of camp atrocities to the Allies. They stitched it into our clothes.

"We had several failures before succeeding. Then an uprising occurred on October 14, 1943. It was time to go. We were hidden in a truck loaded with large tubular shaped bales of human hair heading for a German textile mill where they would weave it into cloth. I never met my partner. We were each curled in a fetal position wrapped in paper inside a bale. The hair around us obscured our shape, but not our weight. A tiny tube glued to the bales' fabric allowed us to breathe. The strongest man had to lift our bales onto the truck without showing any physical strain.

"The SS habitually poked the bales with their bayonets. I held my breath as another prisoner distracted the Nazi guards. He offered them expensive cigars confiscated from a Jewish valise. The SS loved cigars and overlooked their security check sniffing their spoils. That prisoner positioned them to look in the opposite direction as the strong man lifted us."

"Was there no other way to escape?" Leclerc is skeptical.

"They had watchtowers, dogs, and electrified fences. They shot to kill. The only way out alive was through the front gate, under Nazi noses. Or else you went up the chimney."

Monsieur Kleinboren makes an upward circular motion with his right index finger to imitate the rise of smoke. His face chills the court; it takes on an eerie, death-like grin. He shakes his head as if to dispel the memory and continues,

"That day the deliveries were to leave early because they were traveling far away, to Germany. This would give us more time before the *Appell*, the roll call in the evening, when they would discover us missing. But it was also the day of the Sobibór revolt. We heard shots fired—then in the chaos: screams and shouts in Lithuanian, Russian, Polish, Yiddish, Dutch, French and German. . . . The other person escaping with me pushed my bundle off the truck and fell on top of me. We heard running nearby. We undid ourselves from the wrappings and stared at each other in the commotion. Miriam, my wife, was the other person."

A quiet "ahh" rises from the gallery, who are engrossed in the witness's testimony. Leclerc smiles.

"Our transport was parked at the open gate. The SS drivers were in their seats, murdered. There were no land mines or barbed wire in front of us. We had no weapons. In that moment of freedom, we clutched our small parcels and ran into the forest."

"How many escaped that day?"

"Hundreds, but in the end, partisans and protectors along our route told us maybe fifty survived. For us it was a miracle."

"Why do you think you survived?"

"We were not known as Jews in the Armia Krajowa. We never registered as Jews, nor admitted we had roots in a Jewish community. Our families had lived in the Aryan district of Warsaw for five generations. They arrested us as they did other Polish insurgents. A few who shielded us on our way might have refused to help us had they known we were Jews."

"How did you get through the borders? What papers did you have?"

"We had false identification. Our friends had sewn a map and compass into our coats. When we were safely in the forest, we buried our camp uniforms. We put on street clothes stolen from suitcases of those murdered upon arrival. They were remade carefully, to fit us. We carried shoes and stockings we put on just before a checkpoint inside the Polish-German border. We had to look decent to offset our obvious malnutrition.

"At the border a Polish guard forced to work for the SS recognized my wife. Miriam took a calculated risk that he was still a Résistant at heart. She asked meekly if he was going to do a body search. He understood and took us to a small building and locked the door. Miriam showed him photos of the Auschwitz and Sobibór crematoria, and the trenches with piles of rotting bodies. I translated the written German documentation. He wept and cursed, and accepted our forged papers.

"He lied to his superior that he needed to transport us personally to the next town because we were under suspicion. He drove us into Deutschland to a rural farm wife. She took us to a partisan bunker where we received a bath, a meal, fresh clothing and newly forged identifications and ration cards in three languages. We met their leader. He studied our evidence of the atrocities. He knew how to get it to the Danes who would send it to the Vice-President of the Swedish Red Cross, Count Folke Bernadotte.

We slept for almost two days. Then we traveled all night and hid all day for several weeks before we were safe in a French farmer's root cellar, three hundred kilometers north of here. When we left there I tripped over a fallen tree in the forest and severely injured my ankle."

"One more question, sir, for the record. The name Kleinboren is German and not Polish. What was your Polish name? And why would you use the German name now?"

"Our Polish name was Malenski, but Kleinboren was my family's name six generations ago, when they lived in Austria. We have relatives in America under the name Kleinboren. We decided to use it as our new name because we can't return to Poland. There's nothing left for us here in Europe. Before our family separated we told our children to change their names. Then we could find each other at the end, but, they are probably dead, Monsieur," his voice wavers with grief, "we must have hope because we have to emigrate."

"Monsieur Kleinboren, for the record, do you recognize the accused in this courtroom?"

"Yes, sir," he points to me, "Madame Henri, ah, Madame Ingrid de Vochard Fellner."

Monsieur Jakub acknowledges me by nodding his head in my direction.

Leclerc smiles warmly, and extends his arm toward me. All eyes shift to the accused as my defense attorney draws me into this grotesque history, "Let the court understand that Ingrid Fellner's nom de guerre in the Résistance was Madame Henri."

"Now that we have your background, sir, describe your meeting with her."

"We met in her basement on the evening of 29 February 1944."

"How many people were there in total that night?"

"Eleven Jews and a French doctor. Someone bandaged the doctor's hands following a Milice torture in Paris. They arrested him for treating Jewish escapees in the hospital's basement."

"Did you know how many had come through Madame Fellner's basement since November of 1941?"

"Yes. Each inscribed his mark on a wall behind a cabinet in the farthest chamber where we slept. I counted four hundred sixty-eight marks before the last twelve."

"What happened that night, sir?"

"I told Madame Fellner the same story I just told you, sir. She was very kind and spoke to us in German. She knew a little Polish too. Then she looked at her watch and excused herself to go upstairs. A minute after she left two short buzzes and one long one went off in the basement. Instantly her butler led us into hidden chambers and explained we had to be absolutely silent. No one could use the toilette or come out into the main room. The Obersturmführer for the eastern Franche-Comté region was upstairs. The butler said he would return to us when the house was safe again."

"How long did it take?"

"Two hours. When he returned, we went back into the main room. On the following evening we left Madame Ingrid's home. She gave us herbs and remedies for my leg."

"Thank you for your testimony, Monsieur."

I stand very still. Tears soak the front of my dress. These two risked their freedom for me. I've worried for years that someone would denounce me. Their story thaws years of worry.

Then the prosecutor announces,

"Your Honors, the court is not convinced. The witness could have made up this story." The gallery appears mute with disbelief.

Leclerc apologizes, pretending obeisance, "Yes, your Honors, you must have proof. Sorry I neglected to provide it at the outset. Monsieur and Madame Kleinboren, would you be so kind? Explain what the court will see."

"Yes, sir. Nazis branded us like animals in Auschwitz. Afterward, we were never allowed to use our names. To dehumanize us the Nazis addressed us by our numbers."

Calmly, with deliberate slowness, the two peel back the cuffs of their left sleeves to show the court their tattooed identification numbers from Auschwitz-Birkenau. The room is silent. People strain to see when Leclerc holds out Monsieur Kleinboren's left arm.

The old lawyer stares at Édouard and the prosecutor, pausing before he reads in a loud ceremonial voice: "Let the court records show Jakub Kleinboren's tattooed identification number is 81,587 and Miriam Kleinboren's tattooed number is 76,925."

Leclerc's eyes sweep across the courtroom. He pauses, allowing the full impact of the couple's indignity to settle into the hearts and minds of all assembled. A collective tremor weaves through the gallery, along with whispers. People blow their noses and cough as Leclerc helps his witnesses to their seats.

Next, he calls the old farmer, Marcel Beauchamp. Everyone in town recognizes their scruffy WWI veteran. Beauchamp is an old bachelor whose large family helps him run his dairy farm. Many people are amazed he was involved in the Underground because of his age.

"Monsieur Beauchamp, please tell us how you know the accused, Madame Fellner?"

"I've known her since she was a bébé. Her mother's land is on the other side of the road along my northern pasturage. In the Occupation I knew of Madame Henri, but I didn't know she was Madame Ingrid officially until recently." He winks at me across the room.

"What do you mean, "officially," Monsieur Beauchamp?" Leclerc wants details.

"I knew from the beginning the woman the refugees described, Madame Henri, had to be Madame Fellner, by the way they expressed their gratitude for the food, herbs, clothes and the lodging she gave them. She listened. She wasn't afraid or disgusted by the sad and horrible things they told her. Look here: I have a list of the four hundred ninety-two refugees who crossed my land from her basement since 1941." He digs into his breast coat pocket, and hands a small booklet to Leclerc, "They're in there, Monsieur."

"It was dangerous to keep written evidence. Why did you do it?"

"Because I knew some of these poor souls might not make it to freedom. At least if we had their names and where they came from at the end of the war we could help the organizations that search for missing people. I hid the evidence in a jar under a manure pile."

"Why did you volunteer for such dangerous work, Monsieur Beauchamp?"

"I fought the Doryphores in the first war. They killed my twin brother Étienne in front of me. I never got over it. It made sense to help innocent civilians. Only *un monstre diabolique* like Hitler could kill civilians. I was too old for sabotage work, but my ancestral property could shield people. I share a frontier for crossing with the Swiss half of my family across the Doubs River. We've shared herds of cows for ten generations on that border. My southern border is safe too. The Boches never checked it because it's too densely forested. Most refugees from Madame Henri's went to Italy through that exit. We made trails and bunkers along a route deep inside that stretch of my land."

Leclerc thanks the farmer, but the spectators anticipate trouble. Their eyes are riveted on their old WWI hero, as he steps down from the witness stand. Marcel walks toward Édouard and his henchman, Antoine. He stops, points his finger at the evil duo, raises his voice and accuses,

"You, Antoine and your drunks, and you, you rich bâtard, deVillement, are the real collaborators in here. How dare you hide behind Vichy and attack these young women! It doesn't matter what they did for a few francs. They aren't murderers who betrayed their neighbors like you and your Milice ass lickers," Snarling, Marcel spits at the prosecution's table. The Underground and farmers in the courtroom are aroused and shout. "Here, here, you tell 'em, old farmer" rises above increasingly angry whisperers.

Édouard is startled and sits back, afraid. Germaine slinks down in her chair, ashamed. The gavel bangs and the court takes a brief recess.

Édouard ogles me as he stands with his hand over his mouth while he talks to the prosecutor. The three judges confer. Leclerc leaves the room again. Despite the testimonies of Jakub Kleinboren and Marcel, I sense doom and helplessness in the gallery. Maman's worried eyes show me how profoundly this proceeding affects her. The judgment won't be about the war or the truth of my actions—but how the town feels toward me, personally. I feel abandoned.

The pro-Vichy judge gavels the room to silence. He announces the court needs more evidence if it's going to exonerate me. I'm aghast that they can make such a harsh demand. The angry gallery boos the main judge. Édouard leans over to confer with the prosecutor, his chest inflated with anticipation, like a hawk in mating season. I twitch from head to toe in a weak effort to repel his leering glances. I'm fearful he'll have his sway over me in the end.

People are becoming very agitated. Barbs of hatred shower the judicial bench and heckling drowns out the gavel.

The sudden opening of the courtroom doors a second time quiets the public. Everyone turns to see Leclerc enter with two more men. One is a young redhead, my beau-fils, Stefan. The other is older, tall, lean, with a salt-and-pepper beard, walking with a hesitating gait. . . .

"Uhhhh . . . Mon Dieu!"

Screaming, I slump to the floor. My breath whistles away in a dead faint. Seconds later, Maman's sharp, stinging, lavender salts pierce my nostrils to revive me. The gavel's fierce banging reverberates in my head, drilling its rhythm into my confusion. My eyes blink in searing pain. A bright shaft of morning sunlight cuts me back into this world. And I see him.

He's here! Suddenly, I'm alive! Dieter's presence grafts me, and everyone, to his heart. The courtroom is ecstatic! We're one thought, one life! I can't divert my eyes from him! I have real hope!

The slimy judges have lost control of this provincial assembly. Marta jumps up and down in the gallery's front row, chanting Dieter's name with everyone else. I catch her eye and shake my head "no." Immediately she quiets down. Maman motions for her to come downstairs and slide in next to her, beside my counsel.

Across the room, Germaine stands spontaneously, crying and applauding. Édouard is furious. His face pales and he stamps his cane into the floor, pulls her arm and forces her to sit. He thrusts her hands into her lap and says something that must be dreadfully abusive. Livid with anger, she turns and slaps his face with a loud smack, shouting, "*Meurtrier!*"

Immediately the room is still. Before he can stop her, she marches to the other side of the courtroom to sit with Agnes. Édouard rubs his smarting cheek. The judge bangs the gavel to stop the whispering, snide whistles, and laughter. The spectators are sobered by her accusation, "murderer." Édouard looks like he's seen a ghost. Ah oui! He has.

Leclerc waits for the public to digest its awe before letting his star witness proceed. Dieter's miraculous return is hailed like a coronation. Slowly, he's guided to the witness box. Appalling how thin he is. He walks as if in pain or unaware of. . . . Why does he need help? No, is it possible? I can't see his face. He appears to have a difficult time even with Stefan leading him.

He walks up the stairs, leaning forward as his hands grip the rails. His legs must be weak. Yes, that's it, his legs. Who did this to him? Stefan walks back quickly to his seat, his face downcast to avoid me. All eyes are on Dieter. Will the townspeople listen to their former mayor?

"Please, sir, give your name and explain your relationship to the accused."

"My name is Dieter Van der Kreuzier. I was, ah, am the head of the local Underground. I know everyone in the organization, what job they did, where they did it and to whom they reported. I devised strategy to move 1,500 Jewish men, women, children and babies, political prisoners and Vichy-assailed clerics across the Doubs—to the frontier of the Juras: east to the Swiss, and south to Italy—since 1940."

"When and why did you involve Madame Ingrid Fellner in the Underground?"

"In the first year, towns north of us had trouble with Nazi infiltrators. In 1941 two dead Jews were uncovered on the Doubs' riverbank in Duchamps, an omen that our escape routes were not sufficiently protected. We needed someone in our community to divert the enemy so we could move people safely. We had to buy time to delay and confuse the Boches. Then our rescuers would not be raided, tortured, or placed in French work camps and deported to Ravensbrück or Struhof-Natzweiler.

"A dozen courageous French farmers and shopkeepers here in Duchamps hid Jews and supplied them with false papers, food, ration cards, medical help and safe passage.

"Ingrid Fellner, alias Madame Henri, became our beacon. She delayed and distracted the enemy to give us time for Jewish adults and children to cross safely. Four hundred ninety-two individuals came through her basement. Among them was a young Jewish woman who birthed her son in her home. Madame Fellner risked deportation and death hiding them with her mother, Madame de Vochard, for the last eighteen months of our Occupation."

He pauses to let the facts sink into the minds and hearts of the spectators. Then Dieter admonishes his old constituents, "And how did you reward this solitary widow for her noble sacrifice? But, as always, with your ugly obsession to envy her and spread scandalous lies about her! She used your moral decay to build a false persona that deceived the Gestapo and Milice. And you accepted that deception without ever thinking anything good of her. You have disgraced the values of Free France."

He takes a long sip of water to soothe his voice. In the pause you can hear a pin drop. Dieter must hope that silence means the sour taste of guilt is choking their throats.

If only he would look at the faces higher up in the gallery where the farm Résistance sits. He barely notices my silhouette across the room. It's odd that he seems to look only straight ahead. I suppose his innate modesty speaks from an internal script. He will not be distracted by or take advantage of the crowd's overwhelming satisfaction to discover their hero is alive.

His appeal to win my acquittal must be very emotional. He can't let these petty tyrants strip me of my good reputation. More than half the people in here did nothing to help the Underground. Please, dear God, help him to redeem me and lift the conscience of this mob.

The murmuring returns, and then stops. He clears his throat, entreats the assembled, and points in my direction, "Remember, *mes amis*, who you are, and who you were only four years ago before this madness began. Ingrid Fellner never hurt any of you. Quite the contrary, she gave of her wealth freely to support your hospital, and your orphanage. She found jobs for you and gave money to your families in times of need. She, Ingrid Fellner, should be honored for her humanity to win life for so many innocent victims. You owe her a public apology and a triumphant procession, not this monkey court run by a corrupted judiciary.

"You are French, and for four years you groveled before the Nazi slogan, 'Arbeit, Familie, Vaterland.' You shrank before the Swastika! Now look at her. Because Madame Fellner did what precious few of you had the courage to do. She sacrificed her reputation on the altar of Liberté, Égalité, et Fraternité, for the values of our beloved free France!"

Dieter pauses and reaches his arms out to protect me from across the room. He must bypass the court and appeal to the populace to win my acquittal. In a voice hoarse with emotion and private contrition he salutes me,

"Madame Fellner, as a servant of the Résistance, as a mother of France, we know you will forgive us and accept our debt of gratitude. For in our hearts we are proud of your example. By your sacrifice, you gave voice to our Marianne, and our secret desire to restore *honneur* to our town, our nation and our God. 'Vive La France!'"

He waits, testing his impact. Has he stung the hearts that vilified "the Vichy bitch . . ." whose bed bought freedom for Jews and safety for the French Underground? Has he cleared their petty jealousy for my wealth and position long enough to see honor in my duplicity?

His exorcism leaves the room silent. Wait, there's a trickle of "Vive La France." Yes, he has energized them. Slowly applause erupts in the gallery and transforms into angry foot stomping. Seconds pass and an avalanche of vengeance heads directly for the judges. The courtroom will explode if they don't rule in my favor. The magistrate, a Milice informer, bangs his gavel in a vain effort to control the gallery. But by now the entire assembly is on its feet with their thumbs up. The magistrate turns and looks at the judges and the prosecutor, and then faces the spectators. In a shaky voice he dismisses the charges against me and the other women. The court adjourns.

Édouard's face sneers with anger. My acquittal has crushed his fantasy. He slides out the door with the prosecution and judicial vermin—bureaucratic criminals that have no legal legs to stand on. I suspect their filthy Milice leanings will subject *them* to scrutiny in the near future.

The room is a sea of excited voices and waving arms. I'm revived. Our camarades de Résistance burst into the "Marseillaise" and carry their jubilation outdoors. A blur of senior men and young Maquisards huddle excitedly around Leclerc and the Kleinborens.

I feel Dieter searching my heart through their chorus. I'm safe. He wants justice, too, but something stands in his way. I watch him knot his brows in a frown and squint his eyes. His face seems to echo a conversation from the past. I sense regret because his heart makes me feel sad. He won't look at me across the room, yet his words have lifted me from pariah to heroine.

My life is bare in front of everyone. Lightheaded, I lean into the railing of the accused, covered in their psoriatic social spittle. The room clears. The bad dream of November 1941 is over, but I'm still afraid to breathe. My body is desiccated like a piece of wood left in a desert too long. My hands are lifeless from gripping the rail of the accused, not for these few hours, *but for three years*. Deep blue veins are raised against my skin, transparent like vellum. My white-ridged fingernails are blood-bitten. Finally the myth of my parasitic collaboration will detach from my anemic soul.

Ridicule will now be exchanged for embarrassment, the new way the town will avoid me. The change comes too quickly after the intensity of yesterday's tribal siege, and I'm too numb to move back into a world I haven't trusted since the war began. I want to reaffirm life with my family: Marta, Sylvia, and Pierre.

Marta touches my face like she's never seen it before. "Maman, forgive me for sneaking in here, but I had to be near you. I lied to Michelle but left a note for her not to worry. I hid in the secret compartment under the rear seat of the sedan when Guy drove Grandmaman, Sylvia, and Pierre into town. I slipped out when he escorted them into the courtroom."

My big smile forgives her escapade but fades when she adds, "Maman, you never shared your danger with me unless it came without your control. In those times when our lives were at risk we stood together. We did it well, Maman. We saved them. Please don't be angry that I came here today. I love you, Maman, and I need you."

I have hurt her and still her young arms envelop me. Then Sylvia and little Pierre join her to hold me firmly. I begin to shake and finally feel safe enough to cry. They part for Maman who comes close to kiss my forehead. She grabs my shoulders and blesses me with a gentle maternal smile. I return her relief with deepest gratitude and embrace the thin wisp of her bony frame. Despite my weakness I almost raise her off the ground in a rush of trust and love.

My dear Stefan is next. Dieter sends him alone from across the aisle. He hesitates, but his eyes beg forgiveness with every step. At close range I see how he has matured. His body is angular, broad, still tense and alert to the enemy. He stands before me, béret in hand, his clothes rumpled like a man obsessed with a mission of soul. I reach up to caress his cheek. He's wary; barely looks at me and says quietly, "Vive La France, Madame Henri."

He bows formally and kisses my hand. I can't speak. I'm too choked up. I run my fingers through his hair. My facial muscles grimace to suppress tears. My silent acknowledgment feels like a mother's love for her newborn. He senses we will begin a new relationship and with great abandon hugs me tightly and pleads softly in my ear, his voice haunted with a little boy's angst, "Forgive me, Maman, for the years of resentment. I was afraid I wasn't good enough, that I'd hurt you as I did Hélène. That was an accident. You're here, thanks be to God, alive and free." He calls me "Maman" for the first time since childhood.

Then Stefan guides Dieter to me, the one person who deserves my most sincere apology. My beau-fils escorts everyone else out of the courtroom to leave us alone. Dieter is very lean, a ghost of his former baritone sinew. I stare into the once perfect blue eyes of my mentor and protector. His sclerae are clouded with red spots. Is it as Amélie saw in her dream? We stand here together for an eternity absorbing the shock of being alive to each other. He embraces me, and his beard rubs against the scarf and wig covering my baldness as he kisses my forehead. He lets me go.

I look up and whisper, "Dieter, I'm sorry about Amélie."

"She had a premonition even before my arrest. I didn't realize until it was too late, Ingrid. Duvette buried me publicly to save the Underground. Beauchamp left me in the forest. The Kleinborens nursed me back to health. I can see some color, mostly light and dark outlines but can't see to read. Each day my vision becomes a tiny bit stronger, but it may never be better than this. Ingrid, I wish I could see your lovely face."

My God, he's blind! I want to hold him in my arms but feel constrained by our public exposure. I long for privacy with Dieter and sense the same from him. I reach for his face and he kisses my fingertips. A tremor runs through me as his deep voice says softly, "Vive La France! You did it, Madame Henri!" He pulls me closer and whispers, "Today, sweet woman, this is all I could pursue. You, my valiant rescuer needed rescuing and my effort was too long overdue. Please, Ingrid, can you forgive me?"

I feel woozy being physically close to him after three months of mourning for him and can only murmur, "Oui, mon ami."

I watch Stefan escort Dieter as Marta takes my hand. I move like a dreamer into the bright sunshine of the warm late summer day. My daughter leads me to Maman at the courthouse curb. Leclerc and the Kleinborens follow Sylvia and Pierre. The old gazogènes build up power to move us up the mountainside. Guy and Stefan will drive us past the haze of gawking crowds. Marta says very gently, "Come, Maman, we will go home now. You can rest. It's over."

But I no longer care to rejoice. I can't think past Dieter's blindness.

Chapter Thirty-One

Reconciliation

9 September 1944, Saturday

Everyone is invited to Maman's for an impromptu feast in her elegant dining salon. Michelle has laid out the best linens and silver. We haven't used them since Emil's funeral in 1939. Huge vases on the old credenzas at each end of the room overflow with late summer flowers. Their fragrance competes with the aroma of liquored chocolates and cooling raspberry tarts on the long side buffet.

We gather around Maman's large U-shaped dining table to eat a hearty lunch prepared by Yvonne and Yves from Le Petit Chat and Annette and Igor from the LaFrance Hotel. The table is crowded with tureens of hearty onion soup; baskets of warm fresh pure whole wheat bread (no fillers today); and platters of salted trout; bowls of salade niçoise; a late summer harvest of fresh fruits; mirabelles; wheels of Comté, Raclette and Fontina; fresh roasted nuts; boiled potatoes with roasted garlic; parsley; and vinaigrette. Stefan supplies wines: Emil's labels. Michelle and Yvonne made crème brûleé to serve with real coffee. A fine brandy awaits my Maman's toast.

This feast required planning. They all believed Dieter would succeed on my behalf. And did everyone know he was alive except me? Oh no, I must stop this ruminating or it will lead me back to old mistrust.

This is their victory celebration. Miriam and Jakub Kleinboren; Marcel Beauchamp; Alain Duvette; Jacques Devoir; Patrice; Jean Claude; Annette and Igor; Jeanne and Mirek; Philippe; Agnes and Charles; Dieter; Maman with her dogs; Marta; Marie and Guy; Michelle; Leclerc; Yves and Yvonne; Stefan; Sylvia and little Pierre; and I sit at the table. For me this will be a repast of relief—the first food that will taste delicious in my mouth in five years, although today I have little appetite for its richness.

Before we begin, Maman tinkles her wine glass. Alain rises slowly to offer thanksgiving. He clears his throat and digs his cigarette butt into a bread dish. How tired he looks wearing the war like an old cloak, its nap frayed and shiny but lined with his impenetrable fidelity.

"Mes amis, we have survived. Thank God. Amen. Some of us are here, alas, without our beloved spouses, family, and friends." His voice softens and falters briefly, "We pray for our departed Amélie. And we beg a thousand pardons for the errors of conscience that this maniacal state of war has pressed from us," turning to me his sad eyes glisten, "Ingrid, forgive me for deceiving you of all people about Dieter's death. It was the only way to save you."

My muscles stiffen and jaw clamps shut. Maman, to my left grasps my hand tightly and Dieter at my right looks away. I am afraid to look at everyone around the table except one person, Patrice. She smiles at me and nods her head toward Alain. I breathe deeply, look up at him and forgive the good doctor from my heart.

Maman's lively eyes crinkle into a myriad of crow's feet. She lightens her grip and smiles broadly at me. Duvette's wary eye catches mine as I digest his plea. I nod, looking down as he sits and then I reach around Dieter and touch the médecin's shoulder. He turns toward me, his eyes full of pain at first. But seeing my smile they shine again, and a small smile lifts Alain's thin cheeks.

I can't hold any grudges. There is recrimination to let go of with those who love me. What we did to save people has to be greater than the dissension that hurt us in the process of regaining our freedom.

Jakub Kleinboren nudges Miriam who rises and walks to my side. Her warm hand, firm on my shoulder, presses her strength into my tired heart. I look up and marvel how her hard features radiate a soft loving spirit when behind them this mother carries the agonizing, incomprehensible loss of her children. Her voice is strong and clear as she makes a toast:

"I have to tell you, Madame Ingrid, of all the Menschen who came through your basement it was no coincidence that we came, escapees from a Gehenna. Everywhere we went all over Europe we were never safe. Each morning that we awoke still free we pinched ourselves to be alive. What Mazel, what luck!

"Mein Jakub asked before we met you what kind of woman is this who doesn't need to do anything for anybody and she rescues? Such risks she takes? Your compassion shielded us. You told us you were terrified, but if you didn't resist the Nazis, your humanity would be worthless, a legacy of fear and selfishness you could not leave to your daughter."

Her Jakub adds, "Testifying for you, Madame Ingrid, was a good deed, a mitzvah."

The room stills as Miriam pauses to swallow a lump of sadness that never leaves her,

"Madame Ingrid, we will never forget what is happening to destroy our children, our family, our home and our people, but may your love and the love from all of you here keep us safe from the abyss of despair, so we can dare to hope for a better tomorrow for this little baby, here, and his young mother."

She runs her fingertips lightly over Pierre's face and bows her head for a moment, lost in her mother's memories, caressing his wavy hair before she raises her glass, and smiles wistfully. We rise in anticipation of her call to a toast. We give her a few seconds to compose herself. She lifts her glass, "To your health, Madame Ingrid and Madame Mathilde," adding the Hebrew phrase, "L'chayim!" The salon rebounds as we lift our glasses and confirm with a jubilant, "L'chayim!"

We turn to each other on either side, embrace and talk a little as we sip our champagne. Our wartime self-discipline fights the demons of loss that would overtake our rejoicing. With the pop of another champagne cork we sit and pass plates of food. Some dishes haven't been served since before the war in 1940.

Midway through the meal, I look at this noble company. The tension of the years of resisting gently disappears. The core of their goodness projects freely past their war-induced wrinkles. A new calm dissolves their forced indignity. Their voices are openly vibrant where formerly hesitant and shielded. Every head has new strands of grey hair.

I am indebted to these brave souls who held the line for me. Whereas our meal is wonderful, after years of silent worry, the revival of freedom in our hearts and laughter on our lips is the greater feast.

I eat what I can before becoming lightheaded, and excuse myself. The others finish their desserts and liqueurs. Cold from the strain, I need to sit outside in the warm afternoon sun on the balcony overlooking the backyard vegetable garden.

My head itches from the wig. I remove it in the toilette mirror and stash it in a hand towel in the small cabinet under the sink. I reposition the scarf. Walking from the toilette past the library my ears perk up, hearing Stefan mention my name to Dieter. The library door is ajar.

"Ingrid's a brilliant actress, Dieter, but you used her sacrifice to protect the Underground and ignored the violent rape she endured. My little half-sister watched her suffer for years."

"Is that what you think, Stefan?" I see Dieter run his hand through his hair nervously.

"Yes, of course. You treated her like a soldier, Dieter. Ingrid wasn't wounded with impersonal bullets from an unidentified enemy. She was lying under her enemy, for Christ-sake! Her body was a battle-field. She endured her wounds alone. Cherished memories loving my father were stained every time she submitted to the bastards. You used her, admit it!"

"I know it appears that way, Stefan. I took control of her when she couldn't control herself. I would have let her go if it had been safe but her

ambivalence jeopardized her life and everyone else's. I had no choice."
Dieter's voice is firm and indignant.

"Well, face it now, and beg her to forgive you."

Dieter responds, defensively, "That's enough! Don't assume what you don't know, Stefan. I've begged her, but she will never forgive me. Why should she?"

"Fine, Dieter. Now that this war is over . . . leave her alone!"

Stefan's words are chilling. He's young and still smarts from not knowing I was in the Résistance. He lacks the charity to understand how Dieter's blindness separates him from the world he knew. Kreuzier's masculine pride is bereft of his Amélie's feminine resilience, the love she infused in him. His heart is torn in two. His destiny is barely visible, and his life is out of his control. If I can forgive him, in time Stefan will do the same.

I wait until their voices die out in mutual frustration and knock on the door.

"Please, Stefan, I need to speak with Dieter alone for a few minutes."

"Bien sûr, Maman," he says sweetly and leaves.

Dieter is gravely silent; perhaps afraid I overheard them just now. We walk outdoors. Finally we have privacy. I can't talk. I just look up at his eyes. Then it hits me. Oh God, he doesn't know about my épuration sauvage. Everyone has kept him in isolation from the truth. He places his hands on my face and slips his fingers under my scarf. I wince.

"Sacrebleu! Ingrid, you're shaved like Jews from the camps! Who did this to you?"

It's too ugly. Telling him what happened will only cause more guilt.

"It will grow back, Dieter."

"Don't avoid the truth with me, Ingrid! Tell me what else was done to you."

His hands feel the many scabs. Afraid he'll tear them open he lifts his fingers from my skull. His face contracts in anguish.

"No one told me. Why didn't you tell me in the courtroom when it was over?"

"Germaine lent me the wig you felt in the courtroom, Dieter. Miriam Kleinboren suggested I wear a perruque like Orthodox women. No one notices," I try to be casual.

"My God, Ingrid . . . you were caught on the street! The town did this to you? *Aye*, mon amie, forgive me," he's undone, horrified.

I hesitate to respond until sorrow pushes me, "My hair's not important, but your eyes, Dieter. How do we get you a new pair of eyes?"

I sigh to suppress a sob and hug him burying my face in his chest. He doesn't react to my words, but holds me gently, stroking my back as I shiver.

I sense someone is looking at us, but cannot pull away from his embrace. Then I recognize the slight, uneven sound of Marta's footsteps.

"Maman, please, you need this," she murmurs tenderly, like an old woman ministering to a child, "feel this Dieter; sir, it's for maman." She places my favorite shawl in his hands and he lays it over my shoulders. "I am very sorry for your loss of vision, Monsieur Dieter."

Marta embraces us, the two pathetic wrecks she must trust to guide her forward out of her war.

"Marta, mon amie, these old eyes will suffice. I don't need eyes for music. Music is in my ears and fingers."

Dieter recovers himself for Marta's sake. He can't let anyone be saddened by his loss. He's had three months to come to grips with blindness. For my daughter and me it's fresh tragedy. He doesn't wish his condition to frighten us; he tries to lift our solemnity.

"Look you two: think about it. You'll never age. You two women will be my precious jewels forever young and beautiful in my inner vision."

He hopes I'm relieved but I feel his desperation.

"Dieter, my vanity thanks you," yet sighing, I think, sweet man, as your smile, embrace, and deep voice heal my lonely soul, why am I forced to discover you now as a blind man?

We sit on the long wooden bench. I hold Dieter's warm hands and lean my head on his shoulder. I remember taking his arm when he escorted me to the corpses on the riverbank in November 1941. I stroke his beautiful square palms, and run my index finger over their deep clear lines. My manic collaborator persona erodes. My thoughts are lighter. But under the spell of his blindness my body feels drained, even if it's finally safe from harm.

Marta pulls me to the present. She points to the butterflies and honeybees hovering among the flowers that tease an imminent frost with their fragrant vitality. She grins at her tired maman, disregarding my courtroom spectacle and years of widowhood. Filled with joy she whirls herself around in a circle like she did as a little child.

"Hey, Maman, I did it and I'm still standing! My balance is better! Oh God, Maman, you must smile. We're safe, all three of us now. We've been given another beautiful day. We can love again, even outside. Aren't we the lucky ones?"

Dieter smiles, squeezes my hand and bows his head. I don't know if I want anything from this noble man. It's enough that he is alive.

Chapter Thirty-Two

A Harvest of Clues

12 September 1944, Tuesday

The days pass since my exoneration. Although the mind knows war in our corner of France is over, the flesh is not convinced. When the doorbell rings or a door closes in the house, my solar plexus cringes. I startle at sudden noises, anxious that a Nazi bent on vengeance is nearby. When nothing happens I take a deep breath to shake off the ingrained response.

When Dieter asked me to join his ranks my heart opened and my trials began. He gave me the opportunity to live what I believed. I risked my comfortable world for others in a hopelessly romantic way—swirled upward in a spiral of love and mercy at the piano in 1941.

I aspired to a purity of purpose I thought impossible while attempting it. I wasn't strong like rescuers across Europe that still search for food and fuel for themselves and their hidden lodgers. They starve and freeze in garrets amidst active warfare without the "benefit" of collusion. Except for a constant fear of betrayal, denouncement, and vicious SS and Milice reprisals, my life has been easier. I've had money and support from fellow believers, food, and shelter in a bomb-free locale with a hidden radio tuned to the BBC.

Commitment appeared easy before the storm. Petty attitudes pierced me. I allowed them to flood my mind and pull me down. Now I will have to grow past my public humiliation at the hands of a town I no longer trust. I'm not proud of my resentment for having to cultivate forgiveness in such hard hearts.

This creates a new sense of separation that sneaks up on me. My rescuer persona must settle into the town's rumor mill, after years as their pariah. I've done something that forever sets me apart from most of my neighbors. Their guilt projects from the corners of their eyes. This guilt will force me to leave Duchamps. Although no other action I take will ever satisfy my soul as deeply, the understanding "earned" here will have to mature me elsewhere in a more honest and enlightened community.

The God I trust now is no longer a childhood figure in a pink and blue heaven carved in marble like Michelangelo's Moses. Nor does He transmit the Holy Spirit with a touch of his finger to Adam on the ceiling of the Sistine Chapel. This God is an infinite source of sublime energy, a pure awareness of love. Months ago in March, I savored a blinding blue-white light. I felt a sacred presence then and don't know how to lift myself to comprehend it or experience its peace again.

I hope this will be the God to sift me from my flesh one day and absorb me into its Holy Spirit, to reflect my few good deeds.

I need to believe I carry that spark and deserve mercy even after taking another's life.

The truth is, I'm less confident of ever feeling that presence again—certain to wobble without the impetus of a humanitarian mission to eke the good out of me. Since I have to "do" to "be" it worries me that my postwar life will disperse into a boring existence. I can't shut out the bitterness from my épuration sauvage. Nor can I let myself die sifting through the ashes of that sacrifice. I won't share myself intimately with anyone who didn't partake of that same struggle, even though I have no wish to talk about the crossings.

The hell of the last three years was like eating a forbidden fruit. I trust only those who challenged me to eat it with them. It's our secret. We paid a price together that has become a measure used against each person I meet now. Was he in the Résistance? Was she in the Résistance? Such judgments are cruel and wrong, and walling myself in with other people's resentment is childish. But this war was a lethal roulette that taught me to resist the rule of maniacal egos. The Fascists won't stop being what they are because their Vichy platform is gone. They'll make a new one.

I've learned to detach myself despite being "soiled in the fray." Forgiveness is easier than choking on blame. Reconciliation takes time but it's the emotional food that grows love.

Stefan and I couldn't reconcile before the war. The paradox is the Occupation exacerbated our ancient misperceptions and drove us to forgive each other. War became a reference point for the survival of our relationship. It pushed my beau-fils out of bottomless self-hatred. I'm grateful to have believed in his essentially loving nature when he reviled me. Stefan and Dieter will make peace. Each sees his weakness in the other. They're too much alike. I will have to guide them toward forgiveness with great tenderness.

Dieter's return revitalizes me, but his blindness is heartbreaking. He consents to stay in my riverside mansion until he decides what to do with his property and his life. He can't take care of himself, yet his days are full of hard work; legal papers to sign, personal affairs about Amélie, and old violin students to meet. I become his eyes—driving, reading, and giving him remedies. Guy helps him bathe, shave and dress. Dieter's sons are Maquis members fighting with de Gaulle's Free French Army units liberating pockets of battle up north.

As we settle into this transition I cannot put deVillement to rest. The court ruled in my favor only because Dieter "rose from the dead." What Édouard said the afternoon he attacked me, and Roemler intervened, still haunts me. My mind is foggy remembering the chaotic months in 1939 after Emil died tragically. The "blood dream" in December of

1941, with its evil smell of death, still holds unanswered clues to my life in the Résistance. Marta, Dieter and I won't be safe in this town until its hideous events can be tied together.

I confide my suspicions to Dieter and he suggests we invite Duvette and Devoir to dine with us on Saturday evening.

⌒

First the good doctor arrives dressed in his three-piece suit with a cigarette dangling from his mouth. Alain's medical bag bursts with fresh garden greens and autumn chestnuts. We laugh at the spectacle of him carrying a baby nappy full of duck eggs—an installment toward payment for a newborn's delivery today. His viands will be a perfect compliment for Marie's dinner. Jacques appears a few minutes later with two old bottles of fine wine.

After a sumptuous meal rowdy with jokes, song, and relief for France's Liberation we retire to my infamous salon. I've reupholstered the divan and chairs, changed carpets and hung new wallpaper to blot out the past indelibly inscribed in its soul. Fresh bouquets adorn end tables and the hearth. Men don't notice such changes. In truth, in my eyes, the newness will never disguise its history.

Duvette and Dieter sit on the divan. Jacques relaxes in the rocker, looking at the bouquet of flowers in front of the fireplace. I curl up in the plush chair adjacent to Dieter with my beloved shawl over my legs. Our liqueurs rest in front of us along with baskets of fresh nutmeats, a few morsels of apple tart and cheese. This would be a cozy evening except for the dire consequences of the last four years resting heavily on our hearts.

We discuss Dieter's prognosis after Alain checks his eyes and gives him more tinctures. The men settle in with cordials, pipes, and Alain with his Gauloises. I nibble on a piece of chocolate, momentarily content. But I feel my relief at the war's end is about to be undone this evening.

I start the conversation by surprising myself, "Gentlemen, let me hear what you think happened to my Emil."

Duvette looks at me over his half-lensed spectacles. His smile turns to a frown. He shakes his wire-haired head, startled by my candor, and begins bluntly, "My dear child, we suspected your husband met with foul play. Didn't you know? Well, I suppose you didn't, or you wouldn't be asking."

"I wasn't allowed near you, Alain, or anyone else who could have told me anything. Everyone guarded me very carefully. I didn't hear any rumors in 1939."

"Yes, Ingrid, but please don't blame us. Your Maman was worried sick. We couldn't get you to eat and Marta was unconscious. You were in deep shock and needed protection."

I listen while the ugly past with its grief-filled memories creeps into our conversation. Édouard's cryptic admission before he attacked me, tenses my chest. Why did I not question my late husband's demise before this war?

"What does Emil's death have to do with your life now, Ingrid?" Jacques asks.

Dieter says guardedly, "Look you two, we can't entrust this information to anyone else. Ingrid believes there is a connection between Édouard deVillement—and Emil's death."

My mind races between the past and present while Dieter talks. Just hearing him utter my dilemma as his energy pulses in my hand makes me bold enough to see startling connections. I can't contain myself. I begin to stutter, staring into these three masculine faces,

"I . . . I . . . ah. . . ."

"What is it, Ingrid? What's the matter?" Dieter presses my hand.

"Édouard not only meant to have me stripped naked and defiled on the day of my public disgrace, but his henchmen implied that later the man who gave them their orders would rape me. They had grabbed the wrong woman. That was the real reason I didn't fight going to jail. I was safer there. They were supposed to take me somewhere else."

"What?" Jacques can't believe what he's heard.

"Yes, he meant it. I never took Édouard's threat seriously. I'll never forget what he said the day he attacked me here in this room. He's very sick. Tell them, please, Dieter."

"Ingrid was invited to the deVillement home for a soirée back in June. She saw old securities for land acquisitions in Emil's name on Édouard's desk in his study. She assumed his plan was to blackmail her and betray her to the Milice."

Dieter turns to me, "In July he made a fatal slip of the tongue when he attacked you, Ingrid. He threatened you. If you didn't go along with him you'd end up dead—like Emil, Amélie, and me."

I watch the two men's faces intently. Devoir tightens his lips and looks down. He knows something but won't say it. He's always too quiet.

As usual, Duvette responds, "That makes sense. I thought all along Édouard was embezzling money and securities from his bank. He had become part owner, *and* the loan officer. When you were the mayor, Dieter, funds were set aside to recondition the old orphanage."

"Two years later while Emil was mayor, he must have discovered those funds were missing. Since I was the senior medical officer at the Orphanage and liaison to the bank, he asked me how much more money he would need. I thought that was odd but never had a chance to investigate before his accident. At the time Emil seemed preoccupied with something. He never told me what it was. Did he tell you, Dieter?"

"No, but on that last ski trip, Alain, he kept saying we needed to speak in private. He insisted he could only tell me outdoors on the slopes—away from everyone. He never got the chance," Dieter shakes his head.

"Yes, and that mysterious private coroner, who became a Vichy-ite accomplice of Klaus Barbie, from Lyon, wrote off his death as an accident," Jacques says suspiciously. "He must have been paid a handsome sum to be quiet."

"Why was there an out-of-town coroner?" I ask innocently.

"Someone in a highly influential position had something to hide, Ingrid. It was too suspicious to be an accident. Did Édouard know you suspected Emil's death was premeditated, Dieter?"

"No, Jacques, but if he thought I knew, or assumed I might learn of it, that would give him motive to pursue me. His embezzlement had to extend beyond municipal funding. It had to affect other landowners.

Rich confrères of Germaine's family owned most of the farms around the orphanage."

Dieter and Emil never told me this. Not a woman's concern, I suppose.

"You knew Emil transferred half of the additional sum to another bank."

Alain looks at Jacques. Devoir shakes his head. "He must have been investigating Édouard at the time of his accident. But could that be a reason to commit murder? You'd think he'd get away with embezzlement. He had many ways to hide it at the bank."

The two men's faces look blank. I grit my jaw, angry and sad.

"What a sordid mess, gentlemen. Why was I left out of it? I feel cheated. Had I known each of you suspected Édouard was behind Emil's death, I would have protected myself. Instead I was dragged by my hair through the streets and suffered the ridicule of a public trial. If nothing else, I never would have opened my front door to him."

Jacques frowns at Alain as if the two have argued about this.

An uneasy quiet suspends the conversation until Duvette speaks apologetically, "Dear Ingrid, we had only our suspicions. Believe me, we tried our best, but with every attempt to uncover the truth, the bureaucracy was against us. Then war broke out and other situations took precedence. You had enough sorrow and worry with Marta gravely injured. Forgive us for excluding you. We didn't want to burden you with a tale that had no substance."

"Burden me? You didn't want to burden me? Perhaps Amélie would be alive today if you *had burdened* me!" A fresh re-cut of the old wound called "being left out" resists forgiveness.

"Typical. Well-intentioned Frenchmen own the privilege to decide what a French woman can handle. How dare you be that smug? Does it finally occur to you, Alain, why I showed up uninvited at the morgue? Three times, Alain, twice without your knowledge."

Duvette is surprised.

"Ingrid, we can always bludgeon ourselves with hindsight," Dieter touches my hand.

"Damn it, Dieter; this isn't about forgiveness or hindsight. I should have known how this happened. Emil was my husband! Perhaps I would have thought twice about my actions during the Occupation. Even using my telephone!"

"What do you mean? You were never given instructions over the telephone."

"Yes, I know. Nor did I ever say anything about our work over the wire. But on the afternoon Marta was attacked I telephoned her friend's family. Maybe the Milice were listening? How else could they have been in that alley? Why would anyone want to hurt my Marta or your Amélie?"

"It was no accident. You're right, Ingrid, but how it connects? We'd have to look again if we suspect a person outside of the Gestapo," Jacques won't reveal anything without proof.

"See what I mean, Dieter? I forgive you, but you made a terrible mistake not entrusting me with the truth. Only now does anyone think about connecting all these circumstances long after the fact. And in the meantime your wife is dead."

"Sorry, Ingrid. It works both ways. I know from my years with Amélie," her widower is defensive, "I have many regrets for not forcing her to talk. I was being respectful when Amélie's silence hurt both of us."

"Forgive me, Dieter. I knew you were preoccupied with arrangements for crossings and had little time for anything else, but I had time to sort through evidence and could have uncovered a great deal. I've learned to run Emil's businesses, oversee his fromageries, and solve all kinds of finance and labor problems. My experience confirms that just because details don't immediately tie into any obvious clues is no reason to dismiss the possibility. Perhaps you men should have considered my position in the Résistance more useful 'upright than supine!'"

I blush as my anger releases the bitter words. Then, to Dieter's relief, I laugh, and his cheeks flush with embarrassment. Alain coughs on his brandy.

Jacques drops his jaw at first, then flashes a supportive smile that makes me continue,

"Hélas, how many years will pass before you understand how the cultural slur of your French paternalism has kept intelligent French women prisoners of your ignorance? Will our demand to know be answered respectfully only after your lot decides we've earned 'our stripes'? Ooh la la! Pardon, Messieurs! That slipped out past my hard-practiced reserve! But I feel better for it."

A sardonic smile curls my lips at Jacques' sheepish admission, "Dear woman, we underestimated your keen intelligence and strength of character. You've shown yourself to be a most extraordinary person. We didn't see 'la Bonne Jeanne' inside you, Ingrid, except . . . maybe Dieter did."

Jacques's candor is humbling and takes me by surprise. I've forgotten how yielding and immature I was five years ago, living in Emil's shadow like a good little wife. Naturally I would have had to be more intelligent than the smartest male to warrant serious entry into a male-dominated enclave of Underground intrigue. I swallow my frustration.

"I'm sorry for the outburst, gentlemen, but not for the truth in what I've said. It's taking too long to uncover. I'm worn out with the years of strain." I choke up suddenly.

So much unexplained loss makes me feel guilty arguing with Dieter in front of his colleagues. Jacques's eyes follow me across the room where I retreat to collect myself in a search for a box of old photos under my writing desk.

"Emil's suspicions could have finished Édouard in this town," Jacques suggests, eager to help me now. Perhaps my outburst was not in vain?

"Do you think you could see something new from old evidence, Jacques? It's been years," I propose, watching Alain look at the coroner with a glint of hope in his eyes.

They *think* Emil would have investigated Édouard, but I *know* my husband would have gone public if I'd told him the truth. My deepest regret—not sharing Édouard's secret perversity—might have doomed my Emil's life. I can't say this in front of these men but I can't let this conversation die here either. I have to be optimistic, so I plop a large box onto the coffee table in front of Jacques.

The answer lies in enticing their minds to the hunt: what men do best.

Jacques pulls out a high-powered jeweler's loupe from his pocket and the two doctors examine the photos.

"Can you see anything?" Dieter asks anxiously. I squeeze his hand gently to diminish his disappointment. Before his blindness he would have been orchestrating this evening. He smiles in my direction.

I say, blushing, "Please, gentlemen, perhaps you'll think me morbidly sentimental but I kept the skis and boots Emil wore that day. I ah, suppose I did it due to the shock of losing my husband at such a young age. Would you care to look at them?"

"Yes, please, Ingrid," Jacques is eager.

While they examine the photos I drag a bag of ski equipment from the closet to the middle of the floor in front of the fireplace.

"Here, Ingrid, let me help you." Jacques unwraps the skis to inspect them, "Remember, Alain, my autopsy evidence never agreed with the doctor from Lyon who took over the forensics. What little I had written was never accepted into the inquest's record."

Duvette gasps and points to an old photo, "Aha, no surprise why, Jacques. Look! The same judge at that inquest presided at your hearing, Ingrid. Édouard's best friend."

"It's just as I told everyone back then," Jacques runs his hands over the underside of Emil's skis, "it didn't make sense that a gifted athlete like Emil could have such a terrible accident on a well-traveled run. Look here, Alain and Ingrid. Feel these skis, Dieter. These scratches in the undersides had to be made during the accident," Jacques examines the marks with his high-powered loupe.

Pointing to the picture with growing suspicion, he says, "Look at this. A public run is always clear of debris, but see the sharp limbs poking up from beneath the snow in the photo? Look closer. See that shadow? It's impossible for the sun to cast that long a shadow at the hour Emil died. That's a large evergreen bough with needles, buried shallowly, maybe just below the snow's surface. See how the branches stick up? How irregular they are? They were buried there to cover over something else with a very sharp metallic edge. Tree limbs can't make ridges like these. Feel them and give me that picture of Emil's body."

Jacques takes over now, piecing together the evidence. I swallow hard and rub the side of my cheekbone briskly. I want to escape this room and these photos.

Jacques senses it, "I'm sorry, Ingrid, don't look. It's my job to figure out times and causes of death. Don't be offended if I seem cold and calculating. The mystery always excites me. I'm sorry if it hurts you. It hurt me too. Emil was my friend and I wasn't allowed to do his forensics. I always thought Édouard paid someone off to dig up what I had discovered before I was able to return to the scene and collect the rest of the evidence."

"Don't worry, Jacques. You're here this evening for this very reason," Dieter confirms.

I move closer, staring through glassy eyes at the history of my husband's premature end. My heart races when I see photos of Emil crumpled in the snow. Jacques lays out the rest of the official ski patrol photos taken by the police. Dieter puts his arm around me.

I sigh an uneven exhalation and force myself to ask, "Jacques, do you think weakened skis and a few hidden stumps of branches obscuring sharp metal edges could have unbalanced Emil enough to throw him into a tree?"

"Actually, Ingrid," Jacques replies, "I don't, because he died almost instantly. He had to be skiing much faster than you think. Marta's tracks show she avoided her father's body and landed in the same tree. She must have been staring at him in her panic and going too fast to change direction. Her fracture was on her right side, not full face like her father."

Duvette speculates, "Something else is missing. I didn't observe the autopsy before the other coroner replaced you, Jacques, but I'd bet Emil had ingested a poisonous substance."

"Right, one that prevented him from saving himself. He was out of control from the start of the run. That's why another coroner was brought in, to avoid disclosure of a lethal toxin in Emil's body. Damn!"

I've never seen Jacques angry. His cheeks enflame and send their energy to his thick center shock of dark brown hair. His deep blue eyes are ablaze with certainty. The clues from my memory begin to fall into place as I sit here alarmed by what I know he must be thinking. He draws me into a straight line of attention to the details I missed all these years.

"Ah oui, yes, it must be," I gasp, covering my mouth.

"What is it, Ingrid?" Alain is concerned this is too much for me.

"At the cemetery, in a fit of pique, Marta said her father was going too fast for her. I completely misread her, interpreting her figuratively to mean he was pulling his life away from her deliberately. But maybe she was being quite literal?"

"Could we find this out for certain?" Dieter asks.

"We'd have to exhume Emil's body and test his tissues," Jacques replies.

Then another unexplained conversation hits me,

"Dieter, on the afternoon at the luncheon with Mueller, just before . . . ah,"

"What, Ingrid?"

"Édouard came to our table to say hello. When he left he hardly spoke to Mueller. He just nodded and murmured, "Obersturmführer," under his breath. I thought Édouard was reserved out of deference to Mueller's power, but now I realize they shared something about me. Was I supposed to die that day? I imagined Mueller was going to have me shot."

"Perhaps Édouard was going to poison your meal, Ingrid, and that's why Mueller wanted you to eat in his private dining room," Jacques smiles, pleased with his deduction. "A poison would not attract public attention. Only at my end, as the coroner."

That's why Édouard influenced the town to hire another coroner for Emil's autopsy," Alain concludes.

"Right, the same one he would have imported for your autopsy, Ingrid," Devoir smiles.

"Now I understand why Édouard wanted to blackmail me and take me with him. He needed to leave France before anyone suspected him." I shake my head at Jacques, who adds,

"This may be difficult, Ingrid, but Emil's death is pivotal if it links Édouard to Dieter's torture. I think Édouard is a master poisoner. I'm sure he's behind your loss of vision, Dieter. Most substances used in torture are intentionally short-lived in their effects."

"He's right, Dieter. Your handling was not typical of Gestapo tactics." Duvette shakes his head. (Alain and Jacques have already spoken about this.) Jacques insists,

"We need to know what happened when the Milice worked you over, Dieter."

"All right, men, I've heard enough. You have my permission to exhume Emil's remains without delay." I set my jaw, resolved to see it through.

"Ingrid, if we take his threat seriously, then Édouard is behind Amélie's death, too. But did he mean to kill her or Marta? If he pursued Emil and then Dieter, who else was he after and why?" Jacques voices my fear. No one has answered this. The three men are silent.

Dieter breaks the pause and says thoughtfully, "You, Ingrid. He has always wanted you."

"But why take my child?" I think of Édouard's sick lust as a little boy and twitch like a rabbit he was about to kill. It's too embarrassing to utter the answer. Dieter has an idea.

"Ingrid, you were stalked like a prey. The Nazis could have arrested you many times and didn't. It suggests that someone else pulled *their* strings. It's hard to believe that Édouard would align himself with the SS, but he was obsessed with vengeance. He could have planned to use Mueller's private dining room to put a sedative in your meal. Then he'd have relations while you were deeply unconscious, and take photos to blackmail you. Killing you doesn't fit if he's obsessed with you."

"Oui, my insistence on eating outdoors changed his plans, which is why he and Franz were muted in their parting exchange at the table," I put it all together. "Édouard must have been furious. Could he have paid an SS underling to shoot Mueller to make it look like an Underground ambush? Then torture you, Dieter, as a fitting reprisal for his evil scheme not working? Certainly the Milice could commit torture even if Roemler refused to ordain it. But rumors said Mueller's own men were behind his death. They hated him for not sharing his 'French booty.' What really happened?"

Dieter's answer is logical, "The other Nazis were petty underlings who would never admit they divided up Mueller's blackmail money. They took it to Germany and now they're fighting along the front. We might find out what they did if we force deVillement to talk."

I promised myself not to discuss Édouard's perversity, but Dieter's scenario pushes me.

"Bonne chance, Messieurs! Everyone would laugh if I accused Édouard of sexual depravity. To Duchamps' society, he's their banker, a pillar of social and financial stability. Oh, and, by the way, a necrophiliac on the sly? Sadly, gentlemen, my sexual notoriety apart from Édouard's ghoulish seduction is much more delectable to this town's baser palette than my noble Underground mission. Édouard blackmailing me would excite them and only continue the scandal," I groan, humiliated, "and I'd still have to live here."

Embittered, I look away; my hand covers my quivering lips.

The room becomes somber. Jacques walks around the coffee table and kneels before me. He grasps my hand. Instantly I feel whole and warm inside. Jacques's forwardness makes Dieter and Duvette sit straighter, alerted, not knowing what to anticipate.

Jacques speaks softly to me for the first time as a man and a friend, not as the coroner or fellow Résistant, "You were a brave soldier, Ingrid. You gave all you had to save innocent civilian lives. The three of us men here together could not muster the courage you showed in this war. We are the ones who are shamed, Ingrid, by your unconditional love for the people you shielded. Can you forgive us?"

Jacques kisses my fingertips and turns to Dieter, reverential for his friend's bravery and blindness, but warning with masculine rebuke, "You are very lucky to have her sympathetic heart so close, old man. Take care how you honor her."

Alain, like an overly protective father refereeing a daughter's suitors quickly offsets the intimate way Jacques delivers his sweet apology to me, and his rutting admonition to Dieter,

"Jacques speaks for all of us, Ingrid. If Édouard did this, he's a poor deranged bastard!"

Devoir doesn't let go of my left hand. I'm stunned. I didn't mean for this to happen. I blush when Dieter gropes for my right hand as if to assert his unspoken ownership.

The two men's subtle competitiveness was good-natured as the evening began. I took it for mere joking. But now Jacques holds my left hand and Dieter my right. Jacques is concerned about Dieter living under my roof. He, like the rest of Duchamps, doesn't believe it's platonic.

I feel nothing especially romantic for either man, except surprise at Devoir's chivalry. I must ignore their attention yet ingratiate them to my present worry.

I take a deep breath and plead, "One more unanswered question eats at me, gentlemen—the Jews on my riverbank," my jaw clenches saying it.

Devoir catches my thought and confirms it, quietly, "Vous êtes formidable, Ingrid! Increased SS presence made us worry more about protecting our secret operation than question how the Jews landed on your riverbank. I couldn't research anything without revealing Édouard's name. A serious accusation needed solid evidence for a Vichy-backed town council."

"And now what do you think, Jacques?" Alain asks cautiously, as though we're still shrouded in the war. Jacques has waited to clarify this mystery openly.

"Those bodies did not float against the tide, Ingrid. They were brought here and buried on your shore . . . deliberately."

"*What?*" Dieter is shocked, "How? Who could have done that, Jacques?"

"Édouard. He must have contacted the same coroner who did the forensics on Emil almost two years earlier. Only a coroner would have access to Jewish bodies if a Jewish community didn't know about them. Refugees were stateless. France was overrun with people who came seeking asylum before Vichy gave up foreign Jews. A coroner was free to. . . ."

"*To sell them!* Mon Dieu, Jacques, he sold them to Édouard, who paid Antoine to bury them on my riverbank before the storm. That week I was at Maman's in the country, and Édouard knew I would be away because of a conversation we had at the bank. We have to prove this. How could he have been such a two-face: filled with revenge?"

I won't reveal my history with Édouard and swallow my disgust for the moment.

"Oui, revenge was his motive, Ingrid, and yes, it can be proven. Leclerc will handle it. Those bodies had been shot and decayed in the air for a week before someone submerged them in water. Their bloating was limited because *they did not drown.* Their discoloration didn't fit drowning and their primary decomposing bacteria were of soil, and not aquatic."

"The stench didn't fit a drowning either. I grew up on that river, Jacques. The odor of water decay is different. Édouard planned that scenario and knew I'd uncover them. He figured I'd be too upset to notice how they got there. He tried to scare me. He hoped to make me leave my property, because the whole thing was so revolting. Why would he do that?"

"Perhaps in his deluded state, Ingrid, he believed you'd come to him for protection. You would finally give him the love he craved. He thought you owed it to him. He trusted you when you were children. You are the only person he has ever trusted."

"Your deduction is close to mine, Jacques. I've carried Édouard's tragic history forever. He was never a happy soul. Thank you for caring, for your integrity. I feel less alone now."

"We have to exhume the Jews, too," Alain says, looking at me with new respect.

"Oh God, now I fear for Germaine's safety. What can we do to get her away from Édouard?"

"Very little, if she can't keep her mouth shut. She's too impulsive!" Duvette mutters.

"Édouard has too much power over her, Ingrid. She collapses under his rule. She's in too much danger for you to be near her right now," Dieter warns.

Jacques tells me, "Ingrid, there's ample evidence to charge Édouard. We have to act quickly. If Germaine felt safe she'd help us. You know about her liver, Alain?"

The old Doc nods "yes."

We can build a case against Édouard, but will these good men be too late?

Chapter Thirty-Three

A Harvest of Death

16 September 1944, Saturday

A knock at the front door startles me. Marie appears, announcing the police have come for Alain and Jacques. My suspicions tie me to a gruesome image, and anxiety rushes me to the vestibule.

I meet the gendarme who arrested me and can barely restrain myself to ask him calmly, "Ah, good evening sir, officer LeBrun, oui? Can you tell me what's happened?"

"Sorry Madame, it's police business." Recalling me, he's uneasy about my request.

"I have a friend who may be in danger this evening. If this is about Madame Germaine deVillement, I am her closest friend. Please, officer, surely you can tell me if she's alive?"

"Oui, Madame, she is," he admits, and squirms—remembering our last encounter.

My two dinner guests appear in the foyer: my friends in their guise as municipal medical officers. They talk in hushed tones with the gendarme—as Dieter quietly feels his way to me.

I return to the fireplace and sit down with him.

"Dieter, I have to go to her. Please understand. A chapter of my life is closing. No one else knows what Germaine has suffered. I'll be back soon," I speak with determination.

"Ingrid, I wish I could help. I feel useless without my eyes. Do you want me to come?"

"No, Dieter, please stay here. What I have to do now is very personal. I have to go alone. I'll tell you later. Don't worry, I'll be fine."

In fact, oddly enough, at this moment I have never felt better. A strange constriction about my shoulders and head gave way to an almost giddy freedom the instant LeBrun announced Germaine was alive.

When the two men return to say good night, I beg them, "Alain, Jacques, take me with you. Please, I have to see Germaine."

"Ingrid, no. It's police work. Probably, a very grisly scene," Alain insists.

"Come on, Alain, old man. Let's take her. She's no stranger to death." Jacques smiles and contradicts him. "I'm sure Germaine would appreciate your support, Ingrid."

As I prepare to leave the house, I go once more to Dieter, who sits alone. I remove the flowers from the hearth. It's getting chilly; I ask Guy to light the logs in the fireplace.

"Ingrid, are you sure of this? Do you have to go?"

"Yes, please, don't worry Dieter. I'll be back soon. Guy can help you to bed. Sleep well."

And for the first time I give him a small spontaneous peck on his cheek. He reaches out as I pull away. His fingers search my face and his eyes strain to see my expression.

"What has happened to you just now, Ingrid? You're suddenly different."

"I can't talk now, Dieter. I must go. Good night, mon ami."

He grasps my hand and kisses my fingertips. These little kisses feel natural. Their spontaneity sparks our first tender moments and hint of a new feeling, a contrast to the claustrophobic Nazi dread that ground my heart into sexual indenture. Suddenly I can forgive everyone, and leave the house with a burst of energy.

LeBrun drives us to the morgue. Jacques and I say nothing in front of him. We transfer to the coroner's vehicle and race to the deVillement estate ahead of Alain. Alone together in the coroner's hearse, Jacques is very quiet.

I gather the courage to speak, "Thanks for letting me come, Jacques. And for your vote of confidence."

"I meant it, Ingrid." It's surprising how relaxed he seems with me. I've known him casually for five years but can't remember being alone with him. The trauma of losing Emil and reviving my daughter cloud my memory of his arrival in Duchamps. Back then, Alain gave me remedies to help me sleep and tonics to fortify me when I wouldn't eat. I was very distressed; my memory played tricks on me. I couldn't differentiate among the days of the week.

But during the time Marta was unconscious, I think Jacques took me to an event one evening. Oh, I hope I can trust him.

"Yes, um, ah, I need to know something, Jacques."

"You have only to ask, Ingrid."

"Where were you when I was on the street being taunted and degraded and having my head sheared?"

He sighs and purses his lips hearing this. I suppose he expected me to ask.

"I was with a farmer who unburied the tractor he had hidden from the Nazis. When he lifted the engine from the barn floor, he slipped under it, on an oil slick. The engine fell on him. He was lucky he only broke his leg, but I had to set it. Alain was already at a birth on the other side of town.

"I should have come to you, Ingrid, but I didn't know the mob had you. I have no excuses. It was the day *before* the actual Liberation and . . . well, the atmosphere became ripe for épuration very quickly. I should have cared enough for your safety to anticipate what the town would do to you—and when. I'm sorry. I understand if you're angry and hurt. We three men abandoned you. We've behaved like Judases. It makes me sick."

"I've been alone too long, Jacques. I'm grateful that Stefan has forgiven me." He hears my voice wither away into silence that ends in a deep sigh. I look out the window so he can't see me fight back tears. Odd, how he used the word "Judas" as I did three months ago.

Then Jacques disappoints me, "I never agreed with Alain and Dieter that Stefan should not be told about you being in the Underground, Ingrid. I was afraid it would be too hard on both of you. But please. . . ."

"*Please don't say anything to Dieter or Alain, right, Jacques?* You boys have to hang together as always. Certainly, I understand." I turn to stare out the window at the starry night sky. Well, there's my answer. He caught the sarcasm in my voice. He's quiet for the remainder of the drive.

Jacques brings the vehicle to a stop in front of the mansion and turns to me. The entrance lights shine on his face. He frowns, measuring his words, "Please Ingrid, forgive me, and understand I meant what I said before. Dieter has become guilt-ridden about the many mistakes he made. When you bring up Stefan, he'll be depressed. His blindness is a bludgeon he uses *not* to forgive himself, but to feel unworthy."

"You cherish his friendship, don't you, Jacques?"

"Oui, Ingrid. Alain and I stayed in the background at Dieter's insistence. It was a mistake, but Dieter was in charge and determined to keep us safe from suspicion because of our public positions. We knew everything about everyone. If we were denounced it would be the end of the whole cell in Duchamps.

"Dieter's role was deeply undercover. No one suspected him for months. It was only after the Résistance killed Heisler that we had trouble concealing his identity from Mueller. All that time you were more vulnerable than any of us, and said nothing. I kept pushing Dieter to talk with you if Alain and I couldn't. But he didn't see the terror inside you. He couldn't appreciate the pressure you bore not being able to let your guard down in your own home."

"How did you know that, Jacques?"

"You see the details other people miss, Ingrid, and keep them inside."

"Oui, like the dead Jews on my riverbank. You are the first person who heard my suspicion, Jacques. You expected to find bullet holes in the backs of that Jewish couple, didn't you? That's why you turned them over. Something was amiss."

"Ingrid, I couldn't tell Alain if there was no way to substantiate my theory. Dead is dead to Alain. Finished, over. He has no interest in forensics. But three years ago I sensed your confusion about the flow of the current right there on the riverbank. You kept staring at the movement of the swollen streambed. You wanted answers."

"Yes, I had no way to understand how the bodies got there or what my future would be. I felt terribly uneasy. At first I thought it was the bodies themselves. Later I thought about Emil. It was weird. I couldn't make the connection, but I knew those two dead people had ties to my destiny. To think Édouard's depravity birthed my noble mission. It's too bizarre."

"That need and curiosity prompted you to risk your cover, Ingrid. Sneaking into the morgue to find out what happened to Dieter and Amélie was madness, but you were recently widowed, alone with a seizuring, hemiplegic child. The Van der Kreuziers were your friends. No one informed you and you were the most vulnerable player. Some Résistants worried about you, pitied you and never judged you a collaborator . . . like our housekeeper, Patrice. She admires your courage and intelligence, as do I, Ingrid. You were very dignified during that travesty in the courtroom after this town hurt you so brutally."

"Patrice told you, didn't she?"

"Yes, Ingrid, and she gave Alain hell when she told him as soon as the trial was over."

"Thank you, for telling me. My needy heart still hurts me," dejection colors my voice.

"Look, Ingrid, the war may be over, but inside us it will never truly be over. We have wounds to carry. They cause regrets and shame. We have to forgive, as Alain said at your mother's, for the 'errors of conscience this maniacal state of war has pressed from us.'"

"Oui, Jacques, I must forgive everyone who wouldn't tell me Dieter was alive and waiting to testify outside the courtroom. I needed to shriek and faint so the town would believe in my innocence, and Dieter could dissolve the resistance between us."

Jacques's eyes reach across his shyness. My sad face must repel him. I hope for another smile, but instead he looks inward. His expression is grave. I can't tell if it's because he's now the coroner or something else inhibits him, but his masculine warmth still envelops me.

The same power supported me when Jacques steered the rescue toboggan down the icy slope in 1939. He had tied my dead husband to my body. I held Marta's bloody head in my lap, and her unconscious body between my legs, lashed to my torso. The memory humbles me.

"Forgive me, Jacques. I am sorry I was short with you. You weren't part of that deception. Thank you, for being honest."

"Of course, Ingrid," he nods. "Give yourself some time to heal, dear woman. Don't rush back into life too fast." He retreats into the shy bachelor. "Let's go in, Ingrid. Let me tell the police why you're here. Stay close to me until we're inside. I have to deal with Édouard's body. Alain will stay with you and Germaine."

I follow him inside without saying a word.

The late September night is unusually chilly. The mansion appears monolithic in the dark: eerie, like a giant mausoleum. The ashen-faced butler leads us to a first floor sitting room where the house staff stands around Germaine. She sits on a Louis XVI chair amidst a lavish interior of cut glass lamps and chandeliers. Antique Delftware—and Meissen and Sèvres porcelains adorn the walls and rest in glass cases. In contrast to the rest of this dreary cave-like villa, the room is ablaze with light. Still it is cold and impersonal, like a museum interior that lacks little tags to identify the displays of its valuables.

Germaine appears pale and rigid—like one of her porcelains. All this luxury seems worthless. My childhood friend sits dejected and alone, caressing a little lump of fur on her lap. Her staff surrounds her, caring and cleaning for her the same way they do this expensive crockery.

Germaine dabs her eyes as we enter. Her little Scottish terrier, Tutu, raises his head and looks at me. He sits on her lap swathed in a hand towel with bandages over his rump. Germaine's hard exterior shatters when she sees me. She holds out her right arm and weeps, "Ingrid. It's over. Come here, please, please."

An officer takes the house staff to another room for questioning and leaves us alone.

Duvette sits opposite Germaine and me. I hold her hands and search her eyes. She looks at me for a long time before speaking. Her tear-stained face is deeply wrinkled. Purplish bags circle her eyes and transparent flesh hangs loosely under her chin. She has aged even more since the trial. Her touch is dry. Her eyes give only a faint flicker of fire.

Blood-spatter stains dull the soft pink sheen and fur-edged cuffs of her satin robe. Someone has hastily bandaged her left arm, and placed it in a sling made with a silk scarf.

Wigless, her hair is short, brittle and wild in all directions like the ends of spent grain stalks. Perhaps she was roused from sleep when the grim encounter took place.

"Germaine, what happened? Did he hurt you?"

Severely shaken, Germaine speaks barely above a whisper, not in her usual loud and obnoxious tone. "Oh no, not physically. Um, well, he tried to kill me—but didn't molest me—if that's what you mean. He shot Tutu right in front of me."

"I can see that; in the rump, oui?"

"Oui, Tutu ran under the bed. He, oh, I can hardly tell you," she looks down at her dear companion. She strokes his neck and he whimpers in appreciation. I dislike interrupting their loving exchange, both alone in this giant cave, but Alain has to know the truth.

"Tell me, Germaine, or I will tell Dr. Duvette for you."

"No. Please don't, Ingrid. It's too shameful, please, not now."

"I'm sorry, Germaine, Alain has to know if Édouard was going to caress the dog's. . . ."

"Please, Ingrid. I know what I must tell the authorities. It's a nightmare. It's over."

"Are you sure, Germaine? I can't let Édouard hurt you any more. You've been through too much. You needn't protect him. Please forgive me for forcing you to admit these things about him, but you must tell Dr. Duvette what happened. All of it or we can't help you."

"Oui, oui, bien sûr. I trust you, Ingrid. You're right. Édouard was sick, Alain."

The old doc is very solemn. He has no idea of the depth of Édouard's mental condition. Watching the two of us with growing interest, he's about to be privy to a noxious tale. Germaine will relive painful details that corrode her memory.

"Please, Ingrid, let me tell you as though it is happening in front of me, in the present. I am still not able to put it into the past. Maybe I will when I finish telling you, but I need you to live it with me again. Hold my hand as I talk, please, mon amie, will you do that?"

"Bien sûr, Germaine. Tell us, especially Alain, in a way that is the least painful for you."

As she speaks, I feel the years of enmity between us melt away. I have to force back tears for my shame . . . not realizing how harsh the poisoning has been on her.

"I was, no, I am . . . here alone. The servants have the night off. Only the butler is on duty. I'm very tired and not eating well, still struggling to regain my energy after months of arsenic poisoning. I have fired the last cook. Whenever I confront Édouard with his dastardly deed he only laughs.

"He never admits he is doing it, but he stops poisoning me as soon as I voice suspicion. After your day in court, Ingrid, it's worse between us. He rarely comes home. When he does, he seldom speaks. I ask him what his intentions are. He frowns and then smiles mysteriously.

"I assume he'll leave me, but not divorce me. He wants my money, although his machinations at the bank have divested me of most of my estate. I still have objets d'art of significant value. I'm under great pressure to place my most prized goods in safekeeping where he can't find them.

"Two days ago I uncover a frightful sight. I'm out walking Tutu on the grounds and come to an old storeroom at the rear of one of our barns. Tutu catches a scent and runs to the door, scratching furiously to get in. If not for him, I would have passed that chamber of horrors without notice.

"The door is locked. Tutu won't quit barking and scratching. I give up rummaging through the drawer of keys in the barn's office until I close it, and feel resistance under the drawer. A slice in the wood wedges a small set of keys.

"Walking to the back of the barn I wave to men coming and going from the harvest. I smile sweetly. They return the greeting. What do they know about Édouard? The rear barn is deserted. I work the lock free. An overreaching sense of evil grabs my heart as I open the door.

"What an image greets my eyes. Bottles everywhere, but meticulously lined up and labeled and shelved. Most are toxins, pills and tinctures. It's a laboratory with a small stove, cheesecloth in drawers, knives, sieves, glasses, beakers, stoppers and strainers. I find magnifying lenses, vellum tracing paper, a small kerosene lamp—and a drawer full of inks and pens.

"But the worst is Tutu. As I open each cabinet, he becomes even wilder with agitation. He cries and paws at a large trunk behind a small table.

"By this point my nerves are undone. The reality of living with Édouard's devilish mind is revolting. Shall I unlock this trunk? I pause for a few seconds before I lift the lid. What will I find in there? A body? My throat is tight and my hands shake, but perhaps Édouard has some of my valuables in it?

"I have to know; my hands push the lid up, and a heavy, musty scent of death fills my nostrils. Rows and rows of shriveled, stiff, dead rabbits, maybe fifty in all—hang in careful groups of three and four, their necks skewered on wires strung across the coffin's bloodstained interior. The rabbits are decapitated, neutered, and labeled. The males are separated from the females. *It's disgusting.*

"I slam the lid down and cover my mouth with a handkerchief. I retch dryly and continue to search the rest of the shelves, looking through unlocked cabinets. Stacks of yellowed, pornographic playing cards with sadistic images of women being molested sit in the corners of the cupboards.

"The room steals my breath away. I know Édouard has a dark side, but I have kept it from the forefront of my thoughts for our entire marriage. It lurks near my own shameful past with my father and uncle, a shame and abuse I've never revealed. Why do some men succumb to that kind of sickness?"

Germaine's voice becomes very soft and penitent as she confides, "Ingrid, you have a right to know. Jealousy contaminates my devotion to you. It reels forward from my incestuous childhood. It made me think the worst of you during the war."

"Germaine, you don't have to tell me. We've made our peace." I don't want to upset her any further.

"No, please hear me out. I did not defend you when I should have, but I never defend myself. I've been a fraud—compliant my whole life. I have a big mouth yet inside I cower, and am afraid. Why am I a willing victim? When someone does something terribly wrong and depraved to me, where is my instinctive outrage? "

Germaine's eyes are swollen and her face reddens. Alain and I are being drawn into an unseemly private hell. She hesitates to go on . . . but clearly wants me to give her permission.

"Germaine, take a deep breath and tell us. You need to get this out of you. You're safe with us." I try to reassure her. Her face is marked with the pain of childhood memories, and those more recent.

"It's very hard to entrust this secret to you and Alain. I should not give voice to such vileness."

I send her compassion and love. Looking into her blurred, brownish-green eyes, dull with poison, I wish I could purify her emotional and physical being. But I know she must do that herself.

She needs fresh air. She takes a deep breath to continue, "By the time I awoke to feeling violated, three agonizing years had passed. I was so unclean it was too late to change. I stopped allowing the crime but the stain was indelible in my psyche. I suppose the revulsion it engendered will have to stand as my highest achievement in this life. I subdued the pattern and the humiliation."

"How did you manage it?"

"I forced my mother to send me to a boarding school and refused to come home for vacations. I got myself invited to friends who lived far away.

"It stopped their attacks but couldn't stamp out the destructive thoughts of guilt, shame and sin. By age twelve I was spoiled like old meat. I had been desired before my bloom and then cast adrift, trapped in flesh able to conceive and give new life for which I had no desire. I arrived at adulthood unable to cultivate a normal, loving relationship with a man."

"Germaine, can you leave that in the past where it belongs?"

"I think maybe now, today, I have hope that I can, Ingrid. Childhood for me was an ugliness that perhaps I can get out of my mind when I shed this relationship, no . . . this sickness that I pretended, no . . . I made it into a marriage. The discovery of Édouard's private world has also unearthed my own victimization. I understand what drove his depravity. Oh, let me go back into it for this last time."

"Yes, of course. Please . . . Germaine, continue."

"I am in his laboratory from Hell. I carefully put away anything I have touched and relock his cabinets, place the keys into their space under the drawer, lock the door, and return to the main house.

"Again I bid good afternoon to a few farmhands. This time I wonder which of them supplies the rabbits? Who keeps count of their numbers when cleaning the hutches? I bury another of Édouard's secrets next to my own where it will not leap out in all its horror."

Germaine takes a sip of water and composes herself.

"Édouard arrives home from out of town quite late tonight, well past dinner. He startles me when he storms into my bedroom brandishing a handgun aimed at Tutu. His face is dark and his features twist in a dreadful scowl.

"I have invaded his chamber of horrors, my little 'adventure,' as he calls it. Tutu is growling. I reach to protect my little love but Tutu jumps to the floor and circles frantically around Édouard who cocks the hammer and kicks him. My baby falls backward and yelps in pain. I try to soothe Tutu, but stop as Édouard aims at me and grumbles,

"You were in my private room."

"I don't know what you're talking about, Édouard."

"Stop lying, Germaine. I found this piece of ribbon from Tutu's collar. See, it matches perfectly. I could feel your presence in there. I will have to kill the dog now."

"What? No Édouard. Why do that?"

"Because he's the only creature you love in this world. Killing him will teach you to leave my things alone. You brought this punishment on yourself, old woman."

"No. Please."

"I rush to Tutu as Édouard fires. My darling little companion cries out and stops running. He looks up at me and drags himself under the bed, bleeding.

"You monster," I cry, "How can you do such a thing?" (I cannot tell how badly Tutu's injured but I can hear him lick himself.)

"Édouard is furious. He wants the dog to come out. Then he can finish him off, the bastard. When I hear Tutu growl I know he will be all right, but I have to get Édouard out of the bedchamber. I need to get to my baby and bind up his wound.

"I start to reach down. I want Tutu to see my fingers, but realize if I coax him out from under the bed, Édouard really will kill him. My mind runs in circles. I imagine my baby, my poor little companion's blood draining from his body, alone and in pain. I'm furious with Édouard but helpless to do anything."

"Leave him alone, Germaine. Step back or you're next," Édouard commands me.

"Then he pushes me as I lean over to see Tutu. He thrusts me backward onto the footboard, knocking me breathless. Édouard has never threatened me physically before. My ribs feel cracked. I retreat to the middle of the bed, gasping for air.

"He starts pacing again with quick, jerky movements like a rodent. The features of his fifty-year-old face begin to fade as a hurt, wicked, little boy swallows his adult personality."

"Stop it, Germaine. I can't stand it. You make me sick. Look at you, decrepit before your time. You're ugly. You can't even grow decent hair on your head. Hah, you've made it easy not to be attracted to you all these years."

"He walks all around the bed, tracking Tutu's blood everywhere. His eyes glaze over. The right eye is bloodshot and the left one diverges to the far corner of the socket. He looks under the bed but can't see anything. By a miracle Tutu is quiet, apparently sensing he is safer in the dark. He has dragged himself deeply under the bed, behind my storage boxes.

"Édouard cocks his head to the side, staring with a strange expression. I think he wants to touch Tutu in some evil way. My mind sees the decapitated, neutered rabbits in that trunk. I can't imagine what to do. He and his gun petrify me. We are alone as he planned. He is sick.

"I feel bilious, but have to get hold of myself. I can't let him defeat me. How can I distract him? Then I have an idea that sickens me even more—yet what choice do I have?

"What did you do, Germaine?" Alain is amazed at her aplomb when dealing with such insanity.

"I have to enter his fantasy and lure him into putting down that gun. I tell him he is right about everything. I agree with him and lead the confrontation to that end."

"He doesn't believe me at first but then asks, 'What do you mean, Germaine?'"

"I mean you're right, Édouard. I have only one attribute you lust after, remember?"

"Your breasts, yes. But you never give them to me, you bitch."

"Yes, I always tease you with them when I'm jealous of your attention to other women, or, ah things."

"And then Ingrid, he started to stammer, and I knew his emotions were too close to the surface."

"He stuttered, 'You are, ah, you're m-m-mean to me, Germaine, y-y-you are.'"

"Well, I'm jealous now, Édouard. And I promise I won't be mean."

"Will you give them to me, now, Germaine, please?"

"He is shrinking into a pubescent boy. He's wild, and I'm not sure he will relax into his other persona. He gazes at me but sees a figure from his past. I know if it doesn't work, I'm as good as dead. I open my robe and gown slowly, to expose my pendulous bosom and then stop suddenly to test him."

"What, you aren't jealous anymore, Germaine? Please, don't stop now," he begs in a childish voice.

"As my chest draws his eyes, . . . slowly, his hand relaxes on the gun."

"He is on his knees . . . his eyes are glued to my bosom. Each time he asks his voice is softer and younger, "Who are you jealous of Delphine . . . ah no . . . Ger-Germaine? You have to answer me."

"I'm jealous of your attention right now to my Tutu, chéri."

"I speak slowly, as if to a small child. He calls me Delphine, his mother's name. I move to the edge of the bed on my stomach to be closer, and lean over. My long, teat-like bosom falls freely. I call to him sweetly. He forgets about Tutu and puts the gun down. He reaches for me with hands that have caressed the dog's blood on the rugs. I lower myself gently toward the floor. Gradually I swing my torso and legs to the side, while he kneads my breasts rhythmically, as though milking a goat. As I keep sliding down the satin sheets my silk negligee rides up and away from my body. My thighs are exposed, as silk against satin ignites tiny sparks of static electricity. The darkened room glows with them. Damn. I don't want this to happen. I'm afraid the little sparks will be too bizarre and throw him out of his fantasy.

"Suddenly, Édouard stiffens and runs from the bedroom. In his panic, he leaves the gun on the floor. I scoop it up into my pocket and quickly lock the doors. I feel shaky, but relieved. I turn and stare at my Tutu crawling toward me, his head out from under the bed. He whimpers, aware of our danger. I stifle tears for him as I clean and bandage his wound in the sink, all the while reminding myself *not* to give in to Édouard.

"My life isn't safe yet. I can't indulge myself as I usually do when sad and hurt. The pattern of a lifetime, my empty self-pity, hits me squarely in the face. Each ugly memory attached to it begins to collapse like a wall of dominoes. Underneath I finally acknowledge my fear, and allow myself to feel the violation through the gunshot wound of my little friend, my Tutu. This time the sickness and desperation force me forward with renewed strength and clarity. I have to endure. My life depends upon it.

"I place Tutu in a soft towel and slide him back under the bed. I climb back and wait for Édouard to return. I'm exhausted and weak from months of poisoning. I try not to doze off. Thirty minutes pass. He doesn't reappear. I lie there in the dark and second-guess what he will do next. He has keys to every room in the house. My two locked doors will make enough noise to alert his return.

"A full hour later I hear him unlock the outer door. My eyes open and I feel for the gun. It has several rounds left. The nightlight is on but my room is dark. He unlocks the inner door. Édouard enters, assumes I'm asleep and removes the mirror over my wall safe. He opens the safe. Oh no, not my Limoges! I can't let him take my Grandmaman's priceless seventeenth-century enamels.

"I pretend to rouse and turn in the bed to see what he's doing. He stops for a moment. The safe is open and the box is exposed. He turns to look and waits for me to resume deep breathing. I don't know if he has another gun so I decide not to stir any further. He turns back to the safe. I hear him close it. And listen to the slight, uneven drag of his slippered feet leaving the room.

"When the outer door shuts I get up and open the safe. The box is still there. It feels heavy. I check its contents. That thief! He replaced my enamels with rocks! He planned this robbery. I can't stand it. He will leave me utterly destitute. Anger gives me courage.

"I open the two doors quietly and tiptoe down the corridor feeling my way in pitch blackness. Gun in hand with hammer cocked, I move toward his rooms at the other end.

"Without warning his voice rings out in the dark like a menace from hell, 'Stop, Germaine! Don't come any closer or I'll shoot. I warn you.

I've sent the butler and servants away. By the time they discover you I'll be long gone. They'll never find me.'"

"Édouard, I love you, don't leave me, please. Talk to me. Let's work out an arrangement we can live with, but don't kill me." (I can't pinpoint his voice in the dark and need to keep him talking. I tiptoe halfway down the corridor—to the old armoire—for cover.)

"I don't care what happens to you, Germaine. Don't come any closer or I'll shoot. I warn you, if you're armed, I'll give you my back and they'll say you did it in cold blood. They will send you to the guillotine."

"Fine, Édouard, here it comes then." I shoot three times into the darkness.

He laughs, "Wasting precious bullets, you silly woman. You have only two more."

"He's correct but I know where he stands now. I take aim as he fires back. Another volley and my bullets from his pistol are spent."

He laughs again. He has one shot left, "And now, Chérie, I'll blind you."

"He flicks on a large German hand torch. Its intense beam of light catches my face and blinds me for a second. After he fires, a burning sensation erupts in my arm. He only grazes me. Numbed, but keen to kill, I raise my other hand and fire repeatedly with the pistol from my nightstand drawer. I close my eyes as I do it, holding my right hand over my left wrist to keep the weapon steady. I hear him fall."

"*Aye*, Germaine," he calls as I move toward him cautiously.

"The torch's powerful beam illuminates my path; he's lying on the floor, near his revolver. As I kick his gun out of reach he looks up at me. My Grandmaman's antique Limoges enamels lie on the hall table by his bedroom door."

"You did well, my dear, I . . . I . . . underesti- . . . mated . . . you . . . *ahhh*," he dies as a thin line of blood escapes from his mouth."

Germaine pauses to breathe, and her body trembles. But she looks relieved.

"Oh, Ingrid, thank God, I can say the rest as if it's in the past."

"My legs buckled and I slumped to the floor. I reached over to close his eyelids and began to shake furiously, perspiring and gasping for air. I couldn't stand. I crawled to the end of the hallway. I called for the butler. No answer. I crawled to the phone by the stairs and pulled it off the table. I called the police. I still couldn't stand. I was soaked in perspiration, and sat with the phone in my lap. I breathed hard, and tried to organize my thoughts. Another minute passed before I was calm enough to speak coherently."

Her voice trails off into silence. She's lost in that last image.

"Germaine? It's over," I massage her shoulders and give her a drink of water, then sit with my arms around her.

She revives from her saga and stares straight ahead, "He was always jealous and covetous: *obsessed* with things and people. He craved physical love but couldn't stand to be touched. He, we, had separate bedrooms all the years of our marriage. We never consummated it. We couldn't. I married him because I didn't want sex or children."

Then she looks at me. "He wanted you, Ingrid, above everyone else. Your father promised you to him. Édouard apparently was the last to know."

She switches the topic back to herself, and leaves me to wonder what Édouard didn't know?

"Dr. Duvette, remember those bruises on my arms as a child? You were the only man to show me tenderness when my nanny told you lies and made excuses. They never left me alone for fear I'd tell you all of it. My mother denied it to her grave.

"I begged her to let me go into religious life but she refused. She didn't wish her estate to end up with anyone else. I was trapped and afraid. I agreed to marry Édouard. His family was thrilled because he got access to my money." She pauses, "It gives me chills to tell you all this."

Alain steadies her with his warm hands on her shoulders.

I thought I knew Germaine—but her suffering gives me pause. Édouard's perversion has been a bigger pivotal link in our friendship than I ever realized. He covered our lives with his darkness. We had to wait a long time to share its exorcism. Now it's clear why I have always forgiven her social clumsiness.

She mutters, coming to grips with a truth she has denied for years, "Ingrid, he was a very, very deranged man. Whoever his victims were, the evidence will be in that locked room in the back of the barn."

My shoulders jerk the second time Édouard is described as deranged.

"Yes, we shall tell Jacques. He'll test everything in the morning," Alain says softly.

I look up as Duvette reassures her. In a gesture of sympathy he holds Germaine's icy cold hands and comforts her, "My dear, you have nothing to fear. What you've said here won't be necessary for the inquest. The evidence in the barn will indict him for sure. My poor angels, as if this war wasn't enough punishment."

Germaine looks at Alain with gratitude and excuses herself.

She smiles and says softly, "Ingrid, when I saw you wearing my wig in the courtroom, I knew I'd be strong enough to subdue him if I had to defend myself. Thank you for believing in me when I was so rude to you."

She carries Tutu from the room with Alain's support. I let go of a deep sigh. I knew he was referring to Amélie and Emil's deaths, and am thankful for his discretion not to mention them in front of Germaine. But what did she mean saying Édouard was the last to know?

Then the memory of my brooch takes shape. When Emil gave it to me in 1923 in lieu of an engagement ring, I was proud, and wore it the next week to a soirée to raise money for the orphanage.

People were commenting behind my back. The real culprit was my own father. *Mon père* had dishonored me. He told everyone I was to wed Édouard when I stated clearly I would not. He never accepted my decision. I was only well-educated chattel.

I remember the look on deVillement's face at the gala when Emil escorted me into the salon. Everyone applauded our engagement except Édouard, who stood there riddled with jealousy. His eyes were fixed on my new brooch. He hadn't believed my threat either. Even after the cow pie incident in the field. I thought I'd shaken off that sick glower of his clutching bondage, but it never left me. Édouard blamed me; not knowing my father had lied to him. In his mind I had betrayed him.

I hid Édouard's depravity rather than expose him, except when I wore that jewel like an amulet in defiance against the SS. I never knew how deeply that brooch was imbued with Édouard's hatred. I wore it as a symbol of my love for Emil.

I should have been more careful dealing with Édouard when he showed such twisted rigidity. You never think a person you've known all your life could be capable of harnessing deep hatred into a meticulous revenge. He made love to me through his hatred—the only genuine feeling he had left.

Someday when we're both stronger I'll tell Germaine my part of this sad history.

>><<

I enter the house quietly at 2:00 a.m. The salon door is ajar. The room is in darkness but the hearth glows weakly.

I go in to smother the embers and hear Dieter's voice, "Are you all right? It's late, Ingrid."

I'm surprised he's still awake. He sits in the rocker, wrapped in my shawl. His feet are resting on the coffee table, just in front of the hearth's dying warmth.

"I'm fine, Dieter. What about you?"

"I dozed off. I sent Guy to bed hours ago. Don't worry. Come here and tell me, please, how did it go with Germaine? Is she all right?"

I flick on a light and place two more logs onto the iron brazier to resurrect the fire while he talks. Switching off the lamp I sit on the floor in the shadows and lean against his soft corduroy pant leg. He reaches down and casually touches my shoulder. He does this often when there's not enough contrast of light and dark to see an outline of my body.

"Dieter, we have no idea the hell Germaine carved for herself married to Édouard," I'm chilled, just saying it.

I reach up to caress his fingers and pause. A fleeting sense of loss drains something from me. Is the room's SS history inflicting itself on me? No, it's not this room. It's him. This is my reaction to a new and unfamiliar awareness of Dieter.

In one week my body has thoroughly taken on his blindness. Now I perceive through touch what he used to say with his beautiful eyes. Is that why I sit here brushing against his leg like an affection-seeking pet? Dieter was like the rest of us before his torture. He showed his emotions through his eyes, or he hid them. Since the torture his feelings show less and less through his eyes. Unable to suppress his emotions, they live in his flesh when he can't speak of them. And when I touch his body I sense his feelings . . . as if I, too, am blind . . . or I am . . . oh God . . . a *dog*? His . . . *pet*?

"Are you all right, Ingrid?" Of course, he reaches down and strokes my head, "I thought you were about to say something, chérie, and you became silent."

He's as aware of my internal being as I am his. How has this happened so quickly? Maybe unearthing Germaine's history with Édouard tonight has forced me to face how close I came to losing myself. I haven't explained my feelings to anyone for years, and now Dieter demands answers from a deeply personal place in my heart.

I'm used to isolation. I hid from everyone's questions and pretended to be safe. My concubinage was a wall of shame. No one wanted to deal with it, and the men who led me to it never took care of me.

Vraiment, speak your mind now, Ingrid. Really girl, you asked this man to live here.

"You feel cold, Ingrid. You're sure you're all right?" He reacts to my fleeting shiver.

"Yes, Dieter. I'm fine." He knows I spent the war trembling.

A knock at the door, when new clandestine action was proposed, after sex with the SS, killing that young Nazi, when Mueller was shot, Dieter was lost, Marta was beaten, Amélie murdered, Édouard attacked me, I was molested in the street, my head was sheared . . . my litany of hell, a lifetime ago. This man brought me to it and recited it with me. Dieter knows what my nervousness means. His query is an old test to measure how desperate I am. Then he can resist touching me. But now, in his blindness his fingers search for me.

"I'm sorry, Ingrid, is this the chill of a 'dark night?'"

"Oui, the darkest. DeVillement is dead, Dieter. His sick obsession with me is finished."

Dieter says nothing but his fingertips release tension. Édouard scared him too. I wonder if he will ever share why with me. My shame makes me swallow hard. I made Dieter into a Lancelot when I was his adulteress.

"Ingrid, I need to tell you something."

"What is it?" I yawn, my voice fatigues, the fire warms me toward the oblivion of sleep.

"It's about losing Amélie. Maybe this isn't the time. You sound very tired."

At the mention of Amélie, I wake up suddenly and am all ears.

"No, Dieter, tell me."

It matters to him and we haven't talked as equals. He's been my leader and I've been his follower. "Go on, I'm listening."

"I cannot get her out of my thoughts, Ingrid. When I realized she was dead, I was already in a casket. I thought we'd be together after the Liberation. It was only a few weeks. I was going to the forest for safety. Alain would tell her once the Boches had left."

"Oui, that was logical, Dieter."

Oh no, the hearse in the yard? Sacrebleu! My ears are on fire! It wasn't Jacques talking out loud to himself. He was talking with Dieter. In that coffin in the hearse, and he doesn't know I was there. I can't tell him. Not tonight.

"Ingrid, she was there, in Alain and Jacques's arms. I couldn't breathe. Her lavender-bergamot talisman choked my breath in that coffin. Thirty-five years of marriage evaporated. I couldn't hold her, say good-bye to her." His voice drops to a whisper.

I touch his shoulder. He withdraws, shredding his heart with guilt and blame, running his hand through his hair, just as Jacques said he would.

"Jesus, Ingrid, my choices nailed me into that coffin. My life in the Résistance left her dead. My noble deed was a colossal waste."

"Dieter, no! You can't blame yourself. You couldn't control what happened. The pain of profound loss eats at you now. You need time to put your life back together."

"My self-doubt is strangling my will to live, Ingrid," his voice is hoarse.

Oh God, I have to keep him talking. If I don't he'll swallow his blame in silence and resent his life as a blind man. I can't believe it! I was there and he was alive in that box.

"What happened when Jacques drove you to the cemetery to meet Jean Claude?"

"The shock was too much for me, Ingrid. I was weak. My energy plummeted and dragged my emotions into retreat. Every time I felt faint I squeezed Amélie's sachet, and its burst of fragrance restored me. That little packet was the last token of love she gave me. Jacques shoved it through the hole in the left side of the coffin."

I remember Jacques's strange sentence that had no context.

Dieter stifles his sobs through clenched teeth. I get up on my knees to embrace his shoulders and whisper into his ear,

"You need time to heal, Dieter."

"I'm lost, Ingrid, useless."

"What happened at the cemetery, Dieter?"

"Jacques told Jean Claude about Amélie's death—that she was killed by a flying brick in an alley. That just as Jacques was leaving with me, the police had brought her to the morgue.

"Then Jean Claude said, 'Sacrebleu, what's going on, sir? This sounds like what happened when I was in Paris.' I can't forget what he said, Ingrid, after that, 'A few highly placed people there used the war as an excuse to vent their private obsessions and take pleasure from denouncing others. Merde! It was a sick vengeance, a political pornography.

"Jean Claude said it was why he had to leave, Ingrid. The bastards were going to silence him, next. 'Strange,' Jean Claude went on, 'as we finally begin winning this damn war, this great man loses everything. He meant *me*, Ingrid. A vendetta is the only way it makes sense.'"

"He was right, Dieter. Look, tuck it away for now. It's late and we both need to rest."

"I don't deserve to rest. I refused to see the obvious. Look what it has cost me, Ingrid."

"Dieter, in time you'll accept it and learn from it. But not tonight, all right? Let it go for now. You need sleep."

"Oui, chérie," his voice full of remorse. A log falls in the hearth. He changes the subject.

"How was Germaine?"

"Exhausted but relieved. The police will report it as self-defense. I'm thankful I never deserted her. Tonight she had to admit to untidy intimacies so Alain would know Édouard's perverted nature. I didn't want to push her. I hope when she awakens this morning she will realize I did it for her sake and Emil's."

"Emil? What do you mean, chérie?"

"Dieter, I should have told Emil about Édouard's sadistic side when he proposed marriage, but I felt safe with him and I abandoned the idea. I never thought my husband's death could be tied to Édouard's depravity. Now it has scarred you, too."

"Ingrid, we have the remainder of the war to deal with," but his fingers tense for a second saying this. His sweeping denial won't work against the pain he carries. Forcing him to reconcile his feelings and his loss—it's not my job.

Before I can say anything to Dieter, I need to understand how Édouard set the stage for my destiny. His vendetta was a seduction . . . screaming his wretched childhood at my young, sympathetic heart. His sickness squeezed me until I feared him, yet I'm grateful he revealed me to myself. I'm sorry for Édouard, despite Emil and Amélie's deaths, and Dieter's blindness. His sickness still makes me squirm, but I cannot hate him.

Dieter and I are silent for a few more minutes, locked into reviewing our private woes.

The fire's heat relaxes me. As it burns stronger I yawn and smile, looking up at Dieter.

"I can see your face in the firelight, Ingrid. You're glowing. I can almost see the details of your features. Why do you appear different tonight?"

"A part of me has been liberated more deeply than France," I answer, closing my eyes and my mind under the weight of this evening's revelations. "Come, Dieter, let me lead you to your room before I retire for the night."

"In a few minutes, please; let's not waste the fire."

We sit quietly for another half hour.

Chapter Thirty-Four

A Ray of Sun Toward Winter

6 October 1944, Friday

Over time Dieter's dependency deepens our friendship. We have long talks about Marta. She does her best to entertain him, playing piano, flute, and singing. With his help I begin to tear down the wall of misunderstanding between my daughter and me—a wall mortared with the indignity of my double life. I ignored her when she needed me.

I want to tell Marta I watched her struggle in that alley, helpless to stop it and prevent Amélie's death, but reliving that pain nauseates me. I know now why other people refuse to talk about the Résistance and the Occupation. I promise not to hide from my history, but I need time to breathe freely again if I'm to forgive my neighbors and reestablish our trust.

Dieter and I attempt to talk about the war and who we are now. We've become suspended in time. We are no longer casual musical colleagues, political Allies or camarades de la Résistance. The immensity of what we shared hangs between us without that impetus to continue the excitement and growth we fostered in each other. We have changed.

Each afternoon he sits quietly, head bowed in contemplation, in front of the receiving room's east window. I nap on the divan, recovering from exhaustion per Duvette's orders, in that same room with Dieter. He practices violin to discipline his fingers to feel their way across the strings. I accompany him on the piano. I read newspapers to him and we listen to the radio reports of allied progress pushing the Wehrmacht back into their lair.

This parallel living goes on for almost three weeks after Édouard's death. Slowly, a strange discomfort grows between us I can't interpret. I want to say something gentle to soothe Dieter as he deals with his devastating injury, but he can't misconstrue it as pity. I have to subdue my desire to speak on a personal note. He's distant when we're alone, without the distraction of perfunctory business. The loss of Amélie and his vision overshadows almost everything Dieter wishes to communicate.

Our freedom becomes increasingly disorienting. Our every touch is complicated by the strain of profound change. The stricture of his marriage, and his conflicting roles as the promoter of and confessor to the pain of my double life are no longer familiar wedges tucked safely between us.

Our closeness feels illicit; too soon and so strong I suppress my heart. I'm hesitant around him. I melt when he negotiates space and brushes lightly against me. These moments of reawakened femininity jar my widowhood. I feel closer to Dieter since Édouard's death, but life does come closer now that I'm genuinely safe after years of hell.

In early October, a month after coming back into my world, Dieter asks me to go with him to gather items of warmer clothing from his home. This is the first time he enters it since his bogus death in May.

Brightly colored autumn perennials in planters beckon us from each side of the front door. They remind me of Amélie and I half expect her to greet us.

"Be careful, Dieter, remember the high spot as you step onto the threshold."

I unlock the front door and lead him inside. We pause as he breathes in the fragrance of his past. What is best for my dear mentor in these poignant moments? He needs to grieve. It's a pity he can't see the afternoon light weave its lovely shadows through his music room's soft peach walls, cobalt blue settee and white curtains. Amélie's delicate embroidery and tatting appliquéd on the armrests and pillows are beyond the grasp of his eyes.

"Do you want to be alone, Dieter?"

"No, Ingrid. Stay, please. Lead me around the house. I need to say my good-byes here."

It's the first time he speaks of not living here. Slowly, I guide him from room to room. He anchors one hand to my shoulder and the other reaches out for his Amélie. I watch his expression as he touches each familiar object. A lifetime of memories must flood his senses. I marvel at his power to surrender to heart-rending loss. Quiet, remote, he searches the familiar patterns of past movements; to pick up an instrument, reach for a tobacco pouch, arrange sheet music on its stand. He's desperate to shape this space that's empty without his vision to define it. He conducts his funeral march in touch and sound with dignified reserve.

I don't want to impose upon Dieter's private mourning, yet I too relive the past, steering him from room to room. The war has left me drained and easily weepy. Emotions stalled by wartime deception three years ago sputter to life again. They drive my consciousness. I fear their power and neediness. I thought to be at peace would be satisfaction enough, but it isn't. I want life back with a fervent yearning like a parched man in a desert craves water. This little home is the past, a mausoleum, charming, yet a tomb like Germaine's sprawling estate.

Dieter leads me slowly through each room.

"Here, sit with me, Ingrid," he pauses by the bedroom window. "This was Amélie's side of the bed. She always looked at the flowers in her garden and never drew the curtains. We had privacy from thick shrubbery and trees. I feel the afternoon sun and see the light now."

Sitting here in his wife's shadow feels odd. I must run away or stake my claim and can do neither. Then why do I feel a deep wave of attraction for him, warmth again as a woman should? These past weeks we've lived in close proximity but never intimately. Only now do I blush. Is he thinking differently of me, too, at this moment? I wonder. Oh well, he's alone now and blind.

An uncomfortably long silence passes until he confesses,

"Please don't be bitter toward me, Ingrid. I apologize for the pain you've suffered. I can't forgive myself for destroying your privacy and self-respect as a woman. I exposed you to too many indignities."

This is about the resistance between us.

"You never gave me the soothing I wanted, Dieter. Instead, you gave me the strength to suffer quietly. I needed that. What else could you do? I would have been arrested had I allowed my rage to flow and then who knows what would have happened?"

I cannot tell him I've been forced to distill the pain of childhood from widowhood and loving desire from sexual degradation. I needed help to see it and he led me to my precipice. Restraint has disciplined my pain. I recognized my fear and had to get past it for the sake of sheer survival. I hardly know myself anymore.

Now Dieter reaches out, afraid I'll shower him with scorn. Gently, he removes the silk scarf and wig and touches my shorn head. I stop my inner chatter, tremble, and let him kiss the scars.

"It's all right, Dieter, it's over," I whisper.

My mind is wild to go forward but my flesh cannot forget. The memory of my disgrace . . . with him close . . . makes me sad. Because of my numbness I do not stop him.

He embraces me, rocks me gently and strokes my shoulders, speaking softly in my ear.

"Chérie, we're free to begin a new life like Marta said. Let it happen. May you be a happy woman once more and may Heaven give you solace for what I've done to you."

I pull back from his embrace, startled by how sincere he is. Is he showing me respect? Or, is this a remembrance of his dead wife that has nothing to do with me? Either way, I must answer.

"Dieter, I made a choice. I'm not sorry. Please, don't blame yourself."

"But I drove you hard. It wasn't right. Look what they did to you."

He touches my face. I grasp his hands and entwine my fingers through his to reiterate that I'm not weak anymore. I hope his concern is for me, for us.

"Dieter, you saved my life. I was drowning in the past and you gave me purpose. You pulled me forward to conquer childish fear and loneliness. I would do it again except for your eyes and your Amélie."

"No, Ingrid, you'd do it regardless of my eyes and my Amélie. She knew she'd sacrifice herself. She saw my torture coming before I disappeared."

"How did you know that?" He looks away.

"Dieter, I'm sorry. I've no right to ask. Please forgive me if I've caused you more pain."

He turns his back to me. I withdraw from his ambivalence. He wants to say something, but can't or won't. I try to be patient, but my need for respect and recognition stand in the way. I push him,

"Why couldn't you trust me with your disappearance after all I risked for everyone in the Underground? Losing you was too frightening, Dieter."

"I surrendered to save the whole operation . . . especially you and Amélie. Beyond the names of your refugees I knew secret Maquis positions in the mountains. The trail of my torture reached back to dark deals that had nothing to do with the war. I suspected Édouard and couldn't prove it. If he thought I was dead, he'd be free to pursue you and he did."

"Why didn't you leave Duchamps for safe hiding, Dieter? You acquiesced to those butchers and lost too much," and I wonder: what would our relationship be like if you weren't blind?

"Ingrid, you would have been too vulnerable if Édouard thought I was alive. Your life would have become a living hell. He would have raped you worse than Mueller did for as long as he could. My 'death' protected you from his real venom. Instead of playing with you before he fled, he concocted a bigger scheme to own you and force you to go with him. He could take his time, justified by the court's conviction. I hoped others would see it and save you even if I couldn't. For your sake, my sweet, for the rest of your life my sacrifice was the only answer. I provoked the viper to strike and he did."

Yes, I think, and SS-Obersturmführer Roemler saved me from murdering a second time.

Dieter pauses, his voice is strong at first, but dies out in his next breath.

"I lost her without so much as a parting word, a kiss or a moment to bury my lips in her neck. Why did I live through that torture when *she* had to die?"

Dieter looks at me, wanting to tell me something yet hesitating.

"Free yourself, Dieter. Let it out. Tell me, mon ami."

"Ingrid, I blinded myself with my choices."

Grief overwhelms him. He bows his head fighting back tears. His heartache is upon us both. I can't hold him in my arms. His frame is so large I kneel on the bed and rest his head on my bosom. His tears moisten the bodice of my dress and his strong arms grip my waist. I stroke his beautiful thick hair and kiss his forehead, cheeks and ears. I'm floating, intoxicated with his masculinity. This is crazy. I'm falling in love with him.

He recovers his composure and kisses my lips softly, then firmly. He lowers me to the bed, embraces my shoulders and stretches his body over me. The pressure of his torso and the heat between us makes my womb contract and ache to receive him, to begin climbing with him. Then I stop, smothered by our sudden passion, and numb just as quickly. I can't go any further and drift away to the time in the Citroën on the side of the road. He lets go of me reluctantly.

"What is it, Ingrid? Why do you seem far away?" He releases my arms and I sit up.

"I'm confused."

"No, you're not. You felt real love and then you stopped. I'm the first man you touch with desire since Emil. You feel violated by my demands of the past, don't you? Ingrid, tell me the truth."

"Sorry, Dieter, I can't say anything more."

He's too distraught. His reserve crumbles. His pain rises up now after months of denial.

"Damn it, woman, talk to me. I can't see your face. You're only a blur."

Insistent, Dieter interrupts my shock at how profound his grief must be. He's frustrated. I shake his shoulders to bring him outside his new blank world. It swirls, anchorless. His eyes can no longer read my familiar face. Our energy is shared—but now it's out of focus.

"I don't have the answers, Dieter. I only know you must stop feeling sorry for yourself. You're a powerful man with a brilliant talent to perform and teach music."

"Thank you, Ingrid, I needed to hear you say that."

This sensation is bizarre. I need love but inside my body is dull, littered with death. Will I ever get past it? Lost, I let him kiss my cheeks. I can't hurt him anymore.

"Chérie, many times I wanted to take you in my arms when you were in pain, but didn't dare. I couldn't complicate your life or undermine my love for Amélie. Now you and I float like wrecks in a dead calm on a moonless night. We shared too much under such grueling conditions. We became too self-protective. And now we're used up."

"Is that what this is about, Dieter? Because I can't help being drawn to you."

He grasps my hands and searches my face through his fog with a new fear in his voice.

"Is that perfectly natural, Ingrid? I'm an old, wounded bull, and not what you deserve." He smiles—nostalgic, but hopeful—against his doubt.

"Oh no, Dieter, it feels right."

I can't leave the wrong impression. He'll be renewed if he knows I want him.

But how could he love me or I him? I don't understand my feelings now. I barely think beyond my flesh. I'm no prize for any man. Can't be put in my place anymore and don't care about convention, power, money or politics. Unpredictable, emotional, opinionated and rooted in myself, unlike Amélie, the saintly woman he lost.

My body recoils from his touch as the intimacy of their bedroom deflates my desire.

"Look at me, Ingrid. Be sure. I'm blind and older by eleven years."

I put my fingers to his lips to stop him.

"No Dieter. Your infirmity and your age are not the resistance between us."

"Then what is?"

"Me, Dieter, it's me. I'm afraid to feel. The war did it. I looked over my shoulder every day and had no private world. I wasn't safe in my home. My every move was calculated to be deliberately unsatisfying. I couldn't risk romantic love."

"My sweet soul, I am very sorry."

"I must have asked for it, Dieter. If it takes the rest of my life I'll find out why."

Looking at him, I think, dear soul, that story may not be shared with you. This Nazi mistress pressed her desire for love into little dregs forced through a sharp metal sieve of endurance. A first pressing of grapes, her feelings were fermenting tears shed in the arms of evil men. Her honest desire to be loved became acrid like vinegar. Dieter will blame himself.

"Dieter, you have no idea what horrible things I've done."

"Ingrid, I listened to you rage. I put you there. I used you. You must forgive me. We were trapped and haunted by our inability to help each other be safe. Just like the Jews we were crossing."

His heart is finally emptied with these last awful words. If he fears he's a piece of my past, his ears will burn to hear my next words.

"Maybe you did use me then, Dieter, but I'm stronger for it. You couldn't get away with it today," laughing lightly, "Perhaps we do belong together."

"Is that bad, chérie?"

"No, not now."

He catches the lilt of hope behind my words. His spirit is humble. He can't accept what I've said. Either he can't believe the suppleness of my heart or he fears I'll be capricious, and ultimately throw him aside.

"Does it make you unhappy, Ingrid?"

"I don't know, Dieter. Be patient and understand I'm estranged from myself, not you."

I lower my head and push my Gestapo demons to the back of my mind.

"I've become coarse; my body won't surrender to love. Maybe it can't recognize it anymore. Or perhaps it's this bedchamber. This was Amélie's side of your bed."

He raises my chin and stares into my weary face that he can no longer see.

"No, no, Ingrid, don't think like that. We need time to heal, to live normal lives. To be certain of our feelings. Please don't let any ghosts come between us."

"I don't want to but I can't wait, Dieter. I don't want another day of emptiness. You've been a widower for three months. I've been alone and abused for five long years. I deserve some joy. If I can't trust a man's touch, your touch, and whoever might figure in my future, I will shrivel inside and *my* 'occupation' in *the* Occupation will have murdered me."

He hears my wild frustration and fears my wicked self-doubt.

"Ingrid, stop this." Exasperated, he grasps my shoulders and forces me to listen,

"My sweet, please, let's go away together, right now. Can you do that?"

"Yes. But, where do we go?"

"Some place where we have no history. We need to start fresh, take long walks in the sunshine and breathe mountain air like free people. Where we can be alone. Are you ready?"

I kiss his cheek, slide off the bed and open the armoire to find his winter clothes.

I drive us to the perimeter of a nearby village tucked away in the foothills of the Juras. We're in the same Citroën I drove that afternoon the Gestapo almost checked our papers. I glance up at its worn cloth ceiling and smile at the faded imprints of my shoes. They hover over us like a hedonist's blessing. I remark about it and we laugh nervously. Dieter is reserved. Perhaps he tries not to expect anything.

He appears lost in the memory of what happened that windy day when his eye was tearing badly; he couldn't see until I plucked out the leaf stem. I reach over and stroke his arm to pull him to the present.

"Dieter, please understand, it was. . ."

And he finishes my thought, "Meant to be? Ingrid, not you, too?"

"What do you mean, not me, too?"

"Did you see then what Amélie already knew about my eyes?"

When I hear this, my first inclination is to stop the car by the side of the road. Then I think better of it. He's realizing a life with me will be an uphill battle if he can't see past the war and make peace with himself. I'm not sure I'm strong enough to drag us both up that mountain or that it's my place to try.

I pause too long and he's on edge, asking,

"What's the matter? You're not answering. You don't agree?"

"Yes and no, Dieter. I didn't have any premonition about your eyes that day."

"What do you mean?"

"What I saw or Amélie saw isn't important. The message was for you. What's done is done. You have to look at your new world from a different perspective."

"This blindness serves no purpose. I'm not finished with my work."

"That depends on how you look at life, Dieter."

"I'm no good, helpless, like this."

I slow the car to a stop. I hear Jacques saying, "Give yourself some time to heal, Ingrid. Don't rush back into life too fast."

I tell Dieter, "If that's how you feel, Monsieur Van der Kreuzier, we can quit right now."

"I don't understand?"

"Your image of life is too narrow. Figure out what's important. Surrender what you think you're made of to find out who you really are. Raising Stefan and Marta taught me to do that, as much as you did pushing me around in the Résistance. I lived by my intuition. Few men ever perceive life that way unless something stops them dead in their tracks."

"Like my blindness?"

"Oui. Congratulations, like your blindness. After all, *you* said I would have to pass the person I was and not resist the one I would become. Maybe now it's your turn?"

I wince for condescending while inside I fight to face my own future. He says nothing but I hope he thinks about it. I reach over and squeeze his hand. He smiles for a second but his face reflects pain, not security. His hand is dull like a lump of clay. Has he given up already? Oh God, I don't want to babysit another consciousness so high and so talented. A stupid man like my father would drink himself to death slowly. A man like Dieter would become suicidal—as I was in the middle of my whoring collaboration.

Sacrebleu! Everything is in reverse now! I am the driver and he is my passenger. The responsibility weighs on me. We travel the rest of the way in silence. By the end of the ride he's regained his composure. He, too, doesn't want anything to spoil this impromptu tryst.

We pull up to a charming inn. The owners know Dieter and are discreet Résistants. We are left to ourselves to hike in the afternoon sun. I teach him to walk with a stick. At first I guide him and then let him walk alone. Dieter doesn't want pity. He has to believe I want him, wounds and all.

He has shared a few fleeting details of his torture. Perhaps the future will unload that brutal story in the dispassionate clinical vocabulary of an ophthalmologist's diagnosis. But today we abandon our wounds of the flesh to become the breeze and the sun that strengthen us. The air is fresh and clean, fragrant with a final blush of autumn wild flowers.

Our conversation weaves a tapestry of events from war years basted together with feelings we couldn't express before. We move through uneven fields, some newly harvested, some readied for new seed and others fallow. Their alternating dormant and fertile patterns intersect as our lonely lives once did.

We were terribly alone, even when surrounded by loving family. The stiff silence resisting the enemy and adhering to risky choices under the axe of Occupation couldn't be shared. There was real danger admitting what one felt in one's heart. Speaking the truth meant risking death to protect that truth. In my darkest moments my flesh wasn't mine, but on loan to save others.

I learned it's impossible to kill an eternal consciousness. How will I handle the guilt from my murder living in half my heart, if I fill the other half with Dieter's blindness? In the midst of these dark thoughts Dieter says,

"I'm blessed to have your wisdom, Ingrid."

"Please, Dieter, stop being dramatic. I had to coach Marta to walk again."

"No, your tenacity and confidence inspire me. I can hear the fear leaving you, Ingrid."

He grasps my hand tightly when the terrain changes unexpectedly under his feet. He strains to see my shadowy figure move with easy grace in contrast to his hesitating gait. We laugh at his clumsiness when a cow in the next meadow moos along as we sing our favorite arias as loud as we like—my plaintive soprano and Dieter's booming baritone. How can we escape assuming what the other thinks after being such an important part of each other's past?

The sun lowers and the mountain breeze turns chilly. We return from our hike. My spirit is tranquil with Dieter beside me. I'm at a crossing, savoring enough peace and freedom to wonder about my future on the other shore. How to cope after the twisted exhilaration of war? Part of me craves that wild life of doing what was honorable and right against a tide of evil. Yet nothing will ever be the same. I must readjust to a semblance of normal existence.

At times I sit and do nothing and find pleasure in it. When the world is crazed with death, whether one actively shields an innocent life or lives in silent witness to the values of love and decency, true resistance becomes a practice of contentment. What's my purpose now?

These thoughts crowd my mind as Dieter and I climb the stairs to separate, but adjoining, rooms. The walk has been tiring. I lie down. The gentle tap of raindrops from a sudden afternoon shower quiets my mind. We just missed being caught in it on the plateau. I watch rapidly shifting clouds move outside the window. In the distance there's a hint of a rainbow. I listen to the wind, tempted to believe in the landscape's message after three years cut off from trusting its trees, clouds, my dear Doubs and myself as part of it.

My mind and body are blank and peaceful tucked under the soft mohair shawl. As I drift off Dieter bangs around next door, finding his way. Somewhere in the oblivion of sleep a hesitant knock at the connecting door rouses me.

"Ingrid, can you help me, please?"

"What is it?" I climb out of a deep slumber, disoriented, and open the door.

"Oh no, Dieter, you've cut yourself shaving. Let me help you."

At home Guy spoils him. Guy does things for Dieter that are impossible for him to do without his vision. Now it's my turn.

"I'm sorry to trouble you, Ingrid, but Guy just sharpened my razor."

He stands there bleeding and rubbing his cheeks, feeling for spots he missed.

"It's all right. Let me get to it. Put your hand down for a second, please."

"No, thanks, I think I can get it now. Watch me."

"No, wait, Dieter, you're applying too much pressure."

Then a flurry of hands moves over his face. Each pair is after its own end and neither work together.

"Ouch! Damn." He snags my finger with his razor and a bright red droplet appears. I put my finger in my mouth to stem the pain. The wound is slow to coagulate.

"Oh, sorry, Ingrid. I didn't mean to cut you."

"Dieter, let me do it, please."

I'm a little perturbed over this minor emergency. He's making a mess of his face and I can't do it for him, or criticize him.

"You know, I'm confident you can do it yourself. Just wash the blood off the side of your cheek. Can you see it in the mirror?"

"Oh sure, thanks."

He closes the door. I wrap my finger in gauze by the sink and stare into the mirror. Then return to bed and snuggle in the shawl like a caterpillar in a cocoon. In less than a minute there's another knock. I would love a nap but. . . .

"Yes, Dieter, I'm coming."

The poor dear stands there like a forlorn little boy with washcloth in hand—too aware and ashamed of his neediness to ask for help. His peripheral vision on the right side isn't clear. He can't see where to wash.

I burst into giddy laughter at this big strong man's little boy helplessness. Immediately, I apologize profusely for being inappropriate. Dieter falls all over me saying he's sorry for not letting me fix it in the first place. Finally he's silent. I shave the uneven areas and whisk the washcloth over the contours of his handsome face. The door closes. Our little emergency is over in a minute. Or is it?

This casual incident leaves a deep impression. I stare into the vanity mirror. Do I have enough love for this? Do I need this relationship because of loneliness? I recall his words,

"For your sake, my sweet, for the rest of your life my sacrifice was the only answer."

Do I owe him my very being? Is this a guilt-driven entanglement when I want freedom? I pull away from such thoughts. I want only today, this evening to discover him without promising anything. Is that possible? The war's over and I'm safe. Yet my finger bled too long. My blood is anemic from years of strain. I'm not ready. We finish dressing and enter the corridor at the same moment to descend the stairs for dinner.

I'm ravenous. During the war I ate in a state of panic and hardly absorbed my food. After a while everything was tasteless. Tonight Dieter and I share a delicious meal with our hosts, capped off with a cognac their grandpère made in 1918 after the Great World War.

This evening I taste liberty. Dieter forced this fragmented little girl to pull herself into a whole woman. She needs to be carefree and drink in the present without shame.

I look at Dieter across the table. His face is flushed with sun and his eyes blaze with life despite their injury. He sparkles as he jokes with our hosts. I listen to his voice and observe every mannerism. I see a man of hope, still positive after devastating loss.

If we're only compatible for this brief interlude, I want to curl up in Dieter's arms—even now, when the ache for him is great, and he can't see me. I whisper my yearning, "Please, Dieter, let's try again."

He hears my thoughts, thanks our hosts rather abruptly and stands behind my chair with his usual chivalry. Slowly he feels our way to the door and leads me outside. We walk a short distance from the farmhouse into the silver white moonlight to the inn's herb and rose gardens.

I lead him across the steppingstones, around a few muddy patches not yet dried from the afternoon shower. The whole valley rolls out below us bathed in a peaceful glow through verdant mists. They soften the jagged shapes of the mountains, barely green-black and charcoal-violet in the moonlight.

He puts his arm around me as we drink in the brisk perfumed night air of autumn.

"Sweet woman," he murmurs into my ear, "let me wipe away your loneliness and hold you close. I need you, Ingrid."

"Yes, my sweet," on my tiptoes to embrace him.

He lifts me up onto the low stone edging around the garden. We're face to face. He removes my wig and touches my stubbly head, kissing my forehead and neck. I tremble with anticipation.

"You are kissing my barren head for the third time, Dieter."

"Your crown, my dove, a symbol of your surrender to love. Your hair grows longer as we move forward. It's a marker of time. You are stronger and more serene each day."

"It's coming in all grey."

"A measure of your compassion and restraint," he strokes my head and face.

I remember Amélie's words in June shortly after the Résistance staged his funeral. In her strange disjointed conversation she told me to share the same devotion I had shown in healing Marta with anyone else who might need it. She was entrusting her beloved Dieter to me. I'm humbled to think this courageous man could find me worthy after sharing his life with her pure spirit. She had grace I don't understand. Perhaps this second opportunity for happiness will nurture genuine gratitude, and a wisp of humility I never had before this war.

That tiny spark of eternal soul deep inside me is hopeful again. Dieter's need binds me to its flame. His light is irresistible. It makes me more afraid of myself than of him. May I honor his spirit and carry his gift of love forward into a new life of healing, together.

And so it begins. I caress his cheek: the one I slapped hundreds of refugees ago, washed clean just now before dinner, and whisper, "I love you."

End of Book One

An Informal Appendix:

Historical References to WWII
and the French Occupation

Chapter One

Page 3

THE DOUBS RIVER, AND THE JURA MOUNTAINS THROUGH WHICH IT
FLOWS, are the settings for this story. The Doubs is 453 km and runs
northeasterly, along the French and Swiss borders, and then turns,
forming a 'u' and moves southwest, down to Besançon, the capital of
the Franche-Comté department—before it feeds into the Saône River.
Dubious as a river, its name is from the Latin: *dubius*. Its course of flow
changes three times. It varies from being a lake to a shallow streamed
to doubled waterways, and almost half of it isn't navigable. The region,
however, is known for its natural beauty and for many waterfalls in the
mountains. Nazi checkpoints were closely guarded because of the area's
proximity to Occupied and Un-Occupied zones. Checkpoints made
ferrying of Jews hidden in vehicles and boats very dangerous.

Page 6

GAUL refers to the ancient Western French region during the Iron Age and Roman eras. Visigoth refers to a nomadic tribe of Germans from 376 AD who sacked Rome in 410. Gaul was Christianized by the 8th century.

Page 8

VICHY—AND OCCUPIED FRANCE: The German Occupation of France, from June 1940 to October 1944, was a result of French defeat. France's democratically elected government was dissolved. German Secret Police, SS, Gestapo, and French military police, the Milice (created in 1943), subjugated the occupied zone of northern France. In the southern, unoccupied zone, the Nazis ruled through MARÉCHAL PÉTAIN'S puppet fascist government in Vichy, France. In November 1942 all of France was occupied—until October 1944. Maréchal Pétain, an eighty-four-year-old veteran of WWI "gave himself to France" to lead the fascist-dictated Vichy government that followed the orders of the German Reich to gradually order Frenchmen to work in German factories as slave labor and to systematically remove the Jewish population, both foreign and naturalized Jewish citizens of France. Accounts vary, but approximately 93,000 Jews in France were deported to, and died, in Nazi death camps. Also under Vichy, Germany commandeered industry and agriculture— leaving the French to subsist on rationed food with no petrol. Pétain was tried and convicted of treason after WWII. He died in jail at 95.

Page 9

HUNS, FRITZIES AND KRAUTS ARE BRITISH SLANG TERMS FOR GERMAN SOLDIERS; MOST FRENCH USED BOCHES, AND DORYPHORES. THE FRENCH USED BOCHES IN WWI AND WWII. It is an alteration of Alboche, a blend of German and a French dialect word caboche meaning cabbage, as in a blockhead, without smarts. Doryphores is a name for potato beetles used in rural French farming areas. The name signifies the simultaneous occupation by the Nazis and potato beetles in 1941. An invasion of beetles exacerbated food shortages requisitioned for the German army, which, like the beetles, ate the French food supply, denigrating the French to rationing. Germans were avid potato eaters, so French children were charged to collect the beetles in the fields and post the slogan: "Death to the Doryphores." Ingrid uses Teuton, a poetic term, to defame the enemy with her sneering upper caste arrogance.

Page 10

OBERSTURMFÜHRER is a rank within the SS, roughly equal to Lieutenant, and had a wide range of responsibilities: staff aide, Gestapo officer, supervisor of a concentration camp, and/or Waffen-SS platoon commander. Obersturmführers were overseers of regions with active French Résistance cells that sabotaged railways, protected British fliers and sheltered Jews.

THE SS (SICHERHEITSPOLIZEI), SECURITY POLICE AND GESTAPO (GEHEIME STAATSPOLIZEI), GERMAN SECRET STATE POLICE WERE ORIGINALLY SEPA-RATE ORGANIZATIONS. THE SS WERE PARAMILITARY SECRET SECURITY SERVICE POLICE OR SCHUTZSTAFFEL. The SS instigated the "Final Solution" and hunted Jews in France. They were the criminal, Nazi element respon-sible for the worst civilian reprisals in WWII France. Heinrich Himmler headed both the SS and Gestapo by 1939. The SS could command Wehrmacht troops. The Gestapo could not, but both investigated cases of treason, espionage and sabotage in France against Nazi domination and outright deported or murdered civilians. The SS specifically targeted Jews. The two groups had similar jobs. THEN, IN 1943, THE FRENCH MILICE, (PARAMILITARY POLICE), BECAME AN EVEN MORE DANGEROUS FRENCH VERSION OF THE SS AND GESTAPO. Hitler's vengeance against the Alsatians for resisting German rule ordered French Alsatians conscripted into the SS and forced them to badger their own French people. Nazis directing the worst French reprisal at Oradour-Sur-Glane ordered Alsatian Waffen SS in their unit to kill French citizens and burn the town. The Alsatians were called maigré-nous, meaning "against our will." (See Chapter Ten, page 486, of this Appendix for more about Milice.)

Page 11

MARIANNE, ALLEGORICAL SYMBOL (ON FRENCH EURO) OF LIBERTY AND REASON was developed in 1792 during the French Revolution. Cultural icon of The Republic of France, Marianne is depicted as a young female wearing a liberty or Phrygian cap, with a deep décolletage, and referred to as a symbol of French sovereignty. Heroine Marianne—soul of French Liberty, was identified with French Republican secret societies dedicated to the overthrow of the Second Empire (Bonaparte regime of 1852 to 1870) before the Third Republic In France.

Page 12

BRITISH WAR BROADCASTS OVER BBC radio gave war news in the French language, "Les Français parlent au Français" to build morale on the continent. Coded messages were sent to the French from the London Resistance headed by General de Gaulle. The Resistance program started with a "Pon pon pon ponnn," the opening of Beethoven's Fifth Symphony that is also the Morse code for the letter 'V' for Victory. Vichy outlawed ownership of radios— especially short wave radios. People hid their radios in closets and attics. French news was censored. Most French presses were forced out of business or closed down in protest. French people in the Doubs and Jura regions so close to Switzerland listened to Swiss radio when they could, along with the BBC.

Page 14

PIERRE LAVAL (28 June 1883 – 15 October 1945) was a French politician who served as Prime Minister of France from January 1931 to February 1932 and from June 1935 to January 1936. Laval was Vice-President of Vichy's Council of Foreign Ministers from 1940 to 1944. He epitomized French collaboration with Hitler. Laval was executed by a firing squad in 1945.

Page 14

COMTÉ FROMAGE IS A FRENCH CHEESE MADE FROM UNPASTEURIZED COW'S MILK. Manufacturing the cheese relied on the neighboring Swiss labor force that crossed the Doubs daily for hundreds of years. The French/Swiss borders closed with the French defeat. The Cooperative lost Swiss workers. French laborers were killed in the war. Cheese production fell into hands of the elderly and very young.

Fromageries were and are centers where milk is brought from local farms for processing into Comté cheese. Nearby are caves or special rooms where cheese is aged. To this day the Franche-Comté cheese farmers work one of the oldest cooperative businesses in Europe, dating back to medieval times.

WEHRMACHT was the name of the German army.

Chapter Two

Page 19

EASTERN MASSACRES REFERS TO EINSATZGRUPPEN MASSACRES IN EASTERN EUROPE from 1940 to 1941 in Lithuania, Latvia, Estonia, the Ukraine, Russia, and Romania. Known as Operation Barbarossa, they were systematic roundups of Jewish inhabitants for mass killing in huge burial pits. Begun secretly as a first wave of the "Final Solution" this genocide led to gas chambers and crematoria to kill more people faster so that the SS had less direct contact with their victims, and thus, might not "break." Entire Jewish populations of towns were wiped out in a single day. (See *Masters of Death* by Richard Rhodes.)

Chapter Three

Page 26

EUTHANIZING OF GERMAN HANDICAPPED CHILDREN in hospitals began in 1939 with injections of barbiturates and opium. Under Himmler the first experiments in carbon monoxide poisoning took place, killing eight adult male handicapped patients in 1939. The Chelmno gas wagons were the next more efficient gassing technology before the gassing and cremation of huge numbers of the elderly, adults, and children in the concentration camps.

VICTOR MARIE HUGO (26 February 1802 – 22 May 1885), a French poet, novelist, and dramatist of the Romantic Movement, one of the greatest French writers. Hugo's poetry ranks first in French literary fame. His novels and plays reached beyond the French language. In English he's known for *Les Miserables* (1862) and *The Hunchback of Notre Dame* (1831). Hugo created over 4,000 drawings; many presaged modern abstract expressionism and the surrealist art movement. Hugo was admired for political/social crusades for the right to literacy and to abolish the death penalty. A royalist when young and later a republican, his work mirrored the artistic, social and political upheaval in Europe. *Les Miserables* spawned musicals, dramas, and films. *Le Dernier Jour d'un Condamné* (*The Last Day of a Condemned Man*) inspired Camus, Dickens and Dostoevsky.

Page 27

MERS-EL-KEBIR, ON THE COAST OF FRENCH ALGERIA. On top of the collapse of the French government in June of 1940, the British, who had been allies in WWI, scuttled the French fleet in port at Mers-el-Kebir on the coast of French Algeria on July 3, 1940. In a controversial move, the British informed the French that they would be attacked unless they sided with the British against Vichy. The Brits did not trust French Admiral Darlan when he said the French Navy would not fall into German hands, despite France's defeat. A stalemate ensued for eight hours without communication from either side before the bombardment started. Six French war ships were sunk and 1,297 French sailors died in the surprise attack. This caused French distrust of former British allies for the duration of the war. De Gaulle was in London and Churchill had kept him in the dark during the tragic blunder. A pity, when de Gaulle was the one person who could have convinced the French fleet to withdraw from Vichy and side with him and England. Churchill was correct in suspecting the depth of Hitler's malevolence; however, excluding de Gaulle from negotiations was a bitter blow to the dignity of the French people. In their eyes, Churchill became a war criminal—responsible for the slaughter of their sailors.

Page 34

KRISTALLNACHT: On November 9, 10, 1938 the Nazis unleashed a major Pogrom in Germany and Austria called The Night of Broken Glass. Jewish businesses and synagogues were desecrated, burned and Jewish people were attacked and local police did nothing to stop the violence. About 100 people were killed. This Nazi state-sanctioned pogrom tested the non-Jewish civilian populations' reactions. It was a scare tactic to force Jews to leave Germany and Austria initiating Hitler's "Final Solution" for European Jews.

Page 36

NOM DE GUERRE, NAME OF WAR, was literally a false name to hide one's identity in the Underground. Disguising true identity protected people in case of SS, Gestapo, Police, or Milice arrest or interrogation.

Chapter Four

Page 43

PARTI POPULAIRE FRANÇAIS (1936 TO FEBRUARY 1945) a French fascist political party and collaborationist front for Nazis in WWII France. The founders, former communists who became nationalists, were against Jews and Free Masons. The PPF was involved in banking, high finance and international industry. Members were extreme right collaborators with Gestapo and Milice. Its leader, Doriot, died in 1945 in an allied attack on his Nazi car.

Chapter Five

Page 45

THE AMIS OR LES AMIS is short for Americans and also the French word for friends, Amis.

Page 57

FELDMATRATZE is derogatory German slang literally meaning field mattress and used to denote a prostitute who would service sexual needs of German Military. FELDMATRATZENDIENST is the German term for battlefield prostitution.

Chapter Six

Page 66

GAZOGÈNE was a vehicle converted to coal or wood-burning fuel in WWII France when petrol was scarce.

Chapter Seven

Page 73

PASSEURS WERE SWISS RESISTANTS who smuggled goods from France to Switzerland, often as a cover for smuggling Jews. For decades French and Swiss held negative attitudes toward these paid smugglers, until recently, when the few surviving Resistants or ferrymen made it clear that without having the usual goods on them for the Germans and Swiss Police to confiscate when they were caught, they would never have succeeded in hiding children and adults along the way. No one suspected men smuggling chocolate and tobacco into France, but empty-handed, they would have been suspicious. If caught, the goods were confiscated and a fine levied. PASSEURS also smuggled weapons into France and returned to Switzerland with microfilm and Jews. The penalty was Dachau concentration camp. Once across the border in the Risoux forest, Passeurs passed their Jews to Underground families—who then passed escapees to the Swiss Red Cross. However, a refugee had to be 10 km inside the border to be safe from deportation and legally able to apply for asylum.

Chapter Nine

Page 96

LE GRAND RAFLE AT VÉLODROME D'HIVER OCCURRED IN PARIS on July 16, and 17, 1942, the largest single pogrom in France. Over 13,152 Jews: men, women and children were placed in an indoor sporting stadium for a week without proper food, sanitation or privacy in blistering heat. Hundreds died, many committed suicide; over 4,000 children were separated from their mothers. The victims were transferred to Drancy, a French detainment camp, and deported east to die in Auschwitz. Paris Police made the arrests with assistance from civil servants. No SS were involved. Only 400 Jews survived.

Page 97

PATOIS IS A MIXED GERMAN AND FRENCH REGIONAL DIALECT of Alsace and Lorraine, two mining regions of mixed French and German heritage. Alsace-Lorraine was held by Bismarck after 1870, was won back by France in 1918, taken again by Hitler in 1940, and ceded to France in 1945. Each country wanted economic control of the coal, iron ore, bauxite, and uranium found in these regions. The narrator's dowager mother rules a family fortune from mining. Her Alsatian family were victims of seventy years of French/German military hopscotch; hence her acerbic, fearless attitude toward the Germans.

Page 104

GENICKSCHUSS, OR NECK SHOT was a deliberate gun shot at close range into the brain stem area at the back of the neck. It caused instant death. Nazis used this extensively to murder Jews in the Eastern massacres (Einsatzgruppen murders) and occasionally in Nazi reprisals against the Underground in occupied countries.

Page 109

EINSATZGRUPPEN MASSACRES (eastern massacres) on page 481 of this Appendix, under Chapter Two, Page 19.

Page 110

LIDICE, CZECHOSLOVAKIA, AND LEZÁKY, WERE TWO VILLAGES destroyed in the German reprisal, May 1942. Ordered by Hitler after the assassination of Reinhard Heydrick, Reichsprotektor of Bohemia and Moravia and Hitler's architect of the "Final Solution" that killed more than five million Jews. Hitler ordered the two towns to be burned to the ground and 1300 men, women and children were killed as well as family pets and farm animals. Two Czech partisans trained in England had parachuted into the area. Their grenade hit Heydrick's vehicle on his way to work. He died of septicemia in a hospital, the same one where four pregnant women from the Lidice massacre had their babies forcibly aborted before they were sent to death camps to be gassed. This ghastly reprisal received wide press coverage and shocked those ignorant of the eastern genocide.

Chapter Ten

Page 119

MILICE, OR THE FRENCH PARAMILITARY POLICE, were created under Vichy leader Pierre Laval on January 30, 1943. Purpose: to be a French Gestapo made up of thugs, mobsters and fascists who hunted down Résistants. Miliciens made illegal searches, arrests, tortures, detainments and deportations of French citizens, foreigners, Jews, and political figures against the Reich and Vichy by French authorities. Hitler feared a strong French Résistance. Milice units operated largely with informers who betrayed their neighbors. The German Gestapo and Milice were counterparts dealing with local French civilians. The Waffen-SS were Wehrmacht Police that often stepped in to handle civilian and military populations, especially regarding the Résistants that killed German SS leaders. The SS were more visible in France in 1939 to 1941. The Gestapo was more directly involved with civilians, as were the homegrown French Milice. (See Chapter One, Page 10; Appendix page 479.)

Page 120

NACHT UND NEBEL OR NIGHT AND FOG, was Hitler's policy of secret civilian arrests of the Reich's political enemies. The Germans came first; later foreign activists, Underground saboteurs, communists, and protectors of Jews. Individuals were shipped to Germany to be prosecuted but in reality were dumped in labor and death camps, their civil rights lost. This clandestine policy intimidated people, whose families had no control or legal recourse to locate or defend them. Political activists simply disappeared, few survived. The policy, decreed in December 1941, was against The Hague Conventions.

Page 126

MAQUISARDS, MAQUIS. From the moment the STO (Service du Travail Obligatoire, also see page 65) existed, men began escaping to the mountains to avoid conscription. Most joined Maquis units, rural guerrilla bands of French Résistance fighters that were known as Maquisards. Maquis translates as "the bush" or scrub plants, typical of thickets in the southeastern French highlands. Later, the Maquis were incorporated into de Gaulle's Fighting Free French and were invaluable for their geographic knowledge, bravery and guerilla stealth, attacking Germans in retreat.

Page 137

MONTEBÉLIARDE COWS are a French dairy breed found in the Juras. Their milk is used to make cheese because its ideal casein protein makes higher yields. The cows are highly prized, hardy, generally healthier than Holsteins but make less milk.

Chapter Eleven

Page 143

SERVICE DU TRAVAIL OBLIGATOIRE, STO, (COMPULSORY WORK SERVICE) forced enlistment and deportation of thousands of French workers into Nazi Germany as slave labor for the German war industry. Created by Vichy to compensate for loss of German manpower for the German army. STO was established 22 June 1942 with a German promise: for every three French workers who volunteered (were conscripted) one French prisoner of war would be released. It didn't happen. Living conditions in Germany were one step above killing camps. Workers often died or were unheard from until war's end.

JEAN MOULIN, A LEADER AND HERO OF THE FRENCH RÈSISTANCE, TRAINED BY DE GAULLE IN LONDON. Parachuted into France to organize local Maquis units into free French Army. Nazi Klaus Barbie, "Butcher of Lyon" captured and tortured Moulin so severely it's believed the Résistant died of internal injuries on a train to Metz from Lyon. Some believe Moulin committed suicide to avoid more interrogation. He knew all the details of the Underground. Moulin died a hero. He didn't betray any knowledge about members, mission, or future. His death was lamented across France. Barbie was apprehended in Bolivia by Nazi hunters and extradited to France where he was convicted of war crimes in 1987. During the War he ordered the murders of thousands of political prisoners and Jews in death camps. He raided an orphanage in Izieu, and deported 44 Jewish children and their 5 adult caretakers to die in Auschwitz. At 77 he died in prison.

LA CITADELLE WAS A FORTRESS USED AS A PRISON BY SS in Besançon, capital of Franche-Comté region. Here Résistant teens Vital Deray, 19, and Henri Fertet, 16, were executed for Résistance activities in July 1943. Fertet wrote, "The soldiers are coming to get me. Judging from my writing, you might think my hand's trembling, but it's not. I'm just using a short pencil. I'm not afraid of death: I have an extremely clear

conscience. But it is hard to die . . . A thousand kisses. Long live France."
(Fertet's letter was read in French history classes in schools for years.)

Chapter Thirteen

Page 172

ARCHBISHOP SALIÈGE denounces the immoral treatment of Les Juifs.
Priests in all churches in his archdiocese of Toulouse read his public
protest, except one reactionary pro-Vichy prelate. The French Roman
Catholic clergy's institutional response to the Third Reich overall was
disappointing to many of the faithful. This courageous Toulouse
Archbishop, Jules Saliège, questioned the Nazi mentality and was among
the few clergy to gain respect. He wrote a pastoral letter immediately
after Le Rafle that inspired **BISHOP THÉAS** of Montauban to do the
same. With the help of his secretary Marie-Rose Gineste, Théas ran an
Underground forgery business to make identification cards, ration cards
and birth certificates to protect Jews passing through their area. The
Bishop was jailed for 10 weeks after a fiery sermon but didn't divulge
any information. A Capuchin, **FR. MARIE-BENOIT** in Marseilles also
ran a forgery operation, and convinced an Italian Commissioner of
Jewish Affairs in Nice to refrain from action against 30,000 Jews there.
He escaped to Italy, and while there he continued forgery operations to
help thousands more Jews escape death through his contacts with Swiss,
Romanian, Hungarian, and Spanish embassies.

Chapter Fourteen

Page 183

AK OR ARMIA KRAJOWA, THE POLISH RÉSISTANCE, was founded in 1942.
Members sabotaged the enemy and sent intelligence to allies during
WWII. The AK was aligned with smaller Polish Résistance groups that
gave aid to Jews in the 1944 Warsaw Uprising.

Page 187

RAVENSBRÜCK, A CONCENTRATION CAMP NOT FAR FROM BERLIN in northern Germany. Many French women from the Résistance were prisoners there, among them de Gaulle's niece, Geneviève, who was held from February 1944 to April of 1945 to be used as an exchange prisoner at war's end because of her politically prominent uncle.

Page 206

ARCHBISHOP SALIÈGE (See Chapter Thirteen, Page 172; this Appendix, page 489.)
LE GRAND RAFLE (See Chapter Nine, Page 96; this Appendix, page 485.)

Chapter Fifteen

Page 195

DACHAU was 16 km northwest of Munich—the first concentration camp in Germany for political prisoners in 1933, before it became a killing camp during the war.

Page 197

BRAUSEBAD: a sign hung on gas chamber buildings that meant shower/ bath room.

Chapter Seventeen

Page 225

JACQUIES is a German slang name for the French.

Chapter Eighteen

Page 233

"PON PON PON PONNN" the opening bars of Beethoven's Fifth Symphony is Morse code for the "V" for victory that introduced the BBC radio program, "Les Français Parlent Aux Français" that transmitted coded messages to the French Underground from London.

Page 234
THE FOSSE ARDEATINE MASSACRE resulted when 16 Roman partisans killed 30-plus German soldiers on Via Rasella in Rome, in March of 1944. In reprisal, Nazis killed 10 Italians for every German; over 300 Italians were murdered in Ardeatine caves by Genickschuss, but civilians were not told of the murders until the next day, causing a political turmoil.

Chapter Twenty-One

Page 292
THE BASCULE AND LUNETTE ARE TWO PARTS OF A GUILLOTINE. The bascule is a vertically tilted springboard upon which the prisoner places his body. His weight flattens a bascule and his head fits over a lunette. It receives a blade that slices through his neck. "*Le Rasoir national*" (the national razor) was a popular sarcastic expression for the guillotine. Death by guillotine was outlawed in 1977.

Chapter Twenty-Two

Page 295
ORADOUR-SUR-GLANE, village in France, scene of worst French reprisal in WWII on June 10, 1944, when all 642 people were murdered as punishment for the death of one Nazi, the commander of Der Führer Battalion III, Sturmbannführer Helmut Kämpfe. Hitler personally commissioned **Der Führer Regiment of the 2nd Waffen-SS Panzer Division Das Reich,** Adolf Diekmann, to kill off the French Résistance, as German forces were fleeing Normandy after the allied D Day landing placed Brits, Amis and French Free Forces in the lead to subdue the Nazis. Diekmann had grown up through the ranks, was highly decorated for bravery and had sustained a bullet in his lung during fighting in France in 1940. He had two iron crosses and many other medals. In the three weeks before Oradour,

he committed ten-for-one reprisals in several small massacres in area towns. But at Oradour the violence was the most brutal. The town's men were shot in the legs and unable to move. They were covered in fuel and burned to death, forced to listen to their women and children scream as they were burned to death, locked in their town church. The whole village was burned to the ground. De Gaulle left it destroyed as sacred ground and made it into a national war memorial. A new town was built a few kilometers away for survivors and residents not there at the time of reprisal. Diekmann had chosen the wrong town for his carnage. The Résistance held Helmut Kämpfe in Oradour Sur Vayres, which should have been the Nazi target. An American eyewitness to the carnage, Raymond J. Murphy, 20 years old, a B-17 navigator downed nearby recorded the massacre and saw a baby that had been crucified. This grotesque barbarism parallels the Lidice massacre in Czechoslovakia after the murder of Reinhard Heydrick, architect of the "Final Solution" for the Jews in June, 1942, when four pregnant women were forced to abort their babies in hospital before they were sent to the gas chambers at Auschwitz.

Page 296

THE GREAT WAR, or the war to end all wars, was later known as World War I—after Hitler's World War II in 1939-1945.

Chapter Twenty-Five

Page 343

MONT-VALÉRIEN is a fort built in 1841 in Paris near the Bois du Boulogne that defended the Parisians during the Franco- Prussian War. The French ultimately lost the fort to Otto Von Bismarck and the Germans. In 1898 a prime forger in the Dreyfus case committed suicide in Mont-Valérien. During the Occupation the fort served as a Wehrmacht prison and execution site for over 800 members of the French Résistance. Abbé Franz Stock, a German Roman Catholic priest for the Nazi conquerors in WWII, living in Paris, was also the chaplain for the Résistance prisoners of the fort. He did his best to protect their families and comrades from arrest by ferrying written and memorized messages for the prisoners. Fr. Stock is in the beatification process for his pastoral care, beloved by French and German alike, despite his nationality.

Chapter Twenty-Nine

Page 380

THE ÉPURATION SAUVAGE was a brief period of public lawlessness and male vengeance when French towns pursued those politically aligned with Vichy, people who dealt in black market sales, or profited from rationing in France. The most notable group was women prostitutes who served the Boches or those who had sexual liaisons with them. These women were publicly disgraced. Their heads were shaved and some were undressed and abused in town squares—and in a few cases, raped or beaten. It was a kind of tribal justice meted out by local street mobs, with gendarmes looking the other way to allow it. In a few rare instances males were similarly disgraced for collaboration. Women were disrespected, treated as property. France was also behind the rest of Europe, with the exception of Switzerland, in granting women the right to vote. Most Western European axis and allies legalized women's suffrage between 1918 and 1920. The French Catholic Church was deeply paternalistic. Women in 1938 were "FEMMES AU FOYER" or housewives. They could not cash a check without a male co-signer, or have a personal bank account without a male in charge of their finances unless stipulated legally. The tribal violence in France at the War's end showed the French had some of the same social rigidity as their enemy.

Chapter Thirty

Page 390

WOMEN'S RIGHT TO VOTE IN FRENCH ELECTIONS WAS SIGNED INTO LAW by CHARLES DE GAULLE, HEAD OF A PROVISIONAL GOVERNMENT IN ALGERIA, ON APRIL 21, 1944. He cited women's contribution to the French Rèsistance, as though women had earned this right. His own niece, Geneviève de Gaulle, was a prisoner in Ravensbrück at that time. For thinking French women, suffrage came 153 years too late. Women had initiated the French Revolution with their Hunger March of 1789, and Olympe de Gouges proposed voting rights for women in her famous declaration of female rights of 1791, just prior to her beheading. France has had a slow acceptance of women's rights compared to many other European nations.

Page 401

FOLKE BERNADOTTE, COUNT OF WISBOURG and a Swedish diplomat, was Vice-Director of the Red Cross in 1945, and credited for negotiations with the enemy to release 31,000 Jews from concentration camps. Militant Zionists assassinated him in 1948 in Jerusalem when he was United Nations Security Council mediator in the Arab-Israeli conflict of 1947-48.

Author Biography

My Jewish grandfather was a seventh-generation goldsmith who worked for Fabergé in Odessa in the Ukraine. After he and his fiancé were caught in crossfire during the murderous pogrom of 1905, they vowed never to raise their children in such peril. He brought his wife, children and in-laws to America.

My Bavarian grandfather, a pacifist Catholic farmer in the tradition of beatified Nazi resister and martyr, Franz Jäggerstätter, refused to fight for Germany in WWI. Germany had suppressed his Czech language, and his nation's freedom of self-rule. He stowed away on a Norwegian sailing ship for two years, before landing in Canada. He walked across the New York State border and met his Lutheran-Hungarian bride in Philadelphia.

Holiday dinner conversations in my youth sparkled in English, Yiddish and high and low German dialects. The old guard's wild tales of life before America underscored strong beliefs in peace, personal responsibility, and the power of love and dignity. They were a cultural mix religiously, economically, and artistically. They shared exuberant diversity and intense belief in learning, along with ironic, heartwarming and sometimes dark, humor.

They rooted dialogue, stories and settings in my heart. Their suffering taught me to give back for blessings received. They championed my love for literature, music and fine arts. I sought spiritual understanding through the Tao, Judaism, Christianity, and Eckankar.

My father, eighth generation jeweler, a platinum smith, was born in the United States. His experience taught me never to forget the Holocaust. As a twenty-one-year-old American tourist, then a sculptor, he and his older brother, a violinist, were in Salzburg, Austria on the eve of Kristallnacht in November 1938. They heard the glass shatter in the looting of Jewish businesses and smelled the synagogue burning. That night my father realized why his parents had fled to the US after the 1905 pogrom in Odessa. The following day in Munich he almost picked a fight with an SS standing in front of a Munich art museum. My uncle, born in Russia, grabbed my dad by the scruff of his neck and whispered, "Moishe, what the hell's the matter with you? You'll get us arrested! My passport is in my Jewish name, Pincus. They'll know we're Jews! We don't know if we have protection as Americans and we're not going to find out—right, boychik?"

Apparently, my dad's oral history would not be my only enlightenment. In 1957, in fourth grade, a boy in my class accosted my neighbor and me on our walk back to school at lunchtime. This classmate called my neighbor a "dirty Jew," and me—the cute little blonde pigtailed gamine with pierced ears who was a carbon copy of her Aryan shiksa mother— had a knee-jerk response and slugged that boy hard in his stomach. He ran home and never returned to my classroom.

Ironically, film footage of the Warsaw Ghetto Uprising had been shown on commercial tv prior to this incident, here in Joseph McCarthy/ Ku-Klux-Klan America (in Philadelphia, the City of Brotherly Love).

My mother brought me through an upsetting childhood experience that ignited my passion for human rights, not unlike my father's reaction to being in Nazi Germany.

After this altercation, my mother made sure I understood non-violent civil disobedience. Wise, tender-hearted and strong-willed, she set high standards. Crippled with Rheumatoid Arthritis for nineteen years, she could not stand for long periods of time. She took me to Quaker meetings of the Women's International League for Peace and Freedom (WILPF).

My mom taught me respect for all people, and explained Civil Rights and Afro-American history to me. In 1959, she sent me to stand in her place, in the municipal courtyard of Philadelphia, with a small group of resisters in silent, weekly anti-nuclear war/peace vigils sponsored by the WILPF.

I was twelve years old. To this day, I remember how people passed us and stared. I looked back and silently gave them love in a piece of my conscience—hoping my message would resonate in their hearts.

That history haunted me into adulthood. My marriage to the late Reginald Libby, a WWII Marine veteran, inspired me further to write the first book of the trilogy, *Ingrid's Wars: The Résistance Between Us* over fifteen years ago.

I worked in Poland and in 2005 visited Auschwitz. It was a devastating reminder. If my grandfather and grandmother and their family had not left the Ukraine, they would likely have died in a pit from gunshots to the back of their necks—Genickschusse, in the Odessa Massacre of 1941.

Yes, I am passionate about human rights. It is my sincere hope that *The Résistance Between Us* will resonate in your conscience, your heart and your soul. May we, in peace, heed the lessons of history—and may we truly learn to love our neighbors, whoever they are, and wherever they may be.

Phyllis Kimmel Libby

CPSIA information can be obtained
at www.ICGtesting.com
Printed in the USA
LVOW11s1538031117
554901LV00001B/207/P